SEA HAVEN

J.M. Simpson

Also by J.M. Simpson

The Castleby Series
Sea State
Sea Change
Sea Shaken

Twitter @JMSimpsonauthor
Instagram @JMSimpsonauthor

ISBN: 9798395455789

Independently published.

Author's Note

I have taken a degree of literary licence when depicting the wonderful work and crew members of the Royal National Lifeboat Institution (RNLI). I have embellished various aspects and fictionalised others to get the story right and to keep pace. Therefore, any and all mischaracterisations are entirely fictional, and any procedural errors are wholly mine.

For Jane

A truly wonderful soul, who once t
'You should tota

Sweet is the remembrance of troubles when you are in safety.

Euripides

PROLOGUE

The torrential November rain lashed heavily against the windscreen, the wipers barely coping with the unrelenting onslaught of water. The wind threw leaves and debris across the car in vicious bursts.

She woke suddenly at her mother's scream. The headlights behind were too bright, too close. Harsh, bright light flooded the front of the sports car; she blinked as it hurt her eyes and she raised an arm to block it. She heard her mother scream again, a screech of brakes and suddenly she felt weightless. She heard metal scraping, glass smashing. She felt the airbag's impact force the air from her lungs: a hard, brutal white-hot impact. Then nothing.

She awoke, cold and wet, and heard sobbing. On the fringes of consciousness, she heard a man's voice shouting bitter, angry words. She tried to move, but the pain was so intense, she passed out.

When she awoke, she turned her head and tried to see in the darkness. She tried to move her arms but couldn't. She couldn't see. She felt wet on her face. Was that rain?

She heard a rustle, and what sounded like breathing… panting. In the darkness she was blinded by a series of bright flashes. She tried to move again, but the pain was excruciating.

Just before she lost consciousness, she realised the sobbing had stopped, the angry voice had stopped and there was silence again.

She had no recollection of the hours the fire crews spent cutting her and her dead mother from the Porsche 911 Carrera. She didn't remember being air lifted to hospital, nor the six hours of surgery, where they tried to save her severely damaged heart.

She didn't remember arresting four times and being put on a bypass unit, while they looked for a donor heart. She didn't remember the transplant nurse informing her and her father that she was now at the top of the transplant list.

All she remembered was her mother telling her how much she hated driving in bad weather. These were the last words she remembered her mother ever saying to her.

CHAPTER 1

Sebastian Scott picked up the last suitcase and heaved it into the back of the BMW estate. He returned to the house and closed the downstairs shutters, seeing the activity prompt interest from the group of paparazzi crowded outside his London home.

'Why don't you all just fuck right off?' he murmured, snapping the last shutter closed, as he saw some of them jostling with their massive telephoto lenses.

Checking the extensive list that Tabatha had given him the day before, he made sure he'd remembered everything. He smiled as he remembered her sitting in her hospital bed, pale, but businesslike with her notepad, issuing instructions carefully to him like she was the adult, and he was the thirteen-year-old.

He realised he needed to put the bin out and pursed his lips. That meant running the gauntlet out front. Grabbing the bin bag, he opened the door hearing the flurry of lenses clicking and the endless questions shouted at him.

'How are you coping after the death of your wife, Sebastian?'

'How's your daughter doing, Sebastian, how do you feel about her nearly dying?'

'Will you give us an exclusive, Sebastian, about coping with the loss of your wife?'

Seb ignored them and kept his face away from the cameras. They'd been pestering him for days on the phone, message after message left. The voices asking the same questions.

'Weren't you supposed to be with them that night?'

'Doesn't all of her fortune now come to you?'

He heard it again and faltered. Rage built inside him. Then he heard her voice.

'Don't let them get to you, darling, they're scum. Don't give them anything they can use. Don't rise to it.'

He closed his eyes for a second and breathed deeply. He calmly wheeled the bin towards the edge of the pavement and then returned to the house, shutting the front door carefully behind him. Leaning against the door he saw his hands were shaking. The voices taunted.

'How much was she worth, Sebastian?'

'How did you do it, Sebastian?'

'Was your wife having an affair with Levinson Lucas?'

He pushed himself away from the door, grabbed the handful of newspapers on the hall table and took them into the kitchen, throwing them in the recycling. The headlines screamed at him in huge black letters. 'Cassie Warner in fatal car crash.' He closed his eyes and turned the paper over, unable to look at the picture of his wife's beautiful face any longer. Blinking away the tears he turned off the lights and stood for a moment in the quiet house, remembering. Remembering Cassie. Bringing Tabatha home for the first time. Christmases together. The fun, the laughter, the love.

Setting the alarm, he let himself out of the back door. As he sat in the car, he tapped out a text to say the list was done and he was just leaving. The response was instant.

Drive safely. Wuv U Dad. XX
He replied. *Wuv U. XX*

He sat for a moment and another text arrived. He smiled. It was from Cassie's best friend and Tabatha's godmother, Gabriella, who everyone called Bree. She was a force of nature, an absolute riot, drank like a fish, swore like a scaffolder and they all adored her.

WTAF? Where are you? Here? There? Call me IMMEDIATELY.
Seb replied.

BOSSY COW. I was here and now I am on my way to there. Stop being so demanding and PUTTING EVERYTHING IN CAPS.
She replied immediately.

I LIKE CAPS! IT'S ME TALKING LOUDLY. DRIVE SAFELY. Call U later.

Seb pulled up towards the rear double gates at the end of the enclosed drive, which slowly opened. He pulled out and they shut silently behind him. Like a door closing on a chapter, he thought as he watched them in the rear-view mirror. Gunning the powerful engine he accelerated down the street, the paparazzi didn't notice his car until it was too late to give chase. Good luck finding him, he thought as he headed towards the motorway.

Seb was making good time. The traffic behaved as he passed the most notorious part of the motorway. His phone rang, and he pressed receive on the steering wheel.

'Where are you?' Tabatha demanded.

'On the motorway, and good morning to you too,' he said, amused. 'How are you feeling?'

'OK,' she replied. 'Nurses have been doing more blood tests, I think I'm empty,' she grumbled.

'What does Doc say? Anything new since we saw him yesterday morning?'

'Gotta wait for bloods, I think. Where are you?'

'Will you even know if I tell you?'

'Give it to me in time then.'

'I reckon probably another three hours or so depending on traffic.'

'Are you coming here or going there?'

'What would you like me to do?'

'Go and unpack, check the house and then come back here.'

'Yes, boss.' Seb had been staying near the hospital for the last three weeks and not in their second home in Castleby, he just hadn't been able to face it and he needed to be near Tabatha.

'Have you eaten?' she demanded.

'Tabs...'

'Have you, Dad? You know you'd live on cereal if you could.'

'I'm going to stop in a minute for a pee and coffee.'

'And food.'

'Yes, and food,' he said, rolling his eyes.

'I can see you rolling your eyes,' she said accusingly.

'Busted.'

'OK, text me when you get there? You know I worry about...'

'I know, sweetheart... I know. Need anything?'

'Nah, I'm going to have a sleep, I'm tired.'

'You alright?'

'Don't fret. I didn't sleep well. Bad dreams.'

'OK. Rest up. See you later, Tabby Cat.'

'Laters, Dad... Wuv you.'

'Wuv you too,' he said.

As Seb drove, he thought about Tabatha and her progress. Three weeks ago she had received a new heart after the car Cass had been driving crashed over the edge of the road and down a steep incline lined with trees, partially impaling Tabatha.

Even now, Tabatha couldn't remember a thing about it. She remembered leaving the road and being frightened, but nothing after

4

that. The police had now concluded there was evidence to suggest it wasn't an accident. Seb tortured himself that his wife must have suffered an agonising death, knowing that Tabatha had also been hurt. He blamed himself. It had been his fault, and he had paid the price with his wife's life.

Cass had hated driving in bad weather. She had asked him twice to come with them, but he had been trying to finish a script and was in the zone. His writing was flying, and he hadn't wanted to stop. He remembered kissing her soundly, calling her a lightweight and teasing her.

He remembered saying, 'If you hate driving in bad weather, you know you could try slowing down a little and drive at the same speed as everyone else, rather than screaming around at full pelt. Take my car if you like, rather than your rocket.'

She had laughed and stroked his face. 'Now where's the fun in that?'

Unexpectedly, his eyes filled, he gripped the wheel and tried to see through the tears. He saw a sign for motorway services and pulled in, managing to stop the car before the crippling onslaught of grief came.

Seb drove down the high street and admired the town's festive lights. Castleby had gone all out for Christmas, he thought. He tried to remember the date and when the 25th actually was. He knew he had at least a couple of weeks. Bree, Tabatha's godmother, had said she might come for a few days if she could get away, but Seb had no idea when that might be. He had lost all track of time. He was exhausted and wrung out on every level.

He pulled into the driveway in front of the tall Georgian house that overlooked the beach one side and the harbour the other. It was a row of four, named Compass Row, and theirs was the end one.

They had rented the house one summer a few years ago for a few weeks and had fallen in love with it so much that Cass had bought it when she had landed her first big Hollywood film. Amazed at the huge fee her agent had managed to negotiate, she had wanted to buy something to mark the occasion. It was a home from home, their secret escape, and they visited whenever they could. Cass had named the house 'Compass Haven'. This was where Cass and Tabatha had been heading the night of the crash. His wife had died within five miles of one of her most favourite places.

He parked out front and sat for a moment, resting his head on the steering wheel, then desperate to see the sea, he roused himself and went inside. As he walked through the spacious rooms towards the back of the house, he smelt his wife's perfume lingering in the air. He stood at the huge windows at the back of the house and drank in the view. He remembered that they often used to stand there together, watching the sea.

He smelt her perfume strongly again and couldn't help but look around. It was his mind playing tricks on him, he was sure of it.

'I wish you were here,' he said softly, the words catching in his throat. 'I don't think I can do this alone.'

He realised he had been lost in thought and hadn't texted Tabatha to say he was there. He tapped out a quick message before unloading the car. His phone rang and he frowned when he saw the number for the hospital.

'Sebastian. It's Dr Carucci. Tabatha tells me you're back from London.'

'I am. Everything OK, Felix?' Seb said, dreading the response.

'Everything is fine. Bloods are good. She's doing well. She can come home in a few days if this carries on. Maybe Saturday?'

'Really?' Seb was delighted.

'Yes. Nothing stressful mind you. Plenty of rest and sea air, I think.'

'Wow. Home for Christmas. That will be amazing. Thanks, Felix. We're staying here for the foreseeable future rather than London.'

'It'll do her good, she needs to be in a healthy environment. Are you in to see her later?'

'I'll be there in a couple of hours.'

'OK, we'll talk then, get the nurse to buzz me when you get here, and we'll tell her together.'

'Will do. See you later, and thanks!'

Seb finished unpacking the car and stood in the hall, thinking. He had time to get a Christmas tree to surprise Tabatha with, plus he had the beginnings of an idea about a present for her. He looked at his watch, he needed to get his act together. There was a load of stuff he needed to get done before he saw Tabatha.

* * *

'Going once, going twice. Sold. Lot sixty-three sold for three hundred and fifteen thousand pounds to paddle number twenty-seven. Madam, please make your way over to the clerk.' The auctioneer motioned to Jenny Miller who was still clutching her paddle and pointed to the corner. 'Now, lot sixty-four. Who will start the bidding at ten thousand pounds?'

Jenny realised that she had been holding her breath and gasped suddenly. *Christ that was quick!* she thought. One minute she had waved her paddle at one hundred and fifty thousand pounds and two minutes later the price had rocketed up. She blinked and it dawned on her that the place was hers. Really hers. Now it *was* time to worry.

Jenny completed the bank transfer and then felt her hand being shaken.

'You can collect the keys from the office as soon as you've had confirmation that the final funds have cleared, and the paperwork is

7

complete. Final completion should be within a week,' the clerk said dismissively.

Jenny left the hall in a daze. It was still sinking in. She had bought a massive run-down place in need of a serious amount of work for three hundred and fifteen thousand pounds. Was she mad? She walked out into the town square and sat down on one of the benches for a moment, enjoying the December sun on her face, but still slightly dazed about the whole proceedings.

'Excuse me.'

An elderly man stood in front of her. 'I don't suppose you know where the registrar's office is? I think the signage, is all wrong,' he said ruefully, pointing to the cast iron tourist signs. 'I know for a fact that the car park is that way.'

Jenny smiled at him. 'The registrar's office is in the library now, which is that way,' she said, pointing. 'Big new building. Can't miss it.'

'Right. Wish they'd stop changing things,' he muttered. 'Thank you.'

'No problem.' She hoped he had happy news to register. She remembered sitting in the registrar's office a few months ago registering her brother's death. Although she lived alone and had never been married, she had never felt so alone as she had then. Her last living relative gone. Many of her hopes and dreams had been tied in with her brother, they had been inseparable. She had to do it alone now. But she had made a solemn promise to him on his deathbed that she would. She would finish their dream, while he watched over her.

He would have been thrilled about today. About two hundred grand under budget too! A great start. Not wanting to get caught up in the sadness of her brother's passing, she decided she would drive to Castleby, have a look at the outside of her new investment and have dinner in the pub opposite, before heading home to begin packing up her rented house.

Jenny strolled down the high street, admiring the Christmas lights. She wandered slowly, looking in shop windows and admiring the display of photographs on the town noticeboard of the recent Carnival of the Sea. The town had been completely transformed for the weekend. She chuckled at some of the pictures and hoped she would be open in time for it next year.

Rounding the corner, she looked at her new investment. She was now the proud owner of the huge end of terrace six-storey house, with orangery, on Compass Row, made up of four tall, elegant Georgian houses. As far as Jenny knew, the other houses were primarily holiday lets, although she was intrigued to see a BMW estate in the driveway at the other end of the terrace.

There was a battered car parked haphazardly in the drive of her property, and she wondered who it belonged to. Every time she had been to the area doing her research, the other properties had looked empty.

Jenny and her brother had spent months searching for the right place and had finally found Compass End; it had suited all of their needs perfectly for conversion into a small luxury hotel and bistro.

Jenny took a few pictures and wandered across the road to the Hope & Anchor pub, where she managed to get a table in the window so she could look at the house and start to make plans.

An hour later, Jenny was worried. She had watched a constant stream of, what her brother would have called, 'the great unwashed' entering the house through the basement and then leaving a few minutes later. Jenny wasn't stupid, she knew what it meant. She also knew that, as soon as she could, she would be getting in touch with the police and requesting they accompany her into the building so she could change the locks and make it secure. Last thing she wanted was to be paying over three hundred grand for a bloody crack den.

CHAPTER 2

Thirty-six-year-old Will Scully sat on the edge of the hotel bed. He took a moment to roll his shoulders to try and loosen his back, which was absolutely killing him. Whenever he slept in a different bed, or drove for too long, his back played up. This morning it was unbearable.

He stood, grimacing at the sharp pain that shot through his spine and went to the bathroom where he stood under the hot shower for as long as he could stand it.

Wrapped in a towel, he looked down at the sleeping woman and wondered how to get rid of her without hurting her feelings too much. He had no desire to see her again, or swap numbers, or pretend he wanted to keep in touch. He had picked her up in the hotel bar last night. It was the usual cliché: she was away on business, they'd drunk wine and ended up in bed.

A fairly usual occurrence since he had never had the urge to settle down, primarily because he travelled so much, often away for months at a time. He'd never found anyone he thought about going the distance with.

Grabbing a bottle of water, he returned to the bathroom where he drank down a handful of painkillers. He needed to be on form today. Big day.

Buttoning up the crisp white shirt, he tied his spotty navy-blue silk tie and looked at himself critically in the mirror. He looked OK. He'd give himself a job. He ran a comb through his hair, which fell into thick layers, finishing just over collar length, and then rubbed some moisturiser into his face. His clear green eyes looked back at him and for once weren't too bloodshot. He packed his bag and shrugged into his suit jacket. He scribbled the woman a quick note and left, closing the door quietly before heading to reception to check out. He needed to be on the road.

Four hours later, Will walked to his car, the interview had gone well, but he couldn't decide whether he was in the running or not. He grimaced as he bent to climb in. Much as he hated to admit it; he needed one that was slightly higher so getting in and out wasn't so damn painful. His back annoyed him. Made him feel like a bloody pensioner. He started the Audi which let out a deep throaty gurgle as the RS6's powerful engine warmed. He texted his sister to say he'd be there in an hour.

How d'it go?

He replied with the emoji of someone shrugging.

She replied with the emoji of a face rolling its eyes.

As he drove, he mentally replayed the interview in his head. They had seemed interested in him and his experience, but kept returning to why he wanted the job. The head of the interview panel had been annoyingly persistent.

'You'll have to excuse me, I feel compelled to ask. Mr Scully, you are a three-time Olympic gold medal winner in sailing, you've won the America's cup, twice, was it? Whatever do you want the harbour master's job in a small seaside town with a small fishing population for?'

Will would have asked himself this too.

'I've retired from professional sailing and racing,' he said. 'I want to put down roots. I've been travelling constantly for the last fifteen years, and I want to do something else. I want to be part of a community. I need some peace.'

'My concern is that this job won't have the thrills for you.'

He remembered smiling through gritted teeth.

'With respect, I wouldn't have applied if I felt that was the case. I have had a lifetime of thrills and high-octane sailing. I don't want to do it anymore, I lost one of my best friends that way and was seriously injured myself. I can categorically say, I am done with that.'

He remembered the panel nodding, but he sensed they weren't convinced. His sister, desperate for him to get the job, to be closer, had told him to get emotional if he needed: try and show a vulnerable side. More often than not, she was absolutely right, but he would never give her the satisfaction of telling her that. He tried her approach and had seen a change in their eyes.

'It probably sounds ridiculous,' he had said, 'but I'm at a stage in my life where I want some quiet. I need some certainty in my days. I don't want to be thinking about the next race. Training for ten hours a day, every day. I want to enjoy life. I want to put down roots and build a home somewhere. Maybe start a family.'

'And harbour master of Castleby is the place?'

'Yes. I know it well. My sister lives locally. They have a good sailing club, good sea cadets. They've also been without a harbour master for over two years now. They even have a youth sailing programme in the summer. What more does a retired professional sailor need?'

The panel had looked at him and Will couldn't tell whether or not they had been convinced. He had decided it was best to push the focus onto something else.

'The job pack said there is subsidised accommodation, can you tell me a bit more about that, please?'

'Ahh, well what that means is, we are happy to contribute to the rent of a property. This is essentially a holiday destination and rental properties are expensive. For what it's worth, we know there is a two-bedroom flat above the sea cadet hall, down in the harbour, which we are happy to contribute to. A local lady owns and manages it for us. If you're successful, you're welcome to have that on the usual tenancy arrangements with the owner direct; but we will subsidise the rent and include that overage as part of your salary. In previous years it actually was the harbour master's home, handy that it's so close to work too.'

Will had asked the burning question. He wasn't good at waiting.

'When will you make a decision?'

'By the end of the day.'

Will arrived at his sister's house. She had an old farmhouse, with an acre of land. She bought the place a few years previously, when her husband had left her for his eighteen-year-old secretary. She divorced him and took half of the money from the highly successful business she had helped create. It meant she had been able to buy her farmhouse outright and do exactly what she wanted, which was to set up a dog grooming and training business, and dog rescue. He parked next to her black van with her *Shoosh the Floof* logo and wandered into the barn.

'Hey,' he called as he saw her putting a very clean and fluffy small white dog into the large indoor pen. She turned in surprise.

'Go on, Fred,' she said, pushing him gently on the backside.

'Hey, trouble,' she said, smiling broadly. She enveloped him in a huge hug. 'Don't you look hot to trot in your suit? I've missed you.'

13

'Me too,' he said, hugging her back. 'Sure it's OK for me to stay a few days?'

'Course not. I've said haven't I. When will you know?' she asked.

'End of today,' he said, pulling a face.

'What's your gut feeling?' she asked.

'Can't call it. They kept banging on about why I would want it and where I'd get my thrills from.'

'You've had enough thrills to last you a lifetime,' she said quietly. 'Did you tell them that?'

'I did. Any food? I'm starving?'

'What am I? A bloody hotel?'

'I'd settle for a cafe at the moment.'

She rolled her eyes. 'Come on. I'll make you some lunch.'

Will had eaten his sister's pasta and surreptitiously taken some more painkillers. If she saw him taking pills, she'd have a fit and subject him to one of her endless lectures. He was on his third coffee when his phone rang, with an unknown number.

'Will Scully.'

'Ahh. Mr Scully. It's David Hill from the interview earlier.'

'Oh, hello.' Will fell silent. This was it.

'Well, it's very good news. I am delighted to offer you the position, Mr Scully.'

Will glanced at Suzy who was stood with an expectant look on her face. He nodded and tried not to laugh as she danced happily around the large kitchen.

'That's wonderful news,' Will said, smiling broadly. 'Thank you very much. I'm thrilled.'

'We'll get the offer letter and paperwork over to you in the next day or so. Do you have an idea of when you might be able to start?'

'I'm always of the mind that sooner is better than later,' Will said. 'I can start almost immediately.'

'Excellent.'

'If you could let me have the details of the place you mentioned to rent, then I can at least get moving on that.'

'Of course. I'll put that in an email too. I forgot to mention, there is a car with the role. I think it's one of the usual trucks, with all the usual markings.'

'OK great. I assume all that's in the paperwork?'

'It is. I'll get it sorted quickly with a mind to you wanting to start soon. I'll also send over the accommodation details for you to look at. Don't feel you have to take the flat if it's not right for you. We will try to be flexible with the subsidy.'

'I'm sure it'll be fine. Look forward to hearing from you.'

'Yes. I'll be in touch. Bye now.'

Will ended the call and pointed at his sister. 'This doesn't mean you can constantly meddle in my life now,' he said as she bounced over to hug him.

'Oh, shut up and give me a hug,' she said happily.

Suzy finished grooming the last dog and put him in the pen with the others. She had some drop offs to make, and she had received a call from a farmer nearby who wanted her to take one of his dogs. He had told her in no uncertain terms to come and get it today or he'd take care of it himself, and she knew what that meant. For many of the older farmers if the young farm collies showed little aptitude or interest in sheep, they saw no point in keeping them and viewed them as an unnecessary overhead. Suzy had a good reputation locally for rescuing difficult dogs, training them and rehoming them.

She emailed out the day's invoices to clients and went to see if her brother fancied a trip into town to help her with her errands.

She found him changed into jeans and a jumper, asleep on the sofa. In sleep, he looked the incredibly handsome, relaxed and carefree man he had been before the accident, when he had been riding high on his numerous successes.

15

As siblings, the two of them couldn't look more different. Will was tall, and wide shouldered with thick light golden-brown hair, light green eyes and a tanned face. Suzy was tiny, not even coming up to Will's shoulder, with very dark hair, a pale complexion and her brother's green eyes. Since adolescence, most of Suzy's friends had thought older brother Will was drop-dead gorgeous and Suzy had to reluctantly agree. He did have a good face on him.

The day of the accident had ended a lot of things. His carefree and wild ways. The pain of his back had left its mark in some of the deep lines that etched his face and the large scars that ran parallel down his spine.

She remembered seeing the accident and being utterly helpless to do anything. She was on the dockside, screaming with excitement as she had watched him take the lead through her binoculars. She had seen the accident happen as if in slow motion, had felt her blood run cold when she saw the racing catamaran break apart and start cartwheeling.

Will had been trapped beneath the heavy mast, while his team mate and best friend, Ian, had been trapped in the sails and netting from the boat. Will had managed to get his head above the water under part of a broken keel finding air, but Ian had been trapped for ten minutes under water and drowned. Will had lived, but had broken his back and spent the next nine months in surgery and physiotherapy. He had never sailed or raced professionally again.

She tousled his thick hair, and he opened an eye sleepily.

'I've gotta go into town and drop off some dogs then pick up a new one? Wanna come with me?'

He stretched and winced. 'Why not? You can buy me a pint to celebrate, and I'll check out this rental place from the outside, see what it's like.'

'Deal,' she said. 'Let's get the dog on the way then.'

Suzy pulled into the muddy farm road and the van bumped up the potholed track. She stopped in the mud-covered yard and spotted a small brown and white collie puppy of about four months sat outside, chained up, shivering in the cold and wet. The small dog looked dangerously thin.

The farmer strode out of the shed frowning and pointed to the terrified puppy. 'Take him. I don't want him.'

'Goodness, he's tiny. Have you named him?' Suzy asked as she approached the tiny collie.

'No point until I know if they'll be any use or not. He'll be no use,' he grumbled. 'Go on. Take him. I've got things to do. I don't want to be chatting.'

'But he's so young. You surely can't tell yet?'

'Years of experience,' barked the farmer. 'I don't want him.'

Suzy bent down and loosened the chain off the dog who had thrown itself at Suzy and was trembling.

'OK now, you're OK,' she said soothingly. She picked him up and he licked her face, snuggling into her arms still trembling.

'Go on then,' said the farmer. 'Away with you.'

'Do you want to know if he goes to a good home?' asked Suzy.

The farmer looked at her. 'No,' he said, turning and walking away.

Suzy opened the van and grabbed an old towel. She climbed back in the driver's side and passed the towel to Will and then passed the puppy over to him.

'Wrap him in this,' she said, passing the bundle over.

'Oh man... he's cute.' Will wrapped the small puppy in the blanket and rubbed him gently. 'He's freezing.'

'That's because he's horrendously underfed and fucking terrified of that bastard farmer,' said Suzy, pulling away, angry, back down the potholed driveway. 'Who keeps a puppy outside in this fucking weather?'

'Does he have a name?' Will asked, holding him up and looking at him.

'No.'

'We'll have to come up with one,' Will said. 'He looks like a pirate with that patch over his eye.'

An hour later, after all the dogs had been dropped off, Suzy pulled up in front of the sea cadet hall, which was a large two-storey brick and flint building, with tall windows. At the end of the building was a bright blue door, with a porthole, that had a plaque next it which read 'Harbour master's Loft'.

'Is this it?' Suzy asked, climbing out. 'Looks cool.'

'It does, doesn't it?' Will looked at the building and liked what he saw. The place looked huge. Perhaps he might be able to indulge in his favourite pastime if he had room for his drawing board. The puppy, who was asleep in his arms, still wrapped in the towel, snored gently. Suzy wandered around.

'Looks nice,' she called, approaching the front door. She pushed it gently and it opened.

'Oh,' she said. 'It's a sign! Shall we have a poke around?'

Will rolled his eyes. 'You can't just invite yourself in.'

Suzy stuck her head in the door. She motioned for Will to be quiet.

'There's someone in there,' she whispered.

'Well the door *is* open,' Will shot back.

The sound of a large crash and an accompanying small scream made them both jump.

'Come on,' Suzy said, pushing open the door and going up the stairs. 'Hello? Everything OK? Can we help?'

'Jesus Suzy—' Will started, but she was already in and at the top.

He followed her up and saw a small, slim, blonde-haired woman lying on the floor with a stepladder to one side.

'Blimey!' Suzy said, rushing over to the woman who looked a little dazed. 'Are you alright? Do you need an ambulance or anything?'

'I'm OK,' the woman said. 'I'm just a bit winded. I'm an idiot.' She looked embarrassed pushing herself up into a sitting position. 'I'm fine. I just slipped off the ladder.'

'Are you OK to try and stand?' Suzy asked.

'I'll be fine. Thanks,' the woman said, standing, helped by Suzy. Will picked up the stepladder and righted it, still holding the puppy.

'I'm fine, honestly! Thank you. Occupational hazard for me. Don't let me hold you up,' the woman said.

'You're not holding us up,' said Will pleasantly, thinking how attractive this woman was but seeing her wedding ring and reprimanding himself.

'Cute puppy,' said the woman, rubbing her wrist. 'Yours?'

'I've taken him off a farmer for rehoming,' Suzy said. 'He's exhausted and terrified, poor thing.'

'Look. I'm fine,' the woman said. 'Thanks for picking me up. I'm Anna by the way.'

'Sure? I'm Suzy and this is my brother, Will. I run the dog groomers and rescue on the outskirts of town. Shoosh the Floof.'

Anna laughed. 'I've seen your van. The name always makes me laugh.'

Suzy smiled. 'When we were kids we always called fluffy dogs floofs. Hence the name.'

'Do you both run the place?' Anna asked.

'No, Will's just been offered the job as the harbour master here,' Suzy said proudly. 'We were just looking at this place as a potential rental when we heard you fall off the ladder.'

Anna went pale. 'I'm sorry,' she said in a shaking voice. She looked around and grabbed her keys with a trembling hand. 'I... I... need to go. Would you mind terribly pulling the door shut for me, it'll lock? I… I can't be here. I've got to go.' She hurried out of the door, not before Will noticed the tears on her face.

'Wait!' he called, worried they had upset her. 'Hang on!'

He watched from the top window as the woman ran across the harbour and up the hill until she was out of sight. Will turned to Suzy.

'You upset her.'

Suzy snorted. 'Oh, bugger off. It was the prospect of looking at your ugly mug that scared her off, I reckon. I saw you totally eyeing her up. What are you like?'

'Wedding ring.'

'Oh, so that stops you these days?'

'Since I saw what it did to you, yes.'

'Aw, you say the nicest things. Come on, let's have a quick poke around.'

The two of them looked around the flat with Will becoming more entranced by the minute. The living area was wide and long with four long windows either side and a kitchen at one end. He mentally placed his drawing board at the other end, and moved the sofa and chairs around to a different position. The bedrooms were a good size, and he was pleased to see what looked like a decent shower.

'I love it,' he said. 'This is brilliant for me.'

'Sure you don't want to stay with me?'

'You cramp my style,' he said.

'More like you cramp mine. Loser.' She shoved him. 'Come on. Let's grab a pint.'

CHAPTER 3

Rob Fox, known as Foxy, to practically the whole town with the exception of one person, left yet another message on his ex-wife's voicemail.

'Carla sweetheart. Call me back. I need to know you're OK. I'm worried about you. You know the drill. If you don't call me back, I'll get in the damn car and come and see for myself.'

Frustrated, Foxy threw the phone down on the front desk of the climbing centre.

The ex-soldier had made a new start after years of fighting wars and killing had taken their toll. He'd struggled with PTSD and suffered a deep personal tragedy when his daughter had died in an accident. His wife Carla had blamed him, divorcing him, but recently they had re-connected when she finally accepted he wasn't to blame.

They now had a close relationship. In the summer they'd briefly rekindled their romance, but she'd not wanted to continue anything long distance and suggested they be friends with benefits if they chose. Foxy still wasn't sure how he felt about it all.

'Still nothing?' Mike asked. He worked with Foxy in the climbing centre and was also a local musician and lifeboat crew.

'No,' Foxy mused. 'I might ring the ward.'

The last time Carla called Foxy had been just over a week ago when she had asked if she could come for Christmas. She said she needed to get away. To Foxy, she hadn't sounded right, and it was unlike her. She was bright, feisty, capable and very little upset her mojo.

He'd heard the catch in her voice. That invariably meant she was one step off tears, but she wouldn't be drawn in to discuss it.

He picked up his phone again and rang the ward, waiting for ages until he heard Carla's voice.

'Hexwood Ward,' she said briskly.

'Sweetheart, it's me,' he said.

'Oh,' she said, sounding relieved. 'It's you. What's up?'

'I've left you like ten messages,' he said grumpily. 'I've been worried.'

'Sorry. I've been getting some weird calls, so I've been ignoring it. My head's just not in the game at the moment.'

'Carls,' he said gently. 'What's up? Weird calls?'

'I can't talk here. I can't get into it.' Her voice broke and she cleared her throat. 'I finish in a few days. Is it OK to come then or is it too early?'

'I've told you before, come anytime.'

'I'll come then, maybe Saturday?'

'Anytime is good.'

'Promise me one thing?' she asked softly.

'Anything.'

'That I get one of your hugs. They make everything better.'

'You said that last time. What's up? What can I make better?'

'Just you being you makes it better. I'll tell you when I see you. I can't talk now, I'm being paged. See you in a few days.'

'Text me when you're on the road.'

'Nag nag.'

'You know it.'

'Bye.' Foxy ended the call.

Mike looked at him. 'Carla's coming for Christmas?'

'She is.'

'She OK?'

Foxy frowned. 'Something's up. She's not right.'

Mike clapped him on the shoulder. 'You'll make it alright, mate. It's what you do.'

'That's what she said,' Foxy said quietly.

* * *

Jenny sat in reception at the police station. She had asked to speak to the local inspector, she didn't want to get fobbed off with some wet-behind-the-ears fool. She was assured the inspector would only be a few more minutes. She scrolled through the pictures she had taken surreptitiously on her phone the previous evening. Noting with satisfaction you'd have had to be some sort of idiot not to realise what was going on.

A door buzzed open and a young man in his mid-twenties wearing uniform stuck his head through the door.

'Jenny Miller?' he asked.

Jenny stood and he motioned her through the door.

'Steve will be a sec, you're in here,' he said, stopping at a door. He opened it and gestured her into the interview room. 'He'll be along.'

Jenny sat down and after a few minutes an attractive blond man with smiley blue eyes in his thirties came in the door, holding a notebook.

'Hi there. Jenny, isn't it? I'm DI Steve Miller.'

Jenny laughed. 'I'm Jenny Miller. Could we be related?'

'Perhaps we are!' Steve said with a smile. 'Right, how can I help? This all sounds very cloak and dagger.'

'I need your help to get a place clean,' she said firmly.

'Clean as in…?'

'Get the junkies out.'

'Ahh. Probably one for uniform. Where are we talking about?'

'Compass Row. Opposite the pub. It's mine now.'

'You've bought it?'

'Yesterday. At auction.'

'Wow. Congratulations. Beautiful along there.'

She smiled. 'Thank you. I'd never been to an auction before, the speed of it was so intense! I wondered for a terrible moment if I'd bought it for a ridiculously high amount or if I'd ended up buying something else completely!'

'What makes you think there are junkies in there?' Steve asked.

Jenny gave him a look that suggested she wasn't stupid and showed him the pictures on her phone.

'I was there for about two hours last night. Constant procession of low lifes in and out. I suppose it's good that they're only dealing and not using in there too much. I'm assuming this is either local druggies or we've got a county line here?'

Steve regarded her with amusement. 'Are you on the force? You've either done your homework or you've dealt with this sort of thing before.'

She waved the comment away. 'I used to do some civilian work for the National Crime Agency years ago, plus a bit of crime reporting. Another life.'

'It's never another life once you've done that. May I?' Steve took her phone and scrolled through the pictures. He grunted at a few of them.

'Jonesey!' he called.

Jonesey stumbled through the door.

'Did you get all that with your ear pressed up to the door?' Steve asked. 'Pull up a chair. Recognise any of these jokers?' He passed the phone to him.

Jonesey scrolled through the pictures and enlarged a couple.

'Ooh that's JJ's brother, isn't it? He's grown. Chip off the old block and all that. And isn't that Lenny the lift going in?'

Steve nodded. 'Yeah. Look isn't that Sniffy there?'

Jonesey peered at the small screen. 'What a surprise. So it is.'

'While this is fascinating. I need them out of my house pronto.' Jenny said. 'I need someone to come with me and a locksmith to change the locks.'

Steve thought for a minute. 'I reckon we should go and have a little looksie. See if we can't encourage them politely to leave.'

Jenny looked at him doubtfully. 'What? Just rock up and say hi guys, howz about you all bugger off?'

Steve grinned. 'Why not? Let's go and have a chat, it's a nice day and I fancy a stroll.'

Jenny walked down the road with Steve and Jonesey. She felt slightly conspicuous and wondered whether people would think she was being frog-marched somewhere since Jonesey was in uniform, and everybody seemed to know Steve.

Steve kept a casual flow of conversation up as they walked down the high street.

'You from around here, Jenny?'

'Me and my brother were born here, but my parents moved about a lot. They're not around any longer, but me and my brother were looking for somewhere to run a hotel and bistro and we fell in love with this place. It's perfect. Nice to be back.'

'You're both taking this on?'

'It's just me now,' Jenny said, then felt compelled to explain. 'He passed away a few months ago. It was… unexpected, very quick.'

'I'm so sorry,' Steve said quietly. 'So, you're going it alone?'

'I promised him I would.'

'Well, whatever we can do to help, don't be afraid to ask. Everybody pitches in here.'

'Thanks. Good to know.'

They arrived at Compass End and Steve and Jonesey wandered around the outside, while Jenny held back.

Steve called to Jenny. 'Whose car is this?' He pointed to a white car with a smashed front and rear headlight, and a dented rear wing.

'No idea, it wasn't here the first time we viewed the place, I reckon it's been there a few weeks.'

'Jonesey. Call it in?'

Jonesey walked off speaking into his radio. Steve carried on walking around the property.

Jonesey reappeared.

'Reported stolen from Pembroke about a month ago now.'

Steve snorted. 'Why aren't I surprised. Jenny, is this where they were going in and out? Here?' He pointed.

Jenny nodded and walked hesitantly over as Steve pushed aside the makeshift plywood door.

'Let the games begin,' he said, smiling broadly. 'Jonesey, chuck me your torch.'

Steve disappeared inside followed by Jonesey. Jenny's curiosity got the better of her and she followed them in.

The large basement was dingy and stank of piss and weed. The place was scattered with cans and carrier bags and general detritus. In one corner on an old mattress lay a small man. His hair was dark and greasy, his fingers yellow and he had very few teeth. He was flat on his back, mouth wide open. Despite looking around sixty, Sniffy was actually in his early thirties.

'Oh God, he's not dead, is he?' Jenny whispered, horrified.

'Course not,' Steve said, chuckling. He gave the man a shove with his foot.

'Sniffy. Wake up.'

The man grunted, sniffed, farted loudly and resumed snoring.

'Sniffy,' Steve whispered urgently. 'Filth are outside.'

The man jumped awake. He tried to stand up and tripped over the edge of the mattress, falling face down with a large grunt.

'Morning, Sniffy,' Steve said, amused. 'How are you today?'

'What d'you want?' Sniffy mumbled, struggling to stand, coughing and hawking up a large globule of phlegm which he spat in Steve's direction.

'Delightful as ever,' Steve said wryly. 'It's a mystery to me why you remain single, Sniffy.' He turned to Jenny. 'Bet you're tempted with this fine figure of a man, eh?'

Sniffy sniffed and wiped the back of his hand across his nose. 'What d'you want?' he said grumpily. 'You here to harass me?'

'You wish,' Steve said dryly, strolling around the room, poking at things with his foot. 'That your car outside?'

'No comment.'

'Don't be a twat, Sniffy. Is that your car or are you borrowing it?'

'No comment.'

Steve sighed. 'Let's try something else. You dossing here permanently now or just dealing from here?'

'None of your fucking filth business, is it?' sneered Sniffy. 'Who's this anyway?' he asked, eyeing Jenny up and down.

'This is Chief Inspector none of your business. Now I repeat. Are you dossing or just dealing? Clock's ticking or it's a trip to B&B at the station.'

'You gonna arrest me?' Sniffy said, sounding bolshy. 'On what grounds?'

'Trespass, squatting, possession of illegal substances, intent to supply, *actual* supply…' Steve said with a long-suffering air.

'OK, OK,' Sniffy said nervously, wiping the back of his hand across his nose again.

'Answer the question.'

'*Maybe* I'm doing a little bit of dossing and maybe some other people are coming in to do a bit of dealing.'

'But you're not dealing, obviously.'

Sniffy looked affronted. 'Course not.'

'Why here?'

'What?'

'To doss and deal.'

'It's empty.'

'Not from this afternoon it isn't.'

Sniffy leered at Jenny. 'This your place? Fancy a lodger?'

Jenny looked at him, inside she was fairly terrified, but it was important not to show it. Her previous crime reporting escapades had taught her that.

'Tempting, but no,' she said.

Steve stifled a laugh. He moved closer to Sniffy. 'Here's the deal. You put the word out that there's no more dealing or dossing to be done here and I don't nick you today. How's that for a deal?'

Sniffy pretended to consider the offer.

'Not much of a deal.'

Steve considered for a moment. 'OK, here's the sweetener. The Old Hotel on King Street, I think one of the downstairs security window panels came loose in the winds last week. How about you explore a change of location?'

Sniffy raised his eyebrows. 'That so?'

'Uh huh. I know you like it there because they left the water on. So, when my very good friend here returns with me tomorrow to make this place secure, you will have moved on, won't you? Along with all of the other pond life you hang out with?'

'Fucking rude,' Sniffy mumbled.

'Deal?' Steve pushed.

'Deal.' Sniffy hawked up phlegm into his hand and held it out to Steve.

Steve regarded his hand with distaste. 'Take my word for it. Now clear up your shit and bugger off.' He pointed at Sniffy. 'I don't want to see you or your mates anywhere around here again. We clear?'

'Crystal,' muttered Sniffy.

'Oh, and you might want to give that car back to whoever you borrowed it from too.'

Steve gestured to the door. 'Jenny, shall we?'

They walked up the steps and out into the fresh air, all three of them gulping in deep breaths.

'Do you really think they'll be gone by tomorrow?' Jenny asked.

'Oh yeah. Now they know they can go to the old hotel, it'll be like rats leaving a sinking ship.'

'I'm really grateful,' Jenny said. 'Thanks so much.'

'No problem. Have you got anyone to make it secure?'

'Not yet,' Jenny admitted.

Steve produced his phone and made a call.

'Teeney? Alright? I'm good thanks. Look my mate Jenny here has just bought Compass End in town… Yeah… opposite the Hope. Any chance you could come tomorrow and get rid of the drug shit in the basement and make it secure? Low lifes have been in, dossing and using.' He listened for a minute and turned to Jenny. 'Nine a.m. OK with you?' She nodded. He went back to the call. 'That's great, mate, thanks very much. I'll meet you here to check they've all left. Cheers then.'

Steve ended the call and turned to Jenny.

'We use Teeney and his crews when we have properties we have to make secure where there's drug paraphernalia. They're the best to clean up and make it safe. You OK with that?'

'I'm sure I could have cleaned up myself,' Jenny said, 'but thanks.'

'Have you got armoured gloves and boots for the needles?'

Jenny gasped. 'No.'

'Then let the professionals do it. It can be really nasty. They're reasonable too. Teeney will most likely give you mates rates since I called for you.'

'Wow. Great. Thanks very much, I really appreciate it.'

'No problem. So, I'll meet you here tomorrow at nine, yes? Look out for Teeney.'

'Is he like massively tall and wide, hence being called Teeney?'

Steve smiled. 'No, just the opposite. Lives up to his name. Literally. See you.'

Jenny watched him and Jonesey walk back up the road, smiling when she saw Steve grab Jonesey and pull him out of the bakers they were passing. She felt good. At least the local coppers were nice, she thought. That was always useful.

CHAPTER 4

Detective Inspector Steve Miller had two jobs to do first thing. He had to check Sniffy had left, and he had to go and see the man who lived on the other end of the terrace from Jenny. Sebastian Scott. The poor guy had lost his wife, and his daughter almost died too. He had to give him an update on the accident investigation, and he wasn't looking forward to it.

He'd kissed Kate, his girlfriend who was the local GP, goodbye and walked up the hill towards Compass Row, noting Sebastian's car was there. Hopefully he'd catch him. He rounded the corner and saw Jenny clutching a coffee and stamping her feet in the chilly morning air.

'Morning,' he said. 'How are you?'

'Raring to go, thanks to you.'

The sound of a loud horn blasted out. Without looking Steve said, 'Teeney's here.'

A large grey van with tinted windows pulled up opposite them, parking on double yellow lines. The hazards were left on, and the door opened.

Teeney, as Steve had warned Jenny the day before, did live up to his name. Born with dwarfism, he had a personality as big as a house, rendering him with enormous charisma, and much appeal to the ladies. He jumped down from the van's cab and ran lightly across the road to Jenny and Steve.

'Morning,' he said charmingly. 'You must be Jenny. Any friend of Steve's is a friend of mine. Shall we get started?'

The three of them went into the basement. Jenny was surprised to see Sniffy had gone and he'd attempted a bit of a tidy up with much of the rubbish piled into a corner.

'Watch where you walk,' Teeney said over his shoulder to Jenny. 'Don't know if there are needles.'

They walked around the basement and found no sign of anyone. Teeney outlined what he would clear and how it would make it safe.

'Do you want me to check the rest of the place?' he asked.

'Please. They've lent me the keys for the day, I've got about a week before it's legally mine, but as it's empty and they knew the police were involved, they were flexible. The owner's going halves on the clean-up and making it secure. We'll have to go in the front door, this basement one won't budge.'

The trio left the basement and walked up the wide stone steps to the front door where Jenny struggled with the rusty lock. She pushed open the door and they looked around the spacious hallway, empty, dated and musty.

'Wow, this place has potential,' said Steve. 'You've got your work cut out for you. Look at that staircase!'

Teeney bustled about moving from room to room. He checked the access into the basement, feeling it was a vulnerable point.

Jenny decided she would start at the very top and work her way downstairs. She wandered into a few empty rooms marvelling again at the tall ceilings, ornate plaster work on the cornices and original fireplaces. She pushed open a small door to a room in the eaves and gasped.

The floor was covered with newspaper cuttings and photographs. They were all of a woman who looked familiar to Jenny, but she couldn't place her. Suddenly she had the most uncomfortable sensation in the back of her neck and whirled around. Nothing there. She walked out onto the landing.

'Steve! Can you come up?' she called.

'Coming.'

She heard his footsteps on the stairs.

'Where are you?' he called.

'Here,' she said, leaning over the banister.

'What's up?'

She motioned with her head to one of the rooms and he followed behind her.

'Blimey.' He stared, before slowly dropping to his haunches to look at the pictures. 'This is Cassie Warner.'

'Isn't she an actress?'

'She was. She died on the outskirts of town nearly a month ago. Fatal car crash.'

'I read about it.'

'I'm sorry, but I'm going to need to get this all collected, and the scene processed. We need to leave this room and be careful not to touch anything.'

Jenny looked confused. 'Why?'

'Cassie Warner's crash is still being investigated. I can't take the chance that this isn't relevant. Give me the name of the agent dealing with this and I'll call them and clear it.'

'Is this a crime scene now?'

'No. We just need to collect the evidence here. Won't take long. By the time forensics have processed the place, it will legally be yours I suspect. I'm going to take a few photos if that's OK?'

The three carefully looked around the rest of the place and found nothing else of concern. Steve allowed Teeney to get started but told him to work with the forensic officer who was on his way.

Steve gave Jenny his mobile number, bade her goodbye and went to speak to Sebastian, a few doors down; the conversation now even more difficult.

Steve exhaled heavily as he pressed the doorbell.

When Sebastian answered the door, he was on the phone. As they hadn't met before, Steve smiled pleasantly and held up his warrant card. Sebastian peered at it and motioned for him to follow him inside.

He walked through to the kitchen and Steve saw the transformation from what he had just seen at Jenny's house to how it could look. He realised Jenny's house was much bigger, and Sebastian's end of terrace was as tall, but narrower.

Seb mouthed an apology and offered Steve a coffee by giving him a mug and pushing the cafetiere towards him. A carton of milk was already on the large table. Steve helped himself to coffee and wandered to the window to soak in the far-reaching views over the bay and the old fort opposite. He tried not to listen to Seb's conversation.

'Yes. I am. Yes. She is. Bree, darling, stop nagging me. I am an adult, and I can look after myself.' He made a sound of exasperation. 'I do not live on cereal. Well, not all the time. Look I have to go. The police are here.' He listened. 'I don't know. If you stop wittering, I'll be able to ask them. Go on. Bugger off. Yeah, you too. Just let me know when you'll be here. Bye.'

Sebastian ended the call and threw the phone down on the table.

'Sorry,' he said ruefully. 'That was Cassie's best friend She's lovely, but she does go on. We've not met, have we?' He offered his hand. 'Seb Scott.'

'Steve Miller.'

'Please sit. What can I do for you, Steve?' he asked. 'Is this about the accident? Is there news? I don't see what's taking so long.'

'There is news I'm afraid,' Steve said, sitting at the table. 'The accident investigator is in court today and he's asked me to come and debrief you. He's reviewed the evidence and he's almost certain that there were other cars involved in the collision. There are some suspicious circumstances implied, hence the coroner being involved. It means we will need to continue and widen the investigation, which has now been given to me to lead.'

Sebastian looked shocked. 'I thought she lost control and veered off the road?'

'She did veer off the road. But the investigator thinks there may have been another car behind, which may have pushed or bumped your wife's car; possibly also a car coming the other way.'

'But they said nobody stopped. Apparently nobody saw anything,' Sebastian said, sitting down suddenly, looking shocked. 'Are you telling me that there were more cars involved and no one stopped or did anything about it?'

'This is what we're trying to establish, Mr Scott, by investigating this further. One person called it in and all they said was that there was a car accident and the location. We can't find that phone registered to anyone. We're running the analysis of the crash site. While we've had the results of the postmortem, there's been a problem with contamination of some of the tests, so they're having to be done again. It's all resulted in a backlog.'

'So can I bury her?'

'That's in the hands of the coroner. The coroner will sometimes issue a burial order, which means you can put her to rest, but the inquest will still be open and ongoing. We can check that for you, but I suspect we'll have to wait for those tests to be complete, just to be sure.'

'Christ, I'll have to tell Tabatha,' Seb said, putting his head in his hands tiredly.

'Do you need to at the moment?'

'I don't know. She doesn't miss a trick.'

'May I ask how she is?' Steve probed.

'She's coming home Saturday. Long road to recovery. Doctors seem happy with her and she's not rejecting the new heart.'

'So, you're relocating here?'

'We are, probably until after summer. Better for Tabs, all the sea air. No paparazzi outside twenty-four hours a day.'

'Any trouble with that, just call me.' Steve passed Seb his card. 'There's something else,' Steve said. 'I'm going to need to spend a little time with you, talking about yours and Cassie's movements on her last day, and perhaps list out anyone who might have had an issue with her, or you. Any nutty fan mail. I've requested her phone records, I'm not sure if her phone was recovered at the scene.'

Seb looked at him. 'Do you think someone tried to kill her?'

'I don't know yet. Honestly, I'm still reviewing the case. But…' He let the word hang in the air.

'But what?' Seb asked, frowning.

'I was in the house at the other end of the terrace this morning, with the new owner, about a completely unrelated matter, and I came across a room that had photos of your wife scattered all over the floor.'

'What?' Seb shot to his feet. 'I want to see it.'

Steve raised his hands to try and calm Sebastian.

'It's newspaper cuttings mainly, a few photos. I've had to get forensics in to process and collate. Once they have finished with the scene, can you spare me some time to tell me when some of the pictures were taken? I need to try and make a timeline.'

'Was anyone there? Any sign of anyone?'

'Few druggies dealing out of the basement, they've relocated now. We've made it secure. I want to get an idea of time though. You've had this place for how long?'

'Three years now. Although we stayed for the summer before that, so we've been coming here for about four years.'

'Right, for all we know, the pictures may be from that initial stay, the place up the road has been empty for so long.'

'Yeah, that would be good to know. It might be one less thing to worry about.'

Steve stood. 'Sorry to worry you. But I wanted all the cards on the table so to speak. I believe in being honest and up front. Will you be able to call in and look at the pictures in the next couple of days? Shouldn't take more than an hour. But I do realise it'll be difficult for you.'

'It's fine,' Seb said. 'Text me when they're in and I'll let you know when I can come. If you call me, Tabatha will want to know the details and she is worse than any interrogator. The less she knows about this, the better at the moment. Take my mobile number.' He grabbed Steve's card and tapped the number into his phone and then sent a text. 'There. You have it now.'

'Thanks,' said Steve, checking his phone. 'Any questions or queries, don't hesitate. OK?'

'Thanks.'

'Tabatha's home for Christmas?' Steve asked, standing.

'Yeah, I thought I might get her a dog. Not a puppy, that might be too much for her, but maybe a rescue. Company, you know? Something that's hers?'

'Good idea,' Steve said. 'Gets her out and about in the fresh air too if that's your plan?'

'Exactly,' Seb said. 'Is it that obvious?'

'There's a woman, Suzy, she runs an informal dog rescue on the outskirts of town. She has a grooming business, it's called Shoosh the Floof. She'll be able to help, I reckon. She trains and rehomes. She's very good I hear. Give her a call.'

'Thanks for the tip.'

'I'll be in touch, by text.'

'Appreciate it. Bye.'

Seb thought about what Steve had said. Had Cassie had a weirdo following her? She hadn't mentioned it. The thought of someone doing something deliberately to his wife and child made a rush of white-hot rage wash over him. He worked to quell the murderous thoughts he had about the kind of person who would do something like that and drive off.

He realised his hands were shaking with rage and sat back down at the table, holding his head in his hands. He had to keep it together. He had to get a Christmas tree and talk to the dog lady today before Tabatha and her bat-like hearing came home.

His phone pinged and he looked to see it was a text from Tabatha.

What u doing?

He texted back her favourite response.

Vibing. What u doing?

She replied.

Vibing. What u doing?

He replied.

I'm going out to do secret things. See you later. x

She sent him an emoji with rolling eyes and added, *Wuv you, Dad. xx*

Wuv you more. Xx.

Seb pulled into Suzy's drive after using the scribbled directions he had jotted down. He parked and got out, unsure of where to go. He saw a large outbuilding, heard strains of music so he opted to head for that.

Suzy was grooming a huge Bernese mountain dog which was almost as tall as her. He had decided he wanted to play, so she was being pulled about like a rag doll.

'For God's sake, Rocco,' she said crossly, yanking him back towards the pen and clipping him in. She spotted Seb in the doorway.

'Oh hello,' she said. 'Sorry, he's a handful. Are you Seb?'

'I am.'

'So,' she said, all business, 'tell me why you want a dog and what sort of dog you're after?'

Thirty minutes later, Seb had outlined Tabatha and her recovery. He was also sure he had seen the penny drop when Suzy realised she knew who he was.

Suzy was thoughtful. 'It would be like a companion for her. Something that she can exercise as well as getting exercise herself. Not too big?'

'Nothing like that,' Seb pointed to Rocco.

'I've got four rescues at the moment,' Suzy said. 'Come see.'

She led him through the barn and into a smaller building, where there was a row of large pens with outside areas for each. As Suzy strolled along, the dogs rushed up to the wire fronts, tails wagging.

'We have Archie here, he's a terrier, corgi cross, he's four. Very nice natured. His owner passed away. We have Bull, he's a staffy, he's two, but I genuinely think he'd be too much for your daughter. He's very strong on the lead and I don't want to damage her chest. Harper's an ex-racing greyhound. He's very affectionate but loves to run. Might be a little stressful for her, when he sees the beach he decides to run the entire length of it. And finally, we have Jack, he's new. He's around four months, Border collie. Farmer didn't want him. He's very affectionate, but I reckon he'll be a handful.'

Seb crouched down to look through the bars at the adorable brown and white pup with a patch over his eye. The pup whined, butting the bars with his head and wagging his tail.

'Oh, he's adorable,' Seb said, smitten instantly.

'Isn't he? He's super bright and has lots of basic commands down pat. He is high energy though and will need a lot of running. Do you have a garden?'

'Small garden.'

'He needs a big space.'

'But I live on the beach… is that big enough?'

'I reckon that would be good.' She opened the cage door and the puppy rushed out, clambering all over Seb and licking his face.

'I think I've been selected,' said Seb.

Suzy laughed. 'He will be a handful. So you need to be sure you have the life where he can flourish.' She looked at him making a fuss of the puppy. 'I'm going to leave you to have a play with him without me breathing down your neck. Have a think about whether he's the right dog for you and your lifestyle. Not just now, but when your daughter is better and back at school etc. What happens then? Something to think about, OK? I'll be back in a bit.'

Seb was so engrossed in the puppy, he lost all track of time. He had completely fallen in love with him, and knew this would be the right dog for Tabatha.

When he finally stood up, Jack had jumped up at Seb to be picked up and cuddled, and had fallen asleep on him instantly.

Suzy reappeared.

'How's it going in here?' she asked.

'I am smitten,' Seb admitted. 'He'd be perfect.'

'Do you mind me asking what you do for a living? Will Jack be locked up all day or will he have company?' Suzy asked.

'I'm a writer for TV and film,' Seb said. 'I work from home, so am pretty much at home all the time.'

'Sounds perfect,' Suzy said. 'Now, before we decide anything I will need to come and do a quick home check. Just want to make sure everything is OK, and perhaps give you a heads up on what might be a danger to him.'

'Great. When do you want to do that?'

'I've got to drop Rocco back later as he's been in day care today. So is around three any good?'

'Perfect,' said Seb. 'I'm off to buy a tree anyway.'

'Right, so you need to think about a tree and a puppy. Perhaps maybe a small one, that sits on something he won't be able to reach?'

'Like a taller table?'

'Exactly. Or he'll have it over. He's into everything. Look, when I come, if it's all OK, we can run over to the pet shop on the edge of town and pick him up the right stuff? Do you need help with that?'

'You read my mind,' he said gratefully. 'Thanks. Just wondering whether we can maybe pay you to do some training for us with him too?'

'Happy to,' said Suzy. 'This one is bright, sooner we start the better. Once this breed is trained they're brilliant. So obedient and responsive.'

'Right. Great. I'll see you at three for a home check?'

'Yup. Where are you?'

'Compass Haven, the row opposite the Hope and Anchor. We're the one at the end, without the orangery.'

'See you later.'

Seb felt happier than he had in a long time. For a minute he had forgotten the crushing grief he often felt since Cass died. He had days

41

where he pretended to himself Cassie was away on location, filming. It was easier to deal with that way. But then the grief would roll in and he would realise he was never going to see her again. Hear her laugh, teasing him. He sat in the car and tapped out a text to Tabatha.

U OK?

She replied instantly.

Soooooooo bored.

He laughed and typed, *Home tomorrow. Special surprise for Christmas!*

Presents?

Perhaps.

Tease. What R they?

Secret. CU later. I'll be in later.

KK. Wuv U. xx

Wuv U. x

Seb drove back via the Christmas tree farm he had seen on the way and selected a small tree, bearing in mind what Suzy had said about the puppy. He ran some other errands and got back just before Suzy had said she would swing by for the home check. He'd just wrestled the tree inside when she rang on the doorbell.

He opened the door. 'Hello again. Come on in.'

She walked through the house, following him into the kitchen.

'Wow, when you said you lived on the beach you weren't wrong!' she said, looking out onto the bay. 'I could stand here for hours!'

'I have done,' Seb admitted. 'I lose all track of time sometimes.'

'And those steps go down to the beach?'

'They do.'

'Wow.' Suzy gestured to the door. 'OK to go out?'

Seb opened the door for her. She stepped down into the garden which was a good size, edged by a flint wall that was around four foot high.

'This will be fine for him for the next few months, but when he's bigger it might be a problem if he's a jumper, but hopefully we'll have trained him by then. Just don't put anything near the wall that he could use to jump up and over it.'

'Understood.'

'This gate is OK too. There's no way he can get through it or over and under it. So outside is good. This garden isn't enough for exercise though. You know that, right? He'll need a lot. But running on the beach every day and swimming will be fine.'

'OK.'

'OK to have a look inside?'

They walked through the house together with Suzy pointing out things that the dog would likely chew and suggesting that various lamps and their leads be moved out of the way or higher. When they reached the Christmas tree Sebastian had been wrestling with, Suzy looked at him.

'Where is this going?' she asked, amused.

'Can't decide,' said Seb.

'OK, which room do you spend the most time in? Relax, watch TV, etc?'

'Kitchen,' said Seb. 'We tend to chill out on the sofa in there mostly.'

'It should be in here then, so you can keep an eye on it,' Suzy said. 'How about we grab the table in that room and put the tree on it? I don't reckon he'd be able to get to it then.'

'Works for me.' Seb fetched the table.

'I reckon that looks pretty good,' Suzy said, admiring their efforts at getting the tree straight. 'You could plug the lights in over there and feed the cable along at a higher level here too. Just to be safe.'

'Consider it done.'

Suzy looked at her watch. 'Right, I've got time to pop to the pet shop with you if you need some help?'

'Great!'

'I've blocked you in so are you OK to go in my van?'

'Of course.' Seb followed her out and climbed into the van.

One hundred and twenty-two pounds later, Seb unloaded the stuff from Suzy's van into the house.

'Who knew such a tiny thing needed so much?' he said, looking around.

'It's just like kids really,' Suzy said, grabbing a handful of things and walking in the house with them.

'You got kids?' Seb asked.

Suzy shook her head. 'Nope.'

Sebastian looked at her from the corner of his eye. 'Sorry, I didn't mean to pry.'

'It's fine.' She waved his comment away. She stood surveying the pile of things. 'You bulk bought the food, so you won't need to worry about that for ages. Put it in a cupboard where he can't chew through the bag though.' She looked at her watch. 'I've got to go.' Her phone rang and she answered it quickly.

'Hey, Will. I'll be two minutes.' She listened for a moment. 'Oh, are you outside? OK, I'm coming now.'

Suzy turned to Sebastian. 'I have to go.' She walked towards the front door and as Seb caught her up he saw, with interest, a handsome man leaning against her van sipping a takeaway drink. Suzy waved at him and turned to Seb.

'When do you want Jack? I could get in some more intensive training over the next few days. Maybe the weekend before Christmas? And then I can give you a bit of a debrief on his training and the work you'll need to do.'

Seb thought for a moment. 'Good idea, Tabs would have been home for a while by then. I'll have to hide everything we've bought today though!'

'OK. I'll drop him over at lunchtime on that Saturday then?'

'Perfect. Thanks,' Seb said. 'Email me the paperwork you were talking about, and I'm going to give you some money for him, whether you like it or not. OK?'

'OK. It's more like a contribution to the pets we rescue though.'

'No probs. However it works best for you.'

'Thank you. See you then.'

She ran down the steps lightly, giving him a wave and blipped the van open. Seb watched while she joked with the handsome man, and they climbed in the van and drove away.

CHAPTER 5

Doug Brodie, skipper of the Castleby lifeboat, closed the door to his office and dialled the number for DI Steve Miller, who was a close mate. He needed to tell him about a woman they had rescued on a shout that morning who claimed she had been pushed off a cliff.

Steve answered on the second ring.

'Miller.'

'Brodie,' Doug replied, amused.

'Hey, buddy,' Steve said. 'What's up? I'm in the car, reception is crap.'

'Where are you going?'

'Morgue.'

'You have all the fun. Look, we had a shout earlier. A woman fell around thirty foot off the cliff near the MOD base. She came around long enough to say she was pushed, and a man had been screaming at her before he pushed her. I've got an errand to run that way, so I was going to call into the hospital to see how she was since she was choppered out. If you're there, perhaps you should join me and ask her about it. I don't want this guy chucking any more people off cliffs.'

'OK, I can see you there in a couple of hours?'

'Yeah. Call me when you're there.'

'See you later.'

Doug left the office and walked back into the kitchen where a few of the crew were gathered.

'Anyone get eyes on the people who were watching on the cliff earlier?' he said. 'Might help identify who did it.'

'I did,' Dan said. 'I took a picture on my phone. Pretty crap quality, because it was so far away, but it might be workable.'

'Can you send it to me?' Doug asked, then I can pass it over to Steve.

Doug and Steve were buzzed into the ward by the sister and were given an update on the woman's condition. Three of her fingers had been dislocated, and two of her ribs had been broken in the fall, and she was very bruised and battered. The nurse said she was lucky and requested Steve keep the questions short.

'Michelle?' The nurse said gently. 'This is a policeman who wants to have a chat with you about your fall. And this is Doug, he was on the lifeboat that helped rescue you earlier.'

Michelle opened her eyes slowly and blinked. She focused on Doug.

'I remember you,' she said croakily. 'Thank you. I just don't know how to thank you.'

'No problem,' Doug said. 'It's good to see you're OK. You said to me you were pushed. This is DI Miller, can you tell him what happened?'

Michelle breathed in shakily, her eyes filling with tears. 'I was running, it was a beautiful day, and I had my music on. I thought I heard some shouting, and I turned around. This man was calling me, shouting at me. He seemed so angry.'

'Can you remember what he was shouting?' Steve was making notes.

'I think it was a name, but my music was on. When I turned around, he stopped shouting.'

'What did he say when you turned around?'

Michelle frowned. 'It was creepy really. He started wailing, like he was in pain type wailing. He was sobbing. He was saying, it's not you, it's not you. Then he asked me why I was pretending to be her. That's when he got angry and pushed me.'

'Can you describe this man?'

'Fairly unremarkable. Young white guy. About your height, jeans, dark waterproof. Reddish hair, normal face. Really. Totally average.'

'Age?'

'Twenties? Thirties, maybe? I struggle to age people.'

'Any marks? Scars?'

'He had a red mark on his forehead.'

'It sounds like he thought you were someone else.'

'I think so too,' Michelle said. 'Maybe explains why he got angry when I wasn't who he thought I was.'

Steve finished making notes. 'I'm going to leave you my number and if you see this man again, or remember anything else, call me. Any time. OK?'

'Should I be worried?'

'I don't think so,' Steve said. 'But call me if you are. We'll talk to the people who called it in and see what they remember.'

* * *

Will was enjoying staying with Suzy. She was funny, a great cook, could drink him under the table and left him alone a lot. He was, however, getting itchy feet, so he had taken himself into town to get the lie of the land with the harbour.

It was a busy little harbour, despite most of the boats being out of the water for the winter. The council were missing out on income from visiting boats that were mooring, and he also noticed a raft of safety issues that he would need rectifying. He clocked some of the local kids tombstoning off the harbour walls, which also made him unhappy.

He was itching to start. He had received all the paperwork for his job, and formally accepted it. That afternoon he had an appointment at the flat with a Mrs Lewis to complete paperwork and exchange keys, so he was assuming Anna, who had fallen off the ladder, would show up or someone else would. He looked at his watch, it was nearly four pm.

Darkness was falling and the Christmas lights around the harbour sparkled prettily: Will had a moment of feeling quite Christmassy. He was looking forward to his first Christmas with Suzy for years; he had always been away or had chosen to be away somewhere warmer. Will and Suzy's parents were both in a retirement community in Cornwall, and for years contact from them had been sparse for both siblings. Will had always felt they believed their job in raising him and Suzy was over and had no desire to be part of their lives anymore.

They hadn't been supportive in any way when Suzy's husband left her, nor had they visited Will in hospital for the nine months he had been there; whereas Suzy had been a permanent fixture whenever she could. Will was pleased that he and Suzy were close, he loved her deeply and had always missed her when he was away. As he rounded

49

the corner to the harbour master's loft, he mused that he really should buy her something nice for Christmas.

He saw the lights were on and knocked loudly on the door.

'Come on up!'

Will walked up the stairs and saw the blonde woman he had met before. She was decorating a small Christmas tree in the corner of the room. She turned as he reached the top of the stairs.

'Hello again,' she said. 'Will, isn't it? Anna.'

'I remember,' Will said, thinking again that this woman was drop-dead gorgeous. 'Nice to see you upright, not sprawled on the floor,' he joked.

Anna pulled a face. 'Totally embarrassing,' she said. 'I'm sorry I rushed out.'

'My sister reckoned it was my ugly mug that scared you off,' he said lightly.

Anna smiled. 'Right, you'd like to take this place on? Hope you don't mind the tree, I do one for all my holiday lets and I thought it would save you a job since you're moving in before Christmas. I'll come and pack it up and take it away afterwards, if that's OK?'

'It's fine. Thanks for doing that. It's lovely. I'm feeling quite Christmassy today.'

Anna put the last decoration on the tree and zipped up a large bag containing the ornament boxes.

'You've checked the paperwork and you're alright with it all?'

Will nodded. 'Seems straightforward enough.'

Anna had laid out the paperwork on the large wooden dining table. 'We just need to go through a couple of bits and pieces, and we'll check the inventory together and the keys are yours. The council has paid the first month for you, don't ask me why, so you're all paid up and good to go. As this is a longer term let, do you want to take over the utilities or are you happy to pay me when I get the bills?'

'Happy to pay you, all you need to do is let me know how much and I can ping it over. I've got your bank details.'

'Great. You need to do council tax though.'

'No problem. Meant to ask, is there a parking space?'

'Yup. Around the back, big enough for the enormous truck they give you. Number 1 is painted on the floor.'

'Great.'

'Right, let's do that walk around and then we're all done.'

They walked around the flat with Anna pointing out various things, and Will mostly not paying attention and wondering instead who this woman was and whether she was single or not. She wore a wedding ring, but not once did she mention a husband or partner. Will was intrigued.

'How many holiday homes do you have?' Will asked.

'I've got three down in the harbour and one really large one opposite the Hope and Anchor on Compass Row. Number 2.'

'Wow. Do you manage them yourself?'

'Yes.' She produced a pen. 'Sign here and here, please, and that one is your copy.'

'What are you doing for Christmas?' Will asked, hoping that this would shine a light on her personal life.

'Putting my feet up! It's been crazy this year!'

'You got family locally?' he asked, signing both contracts.

'Yup,' she said. 'I expect they'll all need looking after, perhaps I won't be putting my feet up after all.' She folded one of the contracts and gave it to him and put the other one in a file.

'OK. All done,' she said. 'Anything else I can do?'

'Er, I've got your number? In case of any issues?'

'On the side of the boiler. List of contacts.'

'Do you mind if I bring some of my own stuff here?'

'Of course. Do you mean furniture? Shall I get rid of some?'

'No. I just want to bring my drawing board. This has such great light. It's pretty big though. I'd put it in that corner and shunt the furniture around a bit. Is that OK?'

'It's fine. Do what you like. Within reason of course.'

'Great. I'll move in over the next few days then. Can I buy you a drink to celebrate my new home and new job?'

The mention of his job made Anna inhale sharply and look away.

'No thanks,' she said stiffly. 'I have to go. Let me know if there are any problems. You've got the keys? Have a good Christmas.'

Will watched in surprise as Anna grabbed the large bag and her files, and made her way awkwardly down the stairs.

'Sorry,' called Will after her, confused. 'I didn't mean to...' he trailed off not knowing what he'd done.

He wandered around the flat and decided that tomorrow he would drive back to his flat and pack up his few belongings and move properly. If he took his drawing board apart, it fitted in his car, and he only had his clothes and a few other things. The rest had been in and out of storage for years. Switching off the lights, he looked around once more and locked up.

CHAPTER 6

Despite having a rare Saturday off and wanting to spend it in bed with his relatively new girlfriend, Kate, Steve forced himself to go to work. He was keen to see the pictures that forensics had collected from Jenny's house, and he needed to get a handle on the case.

He thought about Michelle, the runner, who'd been pushed off the cliff that morning and as he sat at his desk, he loaded the photos the lifeboat team had taken and tried to improve the quality of the image. Frustrated, he realised the figures were just too far away and too blurry, so he filed them away.

Jonesey had been tasked with following up the people that had called the coastguard and hopefully seen her assailant.

Steve grabbed the box of photographs collected from Jenny's house and headed to the large conference table where he could spread out the pictures properly. He texted Sebastian to ask him if he was free to pop in for an hour that morning. Sebastian replied that he could make it in at ten to see the pictures, before he went to pick up Tabatha from hospital.

Steve hummed an annoying Christmas song as he spread out the array of photographs and newspaper cuttings. He spent time methodically separating them out into two piles and then focused on the photographs. Three black-and-white photographs caught his eye.

Every now and again, during a case, something in Steve's psyche rang alarm bells and he would experience a weird sensation. He could only describe it as a sense of icy dread settling gently on his shoulders. This was one of those moments. He looked at the photos more closely.

They were clumsy; taken in a hurry. The flash cast a harsh white light to the immediate surroundings. Steve stared in horror at what he saw.

Someone had been at the crash! Right there. Taking pictures of a dead woman and a badly injured young girl.

The photos showed Cassie Warner, blood on her head, her face smashed, clearly dead or unconscious. Beside her, in the wreckage of the Porsche, at an odd angle, was Tabatha Scott, impaled by a tree, blood over her face and trickling from her mouth. Steve grabbed his phone and made a call.

'Adam. Steve Miller,' he said without ceremony.

'Steve. You know it's Saturday, right?'

'I know but listen. Cassie Warner's crash. I've found photos from someone who was there.'

'From the emergency team?'

'No. Actually *there*. Before the emergency services, it must have been just after it happened.'

'But there were no other records of anyone calling it in, apart from that one caller.'

'Did you see any evidence, like footprints or anything like that when you were there?'

'No way. It took the fire crews hours to get them out and stabilise the girl. Any evidence would have been trampled.'

'Christ,' Steve said, frustrated.

'Steve, where did you find the photos?'

'In an empty house. There must have been a hundred pictures in there of Cassie Warner and these were among them.'

'How many?'

'Three.'

'Can you scan them and send them to me? Might help.'

'No problem. You know what this means though?'

'We're even more sure it wasn't an accident,' Adam said quietly.

'Damn right. These pictures are sick. You said you weren't sure. You said maybe there's evidence of another car, maybe paint on the bumper of the Porsche. It all smacks of something suspicious you said.'

'I did.'

'These photos suggest that someone was *there*. Before the emergency services. What does that add up to in your book?'

'It adds up to a fucking shit storm,' Adam said grimly. 'I'm going to review the findings again. We'll need to tell the super that this is likely to be a murder and attempted murder investigation.'

'OK.'

Steve ended the call to see PC Warren hurrying towards him, her eyes wide.

'Oh… Sebastian Scott's here,' she said, grinning. 'Oh my God. He is like, *proper* fit! Where do you want him, and can I stay and perv?'

'Give me five and bring him up, and no to perving,' Steve said, trying not to smile. 'Poor man's just lost his wife.'

'I'd happily give him some comfort,' muttered PC Warren as she walked off.

She returned with Sebastian a few minutes later, just as Steve had carefully hidden the three photographs. She asked him sweetly if he would like coffee and then left, disappointed when he declined.

'How are you?' Steve asked as Seb sat down wearily at the large table.

'OK,' said Seb. 'I'm getting Tabatha in a minute. Can't wait to get her home. By the way, thanks for suggesting Suzy at the dog rescue place. She's fantastic. I've got it all sorted out and Suzy is bringing the puppy over just before Christmas, so it's a big secret.'

'What did you get?'

'Little collie pup called Jack.'

'Lovely dogs. Jesse at the lifeboat has one called Brock. He's gorgeous. How's Tabatha doing?'

'Good. She's going stir crazy in there. She can't wait to get home.'

'Right. Let's be quick then. Can you look at these and estimate a timeline for me?' Steve gestured to the array of photographs scattered across the table.

Seb inhaled sharply as he looked at them.

Steve studied him from the corner of his eye. 'I'm happy to leave you to look at them alone if that's better? I can give you a pen and Post-its?'

Seb took a deep breath. 'It's fine.' He pored over the photographs and started to move them about until they were in a line of sorts.

'OK,' he said. 'This is the oldest, going up to the most recent.'

'Oldest. How long ago? Can you place it?'

'Last Christmas. We were here for around two weeks. Cassie stayed longer as she had a difficult script to learn.' Seb scrutinised them again. 'They were all taken here. Over Christmas, then February half term, Cassie made it back from filming in Belfast for two days. Then we have Easter. We were here for two weeks then. Cassie came for the last week… See her hair is a different colour? That was for the film. Then we have the summer holidays. She left to come here early, she'd been on the most gruelling shoot in Germany, so she wanted to sleep and chill. Her friend Bree met her down here. See? That's her there with Cass in that photo. Then we came down for a few weeks in October and Bree came again too. Tabs had a few inset days at school, so we made the most of the school break.'

'This completely follows your patterns of being here. No pictures of home in London?'

'Nope. The only one I don't recognise is this one.' Sebastian held up a photograph. 'I don't know where this is, but I think she was wearing this on the day…'

Steve looked closely at the photograph. 'Hang on. I think this is the petrol station off the main road about five miles out of Castleby. She must have stopped for petrol,' he said, making a note to get the CCTV from the petrol station and surrounding businesses.

'Is this everything?' Seb asked.

Steve didn't want to tell him about the other photographs. 'There were newspaper cuttings too.'

'All in that house on the end?'

'Yes. It's empty and secure now. Jenny Miller is the new owner, she's turning it into a hotel and bistro.'

'Hers is double fronted, isn't it? Effectively twice the size of ours,' mused Seb. 'Bet it'll be lovely.'

'Pop in and say hi,' Steve said. 'She's just lost her brother, so she'd be happy to see a friendly face, I suspect.'

Seb glanced at Steve frowning. 'I'm not being set up as part of some local bereavement support group, am I?'

'No,' Steve said levelly. 'I'm just saying she's a nice lady. It's a big house. Tough to do it all on your own. That's all.'

'Sorry.' Seb rubbed his eyes. 'Bit touchy.' He glanced at his watch. 'I need to go. Anything else?'

'No, all good. Thanks for your help.'

Steve called PC Warren to come and see Seb out. She was delighted to oblige.

'I'll be in touch,' Steve promised as Seb left.

As soon as Seb had gone, Steve ran into his office and called the petrol station to get the CCTV sent over. He google mapped the area and then rang the other businesses and asked for the same thing. He told them it was urgent and sat impatiently at his desk to wait.

* * *

Foxy's ex-wife, Carla, parked her car outside the climbing centre and grabbed her suitcase and rucksack from the boot. As she slammed the boot, Solo, Foxy's large Alsatian ran out and nuzzled her legs, his tail thumping against her.

'Hello, gorgeous boy,' she said, crouching down to make a fuss of him.

'You know, I think you only come to see the dog,' a dry voice said behind her. She turned to see her ex-husband leaning against the wall with his arms folded, smiling indulgently at her.

'Hey, you,' she said, a sense of relief washing over her. She suddenly felt close to tears.

'Hey, you,' he said, pushing himself off the wall and coming over to envelop her in a massive hug.

Carla leant into the hug and breathed in his scent deeply. The sensation of being in his strong arms had always made her feel safe. She buried her face in his wide chest and tried to soak up his strength.

'You OK?' he asked, pulling apart and seeing tears in her eyes. 'Christ, Carls, what's the matter?'

For Carla, the expression on his face, the strength of his hug and the effort of trying to hold herself together for the past two months was too much. She clamped a hand over her mouth to stop herself from sobbing loudly as tears poured from her eyes.

'Upstairs now,' Foxy said. 'Mike!' he shouted. 'You're in the chair for a bit. OK?'

'OK,' called Mike as he poked his head out the climbing centre doors.

'Hey, Carla,' he called and received a wave in return.

Foxy steered Carla into his flat and sat her in one of the big leather chairs that overlooked the bay. He pushed aside the fleeting thought that it was where Sophie always sat when she was over.

'Wine, brandy or hot drink?' he asked.

'Tea.'

'Tea it is,' he said.

He made it quickly and brought it over to her along with a box of tissues and sat in the chair opposite her.

'I'm listening,' he said.

Carla took a few deep breaths and blew her nose. She sipped the drink, her hand shaking as it held the mug.

'You're scaring me now, Carla,' Foxy said, his face serious.

Carla took a deep breath.

'Remember when you came to see me at work a couple of months back?'

'Yes. When you ruthlessly admitted to using me for sex and a free holiday?'

She rolled her eyes. 'Get over it.'

'I met that guy who offered to help with Sam,' he recalled.

'Jamie. I went to a party that weekend. He was leaving to go to the Sudan, and it was a joint birthday/leaving party, so I went with another friend who's a nurse.' She looked up at Foxy. 'By the way, how is Sam?'

'Didn't make it. I'll tell you later. Carry on.'

'Oh, poor Sophie,' she said sadly.

59

'Back to the party,' said Foxy, frustrated. 'Something happen?'

Carla took another sip of tea, her hand shaking.

'I think something happened,' she said, tears rolling down her face. 'Well, turns out, I now *know* something happened.'

'Sweetheart, you're not making any sense,' Foxy said softly.

'I think I was raped,' she blurted out. 'But I don't remember. I just don't remember!' she wailed, a fresh wave of tears coming.

Foxy sat very still for a moment. His first reaction was to hit something. Preferably the Jamie guy that he had met. But that was the old Foxy and it wouldn't help Carla.

'Tell me what you do remember,' he said calmly.

She scrubbed her eyes with a tissue and blew her nose.

'I remember going with a girlfriend. We shared a cab. It was in one of the surgeon's flats on the water. It was OK, lots of people there. Jamie started to chat to me and my friend, we had a good laugh, few drinks. My girlfriend had gone off with a bloke she had her eye on. Jamie lived fairly near me, so he suggested we shared a cab home. I agreed and he said let's have one for the road and I don't remember anything else.'

'What happened the next morning?'

'I woke up. Naked. On the wrong side of the bed.'

Foxy snorted. 'You never sleep on the wrong side; you are weirdly particular about that.'

'Exactly. I never sleep naked, and I always sleep on my side.' She wiped the tears with a shaking hand. 'I had some bruises on my upper arms and a bruise on my forehead. I couldn't think how I got them.'

'Did you go and get a rape kit done?'

'I wasn't sure… I didn't know… I wasn't sore or anything… I thought maybe he had just dropped me off and I'd managed to get into my house.'

'So you didn't.'

'No.'

'Sweetie, so why now do you think you know for sure that you were raped?' Foxy said, half knowing and dreading the answer.

'Because I'm pregnant,' she gulped and started sobbing again. 'And I just don't know what to do about it.'

CHAPTER 7

Seb gently helped Tabatha out of the car and into the house.

'Dad, I can walk. OK? Stop fussing,' she moaned as he held her arm while they walked up the steps to the front door.

'Considering you've come home today and it's nearly Christmas, you're exceptionally grumpy,' Seb observed as he unlocked the front door.

'I'm OK. I just want to be normal.'

'Sweetie, until you're totally the other side of this and we've had the all-clear, you're not normal. Stop fighting it.'

'I'm not a bloody pensioner,' she muttered moodily.

'No, you're a stroppy teenager with a new bloody heart. Take it easy and stop fighting it.'

Tabatha plonked herself down in the kitchen on the large sofa and looked at the bare Christmas tree.

'Cool tree, Dad. Shall we decorate it later? Why's it up so high?'

'Er. I thought we'd try something different this year, but we'll decorate it later if you're up to it. Now, do you want anything to eat?'

'Yes. One of Maggie's heart-attack-in-a-roll breakfasts.'

'Seriously? Hardly appropriate considering,' he said dryly.

'I've been dreaming about it. Hospital food for weeks on end. I deserve it.'

'Shall I go and get it?'

'No. I want to go out. I *need* to go out. Do you understand, Dad?'

'I'm worried about you catching an infection.'

'We'll sit away from people.' Her stomach rumbled noisily. 'See? Starving.'

'OK,' he said, laughing. 'Now?'

'Now.' She stood slowly. 'Come on.'

Together they walked slowly down the hill to Maggie's cafe, passing the climbing centre. Seb looked longingly at it. He loved to climb, but he hadn't had a chance to for months. Before the accident, the centre near him in London had closed, curtailing his favourite hobby. He loved the fact that climbing cleared his mind. He focused on what was in front of him and everything else faded away.

'You should book in. You love to climb,' Tabatha said, nudging him. 'Be good for you.'

'I might,' Seb mused.

He opened the door to Maggie's café, and Tabatha stepped inside.

'Tabatha, darling!' shrieked Maggie, ignoring a line of customers and rushing around to hug her gently. 'How are you, my love? I've been so worried!'

Maggie then kissed Seb on the cheek and hugged him. 'So sad about Cassie. She was so wonderful. You must be devastated, my darlings.'

Seb felt his eyes filling up and hoped he wouldn't fall apart in front of everyone. Maggie, intuitive to everything, ushered them

63

gently over to a table before people realised who they were, promising she'd come and take their order in a moment.

Maggie had befriended the family the first time they had come to Castleby as they had been regular visitors to the cafe. She was always delighted to see them back and made a huge fuss of them all. She had even made sure Cassie had eaten properly when she knew that she was at the house on her own, learning lines. Maggie had been heartbroken to hear of Cassie's death and Tabatha's injuries.

Seb settled down with his back to the cafe and looked out to the beach and the grey December sky. The sea was rolling in, the waves were strong and powerful. Perfect for a walk later. He could lose himself in the sea, the beach and not have to think–

'Dad,' Tabatha said. 'Hello?'

'Sorry, love, what's up?'

'You need to decide. Maggie's coming over.'

'Right, my lovely people, what are you having? And what can I do to help with anything?'

Seb smiled. 'It's fine, Mags. We've closed up the house in London, so we're here now. We're focusing on Tabby Cat's recovery.'

'Months off school?' Maggie whispered. 'Result!'

'No such luck,' said Tabatha, pulling a face. 'Remote learning and a tutor!'

'Maybe talk nicely to the local school, they'll let you go there for a while,' Maggie suggested.

'It's certainly an idea,' said Seb. 'We'll see how things go.'

They placed their order and Maggie bustled off to get their drinks.

'Aunty Bree wants to know if you're doing OK,' Tabatha announced, looking at her phone.

Seb pulled a face. 'That's funny. Aunt Bree wants to know if *you're* doing OK.' He smirked.

Tabatha smiled. 'She's been calling most days. She's so funny. I miss her.'

'I know, I do. When her and your mum used to get together it was a riot. They were always laughing about something.'

'She said she might make it down for a few days over Christmas.'

'Yeah. That'll be nice,' Seb said, absently thinking about Cassie laughing with Bree on the beach and feeling a physical ache in his chest.

'Dad, on the way home, book in for a climb. You know you miss it.'

'Maybe another time.'

'Nope. We're booking it in a minute. No arguments.'

Seb looked at her, pale and drawn but smiling, and her eyes were bright.

'God, you're bossy.'

'Apple doesn't fall far from the tree, Dad.'

'Hmm.'

Tabatha pushed Sebastian into the climbing centre. They stood and looked around at the space. Ropes hung down, walls were contoured and covered with handholds in various colours. Parts of walls jutted out with large coloured shaped blocks in what looked like impossible positions. A large window had been installed in the back wall to highlight the enormous outside climbing wall. Seb breathed out in delight.

'Oh man,' he said. 'Heaven on the doorstep.'

'Help you guys?' Foxy approached them, wiping some chalk off his hands. 'Hi there. I'm Foxy. I've seen you around a bit, I think... Compass Row?'

'That's right. Seb and Tabatha,' said Seb.

'Did you want to do some climbing?' He looked at Tabatha who had suddenly gone pale. 'Hey, are you alright?' He stepped forward, catching her arm and steered her to a bench. 'Sit down. I'll grab a water.'

'Tabs?' Seb knelt in front of her. 'What's up?'

'Just a bit dizzy,' Tabatha said quietly. 'Thanks.' She accepted the water Foxy offered.

'Does the thought of climbing always make you dizzy?' Foxy enquired and Tabatha gave a wan smile.

'You've done too much today,' Seb said. 'Come on, I'm taking you home.'

'Book in to climb, Dad. We're here now. Go on.'

'Climbing for you?' Foxy asked Seb.

'Yes, been a while. Fancy that outside wall though.'

'Experience?' Foxy asked. 'You've climbed before?'

'For years,' Seb said and outlined his experience.

Foxy beckoned him over to the counter, where he flicked through an iPad.

'OK. We've got free slots tomorrow or day after.'

Seb thought for a minute. 'Let's do day after. Couple of hours. Earlyish morning?'

Foxy tapped it in. 'Tabatha climbing?'

'No way. She's just had major surgery. She won't be climbing for months.'

'Oh, I'm sorry to hear that,' said Foxy. 'Is she on the mend?'

'Hope so.' Seb looked worried. 'She's done too much today, and we only walked down to Maggie's for brunch.'

Foxy frowned. 'What sort of surgery if you don't mind me being nosey?'

'New heart surgery, about a month ago now.'

'Christ, that's tough for a kid. Look, anything I can do to help.' Foxy looked over at Tabatha with concern. 'She looks exhausted. The truck's outside, let me run you up the hill. She doesn't look like she'll make it.'

Seb looked at Tabatha. 'Appreciate it.'

* * *

Will had got up early and driven through darkness to his old flat, where he'd packed up his stuff, taken apart his drawing board and loaded his car. He stood in the flat and realised he felt no emotional attachment to the place whatsoever. When he thought about it in more detail, he was pleased to be rid of it. Leaving the keys in the key safe, he headed back to Castleby.

He was wrestling his drawing board out of the back of his car when the edge slipped, and he almost dropped it. As he clutched it desperately, trying to preserve the corners from being smashed on the ground, he felt his back going into spasm and gasped out loud, trying to move position without dropping the board.

'Whoa! Need a hand with that?' a voice called.

Foxy was returning from dropping some flyers into the sea cadets centre, after dropping Tabatha and Seb home and had spotted Will struggling. He stopped the Land Rover and hopped out, quickly grabbing the other side of the drawing board from Will.

'Thanks,' Will said gratefully. 'Can't seem to get a grip on it.'

'It's awkward all right,' Foxy said, clutching the corner as it slipped. 'Where are we going with it?'

'Up here,' said Will. 'It's OK though, I can manage.'

'Don't worry about it,' said Foxy, heaving up his end. 'I've got it, it's no problem.'

Together they manoeuvred the large drawing board up the stairs and into the corner. Will had already set up the stand, so between them they balanced the board gently on until Will could secure it.

'Thanks very much. I'm Will.'

'Foxy,' said Foxy. 'Sorry, it's Rob… Rob Fox, everyone calls me Foxy. You an architect or something?'

'Nope. New harbour master. I design racing boats as a hobby.'

Foxy stared at Will. 'Christ, you're Will Scully, aren't you? I saw you race in Sydney. Man, you raced like you were possessed or something,' he said in admiration.

Will pulled a face. 'I was just probably in the zone.'

'Amen to that. How are you? Didn't you break your back or something?'

'I did,' Will acknowledged. 'I'm fine now. All recovered. Retired from racing.'

'So you're the new harbour master?'

'I am.'

'Quite the change then?'

'Yup,' Will said.

'I can relate.'

'How so?'

'Ex special forces. I own the climbing centre opposite Maggie's.'

'Endure?'

'That's me. You should come in. We can stretch that back of yours right out.'

Will almost winced at the very idea of it. 'Maybe,' he said guardedly. 'Look, thanks again for the help.'

'No probs. Anything else need bringing up?'

'No. All good. Thanks.'

Foxy headed for the stairs. 'Next time you're passing, swing by and I'll buy you a settling-in pint.'

Will smiled at him. 'I like the sound of that.'

'See you.' Foxy disappeared down the stairs.

Will collapsed on the sofa and looked around his new flat happily. He grabbed the rucksack next to him and shook out a few painkillers, downing them dry. He was happy here already, he thought, and he would definitely take Foxy up on the offer of a pint.

Will could hear the rain. His brain transported him back to the scene. The sound of the rain hammering on the upturned keel of the boat, him lying awkwardly beneath it, clutching on, suffering pain like he had never experienced before and knowing instinctively that he had injuries he may not recover from.

His brain told him to breathe shallowly, there was only a small pocket of air left in the keel. He felt coldness surround and enclose him. Felt the chill seeping into his bones. He tried to move but couldn't. Pain seared through him like a hot branding iron.

He heard a phone ringing. For a moment his brain struggled to comprehend why a phone would be ringing underwater and then he realised he was in his flat and had fallen asleep on the sofa.

He struggled to wake, fumbling for his phone in the rucksack, dragging it out and answering it.

'What ya doing?' Suzy asked him.

'Napping,' he said dryly, trying to calm down his hammering heart.

'Lightweight. You OK? You sound weird. Look, I'm dropping a dog off, wanna get dinner?'

'Yup. Where?'

'I'll come to you, and we can decide from there. See you in a bit. Get your lazy arse moving, bruv.'

'Yes, boss,' he said, ending the call. He leaned back on the sofa, realised his hands were still shaking from the dream.

* * *

Steve was at the police station, sitting at the large conference table, waiting for a video call from Adam, the accident investigator. They were reviewing his report.

Earlier, Steve had received the CCTV footage from the garage and seen a number of things that had piqued his interest. There were some numberplates he needed to run, and he'd seen what looked like someone taking pictures, but the camera obscured their face. They were sat in a car across the road from the garage. He quickly checked his email again to see if the file of the CCTV footage showing the inside of the garage had arrived.

He summoned Jonesey who arrived within seconds holding a coffee and eating a large iced bun.

'Christ, Jonesey, are you eating again?'

'It's PC Garland's birthday, I'm just showing willing. Do you want one? There's plenty going.'

Steve thrust a list towards him. 'Names, addresses and status of all of these plates, please. Quick smart. Anything on witnesses to the runner pushed off the cliff?'

Jonesey crammed the last enormous piece of bun into his mouth so that his cheeks bulged.

'No,' he managed through the bun. 'People gave a description very similar to the one she gave. Average-looking bloke with reddish hair. Odd behaviour. Crying and muttering. He ran off when they tried to approach him.'

'Hmm, go through known offenders when you get a minute, you might be able to narrow it down with the hair colour at least.'

Jonesey nodded. 'On it.'

Adam appeared on Steve's laptop screen. After exchanging pleasantries, Steve pushed on.

'Can you share your screen and talk me through where you think the other cars were?'

Adam took his time reconstructing what he thought had happened for Steve. In simple terms, he had modelled that Cassie's car had been bumped from the back. With the trajectory of the push and the approaching bend of the road, this had pushed the Porsche into the lane for oncoming traffic and it had swerved off the road.

Adam concluded that there had been some initial evidence of an oncoming car, but there was no evidence of it braking hard.

'Is that usual?' Steve asked. 'Why wouldn't someone brake?'

'Hard to say. There are a myriad of reasons. It could have been a car with crap brakes, the driver was blind drunk or stoned, they were texting or just not paying attention. But I also wonder, maybe this might be what you would see if a car had overtaken Cassie's and had maybe pulled in front of her. Perhaps if it had happened that way, Cassie might have swerved to avoid it. But there is definitive evidence of another car at the scene, perhaps pushing her from behind.'

'Wait. Pushing the car from behind on a blind bend?' Steve said doubtfully.

'I said it's a possibility. I'll need to wait for paint residue analysis on the Porsche though.'

'Jesus,' said Steve. 'Some of those bends are nasty on that road, who would overtake?'

'No one in their right mind would. Unless…'

'Unless what?'

'Unless they were doing it deliberately.'

'Then that makes it murder,' Steve said quietly.

CHAPTER 8

Doug Brodie was sat at his desk, in the lifeboat station with his feet up, looking out to sea as he chatted to his partner Jesse on the phone. She was away looking after her elderly parents and Doug was missing her badly.

'SKIP!' a voice called.

'I'd better go. I'll call you later,' he murmured into the phone. 'Love ya.'

Doug ended the call and walked out of his office. 'What?' he called.

'Special visitor, Skip!'

Doug looked behind Tom's shoulder and saw Anna. The widow of his late best friend Gavin.

'Anna!' Doug was genuinely pleased to see her and enveloped her in a hug. 'I never get to see you these days, you're always rushing off somewhere or waving as you drive past. How are you?'

'I'm doing OK,' she said. 'You got a minute?'

'For you? Always.'

Doug gestured to his office and she followed him in.

'Do you want a coffee?'

'Not if you're making it,' she said, shutting the door behind her. She eyed him. 'Look, Doug. Did you know and just not tell me?'

Doug looked confused. 'Did I know what?'

'That they've replaced Gav?'

Doug's eyes widened in surprise. 'A new harbour master?'

'Uh huh. He's taken the loft too.'

'Wow. You've met him then?'

'Yes.'

'And?'

She shrugged. 'He's a nice man. Pleasant.'

'But?' Doug said, missing nothing.

Anna sat down heavily in the chair. 'But he reminds me that Gav's gone!' she wailed. 'And that things have moved on and people have forgotten him.' Tears ran down her face and she fumbled for a tissue.

'Hey, come on now,' Doug said, coming around the desk to give her another hug.

'No one is going to forget Gav. I miss that ugly mug every day,' he said, gesturing to a photograph on the wall of Doug and another guy grinning broadly. 'See? Who can forget that?'

Anna sniffed and gave a halfhearted laugh. 'I went to pieces when I met the new guy. Soon as he said that he was taking the harbour master's post I lost the plot and ran out of the loft like a right idiot.'

'I'm sure he didn't think that.'

'Oh, I'm sure he did,' she said dryly.

'Have you seen him again since then?'

'We met at the loft when he got the keys. He tried to be nice, and I just wanted to get out. It was all I could do to hold it together...

seeing him there. Standing where Gav used to stand. I just couldn't do it.'

'Oh, Anna. What can I do?'

Anna sniffed and blew her nose. 'You can tell me to stop being so damn stupid.' She sniffed. 'It had to happen sooner or later. We can't do another summer without a harbour master. It's not good for the town.'

'You're right.'

'I miss him so much, the fun we used to have together,' she said sadly.

Doug took her gently by the shoulders. 'Anna, you will always be part of this crew's family, you and Danny. Always. Just because Gav's gone, it doesn't mean you need to stay away or not see any of us.'

'I know. But it's so hard to see everyone without him there goofing about in the background.'

Doug smiled. 'I know. But we all miss you. Why don't you come to Maggie's bash Christmas Eve? You can get to know some of the new faces.'

Anna thought for a moment.

'Come on,' said Doug. 'It'll be good to see you out and about.'

She bit her lip for a moment. 'You're on,' she said firmly. 'My social life is nonexistent, so I would love to.' She looked worried for a moment. 'You might need to hold my hand, I'm a bit rusty at meeting new people.'

'Whatever you need,' Doug said. 'I'll hold on for as long as you need me to.'

'Thanks. How's Jesse? She not around?'

'Her dad had a bad fall, and her mum's ill, so she's taking her turn to look after them. She'll be back in a week or so hopefully.'

'You're missing her like crazy?'

Doug looked sheepish. 'Yup.'

'I'm happy for you, Doug. No one deserves it more than you. Right, I must go. I've got stuff to do. See you later and thanks for the chat.'

As Anna left, Doug pondered what Anna had said about a new harbour master. He wondered who it was and made a mental note to wander around to the harbour master's office for a nosey later that day.

He busied himself making a couple of calls and heard laughter and a light tap on his open office door. He looked up to see a handsome, tall man, with light brown hair and intense green eyes standing in the doorway.

'Doug Brodie?' the man asked pleasantly.

'Guilty as charged,' Doug said. 'How can I help?'

'I'm Will Scully. New harbour master. Thought I'd come and introduce myself.'

Doug regarded the tall, green-eyed man standing in his doorway with a mixture of emotions.

'Good to meet you,' he said, shaking his hand. 'I've only just heard there's a new harbour master.'

'I start officially in a couple of days, but I thought I'd get a head start. Your lifeboat is a beauty. I've been admiring her. Bet she goes well.'

'She does.'

'She's a self-righter, isn't she?' Will asked, looking out of the door and down into the pit where the lifeboat sat.

'Yup.'

'Ever been in one when it does that?'

'I have. Wasn't great. For the first time ever at sea I wondered whether I would lose my breakfast,' Doug said, smiling.

'I'll bet. Can I buy you a coffee? Be good to pick your brains a bit if you can spare the time.'

'Happy to,' Doug said and grabbed his jacket. 'Let's go and bother Maggie.'

Doug called out to Tom that he would be at Maggie's and the two left the station and walked to the cafe.

'Do you know the place?' Doug asked as they walked.

'Yeah,' Will said. 'My sister lives here. She's on a farm on the outskirts of town, runs a dog grooming business and rescue.'

'Ah, so you're not a complete outsider.' Doug chuckled. 'Previous harbour master had been in the job fifteen years and the locals still called him the new harbour master, so be prepared for it to take some time to be accepted, especially by the old locals.'

'I'm not expecting it to be easy to integrate at all, to be honest.'

'Why do you say that?'

Will looked rueful. 'You know how it is. Much loved predecessor, tragic death, everyone mourning, no one wants to move on. No one wants it to look like he's being replaced. No one wants anyone to think he'll be forgotten.'

Doug's opinion of Will shot up a few notches. This guy was perceptive.

'Nothing you can do about what people think,' he muttered. 'People always have an opinion, whether you want it or not.' He opened the door to Maggie's and gestured Will in.

'Hello, handsome,' Maggie called from behind the counter.

'Hey, Mags,' Doug said. 'Come and say hello to Will. He's the new harbour master.'

Maggie raised an eyebrow. 'Nice to meet you Will. You've got big old boots to fill,' she said pleasantly.

'I'm aware,' Will said ruefully. 'Nice to meet you, Maggie, is this cafe the best kept secret in town by any chance?' he asked, looking around. 'It might well be my new favourite place.'

'Much more talk like that and you might be my new favourite person,' she said, preening. 'What can I get you?'

76

'Two coffees, please,' said Will. 'I'm unashamedly pumping Doug for information before I start next week.'

'You two sit, I'll bring them over.'

'Are you living with your sister?' Doug asked as they sat by the window, knowing full well Will had taken the flat.

'No, I've taken the loft over the sea cadets hall.'

'Nice little place.'

'It is.'

'You've met Anna then.'

'Yes. Small blonde lady?'

'The very same.'

'I think every time I speak to her, I say something wrong though. Don't know what it is I seem to do.' Will shook his head.

'Pay no mind to it.'

'You know her well?'

'I do.'

'Is she OK?'

'She's struggling to adjust if the truth be known. Struggling to get her head around a new harbour master.'

Will looked confused. 'Why would she be struggling to adjust to a... Oh God... Who is she?'

'She was his wife.'

Will sighed. 'And suddenly everything makes sense. It didn't occur to me that she would be his–'

'Widow,' Doug finished.

One of Maggie's staff delivered their coffees.

'She's OK about it. She needs to move on. Perhaps just bear it in mind if you see her around,' Doug said, picking up his drink.

'Has she got family?'

'Not immediate. Gavin's nephew, Danny, lives with her. He's in his twenties. He has some learning disabilities, he's a lot younger than he is if you get my drift. Gavin's older brother was not a nice man.

Social services took Danny away and Gavin gave him a home when he was a teenager. He's been there ever since. He's a lovely chap. He used to help Gav out every now and again at work. Gav got him a fleece made that read Deputy Harbour Master and he always wore it. He loved helping Gav out. He misses him.'

'What about you? Do you miss him?'

Doug took a sip of his coffee to get his emotions under control. 'I do. Every day.'

'You were close?'

'Best mates.'

'I'm sorry.'

'Don't be.'

'Can I ask what happened on the shout?'

Doug knew that whoever filled Gav's boots would always want to know what happened that dreadful night. Doug hated talking about it, but every time he did, it got a little easier. Quietly he told Will what had happened.

'Blimey,' Will said and drained his coffee. He had listened raptly as Doug talked. 'So you lost Gav and Jeff, Billy had a stroke, and you were injured too?'

Doug nodded.

'How bad were you?' Will asked.

Doug's phone rang and he looked at the screen. 'I just need to take this,' he said. 'I'll be back in a mo.'

He took the call outside and Maggie came bustling over with another two coffees.

'Oh,' Will said, surprised, 'thanks.'

'On the house,' she said. 'You too looked in such deep conversation I figured you could do with another drink.'

'Doug was filling me in on the rescue where they lost Gav and Jeff.'

Maggie frowned. 'Did he tell you he almost died too, just trying to get the last one out? Piece of metal nearly sliced him in half, but he held on, made sure everyone got to safety. That man was a bloody hero. He was in hospital for weeks. He discharged himself to come to Gav and Jeff's funerals, say some words and be there for the crew. The man could barely stand. Looked like a train wreck, I can tell you. He was on his feet all day. I don't know how he did it, but he said he did it for them.' She looked affectionately at Doug through the window. 'He is a very special man that one. Salt of the earth,' she said wistfully. 'Anyway, enjoy. Oh, by the way, Christmas Eve I'm having a party here, we have a fire on the beach, and I do a spit roast. Come and meet everyone. It will be good to have you here.'

'Thanks. Can I bring my sister? She lives in town.'

Maggie looked confused. 'I know everyone in town.'

'She runs a dog grooming place…'

'Suzy? Shoosh the Floof and dog rescue Suzy?'

'The very same.'

'Yes! I see it in the eyes now. I like Suzy. She's more than welcome here. Starts at 7 p.m.'

'Look forward to it.'

Doug slid into the seat across from Will again.

'Thanks for the coffee, Mags,' he called. He looked at Will. 'She been gossiping?'

'Oh yeah.'

Doug picked up his cup. 'Right, I've shown you mine, now you show me yours. Tell me about you. You interested in being crew?'

'I was on my local crew for years, when I was actually at home long enough to help out. I'd be really happy to help out if you need me, but I come with a warning though. I broke my back a couple of years ago, so I have to be pretty careful about what I do.'

Doug winced. 'Ouch. How did you manage that?'

'I was racing a catamaran for the America's Cup. It cartwheeled, broke apart.'

Doug put his cup down suddenly. 'Fuck me, you're that Will Scully. Olympic medal, Will Scully.'

'Guilty as charged,' Will said wryly.

* * *

Sebastian had awoken to a wave of grief. Used to Cassie being away, or not around, he had still known he could call her at pretty much any hour, and she would talk, even if she had been sleeping. She would always text him before they started filming so he knew not to call, but most of the time they spoke whenever they could when she was away.

He had awoken realising he couldn't ever call her again. He looked at the black-and-white photograph of her in the silver frame on his bedside table. The wave of grief that washed over him had been so powerful that he had cried himself out and fallen back to sleep for another few hours. Deep down, he knew he had to stop pretending she was away and actually deal with it. But he wasn't sure he could.

He lay for a while thinking about her and suddenly realised he hadn't heard any noise from Tabatha, who rarely did anything quietly. Panicked, he stumbled out of bed and ran along to her room to find her bed empty. He ran downstairs and half skidded into the kitchen, coming to a surprised halt when he found her decorating the Christmas tree.

'What's the matter?' she asked, looking at him in surprise.

'Nothing. Just checking you were OK before I hit the shower,' he said, trying not to mother her too much, he knew it irritated her. 'How are you today?'

'Fine. I literally slept right through from when we got back from Maggie's to about an hour ago.'

'Taken your meds?'

She rolled her eyes. 'Yes. Nag, nag, nag.'

'Right then. I'll go in the shower then.'

Tabatha looked at him strangely. 'OK. Why are you being weird?'

'I'm not being weird.'

'Yes, you are. Go on then.' She made a shooing gesture.

'OK, I'm going,' he said, slightly grumpy at being dismissed.

Seb made his way upstairs and showered trying to not think about Cassie too much, he knew he would break down again and in his view, Tabatha didn't need him doing that just now. As he made the bed and finished dressing, his phone pinged with a text from Steve Miller, the local inspector.

Sebastian. Are you free for a quick chat?'

Sebastian kicked the door to his bedroom shut and dialled Steve, who answered after the first ring.

'Hi Sebastian, thanks for calling back so promptly.'

'It's fine. Call me Seb. Any news?'

Steve exhaled heavily. 'There is. It's not great news either, but first, how's Tabatha?'

'She's good, thanks. Very tired yesterday, which was a worry, but she's sparky this morning.'

'Great. So, I want to be as transparent as I can be with you, so I need you to trust me.'

'OK.'

'By this I mean that what I'm about to tell you isn't general knowledge. It won't be general knowledge for as long as I can keep it that way. So this has to remain confidential.'

'Right.'

'I mean it, Seb.'

'You have my word.'

'Seb, I'm sorry to inform you, but we're treating Cassie's death as suspicious.'

Seb sat down suddenly on the edge of the bed.

'Suspicious? What does that really mean? Are you saying it wasn't an accident?'

'It's important to be calm. It might mean nothing. Let's hope it was just an accident, but there are some things that the accident investigator and I aren't happy with, so we've moved this to the next stage. We have to treat it as suspicious, so we can continue to investigate.'

'What aren't you happy with?'

'Seb, you have to trust me. When I have something concrete to tell you, then I'll sit down and talk you through it. At the moment, it's all supposition and I need to try and turn that into evidence. Can you trust me?'

'I don't see how I have a choice.'

'I'll try and be as honest as I can, when I can. OK?'

'OK. Does this mean I can bury her?'

'It's still with the coroner. I'll push for a burial order, so bear with me. I don't think it stops you from making certain arrangements though, things can be organised as much as possible and then when you get the nod all that's needed is a date.'

'Oh OK, I didn't know that.'

'Something to think about perhaps. I know it helps some people with the process.'

'OK. Perhaps I'll give it some thought then, try and get organised.'

'I'll keep you posted as much as I can. I just ask that you trust that I am doing everything I can.'

'I feel pretty helpless here, so I can't do much else except put my faith in you. Keep me in the loop though?'

'Will do. I'm on it and I'll be in touch. Look after yourselves, won't you?'

'Thanks, Steve.'

He ended the call and sat thinking for a moment. He *could* get stuff organised. He needed to discuss it with Tabatha though.

Seb dished up a boiled egg for Tabatha and watched, amused, as she buttered toast and cut it into soldiers.

'Aren't you a bit old for soldiers?'

'Dad,' she said sternly. 'You are never too old for soldiers.'

Seb refilled his coffee and sat at the table.

'Tabby Cat, did you have any preferences about a funeral for Mum?' he asked softly. 'I don't want to be making all the decisions here.'

Tabatha dipped her soldier in the egg. 'I wondered when we were going to talk about this,' she said, matter-of-factly. 'I have had some thoughts. I think we should ask Aunty Bree too.'

Seb looked surprised. 'Really?'

'Absolutely. They used to talk about these sorts of things. What songs they would have played. Mum used to love that song… oh what was it? Bill Withers. "Ain't No Sunshine When She's Gone". She always used to joke that she would like that played at her funeral.'

Seb swallowed heavily. 'I had no idea.'

'Did you never listen to the crazy conversations they used to have?' Tabatha asked.

'Clearly I didn't listen closely enough,' he said sadly.

'We have to get organised, Dad,' Tabatha said, leaning over and patting his hand. 'So, funeral or cremation? Did she ever say what she wanted?'

'When we used to stand here and look out at the sea, she always said she wanted to be scattered on this beach, in her favourite place.' Seb said quietly.

'Then that's what we shall do. So she will always be here with us,' Tabatha said firmly. 'Cremation for Mum and then you and me to scatter her.'

'Not Aunt Bree?'

'She'd probably drop her. But yes, Aunty Bree too.'

Tabatha dipped another soldier. 'Good, so that's decided. Flowers. Mum hated lilies. Loved daffodils, peonies, sunflowers so we'll need to find out what flowers will be around when we can do it. Do we know yet? Did you say it was the coroner who decides if we can bury her?'

'Still waiting to hear.'

'OK. But we can plan a service, can't we? What we want to say, who we want there? What songs?'

Seb tried to hold back the tears. 'Yes, love. We can plan all that.'

'Good. We should FaceTime Aunty Bree, see what she says. Or talk to her when she comes down.'

CHAPTER 9

Carla sat in the big leather armchair and watched the weather whip across the horizon. Unable to sleep, she had risen, made herself coffee and was wrapped in a cosy blanket. Solo, forever sensitive to emotional upset, was curled up on her feet.

Carla was genuinely at a loss about what to do. She felt calmer now she was with Foxy. She could think straight. She was an emotional wreck though. She had a baby of a rapist growing inside of her. She didn't know how to feel. Didn't know what to think. Did she want it? What if it was a monster?

She had told Foxy everything. She had half expected him to get in the car and track down Jamie. Instead, Foxy had been calm and composed, and focused on where she would go from now and getting through it together. He had come a long way.

Foxy walked in yawning and rubbing his hair.

'What's up?' he asked. 'You were restless in the night.'

Carla felt a surge of love for him. She had asked him if he minded if she slept in his bed with him. Not for sex, but just to be close. He had said whatever she needed. Being next to him made her feel safe.

'Couldn't sleep. Too much thinking, not enough sleeping.'

Foxy poured coffee before sitting opposite her, cradling his mug in his enormous hands.

'So, what's the upshot of all this thinking?'

Carla felt tears threatening. 'I just don't know what to do. What to think,' she said, a rogue tear rolling down her face.

Foxy leant forward to brush it away.

'Carls, listen. Think about this a different way. If you had the choice, would you want another baby?'

Carla sighed. 'No. I'm too old.'

'Even if Tom Hardy rocked up and said, "Carla, I want you to have my babies"?'

Carla snorted with laughter. 'Even then. I'd have to say sorry, Tom, it's a no from me, but I'm happy to practice.'

Foxy looked serious.

'This isn't about whether you want a child or not. This is the question of whether you want to have the pregnancy terminated?'

'I guess so. I keep thinking, I know it's early days, but in my view this is a living being, it's not the baby's fault how it came about.'

Foxy frowned. 'Yes, but it happened against your will. I'd understand the dilemma a bit more if it was an accident in a consenting relationship. But this man drugged you and took you against your will.'

Fresh tears rolled down Carla's face.

'I know all that. I think about nothing else. I can't do anything about it, can I?'

Foxy studied her in silence.

'I want you to have a chat with Steve.'

'Steve?'

'You know, Steve the copper. He's a good mate.'

'And say what?'

'Tell him what happened. Find out what your options are.'

'I'm pretty clear on what my options are.'

'No, Carls, I meant, your options with Jamie.'

Carla pushed herself up out of the chair and paced around.

'But I don't remember! There is no evidence. Well, nothing…' She searched for the word. 'Immediate.'

'There's your word Carla and the fact you're pregnant.' Foxy walked over and held her upper arms. 'Come on. We can't just accept this. You might feel better if you know there's something you can do.'

Carla thought for a minute.

'Who's going to believe the word of a lowly nurse against an ex-soldier heroic surgeon?' she said, frustrated.

'I do. Other women will come forward. I bet you.'

'What, and have everyone know it was me? Pointing fingers and gossiping? My God. My career would be over. It would follow me *everywhere*. I'd always be the nurse who accused the surgeon. No one would want to work with me.'

'I'm sure there are ways it can be done so everyone doesn't know. This is why we need to talk to Steve.' He looked at her imploringly. 'Come on, at least talk to the man.'

'Only if it's off the record at this stage.'

'Done. I'll call him now.'

Steve left Foxy's flat, frustrated on a number of levels. He had spent an hour or so with Foxy and Carla and had been highly distressed to hear what had happened to her and the resultant situation. His heart ached for Carla, he couldn't imagine how awful it must feel to be in her situation and to then be faced with one of life's true moral dilemmas.

He felt a surge of anger towards the low life scum who would do anything like that to a woman. He pondered what he could do for her as he walked. He had explained the process, all of which was made even more difficult with Carla not remembering, or having any sort of rape kit or tox screen performed as soon as she realised. The only evidence in truth after all this time was the DNA of the baby and obviously, Carla's word. Sometimes he felt the justice system gave out no justice whatsoever in situations such as this.

'Steve! Wait up!' Steve turned and saw Foxy jogging up the road behind him.

'You forget something?' Steve asked.

'Thanks for just now,' Foxy said, standing with his hands in his pockets. 'I've had to stop myself from getting on the road, finding this guy and beating him to a fucking pulp.'

'I would feel the same, I think,' said Steve.

'I have to think about Carla and her career though. I can't sabotage that in any way by going on a crusade with the lads to kill him.'

'I didn't hear that last bit,' Steve said. 'Mind you, in this situation I think I'd bring a shovel and help you bury the body.'

'Top man.'

'I've got a colleague I worked with in Cardiff who now works in this area. Penny Morton. I know she would pick this up as a fishing exercise. This is the sort of criminal that often gets away with it. The worst kind. Highly intelligent, arrogant – it's a combination that's like catnip to her. She will be out for blood. She would happily go fishing and try to speak to a few of Carla's colleagues and ask them if they've experienced anything like this or have heard of anyone it's happened to.'

'OK. Sounds good. What do you need from us?' Foxy asked.

'A list of nurses who were at the party and their wards.'

'OK. Carla will want to know this still isn't official though.'

'Doesn't need to be at this stage. We're gathering evidence, going fishing.'

'Will she want to talk to Carla?'

'She will. She's fantastic though. She'll be gentle. Trust me.'

'I'll get Carla to make a list. I'll give you Carla's number too.'

'Sounds like a plan. I'll call Penny later and brief her. Check it over with Carla though when you get back and let me know if it's alright?'

'Will do. Thanks, Steve.'

* * *

Sniffy was having a bad morning. Currently he was having his head bashed against a wall by a large man he didn't know. Sniffy couldn't decide which he was likely to succumb to first: his dangerously full bladder, or a state of blissful unconsciousness. Either was welcome if it made the man stop.

Sniffy had been minding his own business, on his way back from his daily ritual of bin rifling at the back of the Loafing About Bakery. They had a new apprentice who tended to leave things in the oven for too long, so there were always rich pickings in the bins. He had been shuffling past Compass Row, where Steve had unceremoniously kicked him out of a few days ago, and a large man had grabbed him by the scruff of the neck and dragged him into a small alleyway.

The man was shouting at him as he bashed his head against the wall, but Sniffy couldn't make out what he was saying. Finally, the large man was tapped on the back and Sniffy saw a smaller man with sharp features, in a smart suit, with slicked back black hair, scary dark eyes and a very pointed, but well-groomed black goatee beard.

'Hello there,' the man said pleasantly in a thick Liverpudlian accent. 'Am I right in thinking your name is Sniffy?'

Sniffy screwed up his face to try and focus on not wetting himself.

'Who's asking?' he said, trying to sound bolshy and unafraid.

The man pushed Sniffy against the wall and produced a long sharp-looking knife from his pocket.

'You can call me Ringo,' he said, pushing the blade of the knife up underneath Sniffy's chin so that he had to stand on tiptoe to stop the knife entering skin.

'Whhaaa… what d'you want?' whimpered Sniffy, desperately thinking that if he lost control of his bladder on this man, then he would absolutely die, no doubt about it.

'I need to have a little chat with you about your dealer,' Ringo said, keeping the pressure on the knife fairly constant. 'I want to change the arrangements here you see.'

'I don't know anything about that,' Sniffy said, sniffing frantically, the fear made his nose run more than usual.

'Oh, I think you do. I also wanna have a chat with a guy called Jimmy.'

'Who's Jimmy?' Sniffy asked innocently.

'I think you know that too. I need to employ the services of the very helpful Jimmy and his boat. Where can I find him?'

'I don't know,' said Sniffy desperately.

'Do you need some help remembering?' Ringo increased the pressure on the knife. Sniffy felt blood trickling down his neck.

'I… I… don't know,' Sniffy gasped. 'I don't do drugs.'

Ringo guffawed loudly. 'Nice one. Very funny. I've been watching the goings on here. I saw the comfy little gig you had over the road. But you've moved on now, haven't you? Well, I've got some boys coming who need a place to stay so they can do their work. I'm thinking, Sniffy, that maybe they can come and stay with you?'

'I don't live anywhere,' Sniffy said, the need to pee at a critical level now.

'I thought you lived wherever you did your dealing? Now, Sniffy, by the way, why do they call you Sniffy?' Ringo tilted his head, waiting for an answer.

'Don't know,' Sniffy said guardedly.

'Perhaps you need your nostrils made bigger.' Ringo moved the tip of the knife into one of Sniffy's nostrils and flicked it, cutting through the side of his nose cleanly. Blood poured from the cut. Sniffy whimpered.

'Might help your sniffing there,' observed Ringo. 'What do you reckon, Paul?'

Paul smiled cruelly. Ringo continued. 'Correct me if I'm wrong, but you were living there...' He pointed with his knife at Jenny's place. 'Looks good enough to me.'

'Builders are c-coming in,' stammered Sniffy. 'I've moved on.'

Ringo pouted. 'But I quite liked it. Bit posh, I thought. I could see myself there. All grand like.'

'I'm in the old hotel now,' said Sniffy desperately. 'Water's been left on.'

'Ahh.' Ringo regarded him. 'Maybe that'll do then. My boys tend to go where they're told. So, let's have the name of this dealer then, and where we might find him so we can have a little chat.'

'He'll kill me,' whined Sniffy.

'Perhaps. But I might get there first, in which case, you won't have to worry, will you?'

Ringo gently inserted the knife into the other nostril. 'So shall we make this one bigger too?'

'No... noooo...' Sniffy pushed against Ringo.

'Now, this *does* look interesting. What's going on here?' Steve said, leaning against the wall at the front of the alleyway and folding his arms. 'Here's me, on my way to the police station, enjoying my morning, and what do I see? Sniffy here locked in, what looks like, an amorous embrace with someone I don't recognise. Oh, and was that

91

a large illegal weapon I saw as well? Now I don't believe we've met, have we?' Steve directed his question coldly to Ringo. 'Detective Inspector Miller, and you are?'

Ringo narrowed his eyes. 'Don't know what you mean, officer,' he said, stepping back from Sniffy and surreptitiously sliding the knife down his cuff. 'I'm an old friend of Sniffy's passing through, with my mate here.'

'Do you have a name?' Steve said pleasantly.

'Ringo. This is my mate, Paul.'

'And will George and John be joining us at some point?'

'Don't know what you mean, officer. Anyway, Sniffy, I've left you my number, let's talk soon, eh?' He moved to walk past Steve and nodded politely as he passed him.

'You have a good day now, officer.'

Steve watched Ringo and Paul walk down the high street towards the harbour road and turned his attention to Sniffy.

'Friends of yours?'

'Not if I can fucking help it,' Sniffy said, pushing past Steve and running off up the road.

Steve watched him go and got his phone out. He made a call and stood watching the harbour as the phone rang.

'Jerry,' he said when it was answered. 'Just come across two scouser thugs feeling up Sniffy.'

Detective Chief Inspector Jerry Reed exhaled loudly into the phone. 'Christ they must be desperate, have you smelt him? What did they look like, did you get a name?'

'One wall of muscle, unremarkable and the other, well groomed, dark eyes, black goatee.'

'He give a name?'

'Ringo. Oh, and his mate was Paul.'

'Were John and George waiting in the wings?'

'That's pretty much what I said, ring any bells?'

'Yup. Not good bells either.'

DCI Jerry Reed headed up the Organised Crime Unit for the area and had been on the case of the Camorra's for some years. Every time Jerry got close to nicking Mickey, he managed to slide out of it somehow. Jerry was obsessed with Mickey to such an extent that it had started to make Steve uncomfortable.

'Is it connected to Mickey?' Steve asked.

'No. It's *competition* to Mickey. Word is, Liverpudlians are muscling in, bringing in county lines to the coastal towns, they're working their way down the coast. Mickey's empire is under threat from what I hear, and he won't be a happy camper. If that happens, I'll never nail the bastard.'

'It's coming our way?'

'Not if I can fucking well help it. I need Mickey to stay around so I can get enough on him to lock him up for good. We need to think about this. It might be something we discuss with Mickey face to face, get him to trust us.'

'Face to face, have you made a will?' Steve was incredulous.

'Mickey is receptive to mutual interests.'

'Rather you than me.'

'Way I'm thinking, it might be better coming from you.'

'No fucking way.'

'Steve, he sent you the gift in the box. Remember? That means you're on his radar. He did you a favour letting you know that scum was dead. I think he'll be more receptive to you.'

'Excuse me if I don't agree.'

'It smacked of Pearl to me though. Perhaps she's the way in. In fact, thinking about it, it had to be Pearl.'

'I'm not keen on this whole idea, just so you know.'

'Get in touch with Jimmy. Get him to call Alexy and set up a meet with Pearl. She's a sucker for a pretty face, so she'll love you. Plus, she'll take it as a personal favour that you've come to chat about mutual issues. Oh, and don't forget to thank her for the gift in the box. It's only polite.'

'I wish I'd never rung you now,' muttered Steve.

'Speak to Jimmy, get him to ring Alexy and set up a meet. Call me before you go. We need to give them information. It's currency. I've got to get this fucker somehow.'

'Jerry, this is your area. I'm busy with other stuff, you know.'

'Suck it up. It all adds up to working your way up the greasy pole of promotion.'

'Can't be promoted up the greasy pole if I'm fucking dead,' Steve grumbled, ending the call, and stomping up the hill angrily.

Steve arrived back at the station to a pile of messages. The petrol station where the photo had been taken of Cassie had finally sent the CCTV from inside. He set about loading the film. He pressed play and scrolled through at speed, whizzing through the preceding customers, until he reached the rough time frame that he was looking for. He sat watching as a stream of customers entered.

Jonesey came in with tea and KitKats, and plonked them down on Steve's desk. He sat down, unwrapped his biscuit, and dipped it in his tea before sucking the chocolate off it noisily. He looked at the black-and-white screen.

'What's this then?' he asked, slurping loudly.

Steve sipped his tea. 'This is…' He pointed suddenly. 'Look there she is. This is Cassie Warner, just before she died.'

'Who's that bloke she's arguing with?' Jonesey asked.

Steve focused in on the slightly blurry image. 'Hello,' he breathed out.

The grainy footage showed Cassie arguing with a tall man, her body language showing she was angry. He repeatedly tried to grab her arm, but she kept pulling it out of reach. He was taller than her, but his back was to the camera, he was wearing a black hoodie, with a baseball hat pulled down low and the hood over that. The man was trying to calm Cassie down and she was pointing a finger at him and talking.

'Do you reckon she's shouting or talking?' Jonesey asked.

'She's talking quietly. Look at the position of this guy's head, he's straining to listen.' Steve took a picture of the enlarged image. 'We need to see if Sebastian knows him.'

Jonesey snorted. 'From the back? I wouldn't know if this was my mum in that get up. Perhaps we should assume he didn't know him?'

Steve frowned at him. 'What?'

Jonesey gestured to the screen. 'Well, you know. What if she was, you know, playing hide the sausage with this bloke? It'll finish him.'

Steve looked at Jonesey aghast. 'Hide the sausage?'

'You know… gettin' jiggy–'

'I know,' Steve snapped. He was angry with himself that it hadn't even occurred to him; he had just assumed all was rosy. That wasn't the objective person he was.

'Either way, I need to know who this bloke is,' he said.

They watched as Cassie said something angrily and then held up her hand to stop the man from following her. She went out of the door and left the man standing there. He disappeared from view and then didn't reappear.

'Where did he go?' Jonesey asked.

'No idea.'

'What's to the left of where they were standing?'

'Dunno.'

'I think we need to find out,' Steve said grimly.

CHAPTER 10

The address for the registration of the car that had been parked opposite the petrol station, where someone had been holding a camera, had come through. Steve had a theory that it was the same person who had taken the picture of Cassie filling up with petrol as well as the three photos taken at the crash. The timing seemed to fit.

He had grabbed Jonesey, and they were headed there to have a chat with the owner.

'Who owns the car?' Jonesey asked, chewing noisily on a toffee as they drove to a house on the outskirts of town. 'What is it? A Fiesta?'

'Yeah. Edwyn Lewis, aged fifty-eight. He's got previous. He's been nicked for drunk and disorderly a few times and there's reports of suspected domestic violence going back some. A good while back social services removed his son because he was physically abusive.'

'Why the look?' asked Jonesey, offering Steve a toffee.

'I know this name from somewhere,' Steve muttered. 'Have a look in that file and tell me the name of the kid.'

Jonesey flicked through the file. 'Daniel Lewis is the son.'

'How old is he?'

'Twenty-six.'

'Daniel Lewis,' Steve mused. 'Why do I know that name?'

Jonesey chewed nosily and Steve suddenly hit the steering wheel. 'Danny. It's Danny. Anna's boy.'

'Anna Lewis?' Jonesey was doubtful. 'Can't be.'

'It is. I remember it now. Danny was the son that social services took away. He's got some learning disabilities. Edwyn was beating him black and blue, rumours were the beatings were half the reason he was the way he was. Social services stepped in when the school reported it and they placed him with Edwyn's brother, Gavin.'

'Gavin Lewis? Lifeboat Gav that died?'

'Yup. Gav was only about thirty when he got Danny. The two brothers were estranged. His brother, Edwyn, was a funny one. I remember the rumours vaguely. Gav helped Edwyn's wife leave. He used to beat her something rotten too. Too much to drink then use her as a punchbag. Gav couldn't stand it. Helped her escape. That's when they fell out finally. Gav took in Danny, and he's been with him ever since. When Gav died, Anna wouldn't hear of him leaving.'

'Danny the only kid?'

'There was an older brother if I recall. He was very like Danny, but a lonely soul. Years ago, people used to call him "Simple Teddy", but these days people have to be a lot more politically correct about it.'

Steve slowed the car and nosed through a gap in a tall overgrown hedge. Before them sat a dirty white bungalow, with a large yard. Several rusty cars lined the hedge, and a scraggy chicken pecked its way across the muddy grass. The windows were dirty, the curtains torn; it looked sad and neglected.

Steve glanced at Jonesey. 'Grim.'

They climbed out of the car and picked their way across the yard, heard a dog barking and made their way to the front door.

Steve knocked and called loudly. 'Police, Mr Lewis. Can you open up, please?'

No answer came from the silent house, except the sound of the dog. Steve knocked again. The dog's barking became more frantic.

'Let's have a poke about,' Steve said. 'Have your cosh ready in case there's a rabid dog about. Last thing I want is something taking a chunk out of my leg.'

The pair turned to walk around the back of the house and came face to face with a man in dirty clothes, sporting long matted grey hair and a beard, and a large weal on his forehead. He was pointing a double-barreled shotgun at them.

Jonesey gasped in fright.

Steve raised an eyebrow. 'Mr Lewis? Here's hoping you have a licence for that firearm.'

The man narrowed his eyes. 'What you want? You here about the boy? What's he fucking said now?'

'We would like a chat with you about a car that's registered to you.' Mindful of the shotgun, Steve slowly drew his notepad out of his pocket. 'A green Ford Fiesta.'

'Don't have it.'

'You've sold it?'

He sniffed. 'I don't have it.'

Steve persisted. 'Who has it?'

He shrugged. 'Teddy uses it sometimes, other folk too. No idea where it is. No idea where Teddy is before you go poking your nose in and asking.'

Steve jotted it down. 'Teddy is your other son?'

The old man narrowed his eyes. 'None of your fucking business.'

Steve raised an eyebrow. 'Our records show that Daniel Lewis is also your son.'

'Dead to me,' he sniffed. 'Was dead to me the day they took him away and he let them. Good riddance. He was a fucking idiot. Always repeating things, arranging things. Muttering. Not the full fucking ticket. Thick as fucking shit. Pleased to be rid of him.'

'Daniel lives locally though still, doesn't he?' Steve pushed his luck. 'You must see him around?'

The old man hawked up phlegm and then spat on the floor. 'I don't go out much. I haven't seen him. S'pose he moved on when Gavin died.'

'He didn't.'

'She's welcome to the fucking idiot then. She's a fucking do gooder.'

'Tell me where I can find Teddy.'

'Why?'

'I need to speak to him about where he was a few weeks back, he might have seen something, just before an accident happened.'

'Don't know where he is.'

'Does he work?'

'Part-time job with the parks. Too thick for anything else. He's slow. Up here. Like a child.'

'Where does he live?'

The old man narrowed his eyes again.

'He comes and goes as he pleases, sometimes I don't see him, sometimes I do. I don't keep tabs on him.'

'If he's like a child, are you not bothered about his welfare?'

'What fucking business is it of yours?'

'What days does he work?'

The old man remained quiet. Steve rolled his eyes.

'You have no idea where he might be right now?'

'Nope.'

'My next stop will be the council to find out when he works, so I'll catch up with him that way.'

'You do that.'

'Right.' Steve glanced at Jonesey. 'We might be back at some point, Mr Lewis.'

'Why's that?'

'For the sheer pleasure of your company. I'll be asking the station to check the licence for that firearm too. If it's not registered and licensed, then we'll be coming back to take it.'

'You can fucking well try.'

Steve gave him a hard look. 'Don't push me. We will take it if we have to, Mr Lewis.'

The old man spat on the ground near Steve.

'Haven't you got other innocent people to bother?' he said rudely.

Steve gave a bright smile. 'Well, it's been an absolute pleasure, Mr Lewis, we'll be going.'

Steve walked back to the car and climbed in, Jonesey followed him at a fast trot. As Steve closed the door, a large mongrel came running around the corner and launched himself at the car, teeth bared, spittle flying, his claws scratching at the paintwork.

'Shit!' Jonesey stared at the dog through the window. 'Look at that thing!'

'You mean look at the state of that thing?' Steve said, undeterred by the animal's ferocity. 'Look, it's thin, covered in open sores. That miserable old fucker shouldn't be allowed to look after anything.'

Steve started the car and drove out of the driveway. Further down the road he pulled over and scrolled through his phone before making a call.

'Well hello there, Inspector Miller,' said an amused female voice over the hands-free speakers. 'I haven't heard from you since you told me about that horse the gypsies left.'

'Rachel, I'd like to think I spoil you with these things,' Steve said dryly. 'Look, I've got another one for you to check in on. Not a horse, a dog.'

'Where and what?' Rachel said, all business.

Steve rattled off Edwyn Lewis's address. 'Dog, looks malnourished, sores all over it. Bit rabid-looking. Bloke's a miserable bastard with a shotgun, so be careful.'

'Poor thing. Mistreated?'

'I'd lay money on it.'

'Is that the place on the edge of the marshes?'

'Yup.'

'OK. I'll call in on my way through in an hour or so, can you give your station a heads up in case I need someone sharpish?'

'Yup. You going with anyone?'

'I'll take one of the guys.'

'Let me know how it goes, yeah?'

'Will do. Thanks for the tip.'

Steve ended the call. 'Jonesey, call the station and give them a heads up about the RSPCA calling in on father of the year back there. Also get them to check the shotgun licence and let me know ASAP. OK?'

'Guv, where are we going now?'

'Fishing, Jonesey. We're going fishing.'

While Jonesey was on the phone to the station, Steve had driven around the town slowly, looking for a parks department person or vehicle. They were often around, tending to flowerbeds, roundabouts, and the town's planters. Finally, he saw two men working on a flowerbed that overlooked the harbour. He pulled over, told Jonesey to hang on and strolled over to the two men.

'Afternoon, lads,' he said pleasantly. 'Either of you Teddy?'

One of the men put his hand up, reminding Steve of a small child at school. 'I'm Teddy.'

Steve smiled. 'Hi, Teddy. I'm Steve, a policeman, can you spare me a minute to have a chat?'

Steve estimated Teddy to be in his late twenties. He had greasy, unkempt dark hair, his face had a slight layer of grime to it, suggesting it wasn't washed that regularly. He was very tall and thin, verging on malnourished. His clothes were worn and dirty, and he had a yellow high visibility coat on that said 'Parks' across the back. The steel toe caps in his boots had worn through the leather and were like shiny eyes peeking out from the boot fronts.

Teddy looked at his colleague doubtfully. 'Well, I don't know if I can, it's not break time… Am I allowed, Barry?'

Barry nodded. 'Go on.'

Steve gestured to a bench. 'Shall we sit here, Teddy?'

Teddy followed him over and sat on the bench. He folded his hands neatly in his lap and clamped his legs tightly together.

'So, Teddy. I'm looking for a car that is a green Ford Fiesta. Is that yours?'

Teddy was silent for so long that Steve wondered if he'd heard him. Finally he spoke.

'It's Dad's,' he said and then whispered, 'I drive it sometimes. Not very often though.'

'Where is it now?'

Teddy frowned. 'I think it's at Dad's place.'

Steve gritted his teeth. Miserable old fucker lied to him.

'Teddy, can you remember where you were about a month ago? It was a Saturday, the 16th November. Might you have taken the car and driven to the petrol station outside town?'

Teddy was silent for a long time; he looked like he was trying to remember.

'Which side of town? The one near caravan park?'

Steve nodded, watching Teddy carefully as he bit his lip to help with his thinking.

'I might have done,' he said slowly. 'But I don't like going that way, I don't like the people over there and the road is very narrow. I only go that way to go bird watching around there. But not very often. The nature reserve has parakeets, you know. Yellow and green ones.'

'Is there any way you can be sure if you were there, Teddy?'

'Why?' Teddy asked.

'I just need to know. It's in connection to an enquiry of ours.'

Teddy frowned. 'I don't know what that means. I take pictures of the birds when I go. I could look at them.'

'Could you, Teddy? Where is your camera now?'

Teddy looked uncomfortable. 'It's in a safe place.'

'At your dad's?'

Teddy shook his head. 'No, he would sell it. I don't let him see it. I have to hide it, so people don't use it without asking me.'

'Right. When can you look, Teddy?'

'Maybe after work?'

'OK,' he said reassuringly. 'Back to the car. Who else uses the car?'

Teddy bit his lip again. 'Few people. Dad's friend uses it too. I'm not supposed to.'

Steve's ears perked up. 'Your dad's friend? Who's that then? Got a name?'

'Lenny.'

'Got a surname?'

Teddy shrugged. 'Lenny. I don't like him though. He smells funny. The car always smells funny when he has it.'

'Do you know where Lenny lives?'

'No. He stays in the caravan around the back of the house sometimes though. Not at the moment. I don't know where he is now.'

103

'How old is Lenny? What does he look like?'

'Older than me and you. About the same age as Barry.' He pointed to Barry who was leaning against the flowerbed smoking and chatting to an older lady.

Steve looked over. 'Does he have grey hair like Barry?'

Teddy nodded.

'A beard?'

Teddy nodded again. 'But it's long and scraggly. He smells. I can't be much longer, or Barry will be cross. I'm not allowed to talk to people when I'm working.'

'I think you'll be OK. Do you have a phone, Teddy?'

Teddy shook his head and said firmly, 'No, they give you head cancer.'

'Right. How can I get in touch with you if I need to?'

Teddy looked panicked. 'Don't ask Dad. He'll be cross and then he'll...'

Steve leant forward. 'And then he'll what, Teddy?'

Teddy closed his eyes. 'He'll be cross.' He thought for a moment. 'Barry has a phone.'

'What days do you work?'

'Always Monday, Tuesday and Friday.'

'Are you always around the town?'

'Always in the town. Always,' Teddy said.

'OK. Can I meet you tomorrow in town and you can tell me about the pictures? Better still, you show me.'

Teddy looked wary. 'You won't take my camera?'

'I won't.'

'Promise?'

'Promise.'

'Cross your heart?'

'Cross my heart.'

'OK then. I will be on the harbour flowerbeds tomorrow morning from 8.30 a.m.,' he said very precisely, showing Steve the hands on his Mickey Mouse watch as he spoke. 'Can I go back to work now?'

'Go for it.'

Steve watched him walk back and start work again. Barry flicked his cigarette away and walked over to Steve.

'Everything OK?' he asked with a little attitude.

'Yup. Just trying to track down a car that Teddy uses.'

Barry looked over to where Teddy was working. 'He's not passed his test, but he can drive. Did you get any sense out of him?'

'Some,' Steve said. 'Pain that he doesn't have a phone though, in case I need to catch up with him.'

Barry sighed. 'They always put me with him, so take my number.' He rattled it off. 'So, you know he's…' He looked over at Teddy. 'Not quite the full ticket, don't you?'

Steve raised an eyebrow. 'Define that for me?'

'Bit slow. Not very worldly. No real common sense. Bit odd.'

'Ah,' said Steve, not wanting to pass comment. 'Barry, thanks for all your help. So, you don't mind if I call you if I need to speak to him?'

'Fine.'

'I'm popping back for a chat tomorrow with him first thing,' Steve said. 'You're on the harbour flowerbeds?'

'Yeah.'

'Right, I'll see you tomorrow then. Bye, Teddy!' he called as he walked back to the car.

Teddy watched him go and gave him a small, embarrassed wave.

'Who was that?' asked Jonesey, ending a call as Steve got in the car.

'That was Teddy, son of the delightful Mr Lewis.'

'What did he have to say?'

'He doesn't know if he was there, he's showing me his camera and pictures tomorrow morning.'

'Why didn't you just take it?' Jonesey asked.

'Softly softly… catchee monkey. He didn't have it, plus he's a little vulnerable. I need to be careful. Anyway, he says the car is at his dad's.'

'Oh, that lying git,' said Jonesey.

'I know. He says he uses it, but not often. He also said others use it too. Anyway, what news?'

'Well, no licence for the shotgun, that's made Sarge quite cross, so he's sending the boys around to confiscate it. By my reckoning his gun will go at the same time as the dog gets taken away.'

Steve started the car. 'I really enjoy this job some days,' he said, chuckling as he pulled away. 'Ask Sarge to have a thorough look around for that green Ford Fiesta while the boys are there.'

* * *

Jenny received a letter that morning from her brother's solicitor. It contained the details of a life insurance policy that he had taken out a few years before he had been diagnosed with a terminal illness. The payout was significant, and he had written her a short note which he had asked the solicitor to enclose. Jenny had read the note, laughed out loud and then cried for an hour.

Alright, Muppet? What can I say? It's a cliché, I know, but you're only reading this now because I've only gone and bloody snuffed it. I've had my suspicions that something wasn't right for years, so I took this out thinking it might help if I croaked. Anyway, buying whatever hotel we pick and doing it up will no doubt be a fucking money pit, so this should help you do it. You need a focus, babe. You need roots and a community. You need to stop being so fucking flaky and get this done. Be around people, let people in. Make friends. Let everyone see the person that I know and love with all my heart. So, here are the rules.

Don't spend it all on wine and Pringles, or chocolate… or rescue animals… you know what you're like. Spend it on an amazing place. You'll make anywhere wonderful. I can see it all in my mind. Now, stop faffing about, get cracking with the hotel and aim to be open in the summer. I love you and I'll be watching.

I'll miss you and your silly frog face. But it's safe to say I won't ever miss your fucking awful cooking, so for everyone's sake employ a chef. Now… come the fuck along and get started!

Love you, Muppet, H. xx

Jenny thought about the note, which was tucked safely in her pocket. She parked her car and got out to greet the small removal van that had followed her through the town. She had legally completed, and was the proud owner of a mountain of debt that would only grow larger in the coming months. She unlocked the door and set about pointing out where she wanted which bits of furniture.

As she stood on the drive directing the removal men, she heard a car horn toot loudly and turned to see Teeney hanging out of the window.

'Jenny!' he called. 'Everything OK? You here for good now?'

She waved. 'I am! It's mine!'

He gave her a thumbs up. 'Keep Christmas Eve free!'

'Why?' She looked wary.

'Maggie's having a party! Everyone's invited. You're our newest resident! I'll knock for you at 7 p.m.!'

'Oh… well…' she stammered.

'See you then!' Teeney shouted and drove off.

Jenny smiled as she turned back to the removal men. Already she felt happy she'd made the decision to go it alone. She ran lightly up the steps and in the front door. She risked a small giggly twirl in the large hallway, when the removal men weren't looking.

CHAPTER 11

Steve had arranged to meet Sebastian at 8 a.m., before his climb and out of earshot of Tabatha. They stood outside Foxy's climbing centre, their breaths clouding in the cold clear air.

'I have to ask you a couple of tricky things, Seb,' Steve said.

'Out with it,' Seb said with a resigned air.

'Did Cassie have any admirers? Anyone who was getting too close that you knew about?'

Seb thought for a minute. 'Not that I know of, she didn't mention anything. You should speak to Bree, she'll remember if Cass said anything to her. She's got the memory of a bloody elephant.'

'OK.' Steve produced his phone. 'Do you know who this is?'

Seb took the phone and enlarged the image with his fingers.

'Where's this from?'

'Petrol station.' Steve didn't want to tell him Cassie and the mystery man were arguing.

Seb frowned. 'I have no idea. You can't really see anyone with that hood up. No other angles?' He glanced at Steve. 'Do you think she knew him?'

'I don't know.'

'Well, no one immediately springs to mind who looks like this. Ask Bree too, she was in and out of Cass's film sets if she was working near, maybe she knew who it was.'

'What does this Bree do?'

'She's PR for some of the big artists. You know the sort, she's the one that puts the positive spin on all the shit that goes down.'

'Ah,' said Steve. 'Can you think back and tell me what you guys did on Cassie's last day, please?'

'OK.' Seb rubbed his face and blinked as if clearing his mind. 'We all got up late. Although Cass said she didn't sleep well, so she was downstairs, looking at a couple of new scripts, I think. We had brunch and then Cassie went out for a few hours. Something to do with the costume for her latest film, a fitting or something. I was pretty much in my office all day getting a script finished. She came home and her and Tabs packed and then they left.' He blinked back the tears that sprung into his eyes. He shook his head and exhaled heavily. 'Tabatha wasn't even supposed to be going with her. She had another few weeks at school, she was supposed to be coming down with me. The heating plant at the school broke down though, so they sent a text to everyone saying the kids could do remote learning for the rest of term as it was a serious thing to replace.'

'So people thought she was going on her own then?'

'People?'

'Anyone who knew she was going away.'

'Maybe.'

'OK. I'll talk to this Bree and try and catch up with her.'

'She's on her way down tomorrow, so if you want a face-to-face, she'll be here tomorrow evening.'

109

'Good to know,' Steve said. 'I'll let you get on.'

'Keep me in the loop?' Seb asked.

'Of course,' said Steve. 'Enjoy your climb.'

'This is a ring-necked parakeet,' Teddy said proudly, showing Steve some pictures he had unwrapped from a brown paper package. 'They like the nature reserve, the heathland and the forest.'

'Wow,' said Steve, nodding, wishing he'd sent Jonesey. 'Teddy, is there a date on these pictures showing when you took them?'

'Not these.'

'When did you take these?'

'I can't remember when it was,' he said quietly. 'Would you like to see my camera?'

'Please.'

Teddy carefully handed over his camera and Steve struggled not to show his disappointment.

'This takes film? Not digital?'

Teddy looked affronted. 'I don't want a digital camera, the microwaves can give you head cancer.'

'Ah,' said Steve. 'This is on number 32, do you remember when you put a new film in?'

Teddy thought about it for a long time.

'How about you think about what pictures were last developed and then maybe what you've taken since then,' Steve urged.

'I took pictures of the sanderlings when they were playing on the low tide, under the jetty,' he said thoughtfully. 'Then I took pictures of the jellyfish on the beach. Then I took...' He looked flushed. 'Then my film ran out.'

'So you put a new film in and what did you take pictures of?'

'I can't remember.'

'When was the last time you saw the parakeets, Teddy?'

'A few weeks ago. Oh yes. But I finished early because the weather was horrible, and I got wet waiting for the bus.'

'What did you do?'

'I ate my picnic lunch in the bus shelter at twelve thirty.' His eyes brightened. 'On bird watching days I have a picnic. I buy a pasty, a sausage roll and a donut from the bakery to have. I save my money all week for my picnic. Lunch is always at twelve thirty. Barry always has lunch then.'

'Don't you have lunch in the week then?' Steve asked.

'No. I don't have any money for lunch,' Teddy said, carefully arranging his photographs and wrapping them precisely back in the crumpled brown paper.

'Why don't you have any money for lunch, Teddy? You have a job.'

'I don't have the money from my job,' Teddy said quietly. 'I find money on the floor, and I save that.'

'Where does your money go?' Steve asked softly.

'Dad has the wages paid into his bank account. I'm not allowed any. He says I can't be trusted. He says I'm not worth it.'

Steve felt the anger rising inside him. 'Do you get a meal at home, Teddy?'

Teddy was repeatedly smoothing the brown paper of his photos and looking agitated.

Teddy shook his head. 'Dad won't cook me food. He says it's a waste, he says I need to man up and know what it's like to be hungry,' he said quietly.

'Does he cook for himself?'

Teddy bobbed his head.

'So what do you eat?'

Teddy bit his lip. 'Promise you won't put me in prison?'

'OK.'

Teddy looked around furtively and whispered, 'I find food in the bins. Sandwiches that people have half eaten and stuff. The new bakery is always throwing things out too. But sometimes they're burnt.' He wrinkled his nose. 'People throw a lot of food away.'

'Why would I put you in prison for that, Teddy?' Steve asked quietly.

'Because it's stealing,' Teddy said wide-eyed. 'And that's wrong.'

Steve sighed deeply. He wanted to do some serious damage to Edwyn Lewis for his unrivalled cruelty to the people and animals around him. He knew from Rachel at the RSPCA they had removed the dog. The old man had threatened Rachel with the shotgun, but as he was brandishing it and yelling at her, the police turned up, cautioned him and removed the gun. A further search found another two shotguns, but no sign of the green Ford Fiesta.

Rachel had said she thought the dog might be beyond help, but she would be prosecuting Edwyn Lewis for animal cruelty and issuing a fine. She was going back the next day to take the ten chickens she had found on the brink of starvation too.

Steve wondered what to do. It was a gamble, but he had to try.

'When will you finish that film, Teddy?'

Teddy looked confused. 'I don't know.'

'Here's an idea. How about you finish that film today and I pay for it to be developed super-fast? They can do it in an hour in the high street.'

Teddy's eyes widened. 'I usually have to wait at least two weeks for mine to come back. Barry helps me with the envelope.'

'What time do you finish today?'

Teddy consulted his Mickey Mouse watch. 'I finish at 2 p.m. today because I am doing an extra morning this week.'

'OK. I'll meet you outside Maggie's Beach Cafe at 3 p.m., yes? Down there?'

Teddy nodded. Steve pointed to 3 p.m. on Teddy's watch.

112

'That gives you a chance to finish the film and then we can go and get it developed together. OK? I'll pay.'

'And I get them back an hour after I put it in?'

'Yup,' Steve said.

'Whoo that's fast,' Teddy said in awe.

'Three p.m. Yes?'

'Three p.m,' echoed Teddy. 'One-hour photos! Goodness, whatever next!'

* * *

Tabatha was restless and fancied some fresh air. She decided to walk down to the climbing centre to watch her dad climb and then maybe wheedle some food out of him at Maggie's. She made her way slowly down the road towards the centre. Pushing open the door, she spied Sebastian at the top of the massive wall. She sat on the bench where she could see him, and relaxed as she watched him climb.

'Foxy'll be around in a minute.' A tall blond boy with a cute face and very light blue eyes walked around the corner, chalking up his hands. At that moment, the door banged open, and another boy of a similar height rushed in. He had brown eyes and a mop of unruly dark hair; he grinned as soon as he spotted the other boy.

'Bro... Can't believe you beat me here.' He laughed.

'Snooze you lose,' replied the blond boy, grinning.

Tabatha watched the two with interest. She missed school. She missed the interaction of kids, and she missed her friends.

'Hey, Tabatha,' Foxy said, appearing from the back. 'Good to see you. How are you feeling?'

'Good thanks, and thanks for taking me home the other day,' she said shyly.

'Happy to help.' He turned to the boys. 'Boys, this is Tabatha. She's just moved here. Tabatha, this is Marcus and Jude. Both ace climbers.'

113

'You here to climb?' Jude asked.

Tabatha looked rueful. 'No not allowed. Just had surgery.'

'Jude had to have surgery a few months back,' Marcus volunteered. 'He's OK now though.'

'Bit different here, chaps,' said Foxy, clapping Marcus on the back. 'And I think Jude would argue that his hands are still healing.'

Jude smiled. 'Damn right.'

'Surgery on your hands? What happened?'

Jude pointed at Marcus. 'This dick fell down an old mine shaft and I had to get him out. I busted my hands up doing it.'

'Worth it though, mate, wasn't it?' Marcus nudged Jude. 'Saving your best mate and getting hero status.'

'Only sometimes,' Jude said, rolling his eyes.

'What surgery did you have?' Marcus asked as he plonked himself down on the bench next to her and started unlacing his shoes.

'New heart,' said Tabatha quietly.

Marcus looked up at her, eyes wide. 'Man, that's hardcore. D'ya hear that, Jude?'

Jude looked at her with his startling blue eyes. 'It is,' he agreed. 'You doing OK? It's a big deal having a new heart, my mum's a surgeon at the hospital. It can take a long time to get over that.'

Tabatha smiled. She couldn't help liking the pair of them. 'Yeah, I'm OK. Miss my friends though, they're all back in London, so it can get pretty lonely here.'

'Come and hang out here then,' Marcus said matter-of-factly. 'There's always someone here and most of the kids that climb here are pretty cool.'

'Apart from that dick Jacob,' interjected Jude.

'Well, yeah, apart from that dick,' agreed Marcus. 'So you can hang out with us? See? That's sorted. Foxy won't mind, will you, Foxy?'

'Nope,' Foxy said, disappearing off to the outside wall to chat to Seb who was nearly at the bottom.

'OK,' said Tabatha. 'I might come and hang out.'

'You should do,' Jude said, smiling at her. 'You can watch me try and beat this guy who had to resort to throwing himself down a hole, just so that I would mess up my hands rescuing him, and he might then have a chance of actually beating me.'

Tabatha giggled. 'Extreme measures.'

'He's a bad loser. What can I say?'

'Yeah yeah,' said Marcus. 'You and your fairy tales. Come on then, money where your mouth is, bro.' He pushed Marcus out the way. 'Last one to the top buys the donuts.'

'Whaaat?' Jude raced after him and together they started climbing the wall.

Tabatha watched in amusement as they raced each other. She felt a little happier than she had in a while; not quite so lonely.

Foxy walked back in with a handful of ropes and sat next to her on the bench.

'You should, you know,' he said, expertly winding the ropes.

'Should what?'

'Come and hang out. You can help out a bit if you want. Bookings, or sorting the shoes and ropes, there's always stuff to do.'

'Really?'

'Really,' he said. 'Those two are great lads. They'll be good friends if you let them.'

Foxy got up and walked over to the reception desk to answer the ringing phone. 'Think about it,' he said over his shoulder, and Tabatha nodded.

Seb emerged looking sweaty but very happy.

'Hello, love,' he exclaimed. 'Alright?'

'I'm good. Fancy breakfast at Maggie's?' she asked cheekily.

Seb rolled his eyes. 'Go on then.'

Local fisherman and sporadic petty criminal Jimmy Ryan was on his boat in the harbour. He was off to pick up his lobster pots, but he was taking his time. He was flush with money due to a particular exceptionally dodgy deal. He had lived to tell the tale and kept himself out of prison.

He was currently serving a suspended sentence for couriering drugs by boat for some highly undesirable Russians. The judge had been lenient because he'd helped the police round up the gang responsible. In Jimmy's view, he was lucky to be alive, but it seemed like Jimmy was born lucky. Hapless, but lucky.

Jimmy's world was good. He had money, his boat was fixed and running sweetly thanks to Jesse from the RNLI crew. He whistled as he sorted out various things on deck and stacked his boxes.

'Jimmy.' His name was whispered.

Jimmy turned to see who was whispering in broad daylight on a virtually empty quayside. He shielded his eyes from the low winter sun and looked for the person responsible.

'Sniffy, you alright? What can I do for you?'

'I've come to warn you,' he said solemnly in a deep whisper.

'You high again, Sniffy?'

Sniffy looked blank. 'No.'

'What have you come to warn me about?' Jimmy said, irritated by him already.

'There's two blokes, called Ringo and Paul.'

Jimmy burst out laughing. 'Fuck's sake, Sniffy. What are you on? Ringo and Paul? You'll be seeing a yellow fucking submarine in the harbour next.'

'I mean it,' Sniffy said angrily. 'They're here, and they want to speak to you about using your boat.'

'Using my boat for what?'

'Bringing in drugs. Well, that's what I think they meant.'

'And where are this Ringo and Paul?'

'I don't know. They want to talk to my dealer. They said things are going to change around here. They're scousers.'

Jimmy pondered for a moment and then dismissed it.

'OK, well thanks for letting us know, Sniffy. Where you hanging out?'

'Old hotel.'

'I thought you were in the boarded-up place opposite the Hope?'

Sniffy looked forlorn. 'Got kicked out. It's OK back at the hotel, they've left the water on.'

'You eaten today?' Jimmy asked.

Sniffy shook his head. 'Nothing in the bins at the bakery,' he said mournfully.

Jimmy dug into his pocket and pulled out a fiver. He passed it up to Sniffy.

'Get breakfast and a drink. Not fucking blow or skunk. I'll check with Mags, you know.'

'Thanks, Jimmy,' Sniffy said, screwing up the fiver and shoving it in his pocket.

'Food, Sniffy. Not shit. You look like death. Hear me?'

'Thanks, Jimmy.'

'See you later.'

Jimmy started the boat and motored out of the harbour. He debated calling his Russian contact Alexy. On reflection, he decided the less he had to do with Alexy, the greater the likelihood he would live a lot longer.

CHAPTER 12

Steve was waiting outside Maggie's cafe at 3 p.m. precisely. He was relieved to see Teddy walking down the road towards him with a carrier bag. He reminded Steve of a rescue dog his parents had rehomed when he was a boy. The dog had been beaten with a stick regularly, his back broken at one point. For years the dog had walked like he was going to be hit at any moment, always in a semi-cowering state. Teddy reminded him of that dog.

'Teddy.' Steve smiled as he approached. 'Did you finish your film?'

'I did. I took a picture of Barry.' He giggled, delighted. 'He was very cross! Then I took some pictures of the beach. I got an extra two pictures as well. Thirty-eight from a thirty-six film.' He held up the film cartridge safe in its black plastic cannister.

'Right. Let's go and put it in then.' Steve steered him up the road and into the photo place.

Teddy looked around the shop in awe.

'An extra set too, please?' Steve said quietly since he was paying.

'No problem,' the woman behind the counter said.

'Hour, right?'

'We're quiet, so more like forty-five minutes,' she said.

Teddy looked at his watch and shook his head. 'Forty-five minutes to develop a *whole* film. I can't believe that. It's amazing. What do you think they'll come up with next?'

'Maybe little printers you can connect to your phone, that print pictures out.'

Teddy snorted. 'Print pictures from a phone? No way. That's just a silly idea.'

'Right, Teddy. You OK to stick with me until we get these?'

Teddy trotted out after Steve and walked with him down the road, keeping up a constant burble about the birds he had seen on the beach that day while he had been working. They arrived at Maggie's, and Steve opened the door and gestured for Teddy to go in.

'I can't,' he stammered, 'I don't have any money.'

'It's OK,' said Steve. 'You're with me.'

He pushed Teddy in gently and pointed to a free table. They sat down and Steve picked up a menu.

'What do you want to eat? It's my treat.'

Teddy looked red in the face and kept looking at the door.

'What's up?' said Steve gently.

Teddy leant forward to whisper.

'I don't know what the words on here say.' He looked close to tears and Steve felt the rage for the boy's father building in his chest.

'It's fine,' Steve said. 'I can read it to you, or you can just tell me what you like.'

'Oh… OK I'll tell you what I like,' he said with relief. He took a deep breath. 'I like sausages, I like eggs, bacon. Chips. I like chips.

Very much. Bread. I like bread, not the brown stuff. I like the things in the red sauce... er...'

'Beans?'

'Yes, I like beans. I don't like mushrooms.' He shuddered. 'And I like fish fingers.'

'Wow,' said Steve. 'How about all of that without the fish fingers?'

'OK,' Teddy said brightly.

'Do you like tea?' Steve asked.

'Yes. I like it with sugar in, but I'm not allowed it at home.'

'Do you want some tea?'

'Oh, that would be lovely.' He sighed.

'Right, leave it with me.' Steve got up to order.

'Hello, darlin',' Maggie said as he approached the counter. She narrowed her eyes. 'Isn't that Teddy, Edwyn Lewis's boy?'

'It is. He's helping me out with something.'

'Needs feeding up. Looks half bloody starved,' Maggie said matter-of-factly. 'He could do with a good bath too.'

'I know.' Steve rattled off their order before he leaned in and said in a low voice, 'You know, Mags, I found out today he doesn't eat. At all. The old man doesn't feed him. He gets his food from the bins. He eats rubbish, Maggie. Can you believe that? That poor boy eating rubbish?'

Maggie's eyes filled with tears. 'That mean old fucking bastard,' she whispered furiously. 'Bad enough what he did to Danny, but now this? Leave it with me, love,' she said, passing over two mugs of tea.

Steve returned to the table to find Teddy gazing out of the window at the seagulls.

'Did you know that there are six species of gulls in Britain?' he said, watching them. 'Fifty species in the world. I like gulls. I like it when they sing. It relaxes me.'

Maggie bustled over to the table.

120

'Food will be over in a minute, but here's some bread and butter for you. Say, Teddy, I was watching you do the flowerbeds earlier in the harbour. They look very nice.'

'Thank you, Mrs Maggie,' said Teddy shyly, but politely.

'I've been meaning to ask you if you would think about coming and looking after all my pots outside, and my troughs around the deck and the patch of flowers on the side? I just don't have time to do it. I've got to buy some new flowers, but I just won't have time to plant them up and look after them.'

'Oh, well I don't know,' said Teddy, flustered. 'I work Monday, Tuesday and Friday.'

A waitress delivered their plates of food and Teddy's eyes widened.

'Is that mine?' he asked in a whisper. 'There's a lot of it.'

'It is,' Steve said. 'Go on, Mags.'

'Well, I couldn't really afford to pay you much to do it, but how about I give you your lunch or dinner every day? So you come and look after the plants when you can. And I give you a main meal every day after you've finished.'

'But my lunch wouldn't be like this though, would it?' Teddy asked doubtfully.

'Of course it would. That's lunch, isn't it? Dinner would be the same. Maybe a pie or something,' Maggie said. 'Do we have a deal, Teddy?'

'Oh, I like pie too. Yes please, Mrs Maggie,' he said, wiping his hands on a napkin carefully before holding out one to shake. 'Thank you very much.'

'My pleasure. Enjoy your food. So I'll see you here tomorrow, after you finish work?'

Teddy nodded, his mouth full. He pointed to his Mickey Mouse watch. 'Four o'clock,' he said. 'I will be here at four o'clock.'

121

Steve winked at her as she passed him by. She was an absolute diamond.

Food finished, the two headed up towards the town and stopped at the photo shop. Steve popped in, grabbed the photo packet and steered Teddy over to a bench.

'One pack for you and one for me,' Steve said, taking the photographs out and flicking through them.

Teddy was going through them slowly, giggling at some of them. He showed the picture of Barry frowning to Steve.

'He looks cross!' he said. 'Look here's a nice one of him smiling.'

'So do we know when you took them?' Steve asked, flicking through them. 'Any of the parrots?'

'Parakeets,' Teddy corrected. 'No, I didn't take any of them on this film.'

Steve was staring at a picture; it was slightly overexposed and blurry in places. It was a shot through a window of part of a man's face. Something that looked like blood was smeared across a cheek. The photo was taken through a car window and there were raindrops on the window. The man's face wasn't fully visible, just an eye and the top of a cheek. The man was touching his face with, what looked like, blood on his hands. What was clear was that the man had a large gold signet ring on his pinky finger with a fleur-de-lis crest on it.

'Teddy,' Steve said gently. 'What's this photograph?'

Teddy fell silent for a moment. 'I don't remember that,' he said, looking at his pictures intently, going red in the face.

'Had this man hurt himself?' Steve asked.

'I said I don't remember.' He avoided Steve's eye.

'Teddy, it's really important that you tell me where you took this photograph,' Steve said firmly. 'We think a lady might have been killed and this might help us.'

'I didn't take the photograph!' Teddy yelled, standing up, fists clenched. 'I don't know who he is. I don't know. I DON'T KNOW! Rusty must have took it! He's not allowed. NOT ALLOWED!' Teddy sobbed and ran up the road clutching his photographs to his chest.

Steve watched him go. He cast his mind back and tried to remember hearing about a Rusty. He frowned. Who the bloody hell was Rusty?

* * *

Carla was manning the reception desk at the climbing centre. She was booking in a couple of women and as she finished up, her mobile rang. She answered it as she wandered towards the picture window at the back of the centre, where Foxy was teaching a class.

'Hello?'

'Carla?'

Carla tried to place the voice. 'Who is this?'

'It's Jamie. How are you? I thought I'd call and see how you were. See if you fancied getting together over Christmas. I'm home for a few days. I'd really love to see you.'

Carla stared at the phone. She felt dizzy and placed a hand against the glass window to steady herself. She caught Foxy's eye through the glass and he mouthed, 'You OK?'

Carla stared back at her phone and suddenly thought she was going to be sick.

'Carla? Hello?' A tinny voice floated out of her phone.

Foxy stood in front of Carla the other side of the glass. His hand pressed against it. He was frowning in concern. 'What?' he mouthed.

Carla's finger hovered over the end call button and then she pressed it firmly. She looked back up at Foxy and mouthed, 'Jamie.'

The phone rang again instantly. Carla noted it was the same number. She fumbled to reject the call and then frantically scrolled

123

through the options to try and block the caller. As she did, she heard the ping of a message informing her she had a voicemail. She stared at the phone, her finger hovering over the voicemail button. She accessed her voicemail and Jamie's voice floated up from the speaker.

'Carla? Something weird going on with your phone. Look, I'm home for a few days. Love to catch up and see you. Shall we get together, I've got no plans for Christmas, I'd love to spend it with you? Call me back! Hope to see you.'

Carla stared at the phone in disbelief.

Foxy rested his hands gently on her shoulders from where he stood behind her. 'You OK? I heard the message,' he murmured in her ear.

She leant back into him, absorbing strength from the contact.

'I've blocked him. I'm going to ignore it,' she said firmly and exhaling heavily.

'Whatever you want to do,' Foxy said soothingly.

'Well, I don't want to see him, do I?' she said crossly. 'I never want to see him again. Ever.'

'Well, I'd better kill him then,' Foxy said with a raised eyebrow. 'Just to be sure.'

'Don't fucking tempt me,' Carla said, pushing away from him and walking out of the centre.

Foxy watched her leave and sighed heavily. He turned to go and finish up with his class.

'Hello, stranger,' a female voice said behind him. Foxy turned to see his best mate Sophie standing there. She looked exhausted was Foxy's first thought.

'Hey, you,' he said, giving her a hug. 'How are you?'

'I thought I'd done something wrong. I've not seen you. Don't tell me you're giving me space to grieve or some such bollocks, because I thought we had established that I didn't want that? By the way, was that Carla I just saw?'

'It was. Look, can you hang about for a bit for a coffee, I'll be five minutes?'

Sophie grinned. 'Love to.'

Foxy left Mike in charge and wandered over to Maggie's with Sophie. They hadn't caught up properly for a couple of weeks. Her husband had recently died, and she was busy trying to sort things out, as well as cope with her father's deepening dementia; Marcus, her teenage son; and her day job.

Foxy and Sophie had been firm friends for a while now, and he had been helping Sophie deal with the recovery, and then later suicide of her soldier husband. About the same time her husband had taken his own life, Foxy realised he was completely and utterly head over heels in love with Sophie. He hadn't done a thing about it, not wanting to hurt her, put pressure on her, or more importantly, lose her as his best mate.

They ordered and sat down at a table. Sophie eyed Foxy.

'What gives?' she said. 'I see Carla's staying. What was it you said? She just used you for no strings sex and a free holiday. You were quite grumpy about that if I recall?'

Foxy snorted. 'Huh.'

'So why the long face? That's every man's dream, isn't it?'

'There's more to it than that.'

'What? More to no strings sex and a free holiday?'

'Not my secret to tell.'

'It seems to be bothering you, so that makes it my business.'

'If I tell you… you tell no one. Not even mention it to Carla.'

'Christ. I'll be signing the official secrets act next.'

'I mean it.' He gave her a stern look.

'OK,' she said in surrender. 'I'll take it to the grave.'

He leant in. 'Carla's in trouble.'

'Is she OK?'

Foxy looked uncomfortable. 'She's here trying to sort her head out.'

'What happened?'

'She was drugged and taken advantage of.'

Sophie frowned. 'What, like a date rape?'

'Exactly like that.'

'Oh God. Poor Carla. What do the police say?'

Foxy pursed his lips. 'It's a bit more complicated than that.'

Sophie pulled a face. 'How?'

'It happened just after we were there. To see Sam? Remember?'

'So it happened then? But that was months ago.'

'The thing is, she didn't exactly know if anything had happened then, she felt a bit weird in that she couldn't remember. But now…'

'Now what? Out with it.'

'Now she's pregnant.'

Sophie's mouth made a small O.

Foxy looked at her wryly. 'See? It's complicated.'

'How's she coping?'

'She isn't really.'

'Does she want it?'

Foxy leant back in his chair, nodding his thanks absently to the waitress who delivered his drink.

'That's the million-dollar question.'

'Shit,' Sophie said softly.

'Couldn't have put it better myself,' said Foxy.

Sophie had missed Foxy. His reassuring presence, his reliability, plus he was fun to be with. She now understood why she hadn't seen him for a while.

'How do you feel about this?' she ventured.

He waved his mug. 'Obviously I'd like to go and kill him with my bare hands,' he said. 'Steve has even said he'd help bury the body.'

Sophie raised an eyebrow. 'Steve knows?'

'Yeah. I persuaded Carla to tell him. He can't do anything formally unless she presses charges and then there's the lack of evidence unless some early DNA test is done. But he has a colleague in Cardiff who lives to prosecute blokes who do this sort of thing, so she's on the case now. She spoke to Carla and she's looking into it without revealing it's Carla behind any accusation. Seeing if any other women come forward.'

'Did that make Carla feel better?'

'For now. It's the idea of going to court and arguing about it. You know what the defence are like… but you went to the party, did nothing the next morning, etc.'

Sophie adopted a grim expression. 'Slimy bastards.'

'Exactly.'

Sophie leant forwards. 'Does Carla want another baby?'

'I asked her that. It was an emphatic no. Then I said even if Tom Hardy rocked up and begged her to have his kids. She still said no.'

'I have to say I'd find it difficult to say no to Tom Hardy. So Carla's struggling with the moral dilemma of it all?'

'Yup.'

'And you?'

Foxy looked blank. 'Me?'

'Yes, you. What if she has it? Is there part of you that thinks you could maybe be a family again, with the new baby?'

Foxy gripped the mug tightly in his hand. 'I can't believe you've asked me that.'

'Why? It's a reasonable question. Has that option not crossed your mind?'

'She doesn't want me. She's made that clear.'

'Yes, but everything's different now. What if she asks you to have the baby together? A new start after Charlie. Have you thought about that?'

Foxy blinked furiously. The mention of his late daughter who died tragically still affected him deeply.

'This isn't a replacement for Charlie,' he said through gritted teeth.

'I'm not saying it is. But this is an innocent child. The child doesn't know the circumstances in which it was made. What if this is a chance for you?'

'It's not my choice to make.'

'But it could be if you wanted it. If you wanted Carla and the baby. It's a choice you make together then.'

'Carla's not said anything.'

'Perhaps she's wondering if you will.'

Foxy dragged his hands through his hair. 'Jesus fucking Christ.'

'I need to go.' She stood and put a hand on his shoulder. 'You need to think about what you want, Rob. I mean it. I don't think this is just Carla's decision, otherwise, why would she have come here? Think about it.' She bent and kissed his cheek and left waving goodbye to Maggie.

Foxy watched her leave the cafe. He wanted to run after and tell her he knew exactly what he wanted. He wanted her. He didn't want Carla and the baby of a rapist. He knew it wasn't fair to think of the child like that, but Foxy wondered whether he would always think of it like that if she had it. Look at unfamiliar features and wonder at the child's nature. Would the child be a psychopath?

He mentally shook himself and left the cafe waving to Maggie. Sophie had given him something else to think about. Now he had to have a conversation with Carla and try to find out exactly what she was thinking and what her plans were. Either way, Foxy couldn't lie to her. He loved Carla and they were close, but their relationship as husband and wife or partners was done. Foxy knew that without a doubt now. He didn't want to lead Carla on, when he was so completely head over heels for Sophie.

CHAPTER 13

Will was three hours into his first day and everything had already gone pear shaped. The ancient computer refused to work, and there was a constant procession of people coming in to drop off large boxes. He had no idea what the boxes were for, or why they were coming.

He had spent a frustrating hour on the phone to IT and had finally cajoled someone into actually coming down to the office from the council offices to give him a new PC. In the middle of it all, a low loader had carefully navigated the narrow harbour roads and arrived outside his office with a brand-new Ford Ranger, complete with high visibility hatching and a light bar across the top.

'No one's gonna miss you coming now,' said one of the older fishermen as he passed by the enormous white truck.

Will decided enough was enough.

'Right. Unload that and park it over there, please,' he said to the low loader delivery man.

'But I have to give you an induction,' said the man.

Will eyed the queue of people holding boxes and said, 'Six o'clock tonight is good for me. Wanna wait?'

'I'll unload and give you the keys,' the driver said and set about the task hurriedly.

Will turned to the throng of people who were noisily chatting.

'Hey! Everyone!' he called loudly.

Silence greeted him.

'Morning, folks. I'm Will, the new harbour master. Now someone please help me out,' he said desperately, 'and tell me what the hell are all these boxes for?'

There was a round of chuckles and murmurs. A stocky, pleasant-faced man in his early sixties stepped forward and shook his hand.

'Nice to meet you, Will. I'm Miles Thomas. All these boxes are for the Kirby supply ferry. Leaves today at 2 p.m. These are all to go on the ferry.'

'All these?' Will looked around frustrated.

Miles laughed. 'This is nothing, the whole quay will be full before it comes, you mark my words. It's not just the abbey there on the island, lots of islanders live there too. So there's always plenty to take. You've got to do the town sweep yet. The harbour master always does it, they'll be even more then.'

'The town sweep?' Will asked, dreading the answer.

'Those buggers didn't tell you, did they?' Miles said, shaking his head. 'I knew they wouldn't. I've been doing the sweep all the time we haven't had a harbour master, but historically the harbour master has always done it. Tell you what. I'll do it with you today and show you the ropes.' He pointed at Will's new truck. 'We'll be needing that, and we need to get a move on.'

Miles turned to the crowd and raised his voice. 'Come on, folks. Fun's over. You know where the boxes go. Leave them neatly and be away.' He called over to a young man in his twenties with dark hair. 'Danny? I'm putting you in charge. Me and Will are doing the sweep and then we'll be back.'

'OK, Miles,' said Danny cheerfully. 'I'll be here. I'll look after them.'

'Good lad. Ring me if you need me.'

'Will do.'

Miles gestured to the truck. 'Come on then.'

Will grabbed the keys from the driver who was just leaving and climbed into the new truck. He sat behind the wheel looking at the array of things in front of him.

'You'll need your top lights on,' said Miles, clipping himself into the passenger seat.

Will looked at the dashboard and buzzed down the window.

'Button for the top lights, mate?' he called. The driver jogged over, leant in, flicked them on and pointed out a couple of other things.

'Cheers. Thanks a lot.' Will started the truck.

'Right,' Miles said, rubbing his hands together. 'Off we go! Really slow though, we need to give people a chance.'

Completely bemused, Will decided to just drive and learn. At Miles's direction, they trundled out of the harbour and turned up one of the narrow streets.

'Honk the horn twice now,' Miles said. Will obliged and looked in amazement as a number of people exited houses and shops with bags and boxes, all with various names scrawled across them.

'Stop up here,' Miles said, and Will pulled to a halt.

Boxes were placed in the bed of the truck and people called out their thanks, some of them introducing themselves to Will. Overall, the sweep took almost an hour. Will was amazed at the boxes piled up in the back of the truck.

When they finally drove back down towards the harbour and quay, Miles said, 'One last stop for two minutes?'

Will stopped and Miles hopped out, returning quickly holding a large white box.

'Thanks,' he said, climbing in.

'Birthday cake to go on the ferry?' Will asked, mildly amused.

'No, I always do it. It's a reward for Danny. He'll have guarded those boxes preciously for the time we've been gone. He'll also help unpack the truck, load the ferry and unload it the other end. This is his reward.'

'Nice of him,' Will remarked as he navigated the narrow quayside.

'He's a great lad. He was the last harbour master's nephew. He liked to help out. It made him feel useful.'

'I know he lives with Anna,' Will said. 'Doug told me about him.'

'He's a great lad,' Miles said.

Will parked and looked around in amazement.

'There's a fridge and a washing machine here… and is that a piece of medical equipment?' he said in disbelief. 'All of this is going over to Kirby in one ferry?'

'The ferry will be able to take the weight,' Danny said very matter-of-factly. 'And that over there is a dialysis machine. It takes your blood, cleans it and puts it back.'

'Wow,' said Will. 'We'd better be super careful with it then.'

Will looked at his watch and saw it was just gone midday, he could see a stream of people with bags and boxes heading down towards the quay. He turned to Miles.

'How often does the ferry go?'

'The supply ferry? Every three weeks, weather permitting. It's different in the winter though, they've not had a ferry out for over a month now.'

Christ,' said Will, thinking he had to cope with this fiasco once a month.

'It's coming,' Danny shouted as he sorted out boxes expertly along the quayside. 'I can hear it.'

Will walked to the end of the quay and looked out to sea, sure enough the bright yellow ferry was approaching the harbour.

'She's lovely, isn't she?' sighed Danny coming to watch the boat approach. 'Ocean Ranger. She's one of my most favourite boats.'

Will watched the ferry moor and people create an efficient human chain, passing boxes and bags along the quayside onto the ferry.

Doug had strolled around the corner and presented Will with a take away coffee.

'Quite something, isn't it?' he said.

'Christ, I wish this was a pint,' said Will desperately. 'But thanks very much. I'm gasping. I literally haven't stopped since I set foot in here this morning.'

'Thought you'd be busy. How about I buy you a pint after work?' Doug suggested.

'Now that is the best offer I've had all day,' Will said, clapping Doug on the back. 'Cheers.'

At quarter to two Danny climbed out of the boat and walked up to Will.

'You need to sound the alarm.'

Will looked confused. 'What?'

'I'll do it!' Danny called and hurried over to the harbour master's office. He leant in the door and gave two large bursts on a loud siren.

'That tells people fifteen minutes till launch,' he said. 'Otherwise people take advantage, you know.'

Will looked in amazement at a flurry of people rushing down the road towards the ferry with various boxes. A man on a scooter

133

balanced what looked like six pizzas on his lap as he steered into the quayside.

'Even pizza?' Will asked.

'The monks like it as a treat,' Danny said. 'I only like cheese and tomato. I don't like pepperoni.' He shuddered. 'Joe's do the best pizza's though, and the waitress is very pretty too. She's called Isabella.' He flushed.

Will watched as a car navigated the throng and drove along the quay, parking as close to the steps for the ferry as possible. Irritated, Will marched over with a view to giving the driver a piece of his mind, when Anna jumped out and ran around to the passenger side.

'Danny?' she called.

Danny ran over and helped her assist a very old man out of the car and onto the quayside. He was dressed warmly in a long brown coat and had a hospital ID bracelet around his wrist. His hands showed papery, liver-spotted skin and his skin seemed stretched taut over his skeletal face.

The old man cautiously approached the steps, swaying on his incredibly thin legs.

'Come here, Brother Joseph,' Danny said. He lifted the monk effortlessly into his arms and walked down the steps and onto the boat. He placed him down gently and wrapped a warm blanket around him that Anna passed to him.

'How old is that guy?' Will whispered to Miles.

'That's Brother Joseph,' said Miles. 'He's the oldest monk on the island. He must be ninety-eight I reckon. He's been very poorly. Dialysis machine is for him. He's basically come home to die.'

'Is he related to Anna in some way?'

'No, Anna helps out with ferrying some of the older folk to and from the hospital. She's a diamond. Do anything for anyone.'

The ferry was finally loaded and sat considerably lower in the water than it had done when it had arrived. Miles gave Will a small salute, jumped down and took the wheel from the attractive middle-aged lady in the wheelhouse.

'Danny, are you coming? Don't forget there's your cake,' she said, waving the white box.

'Yes, Gemma!' Danny laughed and rushed down the steps. He sat outside the wheelhouse and Will watched as the woman carefully opened the box in front of Danny's delighted eyes.

'My favourite!' he said, grinning happily.

She touched his face indulgently. 'You dig in, my love,' she said.

Will stood on the edge and looked down at the ferry.

'Safe crossing!' Will called. He watched as Miles started the engine and expertly manoeuvred the boat around and out of the harbour.

A few minutes later, Will saw three lads clamber drunkenly into one of the small speedboats for hire. He tutted and strolled over to the quayside. He watched them bump into two other boats as they tried to turn theirs around.

'Hey! Careful!' he called as he watched them push themselves off against one of the boats they had bumped into.

'Who the fuck are you?' one of them sneered.

'Watch the boats. Have a bit of respect.'

'Fuck off, wanker,' another retorted. The other boy revved the boat's engine and it surged forwards bumping into yet another boat and then wonkily headed for the harbour entrance.

'Pricks,' muttered Will. He walked around the quayside and stood on the higher stone ledge of the harbour wall and tracked their progress out of the bay. They swerved crazily around other boats, whooping and calling out insults as they went.

Will tutted and shook his head; he decided it might be an idea to warn Doug there were idiots in a fast boat around the bay. He rang Doug's number.

'Brodie,' Doug answered.

'It's Will. Look out of your office window.'

'Already am. I see a trio of fucking idiots in a boat they can't control.'

'Bingo.'

'Let's hope I don't have to go and get them.'

'If you do, let me know and I might tag along,' said Will mildly. 'They were a little bit rude earlier, and it might be nice to have a chat about being rude if the time comes.'

Doug chuckled. 'I love chats like that. You're on, buddy.'

* * *

Mickey Camorra, head of the regional crime mafia was on the phone and pacing angrily in his multi-million-pound purpose-built house which sat high on the hill overlooking Castleby.

Architect designed, the house nestled into the hillside and the clean lines cascaded down the expertly manicured and landscaped garden towards the cliffs. Outside of the main living area, through the massive bifold doors, sat the infinity swimming pool where steam was gently rising, and Mickey's wife, Pearl, completed her daily swim.

He finished the call and threw the phone across the patio where it bounced off a stone wall and shattered into pieces. Pearl, who had been watching his conversation while she completed her fifty lengths, swam over and retrieved a piece of the phone from the pool, placing it on the side.

'Something up, darling?' she asked gently.

Mickey paced furiously, going red in the face, his fists clenching and unclenching as he strode about. Mickey was a large broad-set, bald-headed man with piercing blue eyes, that always softened the moment he laid eyes on his beloved wife.

Mickey jabbed a finger in the air angrily. 'I'm gonna kill him. Kill his friends. Kill his family. Kill anyone that knows him,' he spat out.

Pearl regarded him with amusement. 'Who has you this upset?'

Mickey continued to pace, his face getting redder. 'Fucking scum scousers are making a move. Sniffing around town. Someone called Ringo.'

'And how do we know this?' Pearl said, floating gently along the side, keeping up with Mickey.

'One of the dealers said his pusher was threatened with a knife. Told him things were going to change.'

'Has anyone else seen them around?'

'No one has said anything.'

'Perhaps they were on a fishing expedition. I suggest we gather the team and Alexy's crew together, and find out exactly what the story is.'

Mickey stopped pacing and looked at her. 'Good idea.'

'There. No need for you to get worked up until we have something to get worked about, is there, darling?'

Mickey studied his wife, he worshipped her and had done ever since he first laid eyes on her in a pub in Shoreditch nearly thirty years ago.

His eyes narrowed. 'Perhaps I like being worked up,' he said, approaching the side of the pool causing Pearl to raise a perfectly groomed eyebrow.

'Question is… what do you plan to do about it?' she said, flicking him with water and then screaming with surprise when Mickey launched himself into the pool fully clothed and grabbed her.

'I've got some ideas,' he said, pulling her in for a kiss.

CHAPTER 14

Danny loved ferry days. He loved helping load and unload all the stuff, but most of all he loved the surprise cake that Miles and Gemma always bought for him. Ferry day was one of his most favourite days.

Currently, Danny had finished his cake and was sipping a cup of tea from a Thermos flask lid. Danny spotted the speedboat as soon as it rounded the point of the old fort and got out into choppier water.

'Miles, there's a boat going too fast past the fort,' called Danny. 'He'll be in trouble if he hits a big wave.'

'He most certainly will,' said Miles, who had been watching the progress of the small boat.

'Can we tell him to slow down?' Danny said, becoming agitated.

'Hopefully he'll go past us, and we won't have to worry,' said Miles soothingly, used to Danny's anxiety spells.

They watched the boat get closer until the three boys in the boat spotted the ferry. They laughed and pointed and started throwing cans of beer towards the ferry.

Danny stood up and gestured for them to get away, his face red.

'Get away. You're too close,' he shouted.

'Calm down, Danny, and sit down, please,' said Miles, picking up the radio and calling the coastguard to report it.

Suddenly the boat swerved and cut across the ferry's prow causing a large wave. The ferry rolled sideways, weighed down with its heavy load. Miles came out of the boat house.

'Gemma, take the wheel and slow her down.'

Miles walked to the edge of the boat and shouted at the boys.

'Slow down and keep clear of this boat. We're hitting your wake.'

The boys laughed and cut across the boat again, the ferry lolling sideways. Then the boys decided to zigzag in front of the boat, causing large wake waves.

'Gemma, turn towards the island away from them. Be mindful of the buoy,' Miles called.

Gemma turned the boat and the ferry headed away from the speedboat.

Undeterred, the boys carried on zigzagging in the wake of the large boat, screaming with laughter as their boat smashed into the huge waves of the wake.

Danny was clutching on to the side of the boat. He was in a highly anxious state and Brother Joseph was sitting silently with his eyes closed, murmuring.

Miles requested assistance over the radio. He was sure there was going to be an accident. He looked over, reassured that Brother Joseph, Gemma and Danny were all wearing lifesavers. The radio informed him that the lifeboat had launched to provide an escort.

Will sat down for the first time in six hours and realised he was absolutely knackered. His phone rang from deep in his pocket and he dragged it out, it was Doug.

'You're up,' Doug said. 'We are launching in five.'

'Speedboat?'

'It's a significant danger to the ferry, they're playing tag with it.'

'On my way.' Will jumped up and slammed the office door before running around the corner towards the lifeboat station.

He arrived in two minutes, just as Doug strode out of the locker room dressed to go. He was followed by three other men.

'Lads, this is Will, the new harbour master. You've got time to get your gear on, Will,' he said. 'Help yourself.'

Will rushed into the locker room.

'Hi, Will, you joining the crew?' Mike asked.

'Will's been crew for years. Stepped out 'cause he broke his back, so let's be mindful and not break him today,' Doug cautioned. 'He's just helping us out.'

In the locker room, Will bent to step into the gear and felt his back instantly spasm. He gritted his teeth, wishing it away as he straightened up, pulling up the zipper on the taped seams. He grabbed a helmet and ran out.

'Look at you, all dressed up with somewhere to go.' Doug held out his hand to help Will onto the boat.

On the boat already, Dan was flicking on controls and the others were strapping themselves in.

'Guys, this is Will, he came across the numpties in the speedboat earlier,' said Doug.

The crew nodded to Will, and Doug pointed to a spare seat.

'Strap in, mate,' he said. 'Launching!'

The launch siren blared out and the boat slid down the steep slipway, hitting the ocean with a thunderous splash. Dan pushed the throttle and the powerful engines surged off.

Miles had taken the ferry's wheel. The boys in the speedboat were becoming increasingly reckless and cutting across the front of the ferry as close as they could. During the last sweep, they had thrown a full can of lager and it had broken through the window of the wheelhouse, flying glass cutting Miles on the forehead.

He looked out of the wheelhouse and saw Danny's eyes were tightly shut and he was pale. Gemma was sat next to him, holding his hand and trying to reassure him.

The three boys were taking turns balancing on the back of the boat as it careered about. Miles shouted at them once more to get away from the boat, but they increased their speed. He shouted to be careful of the large buoy that was looming, but they threw more cans at the ferry and sped up again. They cut across the prow of the ferry again, making it roll dangerously in the wake and then turned quickly in a small circle to head back towards the ferry.

To Miles, everything began happening in slow motion. He spotted the lifeboat in the distance with relief. He turned to the front of the boat to see the boys were running too close to the buoy. He realised they were racing to see if they could get through the gap between the ferry and the buoy before the gap closed.

Miles watched as the boat drew alongside it at speed, but the wake of their earlier turn pushed the speedboat up at an angle. The speedboat clipped the buoy, and flipped, rearing up out of the water and ploughing into the back edge of the ferry as it passed them. The force of the boat landing on the corner of the ferry meant its prow raised up and the weight of the cargo turned it over. Eventually settling upside down on the surface.

'She's gone over!' Doug shouted as they helplessly watched the crash happen. Doug ordered Dan to increase speed to reach them and to get the small Y boat stored in the rear of the lifeboat, ready to launch.

'I can't see anyone,' Bob shouted as they slowed to approach the upturned ferry. He craned his neck over the side.

'There,' said Will. 'I'm going in.' He leapt over the side and swam powerfully towards where he had spotted Danny face down in the water.

He grabbed Danny, turned him over and towed him back towards the large lifeboat. Bob and Mike hooked him in and pulled Danny up out of the water. Still in the water, Will looked around him for signs of the others. He saw the small Y boat being launched to look for the boys from the speedboat around the other side of the wreckage.

'I'll look underneath the ferry,' called Will, swimming away, back to the ferry.

Doug was in the water looking for the boys. One of them was swimming towards the lifeboat, but the one that had been balancing on the back was nowhere to be seen. Doug spotted another one floating face down and struck out to turn him over, waiting for the Y to pick him up. The small boat picked up two of the boys and took them back to the lifeboat.

They finally found the third boy, half covered in debris, floating face up in the water, but barely conscious.

Will was shattered. He tried to think how many were on the ferry. Miles, Gemma, Danny and the old man. He took a deep breath and dived down to try and get up underneath the ferry in the hope that there was an air pocket.

He was in luck; the water was clear, and above him he saw two pairs of legs. He came up next to them, it was Gemma and Miles.

'Are you OK?' he said, gasping for air. 'Where's Joseph?'

Gemma sobbed. 'We've been looking for him. Miles has hit his head, he's a bit dazed. He's not making sense.'

Will's senses were in overload. Being underneath a boat was not good for him. He felt himself on the verge of a panic attack and he knew that if he closed his eyes and thought about it, he'd lose it. He'd be transported back to being trapped under the racing catamaran with a broken back, and his best friend drowning. He tried to breathe deeply and focus on what was in front of him and what he needed to do.

'Let's get out. Lifeboat's close. I've already got Danny. Gemma, Miles isn't looking too good, I'm going to take him first unless you're confident to swim with me?'

'I'm fine, I'll help,' she said breathlessly. Together they took deep breaths. Will gently pulled them down and then guided them past the boat and up into the water near the lifeboat. Bob and Mike spotted them instantly and hooked them in as soon as they were close. Will was relieved to see Danny sitting up coughing. Bob looked over at him.

'No Joseph?'

'I'll take another look,' Will said, swimming off.

'WAIT!' Bob called and threw him a rope. 'Rope up. Doug will have kittens if you don't. Boat rules.'

Will quickly tied the rope to himself and swam back towards the ferry wreckage, the rope playing out behind him. He took a few deep breaths and dived down again, blinking in the clear water. He swam around, pieces of clothing and cardboard floated past him, he caught sight of Danny's white cake box floating away.

Then he saw him. Hanging in the sea, something caught around his foot, weighing him down, his eyes closed. A large weal on his head. His brown coat billowed around him like dark angel wings.

Will swam towards him and pulled him close, unhooking his foot. Dragging him, he swam away from the underneath of the boat, his lungs screaming for air.

He surfaced and took in a huge breath, coughing and gasping

for air. The old man lolled against him. Will looked over to the lifeboat and saw Bob standing holding the rope.

Will hoped Bob was bright as he held up a hand and made a circular motion. Bob pulled the rope in, assisted by Mike. Will reached the lifeboat in seconds. Bob pulled Joseph aboard and Will rested his head against the side of the boat, exhausted.

'Coming in?' said Bob, grinning over the side.

'I'll do the ladder at the rear,' Will said, thinking about his back.

'OK,' Bob said, dragging Will towards the back of the boat on the rope.

Wearily Will climbed the ladder and sat down heavily on the deck. He watched Dan and Mike trying to resuscitate the elderly monk.

'I wish I'd found him sooner,' he said, shaking water off his hair and eyes.

'Lucky to find him at all,' Mike called as he pumped on the old man's chest.

'His foot was caught.'

'Quite the hero,' said Bob. 'You can stay if you want.'

'What about the boys?' Will asked.

'Below decks. All three.'

Doug approached Will and sat down heavily next to him. They watched as Brother Joseph was taken below decks.

'You,' Doug said solemnly, nudging Will, 'can come again. Thank you. You got them all back safe.'

'Not sure Brother Joseph's going to make it.'

'He'd say it's in God's hands. The water's cold. It might be in his favour.' Doug turned and called. 'Dan?'

'Skip?'

'Home, please. Quick as you like.'

Doug looked over at Danny. 'I'd better call Anna, if she doesn't know already,' he said ruefully.

Doug headed off below decks and Will took a moment to stand and watch the yellow hull of the ferry as the boat moved away from it.

He felt sadness for all the town's efforts now lying at the bottom of the sea, as a result of three idiots in a speedboat who should have known better. He walked back along the boat to where Danny was sitting, looking shocked, wrapped in a red blanket. Gemma was holding his hand and murmuring to him. Miles was below decks in the warmth with Brother Joseph.

'How are you doing, Danny?' Will asked. 'Do you want to go below decks, it's much warmer?'

'I'm very cold and very frightened,' Danny said in a matter-of-fact voice. 'I don't remember the crash. I just remember hurting my head and waking up on the lifeboat. I'm too frightened to go below deck in case we crash again, and I can't get out. Anna can't lose anyone else.'

'Well, I'm glad we found you,' Will said, sitting down. 'Just think, Danny, all the things that were supposed to go out today will have to be replaced and go out again.'

'I don't know if I want to do ferry day again,' Danny said, frowning. 'It's too frightening.'

'Uh huh,' Will said. 'Danny, how many ferry days have you done?'

Danny thought hard. 'One hundred and seventy-four.'

Will pretended to look surprised. 'That many?'

Danny nodded proudly.

'And in that time, how many times has it been frightening?'

'Never.'

'Well then. Maybe this was just a one-off and it'll be fine again for at least the next one hundred and seventy-four times.'

Danny thought for a moment. 'Maybe, but I think you should come on the next one. Then I won't be scared because you rescued me this time. Bob said you saw me floating and jumped right in.'

Will glanced at Gemma. 'Maybe I will,' he said.

He looked towards the shoreline as the powerful lifeboat surged through the water and saw a line of spectators on the beach who must have witnessed the whole thing. He took comfort from that, hoping some sort of mobile phone footage would appear that would likely highlight the stupidity of the boys in the motorboat.

Dan and Mike had managed to bring Brother Joseph around, but he was very cold, and they were doubtful he would make it due to his underlying illness.

As they approached the mouth of the harbour, Will spotted two ambulances on the quayside. Suddenly he felt exhausted, he grabbed the rail of the boat and willed his legs to work as the boat drew up to the quayside.

The crew expertly moved Brother Joseph and one of the boys from the speedboat into an ambulance. Miles, Danny and Gemma piled into the other one to be taken to the hospital. With his back throbbing, Will found somewhere to sit down and was almost asleep when Doug tapped him on the shoulder.

'Will?'

Will focused. He stood painfully, his back in spasms. He realised he hadn't taken any painkillers since first thing that morning and his back was killing him.

The boat returned to the station where it was pulled back up the ramp with the winch. The crew headed into the locker room, while the slip crew hosed down the boat.

Will and the others changed out of their gear; the mood in the locker room was subdued.

'Welcome to the town, Will. I don't want this to sound patronising, but thanks for today, you did really well,' Mike said as he was leaving.

The others murmured in agreement.

'I'm happy to help out,' Will said. 'But this isn't a regular thing. I'm an old man with my back.'

Dan laughed. 'There's only room for one grumpy old man on the crew isn't there, Bob?'

Bob looked affronted and snorted.

'Right, I'm going for a pint. Will, are you in? Anyone else?' said Doug, looking at his watch.

There were some murmurs and Will said, 'I'm in. I just need to go and lock up the office. See you there?'

'What's your poison? I'll get them in,' asked Doug, shrugging on his coat.

'I'll have a pint. Lager, please. See you in five.'

Will left the lifeboat station and thought about the rescue as he walked back down to his office. He felt his phone buzz and saw a text from Suzy asking what he was up to. He replied that he was having a pint with the lifeboat crew, and he'd call her later.

The pub was busy, but the crew had nabbed a table. Doug was at the bar chatting to an attractive girl who was busy pulling pints. Will approached the bar.

'Need a hand?' he asked Doug.

'Will, meet the lovely Genevieve. She's one of our lifeguards in the summer and a permanent fixture here too most of the time.'

Gen flashed a smile. 'Good to meet you, Will. I heard what you did on the rescue earlier. Well done you.'

Will looked embarrassed. 'Thanks. Nothing really.'

'Everyone on that ferry matters to people here. So thank you.'

Doug paid and Will helped carry the drinks over to the table. He grabbed a chair and was just about to have a sip of his drink when Doug stood.

'Welcome to Will and let's toast our newest occasional crew member!'

The crew raised their glasses in agreement. 'To Will, welcome to the family.'

Will smiled, feeling a little embarrassed. He heard the door bang and turned to see Foxy walking over. He sighed with relief at the spotlight being focused on someone else for a moment.

'Hey, Will,' Foxy said. 'Heard about earlier. Let me get you a welcome pint in.'

CHAPTER 15

Will had slept like the dead, awakening with incredibly stiff shoulders and back. He was going about his daily ritual of rubbing in Bio-Oil into his scars to stop them itching but was having trouble reaching around to do it. This was a legacy from the day before: towing Danny in the water and heaving him up the side of the boat had left its mark.

His doorbell rang and Will debated what to do for a second. He had his trousers on, half done up, but no shirt and his hands were oil covered. He called out for whoever it was to come in, fully expecting Suzy who said she would drop by that morning.

He carried on, awkwardly, trying to get the oil to cover his back. When he heard footsteps at the top of the stairs, he said without turning, 'Suze… Can you give me a hand with this stuff? I can't reach round this morning, I'm too stiff from yesterday.'

'Er, *not* Suzy. Sorry.'

Will whirled around and came face to face with a very red-faced Anna, who was holding a bottle of wine.

'God, s-sorry,' Will stammered, at a loss for a moment, oily hands in the air.

'I'll come back?' she said, embarrassed. She had seen the two large scars that ran parallel down his spine.

'No, it's fine. I'll just get this oil off and get a shirt on. Give me two minutes.'

'Is that Bio-Oil?'

'Yeah. Stops them itching.' Will turned and ripped off a piece of kitchen roll and wiped his hands.

Anna pointed to his back. 'You've got big areas of oil all over your back, that'll go all over your shirt.'

Will tried to peer over his shoulder and then winced.

'Look, bit awkward, but do you want me to rub it in for you? You look like you're in a bit of pain this morning.'

Will grimaced. 'Normally I can do it. I'm just really stiff this morning. Sure you don't mind?'

Anna shook her head and dumped her bag and the wine on the counter. Will faced away from her and jumped when she put her hands on his back.

'Did I hurt you?'

'Cold hands.'

'Sorry,' she said, rubbing her hands together and trying again. 'Better?'

'Uh huh.'

'These are some serious war wounds,' she said, gently rubbing the oil in. 'Did you have a curvature of the spine or something?'

'I broke my back.'

'Goodness. How did you manage that?'

'I was in a racing boat, and it cartwheeled. I was trapped in the wreckage under the mast.'

150

'You got out though.'

'I did.'

'You were lucky.'

'Sometimes on the recovery journey I questioned that.'

Anna tapped him lightly on the shoulder. 'All done.'

'Thanks,' he said, shrugging into his white shirt that was hanging over the back of the chair.

'I just wanted to come and say a really big thank you for all you did yesterday,' she said, washing her hands and gesturing to the wine.

'Bob told me what you did for Danny. How you just jumped straight in and got him.' She gulped. 'I just can't thank you enough. I couldn't lose...'

Will buttoned up his shirt and grabbed the navy-blue sweater that formed part of his uniform. He yanked it on before flicking on the kettle while Anna fumbled for a tissue in her bag.

'Sit down, Anna,' Will said gently. 'Coffee?'

'OK.'

Will made coffee and sat opposite Anna at the table.

'Why didn't you tell me who you were?' he said softly. 'That you were Gavin's widow?'

'You wouldn't have done or said anything differently,' she said, looking at him directly.

'No, but I wouldn't have spent a week picking apart what I did wrong to make you run out of the flat like I'd threatened you with a weapon.'

Anna sipped her coffee, saying nothing.

'You could've been straight with me,' he chided.

Anna shrugged. 'It's done now. Can't look back, can we?'

Will gave a wry smile. 'I find looking back is always filled with regret, lost chances and things I could have done better, said differently or said earlier.'

Anna raised her mug. 'Exactly.'

'Which is why we should look forward. A very wise woman said to me once that we were given eyes in the front to always be looking forward. If we were meant to spend a lifetime looking behind us, we would have had an eye there too.'

'That sounds like it should be in a fortune cookie,' Anna said.

'I know, but the sentiment is right.'

'OK. Sorry for running out on you once.'

'Twice actually.'

She rolled her eyes. 'OK. Twice then.'

Will wrapped his hands around the mug, his clear bright green eyes serious.

'I'm sorry for taking the harbour master's job. I should have done more homework and been more sensitive to you when I met you.'

'Rubbish,' she said. 'You couldn't have known. It was me being stupid. I thought a new harbour master meant people would forget Gav, but I've realised they won't. It's me being stupid. He would've hated me being this way.'

'Quite right. He sounded a top bloke,' Will said.

Anna smiled. 'Look, thanks so much for what you did for Danny and the others. Brother Joseph is still in hospital, but they are hopeful he'll make it back to the island. Miles was sent home, with a mild concussion. Him and Gemma said you were wonderful.'

'I really wasn't.' Will was embarrassed.

'Danny said he's asked you to come on the next ferry day. He said it will make him feel safer. You shouldn't feel obligated though.'

'I'll see if I can swing it,' Will mused.

'You're very kind,' said Anna. 'Right, I must go.'

'Always running out on me,' Will said theatrically.

'Some of us have got work to do!' she teased and finished her coffee. 'Thanks again. Enjoy the wine.'

'You're welcome to join me in drinking it?' Will said hopefully. 'I'd like to get to know you more.'

Hesitating for a moment, she said, 'Sometime. Maybe, thanks.' She walked over to the stairs and started down them. 'See you,' she said over her shoulder.

'Looking forwards, Anna, not backwards,' called Will. 'Have a good day.'

* * *

Steve was sitting in his office, lolling about in his chair on the phone to Jim Murphy the pathologist.

'Seriously, Murph? I thought the scene was really bad. How can you be sure?'

'Do I question your work, you cheeky fucker?' Murphy came back grumpily. 'It's murder. Without a shadow of a doubt. I have even found you a bloody fingerprint. It's not great, but it might be enough.'

Steve sat upright instantly. 'Where?'

'Back of the jawline. The beautiful and talented Ms Cassie Warner was murdered.'

'How?'

'She would have most likely died from her injuries, relatively soon after the crash, however, someone decided to hurry it along. She was suffocated.'

'What?'

'Simple really. Held her nose and covered her mouth. I'm not going to get all technical with you, there's evidence of petechial haemorrhaging, but ultimately suffocation is being recorded as the primary cause of death.'

There was a knock and Jonesey stuck his head around the door. Steve motioned him in and pointed to a chair.

'Have you sent the print off?' Steve asked Murphy. He looked at Jonesey who was picking his way through a large bag of Maltesers.

Steve clicked his fingers and held his hand out. Jonesey frowned and picked one Malteser out and placed it on Steve's hand. Steve clicked his fingers again and gave Jonesey a death stare.

'Course.'

'Anything else from the scene?' Steve asked, chucking the Maltesers in his mouth and winking at Jonesey.

'Some very pronounced marks on her upper arms that are consistent with her being grabbed tightly there. I would estimate that they occurred earlier on the day she was killed.'

'OK. I know she went out somewhere earlier that day. I wonder if that's connected. Anything else?'

Murphy hesitated. 'She was about eight weeks pregnant. I'll be needing DNA from hubby, I assume it's his.'

'No problem.'

'Suggest you don't tell him just yet though. You know, just in case. So, the plot thickens as you plod say. Over to you to wrap it all up nicely with a bow.'

'If only it were that simple.'

'Stop making it look easy then. See ya, buddy. I'd like that DNA asap.'

'Bye, Murph.'

Steve ended the call and held his hand out for more Maltesers. Jonesey handed a few more over grumpily.

'I only bought these to get in with PC Warren, she's not on shift yet.'

'Ah plying the ladies with sweets. There's a name for people like you,' Steve said, snatching the packet from Jonesey and emptying it into his mouth. 'Right, you need to get busy. I need a search on Edwyn Lewis and all extended family. I want birth and deaths and anything social services has on him.'

'What are you looking for?'

'Someone called Rusty.'

Jonesey scowled. 'How far back do I need to go?'

'Thirty-five years maybe?'

'Fuck's sake.'

Steve grabbed his jacket. 'If I'm not mistaken, what I heard then was you saying, "Of course, Inspector Miller, anything I can do to help…" Rather than, fuck's sake?'

Jonesey grinned. 'Nope. You definitely heard me saying for fuck's sake.'

Steve rolled his eyes and ushered him out of his office. 'I'll be back in a bit. Get started. Also, that photograph, the one of half a face, get the geeks to run it through facial recognition for any hits.'

'Yes, Guv.'

Steve strolled out of the station and set about his search for Jimmy. He looked at his watch. Harbour or pub would be his first guesses, he thought as he strolled down through the town and into the harbour.

Spotting Jimmy on the quayside, he wandered over.

'Jimmy,' he said. 'How are you?'

'Popular,' muttered Jimmy.

'Nice to be popular.'

'What do you want?'

'A favour.'

'I don't fucking think so.'

'I do. I need you to talk to your mate Alexy for me.'

Jimmy almost sobbed like a small child. 'I don't want to talk to him. He gets me in trouble.'

'It's just a call, Jimmy.'

'What for?'

'I want to broker a meeting. I would like a friendly meeting with Alexy and the Camorra. I don't wanna just turn up, I want to do this so everyone knows it's a friendly chat.'

Jimmy looked at Steve in amazement. 'You got a fucking death wish, mate? They'd fucking kill filth like you.'

'I was hoping for a slightly warmer welcome.'

'What aren't you hearing? They will fucking *kill* you.'

'They might not. We have a mutual problem to solve that has interests for both sides.'

'What's that then?'

'Liverpool drug cartels looking to muscle in on Mickey.'

'Shit.'

'Precisely. So call him.'

'Now?'

'Now.'

Jimmy dragged his phone out of his pocket and reluctantly dialled a number which was answered almost instantly.

'Jimmy the fisherman!' said Alexy delightedly. 'How is the hanging?'

Jimmy rolled his eyes at Alexy's pidgin English.

'It's "how is it hanging", Alexy,' he said, smiling.

'Ah… my mistake. How are you, Jimmy?'

'I'm good.'

'I thought we were the friends who did not call anymore. This was your wish, no?'

'Well yes. But something has come up.'

'I am thinking this is something Alexy will like, no?'

'Yes and no. Look, there's rumours that the Liverpool cartels are looking to muscle in on Mickey—'

'What is this "muscle in" word mean?' Alexy said, interrupting Jimmy.

'Take over. Get him out.'

'I am thinking this is not good for Mickey,' Alexy said solemnly.

'Look, the local police want a meet. You and Mickey. To talk about how to keep them out. It's in everyone's interests. They say it's information sharing.'

'Who?'

'Steve Miller.'

Alexy was silent for a while. 'Mickey will want meet to be safe. Pearl too. No funny business.'

'That's what he wants.'

'OK. I speak to Mickey and Pearl and talk to this Steve Miller.'

'You want his number?'

'I'll find it. Goodbye, Jimmy the fisherman.'

Jimmy looked at his phone as Alexy ended the call.

'He's gonna talk to Mickey and Pearl.'

'Good. Thanks, Jimmy.'

'Fucking keep me out of it. I've had it with that lot.'

Steve made his way back to the station. Jonesey was in the kitchen picking his way through a large biscuit tin.

'Tea, please,' Steve said, leaning against the doorjamb.

Jonesey jumped and tutted flicking on the kettle.

'Jammie Dodger?'

'I'll pass. What did you find out?'

'Lots.'

Jonesey made tea, filled his pockets with more biscuits and walked back to Steve's office.

'OK, potted version.' He settled himself down and dipped a custard cream biscuit in his tea, sucking it loudly. 'Edwyn Lewis married his school sweetheart, they start life by having a baby that later dies. No real explanation as to why, apart from a social worker's comment about possibly a parent shaking a baby. Nothing further seen on that, bear in mind this was back in the dark ages. They try again and have twins. Edward and Russell. Can't find any real records for Russell, a few school records for Edward, but they tail off into primary school, nothing for secondary school. A few hospital records, broken bones, etc., then Daniel comes along. Few records for him, vaccinations, some school records. He broke his arm twice, so there's hospital records, he also had a few broken ribs too. Social services alerted by the school, and he was removed as a teenager to Edwyn's younger brother, Gavin. Then we have another visit by social services as the wife has left and a concerned neighbour hears shouting, screaming and children crying with a regularity. We have a disturbing the peace when Edwyn attacked Gavin and threatened to kill him, Edwyn believed Gavin helped his wife leave.'

'Quite the family saga.'

'So, Rosemary, Edwyn's wife. She's dead now, cancer, I think. She had some serious medical records. All broken bones, concussion, two miscarriages following trauma, skull fracture, broken ribs, fingers, shattered kneecap...' He dunked another biscuit. 'The list goes on. Social services kept up contact regarding Danny as he was with Anna, but he's over eighteen now, so the file is closed since he's considered an adult, albeit vulnerable.' He slurped his tea. 'I'm at a complete dead end, and can't find any real records on the twins, Teddy and Russell. I know Teddy is around, but there's nothing for Russell. I wonder if...'

Steve frowned at Jonesey. 'Wonder if what?'

Jonesey pulled a face. 'I wonder if maybe he died somehow and Edwyn just hid the body. You know, one child dying is one thing, but two is...'

'The man is a fucking animal. Keep digging. There'll be something. Focus on the twins.'

CHAPTER 16

Jenny was stripping wallpaper. She'd set herself a task of stripping a room a day and had started at the top where the rooms were slightly smaller, so realistically she felt she could achieve her goal.

A radio was set up on the landing and she whistled tunelessly to a Christmas song as she worked. She was settling into the place and getting used to all its noises, which frightened the life out of her at night sometimes. She had created herself a mini bedsit type arrangement in one of the huge rooms with massive bay windows that overlooked the beach. There was a small en suite bathroom attached and at night she locked the door tightly and jammed a chair underneath the lock plate just to be safe.

She was making good progress and had received the last of the quotes for building work. She had cheekily called Teeney and asked him which of the local builders he knew and which he would recommend. Teeney had offered to pop in and cast an eye over the quotes for her, to check no one was trying to swindle her.

Jenny finished stripping the last piece of wallpaper and went into the room next door to retrieve the large black rubbish sack and broom when she heard a door slam loudly in the house. She frowned and wondered if someone had got in. Cautiously she walked down the stairs clutching the broom as a weapon. She caught sight of herself in a glass-panelled door and realised how ridiculous she looked.

Scolding herself, she then proceeded to go through the house from top to bottom and found no sign of anyone. She stood for a moment wondering what to do next and felt her stomach rumble. Lunchtime.

Dumping the broom, she went to the fridge for the pasta salad she had bought yesterday. She couldn't find it anywhere. She stared into the small half-empty fridge and tried to remember. Had she paid for it and forgotten to pick it up? Sounded like the sort of thing she would do.

Frowning, she went to wash her hands. Entering the bathroom, she stopped in her tracks. The toilet seat was up. She looked around cautiously and then stared at the toilet seat. No way she would have done that. Slightly spooked, she backed out of the room and checked the house thoroughly again clutching a large claw hammer, even venturing into the basement. She checked the front door and tried to remember when she had last used the bathroom. Was it first thing? No one had visited her that day, so how was the loo seat up?

She made herself a sandwich and sat eating at the window, watching the sea. What the hell was that about? Who had put the loo seat up? In her mind she heard her brother's voice. '*Stop being a bloody muppet, bet you tipped something down the loo and just weren't thinking about it. There's no one in the house. Stop bloody obsessing and get going!*'

Jenny finished her sandwich, decided she was being stupid and headed back upstairs to finish clearing up.

Sebastian finished a call with a production company he was working with. They were after a first draft of a pilot episode in early March, which suited him fine. He had outlined a rough idea of the plot, and everyone seemed happy for him to flesh it out. He was sitting in his makeshift office when his mobile rang: he didn't recognise the number.

'Hello?' he said guardedly, expecting it to be a reporter.

'Sebastian?'

'Yes?'

'It's Levinson Lucas. I don't know if you remember me. I was playing opposite Cass in her latest film.'

'I don't think we actually met, did we?'

'No.'

'What can I do for you?'

'I just wanted to say that I am really sorry about Cass. You must be devastated... well, *I'm* devastated. We all are. Our beautiful girl. How is Tabatha doing?'

'Good. It's early days.'

'That's good to hear,' Levinson said quietly. 'I feel at a bit of a loss really. With Cassie gone... I... I can't believe it really. I miss her terribly, you know. So much.'

Sebastian didn't really know what to say.

'Is there a funeral?' Levison finally ventured.

'Coroner won't release the body yet.'

'Why's that? It was an accident surely?'

'Apparently not. The police are investigating.'

'That's preposterous!'

'If the police think it wasn't an accident, I'm happy for them to investigate.'

'What have they said?'

'They're keeping me in the loop. Look I haven't got much time, thanks for the call.'

'Yes, but what have the police said?'

'I can't share that.'

'Right, yes. Well, let me know when the funeral is though, won't you?'

'We might just have a very small ceremony.'

'In London though, of course, with all her friends.'

'Possibly not.'

'But everyone will be expecting to come. Cassie would have wanted everyone there.'

Seb was silent for a moment, the anger building. 'I will decide, along with my daughter, what will be the most fitting farewell to Cassie. I hardly think a star-studded turnout is appropriate under the circumstances.'

'But she'd want us all to be there. She would have loved that.'

'I disagree, we'll have to beg to differ, particularly as it's my choice, as she was my wife. Thanks for the call.' Seb ended the call and threw the phone down on the desk in frustration.

Sanctimonious prick thinking that he knew Cassie and what she would want over her own family. He pulled his chair closer to the desk, woke up the computer and typed in Levinson's name. Various images and headlines screamed at him from the page. All suggesting that Lev and Cassie were involved. Sources close to the couple said this and that, and Seb swore under his breath.

Various stills from their recent film had been doctored to make it look like they were together, easy because the film was a love story. Seb scrolled through the images not wanting to see anything that suggested it wasn't just work. He frowned at a series of small pictures, recognising the dress as the one she had been wearing on the day she died. It showed Cassie stepping out of a front door, sunglasses on and Levinson following her. The next photo showed Cassie pointing,

162

what looked like, an angry finger at him, and the third was her brushing off his hand as she walked away.

Sebastian copied the pictures and rang Steve's mobile, making sure the door was shut.

'Hi, Seb, how are you doing?' Steve's voice was friendly.

'Yeah. Good thanks.'

'Tabatha good?'

'Yup.'

'When's the surprise bundle coming?'

'Tomorrow.'

'I was just about to call you, Seb. I need some DNA from you, just for elimination purposes, can we arrange that pretty soon?'

'No problem.'

'Were you ringing for an update?'

'Bit of info really. Just had a call from Cassie's co-star in the film she was working on. Bloke called Levinson Lucas, complete sanctimonious twat. But I've just googled him, and I think he saw her on the day she died. Looked like an argument. Give me your email and I'll send them over and his mobile number.'

Steve gave him his email address. A few seconds later he said, 'Got it. You think this was the day she died?'

'Yeah. She said she popped out for a work thing. She was gone a few hours.'

'You don't know where?'

'Nope.'

'OK. We'll have a chat with him.'

'Great.'

'If you're passing, come in and do a quick swab?'

'No problem, I've got to go out in a minute. Shall I just ask at the desk?'

'Ask for PC Warren or Jones. Either will be able to help you.'

'OK, thanks.'

'I'll be in touch. Bye now.'

Sebastian went to find Tabatha; she was in the kitchen making some concoction.

'What's that?' Seb asked, peering at it doubtfully.

'Mince pies. I'm feeling Christmassy. Aunty Bree will be here around seven. I've made her up a room.'

'I could have done that.'

'We are having pasta for tea. OK?'

'Great. What can I do?'

'You need to buy some wine; you know how much she knocks it back.'

'Right. Yes. Anything else?'

'Garlic bread and a nice pudding, please. Something chocolatey.'

'Yes, boss.'

'Dad, have you seen the photo of Mum that's by my bed? The black-and-white one? I can't find it anywhere.'

Seb shrugged. 'Under your bed? You might have knocked it off?'

'I didn't think of that. I'll have a look.'

He picked his wallet up off the side. 'Garlic bread, wine and pudding.'

'Yup.'

'Got it. See you in a bit.'

Seb closed the door behind him and made a note of what he needed on his phone. First stop was the police station.

Steve ended the call and went to find PC Warren and Jonesey. Both were in the kitchen; Jonesey was busying himself opening a pack of KitKats and making tea while PC Warren was leaning against the doorjamb.

'Mine's a tea, oh and thanks very much,' Steve said, helping himself to a KitKat. 'How are you, PC Warren?'

164

PC Warren blushed. 'Fine, thanks.'

'PC Warren, it's your lucky day.'

'Is it?' she asked sceptically.

'Sebastian Scott is on his way in for a DNA swab. Reckon you're up to it?'

PC Warren's eyes widened. 'With bells on,' she said, then added, 'thanks, Guv.'

'Go get a kit ready.'

'Happy to,' she said, walking off without a backward glance to Jonesey.

'Oi,' Jonesey said to Steve, adopting a hurt expression. 'I was almost in there.'

'Dream on, Jonesey. You'll need more than some Maltesers and a packet of choccy Hobnobs to nab that one. I'll be in my office.'

Steve was reading idle gossip on the internet about Levinson Lucas and Cassie. Levinson seemed quite the lothario when it came to his leading ladies, but the press also liked to suggest the same about Cassie and her leading men. Steve wanted a DNA sample from Levinson too, but he wondered how he would achieve it without alerting him as to why. He was just about to call Levinson Lucas's mobile and have a chat when his phone rang with an unfamiliar number.

'Miller,' he answered absently.

'Good afternoon, Inspector Miller,' said a female voice. 'This is Pearl Camorra. How are you?'

Steve sat a little straighter in his chair. 'I'm very well, thanks. And yourself?'

'Excellent. Looking forward to Christmas.'

'As am I,' Steve said. 'Pearl... is it OK to call you Pearl or would you prefer me to be more formal?'

Pearl chuckled. 'Well, I like to think we're almost friends, Steve, so Pearl is fine.'

'I did want to thank you for the kind package you sent a few weeks back. Very public spirited of you, I appreciated the gesture.'

'It was, wasn't it?' she said warmly. 'I like to think there was another lady locally who appreciated it.'

'There was. She will be forever grateful, I think.'

'Good. Now on to business. Alexy tells me that you would like to meet me and my husband and Alexy to discuss an impending problem.'

'Yes. I would like to discuss it. I see it as a shared problem.'

'Interesting,' Pearl said approvingly. 'We are happy to meet, but we must have some guarantees about safety and not walking into some sort of foolish ambush.'

'I don't operate that way, Pearl.'

'I've heard that you are a fair man with principles. It's some of your colleagues we don't trust.'

'I'm sorry to hear that. I can assure you, I just want to have a discussion, nothing more.'

'OK. We need somewhere totally private, so I suggest you come to the house. Alexy will be here too.'

'Your house?'

'Well, dear, I don't think yours will be big enough for all of us, nice though it is.'

Steve frowned. Of course they knew where he lived.

'And your address?'

Pearl laughed. 'You know exactly where we are, sweet man. Tomorrow night at say 6 p.m. for drinks?'

'Tomorrow night it is.'

'I look forward to it, Steve.'

Steve ended the call and sat pondering. He picked up the phone and dialled DCI Jerry Reed from the Organised Crime Unit.

'Jerry, got a meet organised.'

'Where and when?'

'I'm not going to share that with you on this occasion. I've given my word.'

Silence greeted him.

'Sorry if that scuppers any plans you had,' Steve said, feeling like Jerry was using him. 'So what info am I sharing with them? Although I suspect they'll know more than me.'

'Share whatever. We need to keep this new lot out before we have a mountain of bodies to deal with and a massive turf war. Plus, I need Mickey to stay here so I can nail him. Here's the deal so far. Listening?'

'Listening.'

'Kingpin in Liverpool calls himself "The Surgeon," aka Nathan White. Operates out of an old disused Victorian hospital. Rumour is he's a failed doctor. Got too handy with the prescription cabinet. But he's seen the light now and is clean, only deals it. He is absolutely untouchable locally. Al Capone eat your heart out. This guy is worse than Mickey. Beyond Teflon. Local plod feel like they're helpless and watching it happen. He's into everything. Guns, drugs, girls, boys, cash. You name it, he's got a finger in it somewhere. He's got loads of plod on the payroll too. He knows everything. He's supported by the Apostle Street Gang. Totally ruthless fuckers. Vaguely reminiscent of some of the punishments we used to see with the South African gangs, or in the Sierra Leone wars. You know, legs and arms being hacked off, black magic sacrifices and all that weird shit, as well as the run-of-the-mill beatings, shootings and stabbings.

'He sounds delightful.'

'He likes to focus on the coast. Get a local boat to ferry it in and set up a county line or two locally. Then he gets the local dealers out and his lads in, and hey presto. If he can't find a boat, he'll send young lads by train. They'll bring it in by the bagful and set themselves up for a few weeks until they're all sold and then they'll change. New blood, new stash and the process begins again. Nine times out of ten what they're selling is shit. It's stuff that's been cut and then cut again. Crap quality. At least with Mickey he has standards. Good quality shit.'

'Who were the two he sent?'

'Ringo and Paul. They're his primary scouts. He sends them to all the new places he's thinking about. They do a bit of wet work, off the local dealers, interrupt the local supply, clear the way and get a line or two going. The Surgeon's right-hand man is Freddy Castro. Makes out he's descended from Fidel Castro, but it's total bollocks. He's basically a chav from Speke. Pure Liverpool. He has delusions of grandeur and big dreams. Lords it up when he can, pretends he runs the joint.'

'Nice bunch. Time is of the essence then.'

'It is. You're not going to tell me where it is or when?'

'No. Gave my word. But I'll make sure someone knows just in case.'

'OK. Can't say fairer than that. Good luck, mate. Keep your wits about you.'

'I'm thinking about taking out a funeral plan beforehand, so Kate doesn't get lumbered.'

'I'll speak at your funeral. Say something nice. Make sure everyone knows you're a hero.'

'You're too kind.'

'Call me the minute you're done. Doesn't matter when it is.'

'Will do.'

'Take care.'

'Nice knowing you.' Steve ended the call and sat at his desk for a moment. He pushed himself out of his chair and went hunting for Jonesey. As he rounded the corridor, he met a beaming PC Warren.

'By the look of your face, PC Warren, Mr Scott has paid you a visit.'

She sighed. 'That is one gorgeous man.'

'Swab sent?'

'Just gone now.'

'Great. Thanks.'

Steve tracked down Jonesey and quietly outlined what would be happening the next night at 6 p.m., where he would be and for roughly how long. He issued Jonesey with strict instructions of what to do if he didn't call him or wasn't seen again. Jonesey looked at him in amazement.

'Christ, Guv. You've got some balls on you. A meeting in the vipers' nest?'

'Apparently, Jerry is going to say something nice at my funeral.'

'Catering better be good,' Jonesey said.

CHAPTER 17

Foxy was wondering how to have the conversation with Carla. It had been bothering him since Sophie mentioned it. Finishing work, he trudged up the stairs to the flat. He found her on the balcony outside, towelling off Solo. She looked flushed and had a healthy glow about her.

'Done for the day?' she asked.

'I am. Fancy going out for dinner?'

'Yes,' she said, her eyes sparkling. 'There's that new place, The Chapel. Let's try that.'

'OK. Shall I book?'

'Go for it.'

The Chapel restaurant was a converted chapel on the edge of the harbour. It had been closed for years until a local restauranter bought it and spent some serious money. It had whitewashed walls, bright blue paintwork inside and reminded Foxy of an upmarket Greek taverna. A cheerful waitress showed them to a table by a large window overlooking the water. They decided on wine, and looked at the menu.

'Now, before you start, I'm only having one glass. Also, I'm not having you steal my food,' Carla announced while she inspected the menu. 'It's your worst habit.'

'I don't consider that bad for a worst habit,' Foxy said lightly. 'It could be worse.'

'I know exactly what I'm having, and you won't be pinching any of mine if you get food envy,' she said firmly.

The waitress returned with their drinks and took their order. Carla raised her wineglass.

'Here's to very accommodating ex-husbands,' she said.

'Welcome,' said Foxy, clinking his glass against hers.

The two were silent for a moment and Foxy took a breath.

'We need to talk about this situation and what your thoughts are... you know... what your expectations are.'

Carla looked at Foxy indulgently. 'I wondered when you would get whatever's been bothering you off your chest.'

Foxy shook his head slightly. She knew him too well.

'I feel like I don't know what you're thinking, Carla.' He scratched his head. 'What you want from me...'

'I don't want anything from you,' she said lightly.

'I need to know where your head's at.'

'My head's at?'

'The baby... where you go from here.'

'Ah.' She eyed him critically. 'OK. I'm going to take a punt and have a guess at what *I think* you're thinking.'

Foxy rolled his eyes. 'I hate playing this game.'

'No you don't,' she insisted. 'Here's what you're thinking. One. Does Carla want to have the baby? Two. Does Carla want me to step up and be a family with her and the baby? Three. Do you want to

171

make a future with the baby of a rapist and the wife who you love, but don't *love* love, like the way you love Sophie?' She looked triumphant at his shocked face.

'And the crowd goes wild,' she said, raising her glass. 'Pretty accurate, huh?'

'How did you know?' he said quietly.

Carla leant forward and took his hand. 'Because I know you, you great lump.'

'Doesn't answer the question though, does it?' Foxy said. 'What are you going to do?'

'I haven't decided yet,' Carla said. 'I need some time to think about it. If I make the wrong decision, I get to live with it forever. So, my options remain the same. Do I have this baby at the age of forty-two and bring it up myself, always knowing how it started, or do I terminate the pregnancy? Whatever I choose, it's an impossible choice.'

'I get that.'

'What made you think I'd want to play happy families?'

Foxy looked uncomfortable. 'It's different now since Charlie died. There's a part of me that wonders if it's not a second chance.'

Carla frowned. 'A second chance at what? Have another child and hope it won't die?'

'That's harsh.'

'But true. This baby will never be a replacement for Charlie. Never. Plus, it wouldn't or hadn't even crossed my mind that we would play happy families together. Why would I even think that?' She looked incredulous. 'I love you and you love me, but not in the way we would need to be able to bring up a baby. I genuinely think we would end up killing each other.' Her face softened as she looked at Foxy and placed her hand on his.

'Look. The way we are now. I love it. I'm so happy when I see you because we can be there for each other without all the other crap that gets in the way. I like being like this with you. And if I was to have the baby, then I would want our relationship to still be the same and if you wanted to, you could be part of the baby's life. But I had no ideas or expectations at all that we would embark on this together, like parents.'

Foxy twirled his wineglass.

'You're off the hook, big guy,' Carla said softly.

Frustrated, Foxy said, 'I feel like I can't help you.'

'You're helping me more than you realise,' she said. 'By letting me stay, no pressure, no opinions being forced on me. It's wonderful, I feel free to think.'

'And what about Jamie, if you decide to have it?'

She snorted. 'I don't want anything to do with him. In fact, Penny rang. You know, the one in sex crimes. She's been doing a little digging and she's found two nurses who think the same sort of thing happened to them. Trouble is, none of them got tested the morning after or have been as unlucky as me. So there's no evidence.'

'So unlikely to make it to court.'

'Exactly. She's sent a confidential email to female nurses alerting them to the date rape drug and how this is going on in the hospital, without mentioning any names. Fingers crossed people will be more wary. I've told her he rang me and left a message, all innocently and she warned me to stay clear. Block his calls.'

She shook her head and looked out of the window, her eyes filling.

'I can't believe I was so stupid to have trusted him.'

'Carla, he fooled you and you're one of the savviest people I know. When I met him for a few brief minutes, he seemed like a decent enough bloke. You didn't know. We will get him for this, you mark my words.'

Carla blew her nose.

173

'We aren't going to talk about him anymore. What we are going to talk about is you.'

'Me?' Foxy looked surprised.

'Yup. And when you're going to get your finger out and tell Sophie how you feel about her.'

'We are not having a conversation about that,' Foxy said grumpily.

'I think we are.'

'I think we aren't.'

'We really are.'

'We really aren't.'

* * *

'Dad, why are you standing there staring at nothing?' Jude's voice interrupted Doug's musings about when Jesse would be home.

Doug blinked and looked at Jude. 'Sorry. You ready to go?'

Jude nodded. 'Uh huh. Come on. I need to warm up.'

'You're very keen to get there. Ooh, is that gel in your hair?' teased Doug, reaching out to touch Jude's carefully coiffed hair. 'It *is* gel in your hair! Oh is there a girl who might be there today?'

'Shut up, Dad.' Jude blushed.

'Tell me who she is,' Doug demanded smirking. 'Or we don't go.'

'Dad, don't be a dick.'

'A what?' Doug said, eyes wide. 'You want me to ferry you about to your climbing thing, with your girl-proof hair and I'm a dick?'

'Dad, can we just go?' Jude said desperately.

'Tell me.'

'Dad... come on.'

'Not budging.'

'OK... she's called Tabatha.'

'See? That wasn't so hard, was it?'

Jude grumpily climbed into the truck.

'So, tell me about Tabatha. How old is she, where does she live?' Doug said, starting the truck.

Jude rolled his eyes.

'God, Dad.'

'Come on.'

'OK. She's just moved here. She lives in the row by the Hope and Anchor, the end one. And she's just had a heart transplant. She misses her friends from London.'

'Why did they move from London?'

'Dunno.'

'How old is she?'

'Dunno. My age, I think.'

'Jeez, have you even had a conversation?'

'Only a bit. Hopefully she'll be there today.'

They parked in Doug's space in the harbour and walked towards the climbing centre where Foxy was running an advanced climber's competition that morning.

'Are you coming in?' asked Jude reluctantly.

'Yup.'

'You don't have to.'

'Oh, I think I do,' said Doug, eyes twinkling. 'I want to check out this Tabatha.' He pushed the door open to the centre and walked in leaving Jude standing outside looking frustrated.

Doug greeted Foxy. 'Hey, buddy. How you doing?'

'I'm good. You here to watch the master in action?'

'Thought I might. I'm gonna grab a quick takeaway coffee. Want one?'

'I'm OK. You go on. Starts in ten. Your boy's up first. Jude, get warmed up,' Foxy called.

Jude sat down, unlaced his Converse and dug out his climbing shoes and chalk bag. He heard the door open but didn't look up until he caught a whiff of perfume and Tabatha sat down next to him.

'Hey,' she said, smiling at him.

'Hey,' he said, feeling ridiculously happy. 'How are you feeling?'

'Good, I've escaped. My godmother is down, and she's doing my head in, fussing around me. I've come in for some peace and quiet.'

'Don't know if you'll get that.'

'Where's your mate?' she asked.

'He's always late,' Jude said just as Marcus fell in the door, out of breath. 'See?'

Marcus plonked himself down next to Tabatha, so she had to move closer to Jude, and proceeded to take off his trainers.

'Hey, Tabatha,' he said. 'You come to hang out with the champion?'

'Haven't you got to win first?' she said, amused.

'That is a tiny, insignificant issue,' he said, cramming his shoes on and jumping up.

Doug walked back in at that moment and saw Tabatha sat next to Jude.

'Hello,' he said.

Jude looked embarrassed. 'Tabatha, this is my dad,' he said, his face reddening.

'Hi, Tabatha, I'm Doug, nice to meet you.'

'You too,' said Tabatha. 'You know you two have the most incredible eyes. Pretty obvious that you're father and son.'

Doug grinned. '*All* the good stuff came from me.'

Jude rolled his eyes. 'You staying for long, Tabatha?'

'I'll stay for the competition, but only if you two talk to me when you can. I don't want to be sat here on my own all morning. I've got to be home by two, Dad says there's a delivery I need to be back for.'

'I'll talk to you,' Jude said. 'Wish me luck.'

'Good luck.'

Doug watched Jude head around the corner, chalking up his hands, and suddenly noticed that his son was no longer a boy, but on the verge of being a man. He'd seriously grown over the last month or so and was as tall as Doug now, complete with enormous feet. He sat down next to Tabatha.

'Jude tells me you've just moved here.'

'Having a break from London.'

'Tough to be away from your friends though.'

'I miss them.'

'I'll bet. Do you climb?'

'Sometimes. But I've just had a new heart, so I can't really do anything like that.'

'Hard for you. You look very well though.'

'I was very lucky,' she said quietly. 'Car accident, before you ask.'

'I'm so sorry. Was anyone else hurt?'

Tabatha swallowed hard and tears filled her eyes. 'My mother,' she said. 'My mother died.'

'Tabatha, I'm so sorry. Mums are important people. I've just lost mine too. Doesn't matter how old you get. Still awful when you lose them, even when you're as ancient as me.'

Tabatha pointed at the pager on Doug's belt. 'Does that mean you work on the lifeboat?'

'Aye. I'm what's called the coxswain which is basically the skipper.'

'Wow. Is it a big boat?'

'Yes. And it's pretty cool. If it gets turned over by a wave, then it rights itself.'

'That's cool,' she said. 'Unless you're, like, really sea sick.'

'If you're around for a bit. We'll see if we can get you a sneaky trip on the boat. Jude will come with you.'

'I'd love that,' she said, her eyes shining brightly. 'I love being on the water.'

'It's a deal,' Doug said. 'Right, Foxy's waving. Shall we go and watch the boys?'

Jude was very pleased with himself. He had beaten Marcus by nearly seven seconds. Marcus had the right hump about it and stormed off home. Jude viewed this as more than a victory since it meant he could spend more time hanging out with Tabatha. They had talked about nothing important, but by the end of the morning, Jude was smitten.

'I've got to go,' she said, looking at the huge clock on the wall. 'Special delivery, whatever that is.'

'See you around then.'

'OK.' She handed him her phone. 'Give me your number then we can message and maybe hang out.'

Jude tapped in his number and handed her the phone.

'Cool,' she said. 'Well done beating Marcus. Is he always a bad loser?'

'Yeah. I'll get the silent treatment for a day and then it'll be like nothing happened.'

'Right. I've really gotta go.'

Doug waited at the door. 'Jude, you good to go?'

'Yeah.'

'Need a lift up the road, Tabatha? You're in Compass Row, aren't you?'

'Thanks! That would be great. Always makes me super breathless getting up the hill.'

'Your carriage awaits then, my lady,' Doug said.

'So embarrassing, Dad.'

The three of them walked around to Doug's RNLI truck.

Tabatha turned to Jude. 'Your dad said he'd take us out on the lifeboat. That'll be epic.'

Jude was surprised Tabatha would enjoy something like that. 'Really? Well, we'll sort it out won't we, Dad?'

'Aye,' said Doug, starting the truck and pulling away. They rumbled up the road and Doug pulled up outside Tabatha's.

'This one?'

'Yeah, thanks.' Tabatha unclipped herself. 'Nice to meet you. See you, Jude.'

Tabatha climbed out and walked up the driveway. Jude watched her go and sighed deeply.

Doug hid a knowing smile.

'Who was that dropping you off?' asked Seb, coming out of the kitchen.

'It was Doug and Jude.'

'Jude's the boy from the climbing centre?'

'Yup. His dad is the skipper on the lifeboat. He said he'd take me out on it! That would be so cool.'

'Come and have a sandwich. You look pale. By the way, where's that photo of Mum that used to be on the piano?'

'No idea.'

Tabatha wandered into the kitchen, Bree, her godmother, was sitting drinking coffee and texting furiously.

'Darling,' Bree said, looking up. 'How was your climbing competition? Were your friends there?'

'Yes.'

'Anyone of interest?' she said slyly. 'I had a little peek out of the window. Either of the two that dropped you off looked pretty bloody gorgeous to me.'

'Aunt Bree!'

She gave a mischievous grin. 'I'm guessing it was the young one?'

Tabatha pretended to rise above it. 'He's nice. Just a friend.'

'Maybe a friend with benefits?'

'Gabriella, please stop leading my daughter astray,' Seb scolded as he walked into the room. 'Tabs, sandwich please.'

The three of them sat eating sandwiches Bree had made with lopsided bread, stuffed with random fillings. Bree was a self-proclaimed horror in the culinary department.

'So what's this special delivery at 2 o'clock then that's so important?' Tabatha said, picking one of Bree's hairs out of her sandwich.

'It's your Christmas present,' Seb said. 'I didn't think you'd want to wait for Christmas Day.'

'Sounds interesting,' Tabatha said, finding another hair and abandoning her sandwich completely.

'It's very exciting,' said Bree, clapping her hands. 'I can't wait.'

'You're in on it too?'

'Of course,' she said gleefully. 'Your father can't keep any secrets from me.'

The doorbell rang. Seb looked at Tabatha and gestured to the door.

'Happy Christmas, kiddo.'

Tabatha opened the door to a tall, attractive man with bright green eyes in what looked like a naval uniform, and a small lady with black hair and the same eyes, holding an enormous cardboard box between them. It had a large red ribbon wrapped around it.

'Special delivery for Miss Tabatha Scott,' the man said.

'I'm Tabatha.'

'Is it OK to bring it in and put it down? It's pretty fragile,' the woman said.

Intrigued and grinning broadly, Tabatha opened the door wider. 'Come on in.'

'Kitchen?' asked the small woman.

'Er. Yes,' Tabatha said, surprised that the woman knew where she was going.

The two carefully carried the large box into the kitchen and placed it down gently on the floor. Seb went to stand next to Suzy and nodded to Will.

'Hi there,' Seb said quietly. 'Thanks for doing this. I didn't expect such a ceremony!'

Will grinned. 'Special effort for a special girl, I hear. I'm Will, Suzy's brother.'

'You in the navy?' Seb asked, gesturing to Will's uniform.

'Harbour master.'

'Ahh.'

'Hello, I'm Bree,' Bree said, walking over and shaking Will's hand for far too long, eyeing him up and down approvingly. 'I do love a man in uniform.'

Will smiled broadly. 'Well, it's my lucky day then, isn't it?'

'Is it OK to open it?' Tabatha said, holding the end of the huge ribbon.

'Go for it,' Seb said.

Tabatha undid the ribbon and carefully opened the leaves of the box. She peered inside and screamed loudly with excitement when a small nose appeared.

'Oh my God. Is he for me?' She squealed with excitement and picked the puppy up out of the box. 'Oh, he is utterly adorable!'

Tabatha sat down with the puppy on her lap and petted him. Jack, clearly thrilled at the attention, wriggled onto his back so she could tickle his tummy.

'What's his name?' Tabatha asked.

'Will named him actually,' Suzy said. 'Captain Jack Sparrow because he reminded us of a pirate. But he answers to Jack. He's a Border collie, nearly five months old now. His training is going well, but we'll need to finish it off together, so he doesn't forget. Your dad has arranged for some lessons on training, but we'll go through the basics in a minute. He's very good, house trained and very bright.'

Jack had decided he wanted to explore so he set off running through the house yipping with excitement. The stairs puzzled him a little. He sat at the bottom of the flight looking up before bounding up them, tripping and falling onto his face.

'He'll get the hang of it,' Suzy observed.

'We need to get a load of stuff for him,' Tabatha said.

'Already sorted,' said Suzy. 'He's all good to go, isn't he, Seb?'

Sebastian didn't hear. Jack had thrown himself at Seb and he was currently nuzzling him like a long-lost friend.

'I'm not sure who is happier about the puppy,' observed Bree, 'Seb or Tabatha.'

'I need to get on,' Will said, turning towards the front door. 'Good to meet you, Seb, Bree. I'll let myself out.'

Bree watched him walk away. He looked familiar, but she couldn't place him. Either way, things were looking up locally if everyone looked like him and the lifeboat guy.

'I think I might start to look for property down here,' she said to herself.

CHAPTER 18

Bree had received a request to attend the police station for an interview. Finding the prospect a little thrilling, she had readily agreed and wandered up towards the police station that afternoon. She asked for Steve at the desk and was shown to an interview room.

Steve arrived and pushed open the door, juggling a cup of tea and some files. He smiled at Bree. 'Gabriella Logan, isn't it? Inspector Steve Miller.'

'Pleased to meet you and please call me Bree,' she said, unashamedly eyeing him up, thinking that he was quite handsome for a police officer. All the police she had ever come across had been old, crusty and boring.

'Thanks for coming in, Bree,' he said. 'You're staying at Sebastian's?'

'I am. It's chaos there today, the Christmas present has arrived.'

'Ah, one of Suzy's rescues. How is it settling in?'

'Very well. I don't know who's more thrilled, Seb or Tabs.'

Steve arranged his files, took a gulp of his tea and looked at his watch.

'I need to record this and there may also be a chance I need to speak to you again. So please don't leave town without checking in first. OK?'

'OK.'

Steve pressed record and went through the preliminaries.

'This all sounds very sinister,' Bree said lightly. 'With respect, why all the questions if it was an accident?'

'We're exploring other avenues, not just the theory that it was an accident. So, I hear from Seb that you were Cassie's best friend and Tabatha's godmother. Known her for nearly twenty years? Can you tell me about the last time you spoke to or actually saw Cassie Warner?'

Bree exhaled heavily and blinked away some tears.

'I spoke to her on the day she died, and I saw her the day before.'

'What did you do the day before?'

Bree shrugged. 'I was seeing a client at Pinewood Studios, and I popped onto set to see her.'

'Who was that client?'

'Levinson Lucas.'

'Was that unusual, that you popped in?'

'Not at all. We spoke most days, or I popped in to see her at work or home whenever I was near.'

'Wasn't Levinson Lucas her leading man?'

'He is… Was.'

'OK. What do you do for Levinson Lucas?'

'His PR. He has a tendency to be a bit of a prick, I'm afraid. I tend to mop up the damage.'

'Occupational hazard, is it?'

'Seems so. I make a pretty good living out of it, and he can't seem to stop being a prick.'

'OK. Do you recall what you and Cassie discussed when you saw her?'

'I don't really remember.'

'Really? You don't remember the last time you spoke to your best friend? According to Seb you've got the memory of an elephant.' He smiled. 'His words, not mine.'

'Kind of him,' she said dryly.

'To be fair he said it affectionately.'

'Oh that makes it all better then,' she said, rolling her eyes.

'So…' Steve prompted. 'What did you talk about?'

'Stupid stuff. Christmas, what to get for Tabs. What I needed to bring when I came down for Christmas. Some bloke I fancied. You know. Nothing important.'

'It's really important that you tell me the truth, Bree.'

She looked shocked. 'What makes you think I wouldn't?'

'I'm just making a point.'

'It was nonsense. Just nonsense. That's what we usually talked about.'

'And the day she died?'

Bree's eyes filled with tears. 'She was angry. She'd had a bad costume fitting. Levinson had been there, and they'd quarrelled about something. A love scene or something. He wanted it one way and she wanted it the other. She said he was being such a dick. He threatened to pull out if it didn't go his way.' She sighed. 'Christ, the man was fucking high maintenance. Anyway, I told her not to drive angry, she always drove terribly fast, especially if she was wound up about something. And that was it. We said we loved each other and said see you soon.'

'Filming had been suspended?'

'Until after Christmas. Then it was on location for another six weeks.'

'Did Cassie have any weird stalkers? Fans who were obsessive?'

Bree smiled sadly. 'Everywhere we went she attracted people. Just by being her. Even before she was famous. But once she was famous, everyone felt they knew her, they felt that they had the right to know her. It didn't matter where we went, there was always someone.'

'Anyone in London that might follow her here?'

Bree shrugged. 'No idea. She was always being hounded by journalists. They often chased her car. You would have thought after Lady Diana the press learnt their lesson, but apparently not.'

'You've been here a lot? See anyone weird hanging about?'

'Not really. We had a summer here once where there was a young guy who hung around. Very shy. I think he might have been a bit vulnerable. He seemed to be wherever we were, just watching. Seemed happy to watch and fairly harmless.'

'Can you remember what he looked like?'

'Not enough to pick him out of a line up. Bad haircut, bit weird.'

'You just saw him one summer, not again.'

Bree thought hard. 'I think I saw him about here and there. As you would see someone you've spotted before in a small town. Nothing that worried me.'

'And what about her marriage to Sebastian?'

'What about it?'

'Was it a good marriage?'

'What does a good marriage look like, Inspector?' she said lightly. 'They loved each other.'

'Either of them playing away?'

'No idea.'

'Anything going on in Cassie's life that might have meant someone held a grudge?' he asked.

Bree looked at him in amazement. 'Everyone held a grudge. Cassie was hailed as the next Hollywood darling. They loved her. She was a younger, better, prettier Julia Roberts. She would have stormed Hollywood. It's quicker to ask who wouldn't have held a grudge. Do you have any kind of idea how big she would have been?'

'Who benefits from her death?'

Bree guffawed loudly. 'Every actress in the world.'

'Seriously.'

Bree leant forward. 'I am being serious. She was averaging staggering amounts for a film. She'd just been offered a trilogy and the fee they were offering was mind blowing.'

'Who benefits directly?'

'No idea. I expect it's Seb and Tabs,' Bree said.

'Did she have family?'

'Nope. It sounds weird, but it's not something she ever talked about or wanted to talk about. She never talked about her parents or her childhood. Just the odd memory, but thinking about it she only mentioned it when she was very blue. She had real bouts of melancholy though. You should probably ask Seb.'

'Did she have a faith?'

'A what?'

'Was she religious?'

Bree gave a long-suffering look. 'That's a resounding no. She's pretty scathing about anything religious, to the point that she was almost religiously against anything religious.'

'She didn't talk about any weird fan mail?'

'Nope. That sort of stuff goes straight to the agents though. You might want to talk to them. Seb has their details.'

'Bree, can I ask where you were on the night Cassie died, please? Just for elimination purposes.'

Bree looked surprised. She got her phone out and fiddled with a calendar app.

'I was at a lunch and then I went home.'

'OK. We'll need to verify that.'

'Am I a suspect?'

Steve looked at her levelly. 'As I said, we're just exploring options. Thanks very much for coming in today. Remember what I said about letting me know if you're heading off. I'll let you get back to play with the puppy.' He opened the door and PC Warren was standing outside.

'PC Warren, can you please see Ms Logan out?'

'Guv.'

'Bree, thanks again.' He let the door close.

He sat down at the table and switched off the tape recorder. He leant back in his chair for a moment and thought. Something was off. He'd been doing this long enough for his nose to be telling him that this wasn't the full story.

He got his phone out and called a colleague who now worked in London.

'Toby,' he said, as they exchanged pleasantries. 'Don't fancy doing an interview for me and getting me prints and DNA?'

'Depends on who it is,' his friend teased.

'Levinson Lucas the actor.'

'Since when did you deal with acting royalty?'

'He's a dick by all accounts. I'm looking into the murder of Cassie Warner. It was on my patch.'

'Didn't know it was murder.'

'It's not common knowledge. Suspicious death at the moment. I'll get it cleared with your gaffer, OK?'

'If he says it's OK, I'll do it in the next couple of days. Send me this bloke's details. I'll bet it's somewhere swanky.'

'Chelsea. I'll send over questions. Gotta go, mate. Thanks again. Oh, and tell him not to leave the country and that we need DNA to eliminate him from some of Cassie's possessions. Just in case he kicks off. I need him to explain a couple of pictures too, they'll all be in the stuff I send.'

'No sweat. I'll ring when I've got him here, give you the low down.'

'Top man.'

Steve gathered up his things and walked to his office. He prepared everything he needed for Toby and sent it off.

Steve then requested phone records and locations of Bree's phone, Levinson's, Sebastian's that was pinged in or around the area of the scene of the accident at the rough time it happened. He also chased the intelligence analysts for the phone location of the unregistered phone that had called 999. He looked at his watch. Five fifteen. Only forty-five minutes until he would most likely be dying horribly at the hands of Mickey and Pearl Camorra.

Steve drove up the hill on the outskirts of town and waited at the large cedarwood gates to be buzzed through. In the car park there was already a variety of cars, including a large black truck with tinted windows, which Steve assumed was Alexy's. He saw a tasteful triple garage with what looked like accommodation above.

He got out of the car and strolled towards the house admiring the design and the use of cedar, steel, glass and pebble-filled gabions. Approaching the front steps, he rang the doorbell. Steve usually wasn't one to be nervous about anything, he was mostly philosophical about things, but he felt the flutter of worry about walking into the vipers' nest.

The door opened to reveal Pearl, who was incredibly attractive for her age, which Steve estimated to be in her late fifties. She was dressed entirely in white, with gold accessories and looked more like an actress than a gangster's wife.

'Inspector Miller,' she said warmly. 'Thank you for coming. Do come in.'

'Steve, please,' he said, bending slightly to accept the light kisses she put on both his cheeks. She hooked her arm through his as she guided him into the main living area.

'I've been admiring your house,' he said as they strolled through it. 'Quite beautiful.'

'I hope you're not chatting up my wife,' Mickey Camorra said, his eyes narrowing as Steve entered the room with Pearl.

'Tempting though it is, I value my life,' Steve said dryly. 'I was admiring your house. It's beautiful and even better from here. I could look at this view all day.'

'I do. Drink?' asked Mickey.

'Beer if you have it?'

Mickey walked to a long counter and flipped the top off a bottle of lager, passing it to Steve.

Alexy walked into the room.

'You are Steve, no? Jimmy the fisherman say you are good bloke. Despite being policeman. I am Alexy.'

'Good to meet everyone,' said Steve, looking around. 'Please don't think me rude, but we have matters to be discussed and I propose we get started so that me being here doesn't eat into your evening too much.'

'I like a man that gets to the point,' Mickey said. 'Let's sit.'

The four of them sat at the table. Pearl eyed Steve approvingly.

'You have a good reputation, Steve,' she said lightly. 'You're considered honest and fair, and your word counts for a lot.'

'Thank you,' said Steve.

'Your girlfriend is the new GP, isn't she?' Pearl probed.

'She is.'

'Does she know you're here with us tonight?'

'No. She knows I'm working. Only one person knows I'm here and is sworn to secrecy.'

Mickey folded his arms. 'You know if you're lying I will fucking end you here.'

Pearl laid a hand on his arm. 'Mickey darling, Steve gave me his word. I trust him.'

'Well I don't trust any of them. Especially that Jerry Reed. He'll manufacture any evidence to try and get me,' Mickey said angrily.

Pearl looked at Steve directly. 'Are we right to trust you?'

'I gave you my word,' Steve said, keeping his cool.

Mickey leant forward and jabbed the table aggressively. 'I want you to tell me exactly what you think my problem is.'

Steve looked thoughtful. 'I suspect you probably know more than me, but I have heard rumours there's a turf war in the offing from Liverpool. Am I right?'

Mickey nodded. 'Go on.'

'I'll be transparent here and tell you what I know. Ringo and Paul are scoping the area. By all accounts they're due to return shortly, looking for the names of the key dealers locally. They've felt up Sniffy, fairly unsuccessfully, and have been trying to watch your local dealers. They will get rid of them in a pretty horrific fashion, and then bring in their dealers and their boys and girls and set up a few lines to get themselves established. Word is, they want to boat it in from Liverpool down the coast so they'll either do it themselves or touch up Jimmy. They've been looking for him.'

'Who's behind it?' Mickey interrupted.

'The Surgeon.' Steve relayed what Jerry had told him almost word for word. He looked at Mickey. 'Is that what you know?'

Mickey stood and walked towards the wall of glass.

'Most of it. He wants to run business locally?'

Steve shook his head. 'No, Mickey. He'll want it all. Everything you have.'

Mickey breathed heavily, pacing the room. 'I'm not having some fucking prick with a perm and a fucking shell suit come and take my business away from me. I don't give a fuck who it is.'

'I agree,' Alexy said. 'We have to stop before it gets out of the hand.'

Steve raised his hands. 'This is where I leave. I don't want to hear what you're planning. The only thing I was concerned about was making you aware of a problem. I don't want a turf war and everything that comes with it.'

'You know there's gonna be killing, right?' Mickey said menacingly.

'Darling,' Pearl said soothingly. 'I think the term we will use is collateral damage. I suspect that will sit better with Steve.' She looked at Steve with a raised eyebrow. 'I think Steve would accept that there will likely be a certain degree of acceptable collateral damage, instead of a huge turf war that will undoubtably turn into a nasty blood bath.'

Steve regarded Pearl. He liked her immensely. He suspected she was the brains behind the whole operation, rather than Mickey. 'Well, collateral damage is never really "acceptable", but I'm unable to argue with that logic.'

'What are your thoughts?' asked Mickey.

Steve walked over to the huge picture window that overlooked the pool and the town. 'It's not for me to even go there. I'm governed by the constraints of the law.'

Pearl interjected. 'I think the priority is to get the king out of his ivory tower and come here, he'll be more vulnerable.'

'Go on,' Mickey said.

'Perhaps send him a message. But Ringo and Paul are his top scouts and setter uppers. What if next time they arrive here, we greet them and then return them slightly damaged with an invitation to come and discuss business? Perhaps he'll think it's worth the risk for the greater reward?'

Mickey narrowed his cold blue eyes. 'I like it.'

Steve faced them. 'None of this sits well with me. At all. But as Pearl so aptly made the point, this is about controlling the collateral damage as well as solving the problem. If we let this run unchecked, we'll have gang war and killings all over the place and Christ knows who'll get hurt. It's that collateral damage of innocent people I worry about. And when that happens, we will come down hard, on them and you.'

Mickey regarded him. 'I appreciate your honesty. I respect it.'

Steve inclined his head. 'Never forget, Mickey, I'm a policeman, and more importantly, I am not a bent policeman. If you push the boundaries and I find evidence of it, I will come for you. I can't say fairer than that. If I find collateral damage, I will be compelled to investigate it fully.'

'Understood,' said Pearl, walking over to Mickey and stroking his shoulder.

Steve sighed. 'Half the reason why we're having this conversation is because the stuff this mob sells is shit. It's cut and then cut again and then cut again. Like it or loathe it, you offer a good and safe product and much as I hate it, I respect you for that and it's the lesser of two evils. So, if I had the choice between very reluctantly looking the other way to *some* of the things you do, or dealing with the fall out of a massive turf war with loads of bad drugs in the area, I choose to look the other way on *some* matters. But if you break the law and I know it's you, can prove it's you, then others will be hard on you, and you know it.'

'Jerry Reed,' Mickey growled.

'Exactly,' Steve said. 'His patch is organised crime, mine isn't.'

'Interesting he sent you though,' Mickey observed. 'I like the idea of a message that invites Mr White to come and discuss his plans and our options. It's smart thinking. I suspect his ego will mean he's likely to say yes.'

'On this subject, I'm going to add one last thing,' Steve said. 'If you cut the head off this snake you need to be sure that you control what's left. Otherwise, we'll continue to have this problem, not just from Liverpool, but from other city cartels. You might need to bring in some outside help from someone who you trust implicitly.'

Mickey walked towards the large windows that overlooked the gently steaming infinity pool and folded his arms as he looked out.

'I'm aware of that. Do we know who Mr White's second in command is?' He looked at Steve.

'Freddy Castro. Delusions of grandeur. Fancies himself as the next surgeon from what I hear. I suspect he has quite the appetite.'

Mickey looked thoughtful. 'OK. I can work with that and who is his right-hand man?'

'I don't know.'

A door opened and Steve watched a huge bald man lumber across the floor to stand in front of Mickey and Pearl. He spoke in a low voice and Pearl murmured in reply.

She turned to Steve. 'Stanley says his contact at the docks says Ringo and Paul are heading this way tomorrow. We'll have to lay out the red welcome carpet won't we, gentlemen?'

Steve raised his hands. 'I'm stepping out.' He turned to Pearl. 'Can we keep the lines of communication open?'

'I'd like that, Steve,' she said, smiling at him. 'I told you we'd be friends.'

'Right, thanks for the beer. Let me know what's going on… er… within reason.' Steve shook Mickey's hand. 'Mickey, good to meet you. Alexy, you too. Night, everyone.'

'I'll see you out,' said Pearl, hooking her arm through his and walking him to the door. 'Thank you for coming, Steve. I appreciate your honesty and Mickey will too when he's thought about it.'

Steve smiled. 'It's nice to be walking out alive,' he said dryly.

'Oh shush.' She nudged him. 'We only kill people who really deserve it. I'll keep you posted, and we can see what can be mutually beneficial for us. Have a good evening now.' She kissed him lightly on the cheek.

Steve walked down the steps and climbed in his car. He drove out of the wide gates and waved at Pearl. Only when he got down the road did he let out a huge sigh of relief and realised that his hands were shaking slightly.

CHAPTER 19

Sunday morning dawned bright and sunny, and Carla awoke on a mission. She showered and dressed without waking Foxy, and let herself out of the flat; Solo insisted on coming with her. She stopped at Maggie's and bought a few takeaway pastries and headed off along the beach. A while later, she stood at Sophie's front door and rang the doorbell.

'Hey, Carla!' Sophie looked surprised as she opened the door. 'Are you OK?' She bent to make a fuss of Solo. 'Hey, gorgeous.'

'I'm good thanks, do you have some time for a chat?'

'Of course! It's great to see you. Come on in. Marcus is still in bed, typical bloody teenager, he won't surface for hours.'

Carla chuckled. 'Charlie was the same. Some days she wouldn't appear until lunchtime. I brought you some croissants,' she said, holding up the bag. 'Fresh from Maggie's.'

'Lovely!' Sophie grabbed some plates and tipped the croissants out. 'Coffee?'

'Please,' Carla said, taking a seat. 'Hope you don't mind me popping in.'

'It's great to see you,' Sophie said.

'Sophie, I was so sorry to hear about Sam. How are you doing?'

Sophie stopped making coffee for a moment. 'I'm OK,' she said thoughtfully. 'It was a shock. He left a letter for each of us. Weirdly that made me feel better.'

'Difficult though. To finally get him back and then this.'

'In all honesty, Carla, he died in the desert years ago. There wasn't much of my Sam left by the time they found him. I think it was only a matter of time before he tried to end it. He couldn't accept the way he was. Kept saying we deserved better.'

'I'm so sorry. How's Marcus doing?'

'He is remarkably resilient. He seems to have accepted it. He leans on Rob a lot.'

'He's a good man to lean on,' Carla said.

Sophie handed Carla a mug of coffee. 'How are *you* doing? Rob's been worried about you.'

Carla swirled her coffee mug. 'He's told you, hasn't he?'

'In absolute confidence and I absolutely had to drag it out of him. He's so worried about you. Seriously, I ended up bribing him with coffee.'

Carla rolled her eyes. 'That'll do it. You should have started with that.'

'Are you OK though? This is a really big deal.'

'I know. And before you ask, I don't have any ideas whatsoever about playing happy families with my ex-husband.'

Sophie buttered a croissant. 'Have you talked about it?'

'Yes. Rob knows I don't want anything from him. We're good as we are.'

Sophie ate some croissant. 'Mmm, they're good. Thank you. What do you think you'll do?'

Carla idly tore off a bit of croissant and dipped it in her coffee. 'I don't know to be honest. I've thought of nothing else really. How I feel about it. I've been trying to unpick it, knowing how the pregnancy started. And then I find myself trying to think of practicalities and how difficult it would be to have a child and work where I work. You know. What do I do about childcare? It's so expensive. I can't afford that on a nurse's salary on my own. But then termination goes against all of my principles. So I just can't decide.'

'Have you thought of having it adopted?'

'Yes, but I think I'd have to move away to do that. Too many questions. Too many people at work asking questions. Too many judgements and, of course, the man who did it is around, he has friends. It's a recipe for a living nightmare.'

'OK. Say you were in a loving relationship and the pregnancy happened. How would you feel then?'

Carla put her head in her hands, resting her elbows on the counter. 'I don't know. I just don't know. I'm too old to have a baby.'

'You're hardly a pensioner, Carla. Is having a termination so bad? Especially as you were raped. If it was me…'

'If it was you what?'

'I think I would have a termination and some counselling. I would think I didn't *choose* this situation; I wasn't responsible. My *choice* was taken away. And to me, that's the important thing. Choice. So, for me personally? I'd have to end the pregnancy. Because someone took away my god given right to choose. Have you thought of having counselling to maybe help you make a decision?'

'I hadn't. But it would probably help. I had a lot after Charlie died. It was the thing that finally made me realise how unfair I'd been to Rob. Blaming him for her death, when he wasn't even there, and he was busy trying to chase away his own demons. Maybe I'll think

198

about that. Anyway, I didn't really come here to bother you with the most difficult decision of the century,' she said lightly. 'I wanted to talk to you about something else.'

'Sounds interesting.'

'I just wanted to say that there isn't anything going on with me and Rob anymore,' Carla said carefully, looking Sophie in the eye.

'Why would you tell me that?' Sophie asked slowly.

'I felt that it was important that you knew. He doesn't want to because he has deep feelings for someone else. He's a deep one that one. Once he falls for someone, he falls hard.'

'He's a good man. A good friend.'

'He told me about the letter, you know,' Carla said suddenly. 'When Sam said about you and him.'

'I don't know what to say, Carla,' Sophie said. 'What you expect me to say.'

'I don't expect you to say anything. Especially to me. I just wanted you to know that me and Rob aren't involved because he's fallen for someone else. You know exactly who that is too. So we won't be playing happy families. We still love each other very much and I expect we always will. Like you will always love Sam. But anything resembling a romantic relationship is over and done with.' She smiled at Sophie. 'Right, I must go. I've stuck my nose in enough, and I'm leaving before I do any more damage.'

'It was good to see you,' Sophie said, smiling.

'I'm so sorry about Sam. It's no comfort whatsoever, but often men think they're cowards when they take this way out. For me? Knowing what Rob was like after he was captured, I think it was pretty damn heroic of Sam to choose to leave you guys. He did it so you both would have a different life without him. Maybe even a better, easier life. It would have been so incredibly hard for all of you if he had come home.'

Sophie's eyes filled with tears. Carla leant over and kissed her cheek.

'Thanks for the coffee, see you around. Grab that last croissant before Marcus smells it from his slumber and comes and inhales it!'

'See you, Carla... thanks,' said Sophie softly to her retreating back.

* * *

Doug stepped out of the shower, dried off and tucked a towel around his waist. He walked back into the bedroom and wondered for a fleeting moment why he could smell coffee.

'You take longer than a woman in the shower.' Jesse grinned from where she sat in the red rocking chair, sipping her coffee. 'But... in my view, it was worth the wait, although I think you can definitely lose the towel.'

Doug raised an eyebrow. 'Oh, so you think I'm that easy, do you? Turn up back home without warning and at the merest mention of whipping off my towel, you expect me to be putty in your hands?'

'Absolutely.'

'What if I want to play hard to get?'

Jesse tried not to smile. 'Oh well, I suppose I'd have to indulge you if you feel that way and let you play at being hard to get.'

She stood, stretched and unbuttoned her shirt, slipping it off. 'I'll go and have a shower and you can think about playing hard to get. Shame to not make the most of the kids being over the road with Claire.'

Doug grabbed her and pulled her close. 'Let's not be too hasty. I think there's things to be discussed first.'

Jesse looked at him innocently. 'Things to be discussed?'

'Important things. I mentioned some pressing matters that needed your attention,' he said.

'I think I might feel these pressing matters,' she said, wrapping her arms around his neck.

'You having too many clothes on is becoming an issue for me.'

'We ought to do something about that and this pressing matter.'

'I think it would be rude not to.' He kissed her deeply. 'Welcome home. God, I missed you.'

She unhooked his towel. 'Exactly how much did you miss me?'

Hair still wet from a slightly delayed shower, Jesse was sitting at the counter in the kitchen and Doug was scrambling eggs.

'How's Brother Joseph now?' she asked.

'He's OK. They're keeping him in for a bit though until another dialysis machine comes. Then they'll let him home.'

'The new harbour master sounds pretty handy. Is he a nice guy?'

Doug nodded. 'Very. It's Will Scully. You know, the Olympic sailor?'

'Vaguely, although I thought he died in a boat crash.'

'Nope. His mate did, Will broke his back. Trapped under the keel and mast for ages.'

Jesse made a face. 'Ouch. That takes some getting over.'

'Exactly. He used to be crew, and he said he'll happily help out, but he has to be pretty careful of his back.'

'He married or got a family?'

'Just him, although his sister is Suzy the dog rescuer and groomer. You know, the black "Shoosh the Floof" van.'

'I know the one. I always laugh when I see it. Perhaps I should give Brock to her for a wash and tidy up.'

Brock sat up from where he was lying on Jesse's feet and slunk off, throwing her a dirty look.

Doug dished up breakfast and Jesse got stuck in.

'Kids OK?'

'Yeah. Meant to tell you, Jude has the hots for a new girl in town.'

Jesse sniggered. 'Spill.'

Doug filled her in on the climbing competition, meeting Tabatha and where she lived. Jesse sat for a moment thinking.

'Did she have a new heart here then?'

Doug shrugged. 'Think so, it's where the accident happened.'

'I just wonder…'

'What?'

'Well, it was about the same time as Sophie switched Sam off. I know he was an organ donor… I wonder if Tabatha…' she trailed off.

Doug's eyes widened. 'You're wondering if Tabatha has Sam's heart?'

'That's what I'm thinking.'

Doug mused for a moment. 'Keep that to yourself. I'm not sure how either Marcus or Jude will feel about that. I'll put it on Claire and Felix's radar.'

'Difficult if it is. I wouldn't want it to drive a wedge between Marcus and Jude.'

'We'll have to play it by ear,' Doug said. 'See how it goes.'

* * *

Jenny was doing well with her wallpaper stripping efforts. So much so, she had given herself the morning off, with the promise of coffee and breakfast at Maggie's and a walk on the beach. She felt things were progressing. Teeney had helped with quotes, and they had decided to proceed, with him offering to help Jenny manage the builders so that she wouldn't get what he called 'shafted'. She had gratefully accepted his help but on the proviso that he charged her for his time and at an agreed rate. Jenny felt like a weight had been lifted off her shoulders.

She pondered as she walked. She was very happy here. She missed her brother terribly, but she knew that what she was doing was the right thing to do. She was so desperately lonely though.

She missed the company of people and knew that she needed to make sure that she got out more and include people in her circle. Teeney had mentioned taking her to Maggie's Christmas Eve party again and she realised she was quite looking forward to it.

She mentally reviewed things as she walked along the beach. She had a good pot of money to tide her over, plus her brother's windfall, which eased her money worries even more. She thought about the other day with the missing food and the loo seat, but still couldn't come to any conclusions. She had even poked her head into the loft space and seen nothing at all, so she figured she either had a friendly ghost or she was losing her mind. If the latter was the case, she hoped she'd get to a point when she didn't know anything about it.

As she walked along the beach she turned and looked up at her house, noting that in the raging storms a large log had fallen against the gate from her property that led down the carved rock steps onto the beach. One of her jobs that weekend was to cut the padlock off so she could use the gate as the key had long been lost. Now she realised that even if she had got the padlock off, she wouldn't have been able to use it because of the log.

She looked along the row of houses and saw the end house had Christmas lights in the window. She had seen a man and a girl go in and out and assumed they lived there permanently. She knew the other two properties were holiday lets. She looked up at the house next to hers and saw a face at a window on the top floor, looking straight at her. Jenny stared back, and the face disappeared, she assumed the cottages must be let for Christmas. She climbed the rocks up to her back gate and tried to shift the log.

'Need a hand?'

Jenny turned to see the man from the end house.

'Hello, neighbour,' she said.

He smiled. 'I've been meaning to move this for you, but now there's two if us it'll be easy.' He turned and called to a girl at the top of the steps to the beach. 'Meet you down there!'

Jenny looked over his shoulder and saw who she assumed was his daughter holding an adorable puppy at the top of the steps.

'Oh, how cute is that puppy!' Jenny said. 'Yours?'

'Present for my daughter. She's been ill, so I'm hoping this'll prompt her to take in the sea air a bit more and leave the phone at home.'

'Wise man,' she agreed. 'Is she OK?'

'She's getting there. I'm Sebastian.' He held out his hand.

She shook it. 'Jenny.'

'I love your place,' he said. 'It's double the width of ours, it must be gorgeous.'

'It is. I'm going to open a boutique hotel and bistro. You're welcome to come and have a nosey.'

'Wow. Love to.' Seb looked impressed. 'Just you? Opening the hotel and doing all the work?'

Jenny looked uncomfortable and swallowed a lump in her throat. 'It was me and my brother, but he passed away suddenly a few months back. So now it's just me.'

Seb looked at her strangely. 'I'm sorry,' he said. 'Must be tough.'

'How about you guys? You lived here long?'

It was Sebastian's turn to look uncomfortable. 'We've had the house a few years. But we're staying here indefinitely now.'

'Just you and your daughter?'

'Yes, my wife passed away recently,' he croaked and then looked away. 'Right let's get this moved.'

'I'm so sorry,' Jenny said. 'Life can be so cruel.'

'Amen to that,' he said and gestured to the log. 'I reckon if we can get it loose, then we can shove it that way and it'll fall down onto the beach by itself.'

Together they hefted the log and managed to drag it until it rolled down the rocks onto the beach.

'Job done,' Jenny said. 'Thanks.'

'Wanna meet the puppy? He's called Jack.'

'Love to!' She followed Seb down the rock steps onto the beach.

Suzy had turned up for a few hours training with Jack, so Jenny was introduced to everyone and ended up helping with the lesson, fielding Jack when he ran off excitedly forgetting what he was supposed to be doing.

Suzy, spotting a lover of dogs, sidled over to Jenny.

'Hey. You seem to love dogs; do you have one?'

Jenny shook her head. 'No, I'd love one though. I'm in that big house up there all alone and I'm beginning to think about it. I couldn't have a puppy though.'

Suzy raised an eyebrow. 'I might be able to help you out. I run a dog rescue and I have an adorable four-year-old terrier/corgi mix. His owner passed way. He loves company, he's quiet and chilled and happy just to be with you. He's called Archie.' Suzy produced her phone. 'Here he is. Cute, huh?'

Jenny looked at Archie. 'Oh, now that is cute. Look at those adorable ears! What happened to him?'

'His owner had a heart attack in her sleep. She lived on her own. She wasn't found for around three days until the milkman turned up and noticed the milk from the last delivery was still there. He rang the police and there she was. Poor Archie hadn't been fed for days and had run out of water. But he didn't want to leave her side.' She pulled a sad face. 'The police rang me and asked me to take him. He's such a lovely boy.'

Jenny looked horrified. 'That's so sad. And he's with you? Can I come and see him?'

'Of course. Tell you what, I've got another half an hour or so of training with these guys, then I've got to go home and pick up some stuff and come back to meet my brother. If you jump in with me you can come and spend some time with Archie, and I'll drop you back later.'

Jenny thought of all the excuses not to go, then remembered her brother's note.

'Love to,' she said.

Suzy's last half an hour of training was a series of games to test Jack's recall that involved everybody. By the end of it, Jenny felt she had made a bunch of new friends and felt better than she had for ages. She was exhausted from running and had a rosy glow that suited her.

Sebastian took one of Jack's toys from her. 'Thanks for sticking around. I've not had that much fun for ages.'

Suzy interjected. 'Seb, Jenny's gonna come and look at Archie. You've given her the dog bug.'

'Oh, Archie is cute,' Seb said. 'Far too calm for our household! Probably perfect for you, I doubt he'd be bothered by builders or any of that stuff. Hope you like him. Are you going to Maggie's party? You should do.'

'Yes, I am!' Jenny exclaimed. 'Looking forward to it.'

'Great. Look, don't be afraid to shout if you need any help with anything in that big old house,' Seb said. 'Right, I need to get Tabatha in for a rest, she looks like she's overdone it.'

'She looks good,' Suzy said. 'Jack's helping, I think! Jenny, you ready to go?'

'I am.'

Jenny had spent an hour with Archie and was smitten. He was quiet and trusting and looked at her with his huge eyes and her heart melted.

'Do you want to try him for a few weeks? See how he works out?' Suzy asked, coming back into the barn.

'Yes,' said Jenny softly. 'Very much so.'

'OK.' Suzy hefted a cardboard box onto the side and put in two bowls and a few trays of dog food and some biscuits. 'This should tide him over until tomorrow, but the pet shop stocks this, it's what he's used to.'

'OK.'

Archie leant against Jenny's leg and looked up at her adoringly.

'I think he's smitten,' Suzy said fondly, tickling his ears. 'I shall miss him.' She clipped his lead on and bent into his cage for a small white floppy rabbit. 'He likes this at night,' she said. 'It's a comfort thing, I think.' She placed it carefully in the box. 'OK. Good to go?'

'Let's go, Archie,' said Jenny. They climbed into Suzy's van and Archie settled himself into the footwell on Jenny's feet.

'That was a stroke of luck you bumping into Seb today,' Suzy said as they pulled away. 'They're a nice family. Tragic considering.'

'I knew his wife died but I didn't ask how,' Jenny said.

'His wife was Cassie Warner. The actress. She died on the outskirts of town in a car accident. Tabatha was in the car and needed a new heart.'

Jenny gasped. 'I thought he looked familiar. It was all over the press. So sad for him and Tabatha. Grief is awful.'

'Have you lost someone?' Suzy asked.

'My brother. Few months back.'

'That's tough. I almost lost my brother in a sailing accident. I watched the boat cartwheel, and he didn't come up again. Longest thirty minutes of my life.'

'He was OK though?'

'Well, he was trapped under the boat, broke his back. Lost his best friend and crew mate who drowned. Took him nearly a year to walk again. He's a different man now. Never sailed again professionally. But I love him something rotten. I just couldn't bear to lose him.'

'We were doing the hotel and bistro together. He was a great chef.'

'So you're doing it alone. Girl power. Well done you.'

'I'm a shit cook though.'

'Oh well, we can't be brilliant at everything.' Suzy laughed, pulling into Jenny's driveway.

Jenny asked, 'Do you need to check the house over to see if Archie will be OK?'

Suzy patted her hand. 'He's not a puppy. He's calm. I can see it's a big house and he'll be on the beach most days. It's all good. I trust you.' She got out of the van and hefted the box from the back and put it on the steps. 'See you around. I'll check in over the next few days, see how you guys are doing.'

'Thanks for everything.'

'See you soon. Bye, Archie!'

'There you are!'

Jenny turned to see an incredibly handsome man with bright green eyes and thick, layered collar-length golden-brown hair, stood outside the pub holding a pint. 'I'm drinking by myself here!'

'Better shut up and get the beers in then!' Suzy turned to Jenny. 'Jenny, this is my brother Will. Will, meet Jenny.'

'Hi,' he said warmly. 'You've taken Archie?'

'He's trying me on for size.' Jenny grinned.

'You'll love him. You coming for a drink?'

Jenny looked uncertain.

'Come on.' Suzy nudged her.

'Why not?' Jenny said, opening the door and pushing the box of Archie's stuff inside and closing it again. 'Come on, Archie. We're off for a drink.'

Dusk was falling and Jenny stood outside the pub, waving at Suzy as she drove off. Will stood next to her.

'Thanks for asking me to join you,' Jenny said. 'I had a great time.' In truth, Jenny had loved every second of her few hours in the pub with Will and Suzy. They had reminded her of her brother–sister relationship and the pair of them were great company.

'It was nice to meet you,' Will said. 'It's not every day that someone special is selected to take Archie.'

'Right, quick trot around the block for this one and then home.'

'I shall be gallant and walk with you, to make sure you're safe,' Will said.

Jenny raised an eyebrow. 'Don't you live around the corner anyway?'

Will pondered for a moment. 'Quite right. So, you can walk me home to check I don't get attacked.'

'That sounds more like it,' Jenny teased. 'Archie and I will protect you.'

Will stuck his arm out for Jenny to take it. 'Come on then. I'll need to get home before all the undesirables come out.'

Together they wandered around the corner with Archie trotting happily along next to Jenny, sniffing and piddling.

'He seems very happy,' Will observed as they strolled.

'How's your first week as harbour master working out?' Jenny asked.

Will thought for a second.

'It's had its moments,' he said, stopping. 'This is me. Thank God I made it home unscathed with you protecting me. You're welcome to come and have coffee if you want?'

'I'd love to, but I need to get home and get Archie settled, I think. Maybe another time? Particularly if you ever need protection again on the way home.'

Will laughed. 'Done. See you around, Jenny.'

'Bye, Will.'

Jenny walked back up the hill and along the terrace of houses. She raised an arm to Sebastian who was carrying something in the front door and noted that the house next to Seb's had lights on; someone had let it for Christmas. The house where she had seen the face in the window stood empty and silent. She wondered for a split second whether she had got confused about which window she had seen the face in.

She let herself into the house, got Archie settled, and didn't give it another thought.

CHAPTER 20

Steve was at the police station chatting to the PC on reception, when a woman he vaguely recognised rushed in.

'You!' she said, pointing at Steve behind the counter. 'I've seen him! I've seen the man who pushed me off the cliff!'

Steve tried to place the woman, and the PC on reception gently stepped sideways murmuring quietly.

'It's nutty hour, you can deal, Guv.'

'Michelle,' he said, suddenly remembering. 'OK. Calm down.'

She clutched the counter, eyes wide, her breathing heavy.

'The man who pushed me off the cliff! I've just seen him!' she said breathlessly. 'Come on.' She turned to leave.

'Where exactly?'

'In town. Outside the beach cafe.'

'Alone?'

She looked blank. 'I don't know.'

Steve put his head around the office door.

'Jonesey! Or Garland! Get your coat!'

'Guv,' a distant voice called and a few seconds later Jonesey appeared, with an iced finger stuck in his mouth as he struggled into his jacket.

Steve rolled his eyes. 'Is there a moment during the day when you're not eating?'

Jonesey grinned. 'Fast metabolism. Birthday buns so it's rude not to. Have to show willing.'

Steve motioned to Michelle. 'This is the lady who was pushed off the cliff; she's just seen the man who pushed her, so we're off for a looksie.'

'Where was he?'

'Outside the beach cafe.'

'Excellent. I haven't had lunch yet,' said Jonesey.

Steve opened the door between reception and the foyer. He and Jonesey stepped through, motioning for Michelle to lead the way.

'What was this man doing when you saw him?' Steve said, jotting down notes in his black notebook as they marched briskly down the road.

'Looked like he was waiting, outside the beach cafe,' she said.

'Maggie's?'

Michelle nodded with a worried expression.

'This way's quicker.' Steve directed her down a steep flight of steps that came out behind Maggie's, a narrow path led from the steps around to the front of the cafe.

As they reached the end of the path, Steve stepped quietly into the road and looked up and down. He couldn't see anyone. He motioned for Michelle to join him, and she looked around frowning.

'He was here,' she said.

'Inside?' He motioned towards the window.

Michelle peered through the glass, turned to Steve and shook her head. 'He must have gone.'

'Maybe on the beach?' Steve suggested and Michelle walked past Maggie's to look at the beach which was scattered with a few people and dogs. Jonesey accompanied her.

'Hello, Mr Steve,' came a nervous voice.

Steve turned to see Teddy holding a tray full of brightly coloured flowers.

'Hey, Teddy, how are you doing?' he said, thinking Teddy looked much better compared to the last time he had seen him.

'Good, thank you. Mrs Maggie is very nice to me. She feeds me a lot of food, there's so much sometimes, I have to take it with me.'

'You look good, Teddy. I'm pleased it's working out for you.'

'I think it was you who asked Mrs Maggie to be nice to me,' Teddy said. 'You were being kind to me. Not many people are nice to me.'

'It was all Maggie,' Steve said.

'I thought you'd be cross with me and tell Mrs Maggie not to help me anymore,' Teddy said, looking worried.

'Why's that, Teddy?'

'I thought you'd be cross about Rusty taking pictures.'

Steve wondered how the hell he was going to get information on this mysterious Rusty out of Teddy.

He took a leap of faith. 'And Rusty is your–'

'There he is!' Michelle cried as she walked back up from the beach, pointing at Teddy, who almost dropped his tray of plants in fright. 'It's him! He pushed me! Wait, he's changed his hair…He's made it darker, it was red.'

Teddy was white faced. 'What's the lady saying, Mr Steve?'

Steve turned to Jonesey. 'Take Michelle inside.'

As Jonesey ushered Michelle into Maggie's, Steve led a shaken Teddy over to one of the outside benches, sat him down and took a seat opposite. He surreptitiously pressed record on the phone in his hand and laid it face down on the bench. He needed an accurate record of Teddy's ramblings.

'Teddy, are you alright?'

'Who was that lady?' asked Teddy, almost in tears. 'What have I done?'

'She thinks someone who looks like you pushed her off a cliff.'

Teddy gasped and put a shaking hand over his mouth. His eyes filled with tears.

'I would never hurt a lady like that,' his voice a shaking whisper. 'I could *never* do that.'

Maggie walked over with a mug that read 'Teddy's Mug' and gave it to Teddy. She stroked his head gently and handed Steve a takeaway coffee.

'Everything OK here?' she asked.

'Thank you, Mrs Maggie,' mumbled Teddy. He held his mug up to Steve. 'Look what Mrs Maggie got for me. It means it's my mug and no one else can drink from it.'

'Very thoughtful,' said Steve. 'Look, Teddy, I think we need to have a proper talk.'

'It's about Rusty, isn't it?' Teddy said quietly.

'Yes, it is. Tell me about Rusty.'

Tears poured down Teddy's face and left two clear tracks in the grime.

'He would have pushed that lady, I bet you,' he said. 'He can be so mean.'

'Is he your twin brother, Teddy?'

Teddy nodded and wiped his nose on his sleeve. He picked up his tea and wrapped his hands around the mug, cradling it tightly as if he was absorbing the warmth.

'Where's Rusty now?' asked Steve.

Teddy shrugged. 'I don't know.'

'Tell me why you don't know, Teddy,' persisted Steve. 'Does he live at home with you and your father?'

Teddy shook his head. 'I don't know.'

'What do you mean, you don't know?' Steve frowned.

Teddy looked tearful again. 'I'm not allowed in the house with Dad. I'm in the room in the barn. He says I have to be there.'

'But it's winter,' Steve said. 'It's freezing. Why do you have to be in the barn?'

'Because I'm not good enough to be in the house,' whispered Teddy. 'I don't always sleep there, sometimes I stay in the council truck if Barry forgets to lock it.'

Steve considered himself pretty hardened to most things in the world but hearing the life that this poor lad endured was almost reducing him to tears. He channelled his anger towards the person responsible and vowed inwardly he would make Edwyn Lewis pay.

'Is Rusty allowed in the house?' he asked.

'Yes. Rusty needs looking after properly Dad says.'

'Why's that?'

Teddy looked up and then said quietly, 'Because Rusty is special, that's why Dad gives him my share of the food. He says he's special and I'm not.'

Steve took a moment.

'Why is Rusty special, Teddy?'

Teddy looked confused. 'I don't know. Dad has always said he was. He lets him in the house and the caravan.'

'Do you get on with Rusty?'

Teddy's eyes filled with tears again. 'No. He doesn't like me.'

'Why's that, Teddy?'

Teddy shrugged. 'I don't know. He hits and kicks me. He steals things of mine. He doesn't care about things.'

'Like what, Teddy? What does he steal?'

'My camera.'

215

'Where did you get your camera from, Teddy? Did you buy it?'

'I found it on the beach one day. It was in a bag that had been left. There was an orange towel and a sandwich. I waited for ages, until it got dark, but no one came back for it.'

'Right, do you remember when that was?'

Teddy shrugged. 'I remember that there were lots of planes in the sky on their way somewhere and I saw the Red Arrows,' he said wistfully. 'The sandwich was nice.'

'Teddy, if I went to your house, would Rusty be there?'

Teddy shook his head. 'He hasn't been home for weeks. Him and Dad had a fight a few weeks ago now.' He shuddered. 'I was in the barn and heard it. They were yelling at each other. The car was still on with the doors open and they were fighting in the yard. It was raining and windy. Dad took a stick to Rusty and beat him and then Rusty threatened Dad with a shotgun.'

'Scary for you.'

'The things they said to each other. Rusty blamed him for something. Dad called him horrible names. Like the ones he called me and used to call Danny.'

'Do you see Danny?'

Teddy looked around fearfully. 'Dad said to me that he would kill me if I saw Danny. But he's my brother. I do see him, but we meet in secret. Sometimes, if I have money, I take Danny a donut. He brings me cookies that Anna makes.' He sighed. 'Danny's very lucky. Gavin and Anna are very nice.' He looked awkward. 'Well, it's just Anna now. But she is lovely. Danny said she gives the best hugs. Nobody hugs me. I don't think I've ever had a proper hug.'

'If Maggie heard that she would give you a proper hug every time she saw you.'

Teddy's face brightened. 'Really? You think so?'

'Yup. So, no idea where Rusty could be?'

Teddy shook his head. 'No.'

'Teddy, it's very important that I talk to Rusty, if you see him can you get Barry to ring me or Maggie if you're here?'

'OK,' said Teddy. 'I'll remember that.'

Maggie bustled out the door.

'Teddy, your lunch is ready. Do you want to eat it out here? Another mug of tea?'

Teddy beamed. 'Yes please, Mrs Maggie.'

Maggie disappeared.

'Right, Teddy, so remember, if you see Rusty anywhere you call me?' Steve pushed.

'Yes. I remember.'

Maggie reappeared with a steaming plate of fish and chips and put it in front of Teddy, with another cup of tea.

'There you go poppet,' she said. 'You eat up.'

Steve stood. 'Take care now, Teddy.'

'Thank you, Mr Steve.'

Steve walked into the cafe where Jonesey was taking note of Michelle's ramblings. He sat down next to her.

'Michelle, I think the man who pushed you off the cliff wasn't Teddy out there, it was his twin brother, who has red hair. I don't think Teddy could do something like that, but I suspect from what I hear, his brother could.'

'The man had red hair and I think he was taller too. He had a red mark on his forehead now I remember. Here.' She pointed to her temple. 'It was quite long now probably about two inches. Very red. I don't know why I didn't remember it before.'

'I'm looking for Rusty as a matter of urgency, but he hasn't been seen for weeks. If you should see him, call me. Doesn't matter day or night.'

'Thanks. Sorry to drag you out of the station.'

'No bother.'

'See you then.'

'Maybe give Teddy a wide berth, eh?'

She pulled an apologetic face. 'Will do.'

They watched her leave and hurry away from Teddy up the road.

A loud frightened cry and smashing crockery sounded outside, and Steve and Jonesey ran out of the cafe at the same time Foxy walked out of the climbing centre door.

Edwyn Lewis had Teddy by the throat bent backwards on one of the outside tables. Teddy's lunch plate was smashed all over the floor.

'What's this, eh? Where do you get the money for this? You're not worthy of a meal like this. You haven't earned it. You fucking waste of space,' he sneered, then spotted Teddy's special tea mug. 'What the hell is this?' He picked it up and threw it down on the floor where it smashed into pieces. 'You don't deserve things like this. Who have you fooled into getting you things and buying you food? You're a useless piece of shit. If I catch you here again, I'll fucking kill you. Now get home.'

Foxy appeared and strode over dragging the man off Teddy. He pushed him up against the wall with his face pressed into the rough stonework.

'How about you go ten rounds with someone nearer your own size?' Foxy said through gritted teeth into his ear. 'Fuckers like you need a good taste of their own medicine and I'm happy to be the one dishing that out today, you miserable shit.'

Teddy was crying, scrabbling about trying to pick up the smashed bits of his mug and plate. Maggie had walked out, nodding approvingly at Foxy's treatment of Teddy's father. She crouched down next to Teddy.

'It's OK, sweetie. I can get you another one.'

'But the plate is broken too, and all the food is ruined,' Teddy wailed. 'I'm so sorry, Mrs Maggie. I'll work extra hard to pay for the broken things and the waste.'

'Now don't you worry about any of that. You come inside and we'll fix you up again quick smart. You leave that nice Foxy to have a chat with your father.' Maggie gently led Teddy inside and sat him in a corner away from the windows.

Steve laid a hand on Foxy's arm. 'Let him go.'

Foxy released him and Edwyn turned, sneering at Foxy.

'You can't touch me.' He looked at Steve. 'You can't either. That fuckwit in there is hardly going to press charges, is he? Doesn't even know what fucking day it is most days. I can do what the fuck I like to him, and you lot can't do a fucking thing.'

Foxy stepped towards Edwyn. 'Time for you to turn your back, Steve,' he said menacingly.

Steve stepped forwards. 'I can touch you, Mr Lewis,' he said quietly. 'I hear the RSPCA paid you a couple of visits, taken your animals and will be prosecuting. We've taken all your guns too. I will keep digging. I hear that you take all Teddy's money, don't feed him or house him properly. There are a raft of charges I'll be bringing against you regarding the treatment of your son, who's a vulnerable adult. So, Mr Lewis, if I hear that you have beaten Teddy again, I will take you into custody.' He jabbed Edwyn in the chest. 'I will be checking in with Teddy every day and if there is so much as a scratch on him, I will come for you. Are we clear?'

Edwyn pushed away from Foxy and Steve angrily. He looked them up and down and then spat at them in disgust and walked off up the hill without a backward glance.

'Nice chap,' said Foxy dryly.

* * *

Jimmy the fisherman was crapping himself. He was steering his boat towards the quayside, and he could see three people, who looked suspiciously like Alexy, Pearl, and Stanley.

219

'Oh fuck, oh fuck, oh fuck,' he chanted to himself as he negotiated various boats and then moored next to the wall. He decided that Pearl would not take kindly to him hefting his catch up onto the quayside, so he reluctantly climbed the metal ladder and went over to them.

'Hello, Pearl, Alexy,' he said, nodding, feeling scruffy in his oilskins. 'Stanley.'

'Jimmy darling,' Pearl said warmly. 'We wondered if we could have a little chat with you. We need your help on a small matter.'

Jimmy swallowed heavily and closed his eyes. He so wanted to be free of this lot, he knew his luck was going to run out sooner or later. He was still on a suspended sentence and lucky to be alive. He croaked out a response.

'Of course.'

Pearl sat delicately on a nearby bench and beckoned Jimmy over.

'Jimmy,' she said, pulling her large coat around her. 'We need you to take a couple of large packages up to Liverpool in the boat for us and leave them in a certain place. Alexy will go with you. All you need to do is drive the boat and we'll make it worth your while.'

'What are the packages, Pearl?' Jimmy asked quietly.

'Couple of people, darling,' she said, lighting a cigarette. 'Don't worry. They'll be alive.' She smiled brightly at him. 'Is that OK with you? We might need you to do the same run twice. So I'm thinking ten thousand will cover your expenses.'

Jimmy almost swallowed his tongue. 'Sounds fine,' he croaked out, mentally spending the cash. 'It'll take a long time by my boat, unless you want to find me a faster one, which I'll happily drive.'

'How long in your boat?' Pearl asked, frowning.

'She's not fast, it'll take hours and hours, but if you have access to a speedboat, it'll be much quicker if we push it. But why not take the packages by road?'

'They'll be expecting that,' she said. 'But they won't be expecting us to arrive at their back door on the water. Plus, I don't want a record of us going by road.'

She thought for a moment. 'Alexy, get a friend to hire whatever you need to get yourselves there and back in the quickest time. I can't afford for you to be away long. Be careful, I don't want any sort of trail to link us being there.'

'OK.'

Pearl beamed at Jimmy and Alexy. 'Excellent,' she said. 'I knew I could rely on you Jimmy.'

Jimmy shuffled from foot to foot. 'When will it happen?'

'Tomorrow. Alexy will let you know, won't you, darling?' Pearl stood and crushed out her cigarette with a stylish Louboutin boot. 'I must get on. Thank you, Jimmy. I'll be seeing you.'

Alexy gestured to Jimmy that he would call him.

Jimmy watched with relief as they climbed into a car and left. He instantly wondered how he would explain the ten grand to Marie, his partner, who was convinced he was keeping his nose clean. She took a dim view of shady dealings, but as this was essentially providing a taxi service for Pearl, in Jimmy's view, there wasn't anything for Marie to have the hump about.

* * *

Steve was having a rare night off and was dozing on the sofa, cuddled up to his girlfriend when his mobile rang.

'Yours, not mine,' murmured Kate as she snuggled into Steve. They were used to her phone often ringing in the middle of something.

Steve picked it up.

'Miller,' he said, stifling a yawn.

'It's Toby. You'd better not have been dozing while I'm out being your bitch.' Toby's voice was amused.

'You alright?' Steve asked, instantly focused and scrabbling to find his notebook in his jacket which had been flung over a chair.

'So, I have your man Levinson Lucas here at the station. Jesus, the guy is a fucking dick. I'd quite like to punch him. Thinks he's God's gift. Anyway, got your samples. He said he saw Cassie Warner the day she died at a wardrobe fitting. He said everything was fine. They discussed different ways of treating a few scenes and she left.'

'How did he explain the pictures? They looked like she was angry with him.'

'He says she was joking. It was a lucky shot that looked like they were arguing but they weren't.'

'Hmm. Where was he that night?'

'Home alone. No alibi, but you've pulled his phone records, right?'

'Waiting on them. Were they having an affair?'

'He says not.'

'What do you think?'

'I think he's full of shit. Something interesting though. Kept moaning about the husband, Sebastian, and how Cassie wasn't going to get a proper funeral.'

'What's his definition of that then?'

'I got the sense of a big turnout, all the celebs... you know. Typical show funeral. Where he would no doubt be the weeping co-star who adored her.'

'So he's missed out on a PR opportunity?'

'That's the vibe I got. But call me an old cynic.'

'How was he about the DNA sample?'

'Really fucking odd. Wanted to call his lawyer. Wanted to know exactly what it was for. Tried to cover it up by suggesting we would lose it or sell it to the highest bidder.'

'How did you get around it?'

'I told him we needed to eliminate him and that perhaps he should focus on the fact that someone had died, and this was helping try to solve that rather than suggesting we were all bent enough to sell his DNA.'

'What a dick.'

'Couldn't have put it better myself. By the way, I asked him if he had a car, and he was odd about it.'

'How?'

'Evasive. I'd look into that more. Twats like him either have a flash motor or tend to use friends' ones that the fans don't know about. Remember that singer we nicked who used to use his gran's old banger?'

'I'd forgotten about that.'

'I thought of that when we were talking, so check that out.'

'OK. Overall sense?'

'Didn't believe a word he said.'

'OK. You've sent me the recording.'

'Yup. Enjoy your viewing.'

'Thanks, Toby. I'll watch it and give you a bell, yes?'

'No probs. I'll let him go.'

'Tell him not to leave the country.'

'He'll ask me if he's a suspect.'

'Tell him yes. That'll frighten the shit out of him.'

'Excellent, made my day. Talk soon.'

'Bye, Toby, and thanks again.'

Steve ended the call and looked at Kate. She raised an eyebrow.

'Let me guess, you're going to the station?'

He pulled a face. 'I am.'

'Can I get one last cuddle at least before you go?' she asked.

'I think we can do better than that,' Steve said, pulling off Kate's jumper. 'I can wait ten minutes before I have to go.'

223

Kate laughed. 'Oh, we'll be doing it twice then?'

'Shut up and get your pants off.'

'Oh, the romance of it all,' Kate said sarcastically and giggled as Steve nuzzled her neck.

CHAPTER 21

Trauma and orthopaedic surgeon Dr Jamie Hunter drove along the coast road admiring the view. The brand-new powerful Range Rover Evoke effortlessly ate up the miles and Jamie let his mind wander. He had returned from the Sudan a few days earlier where he had been training army surgeons on new and emerging trauma surgery techniques. He had then gone to see his mother briefly in Liverpool, citing work as the reason he couldn't stay for Christmas.

If the truth be known, he would like to pretend he had no family whatsoever, rather than the scrag-end chav his mother actually was. In his mind, the scummy council house she insisted on living in, surrounded by hideous time-wasting fat gobby chavs, was an environment he didn't want to be associated with in any way whatsoever.

He had worked hard to lose the Liverpool accent; worked hard to rise above a childhood of penny pinching, shit food, second-hand clothes, no father, and a pissed mother who lived on cheap cider, processed food and cigarettes. He had never brought anyone home to visit, and had only been home four times in the last six years.

He'd worked hard to get a scholarship in order to attend university, leaving home and never looking back. He was committed to his work, and it was the only thing he was truly passionate about. He lived in constant hope that his mother would die and then he would never have to return to that area again. He dreamt of a time when she died, and he would rock up, toss a petrol bomb in her house, and walk away. It would be a fitting Tarantino-style ending to his shit childhood.

His mind wandered to where he was going. He was on his way to see Carla Fox. He liked Carla, he found her bright, attractive and excellent company. They had gone out a couple of times, but Carla had resisted his advances since she was still involved with someone else. He remembered the last time he had seen her. No more had she resisted his advances. He was pleased that she clearly had no recollection of what he'd done. It was like looking at someone and knowing a deliciously wicked secret.

He had carefully inspected every inch of her body when she lay unconscious and yielding. He had taken her more than once and enjoyed the feeling that he had the power and she could do nothing about it. He felt he knew her. Every inch of her. Despite this, he was drawn to her. He liked her and felt she would be fun to have while she was awake, hence his efforts in coming to see her.

While she had been unconscious, Jamie had activated her phone and installed the find my device software; which is how he knew she had been in Castleby for the past few days. He suspected it was a small town and he would find her fairly easily. He'd searched for somewhere to stay and found an exclusive hotel on the cliffs overlooking the town and booked himself in for a few nights.

As he approached Castleby, he thought he might check into the hotel and freshen up before heading out to see if he could find Carla.

The satnav guided him up a narrow road, lined with trees, and he pulled into the grounds of the hotel. He nodded approvingly. Very classy. Exactly what was needed after his mother's house.

He parked, headed for reception, and admired the house he could see a few thousand yards away, it was clearly architect designed. It was a wonder of wood, glass, and the design had it fitting snugly into the hillside with a perfectly manicured garden and a beautiful infinity pool. Jamie approached the reception desk where a pretty young lady sat and activated his most winning smile.

* * *

Mickey was stood in the cavernous farm building he favoured when he needed to inflict serious pain on people. He liked it because it was in the middle of nowhere and had surprisingly thick walls, which meant sound didn't carry. In front of him, sat in chairs with their hands nailed to the table, were Ringo and Paul. Both were bloody, sweaty, and clearly terrified. Mickey regarded them coldly through narrowed eyes as he stood in front of them.

'Word is, you're looking to off some of my dealers,' he said.

Ringo opened his mouth to speak, and Mickey roared, 'I haven't finished talking, interrupt me once more and I will nail your fucking tongue to the table! Are we clear?'

Ringo swallowed heavily. Mickey continued.

'I was going to go on about the perils of coming into my community and throwing your weight about, telling my people that things are changing etc., but I don't see the value in that because I'm quite a busy person, plus I have dinner plans. So this is what's going to happen.' He pointed to three men stood in the shadows. 'Maxim, Gorka and Stanley are going to have a little chat with you. They're

227

going to break some bits and pieces of yours and then we'll take you on a trip. You see, boys, you are a message.' He gave a cruel smile.

'Now, I consider myself to be a reasonable man, and as a result I'm sending what I consider to be a reasonable message.' He laughed. 'I mean, I could send you back "return to sender" without your arms and legs, or maybe even put your legs where your arms should be and vice versa. But as I said, I'm reasonable. I could send you back dead, but then what's the point of that because I'd have to send another message to make it clear what I wanted, and that would be a waste of my very precious time. This way, you're the message.'

He beckoned Maxim and Gorka over.

'Boys, you choose what you do, I don't mind how much it hurts or creative you are, but that's all. OK?' He eyed Maxim. 'Maxim, none of the funny stuff, OK?'

Maxim looked disappointed.

'Maybe next time?' Mickey said and Maxim happily nodded. Mickey folded his large arms and stood in front of the two men. 'Pay attention, because this is my message for you to take back. You listening?'

He waited for them both to acknowledge.

'I will not have a bloodbath on my patch. If your boss wants my business, then your boss will show me the respect I deserve and will come and talk to me properly, because my business might be for sale at the right price. I suggest he comes and has dinner with us in a civilised way, and we will discuss business and terms of sale. That way, all the infrastructure remains and it's what they call a seamless transition.' He leant forward to look at them. 'We clear, boys? Did you get all that? No long words that need explaining?'

Ringo and Paul nodded.

'Good. It's not difficult.' He pointed to Ringo. 'You will call Stanley here and tell him when your boss will be arriving. I suggest it's soon. Outside of Christmas, of course, I suggest we put business on hold until at least Friday.' He turned. 'Right, I'm off. See you, lads.' Mickey picked up his coat and left the building.

* * *

Will's feet hadn't touched the ground that day, his back was killing him, and he was shattered. It seemed everyone in the town wanted to know when the next Kirby ferry would leave, and Will couldn't give them an answer. He needed to talk to Miles, but that didn't stop a raft of people bringing down boxes for the next ferry and leaving them stacked high in Will's office.

As well as fielding box arrivals, he had been flat out busy issuing various notices and getting to grips with the huge volume of paperwork that had been left unattended for so long.

He'd also had to control a bunch of kids in wetsuits who were busy tombstoning off the harbour wall because of the high tide. The fishing boats were returning, and this was a recipe for disaster.

Once he had got the boys out of the water, he'd walked back to the office and realised he was completely shattered.

He chuckled to himself remembering the day he was interviewed, when the panel told him they weren't convinced Castleby had enough excitement for him. What with everything going on and the ferry disaster, he'd had more than enough excitement.

Glancing at his watch he realised it was early evening. He was starving hungry and wanted a hot shower on his aching back. Grabbing the laptop, he pulled his office door shut and tiredly walked around the harbour towards his loft. After a few minutes, he noticed a small car was slowly following him, but it was too dark to see inside. He assumed it was just someone driving slowly and carefully around the narrow streets.

Arriving home, he stripped off and went and stood under a hot shower for ten minutes. Feeling his back ease a little, he chucked on

229

jeans and a jumper and wandered into the kitchen, smiling when he saw Suzy had been and had put a few things in his fridge. She had left a note in the fridge on three tupperware containers saying, *Beef Stew, Chicken Curry and Lasagna. Fill your boots, bruv. Love ya.*

He dragged out the beef stew, put it in the microwave and texted her.

I knew my cunning plan of giving you a key would work. Thanks for my dinner. You are the best sis ever. Love you.

She replied instantly.

You're welcome. Love you too. Enjoy.

Will eyed up the bottle of red wine that Anna had left on the counter the other day and decided that he would open it. The microwave dinged and Will ate the stew straight from the Tupperware standing at the kitchen counter, with a large glass of red next to him. His doorbell rang and he went down the stairs to answer it.

'Hello, Will.'

Will wasn't expecting to see the widow of his best friend and crewmate who had drowned, standing on his doorstep at eight o'clock on a Monday night.

'Gina. What the hell are you doing here?' he exclaimed, opening the door wider and gesturing for her to come in.

She followed him up the stairs and in the light he saw she had been crying.

'Gina… Give me your coat. Do you want a drink?'

She held up a shaking hand to Will and backed away from him.

'No,' she said loudly. 'I came here… because…' Tears ran down her face and she took a deep breath. 'Because I couldn't believe what I read in the paper.'

'What are you talking about?' Will was genuinely confused on a few levels. Firstly, what Gina was doing at his flat, and secondly, what she was on about. He hadn't seen her since the funeral which he'd attended in a wheelchair, and they had rowed bitterly when she had

230

blamed him for Ian's death. Will had tried to explain but had eventually left to try and keep the peace.

'The paper. The report about the ferry accident. The piece about you being a fucking hero and saving those people and a *monk* of all people.'

'What? Gina, I didn't know it was in the paper. It was nothing. Why are you so angry?' he said, trying to placate her. 'Come on, have a drink.'

'I don't want anything,' she shouted. 'I want to know how it is that you can save four people from a ferry accident, but you let my husband die in your race. You were the one pushing the boat. You were the skipper. It was *your* decisions and *your* choices that day.'

'It was an accident!' Will said desperately, trying to remain calm at the barrage of blame. 'Do you think I don't blame myself? Every day? I've watched the footage over and over. We hit a freak wave. The hull cracked and the force of it sent us upwards. There isn't a day I don't wish it was me and not Ian who died.'

She pointed a shaking finger at him. 'Your fault. Entirely. You killed my husband.'

Will sighed deeply. 'We've been through this. It was an accident. Ian knew what he was doing, Gina. He loved the risk. He loved the danger. He told me you wanted him to give it all up, but he couldn't do it. He said he'd feel like half a man. He knew he would die inside.'

'Rubbish. You ended his life. It was your fault. You were careless.'

Will had had enough. He had been fighting with Gina about this for too long. He rounded on her.

'FINE! If it makes you feel better. Blame me. How long are you going to carry this around for, Gina? Forever? Well, I don't need you blaming me for Ian's death because I blame myself for it. For the record though, I was never, *ever* careless when I sailed. Do you think I wish that he'd found a pocket of air instead of me? I do. Every fucking day. When I hear rain I'm back there. Trapped under that keel and mast, in that tiny air pocket, the rain hammering down on the keel. Thinking I'm going to die in there and I don't know if anyone else has made it out. But I know I can't move my arms and legs. I would have happily died in there if it meant that Ian could have lived. He was my best friend and I loved him.'

'You were careless with his life!' she shouted, breathing heavily.

Will approached her. 'No,' he said firmly. He was close to her face and spoke quietly but firmly. 'I was never careless about sailing or careless with anyone's life.' He raked his hands through his hair. '*He* was careless that day. He wasn't where he was supposed to be because he was arsing about! Four times I told him to stop and to get back to where he was supposed to be, but he wouldn't listen. He died, Gina, because he was being a fucking dick and he was arsing about.'

Will stopped suddenly. He knew he had said too much. Gina looked like he had slapped her.

'Is that how it was?' she demanded. 'Really?'

Will was breathing heavily and wishing that he hadn't said anything.

'Will, I said, is that how it really was?'

Will looked at the floor and nodded. He didn't trust himself to speak. He felt his eyes filling as he remembered yelling at Ian to stop dicking around and focus. He remembered Ian ignoring him and trying to impress the pretty crew member he had been sleeping with.

'Will,' she said sharply. 'Answer me.'

'Yes, it's how it was,' he said quietly.

'I see,' Gina said. She slipped off her coat, dumped it on a chair and picked up Will's wineglass. She drank deeply. 'He was trying to impress that girl on the crew, wasn't he?'

Will didn't meet her gaze.

'Wasn't he?' she persisted.

Will remained silent.

'Will Scully,' she warned in a dangerous tone.

'Yes, he was.'

'He was sleeping with her, wasn't he?'

Will didn't say anything.

'Wasn't he?'

Will nodded.

'Was he trying to impress her? Showing off?'

Will exhaled deeply.

'That tells me what I need to know.'

Gina filled the glass again and drank deeply. She put the glass down and walked towards him.

'I've not been fair to you. I'm sorry,' she said, putting her hands on his chest and kissing him gently on the cheek. She lingered as they were cheek to cheek. 'I should never have said those things. I'm sorry.'

Moonlight streamed through the window and Will looked over at Gina who was sprawled face down, her blonde hair cascading around her shoulders, the duvet around her hips showing off her smooth back. He felt another twinge of desire and then shook his head. God he was weak. She had looked at him, all big eyes, stood close to him and said sorry. Her hands were on him and all he had to do was turn his head to kiss her. He hadn't been able to help himself. She shifted in her sleep and threw a careless arm across his chest and then woke sleepily.

'Why are you awake?' she asked.

'Thinking,' he replied.

'There's better things to do than think,' she said, trailing her hand down his chest. 'Isn't there?'

When Will awoke the next morning, she had gone. There was no note. Will wondered what to do about that and then concluded it was probably safer all around to do nothing. He showered, dressed, and headed into work.

CHAPTER 22

Tabatha had risen before Seb and was on the beach with Jack. His training was improving, but he tended to run off if there was another dog about that took his interest, or if he was frightened. Tabatha had been working on his recall, rewarding him with the odd treat, when suddenly a man appeared with a huge dog that snarled at Jack for no reason.

Terrified, Jack ran off. Tabatha started to chase, but then felt a sharp pain in her heart that made her gasp and drop to her knees.

'Jack,' she cried weakly. 'Jack!' Desperately, she watched him running flat out across the sand.

Tabatha knelt in the sand and tried to breathe slowly as they taught her in hospital. She felt sick and dizzy, so she dropped her head down and focused on her breathing. She saw black spots before her eyes and tried to calm herself down. She jumped as she felt a hand on her shoulder.

'Hey,' Jude knelt down next to her, his face full of concern. 'You OK?'

Tabatha said between breaths, 'Jack was attacked. He's run off.'

'We saw him go, Marcus is after him. Look, you're going to freeze here,' he said, helping her stand. She swayed so he lifted her effortlessly and walked across the sand with her.

Since the accident where Jude had helped Marcus climb out of the sink hole he had fallen into, Jude had been working hard to build up his strength in his arms, shoulders and hands so he could climb again. Lifting Tabatha, who was pretty light, was easy for him.

He looked up to see Seb at the top of the rocky steps to the house.

'Did that dog attack Jack? Tabs, are you OK?'

'You can put me down,' Tabatha mumbled, embarrassed.

'You don't weigh much,' he said, striding up the rocky steps and accidentally banging her head on the gate as he walked past.

'Ow,' she grumbled. 'Save me from catching a cold on the beach but give me a concussion.'

Seb was touching her face looking worried.

'I'll call Felix,' he said.

'I'm OK, Dad. I just need to lie down for a bit, maybe take a tablet.'

Jude had placed her carefully on the sofa. Seb hovered about.

'Thank you so much. Jude, isn't it?' Seb asked.

'Yeah.' He looked out of the window. 'I need to tell Marcus to come here when he gets Jack,' he said, turning to Seb. 'Is it OK to come back and check on her?'

'Fine,' Seb said, fussing over Tabatha.

Jude smiled at Tabatha. 'Don't worry, we'll be back with Jack.'

Jude disappeared. 'That boy is hot to trot,' Bree said, looking at Tabatha approvingly as she walked into the kitchen. 'He likes you.'

'Aunty Bree,' Tabatha scolded. 'You're *so* inappropriate.'

235

'Rubbish.' She watched Jude run across the sand effortlessly. 'Goodness, that boy is cute,' she murmured wistfully.

'Stop it. You're old enough to be his mother,' Seb called and received a cushion to the face from across the room.

Tabatha was feeling better, but Seb had insisted on calling Felix, who instructed him to take her blood pressure and heart rate. Seb relayed the readings.

Jude and Marcus returned with a wriggling Jack, both boys were rosy faced and breathless from chasing him.

'Oh, thank you so much!' whispered Tabatha while Seb was on the phone. She held her hands out for Jack who nuzzled her and then scampered off to his water bowl.

'Alright?' Jude asked in a low voice.

'I'm fine. Dad's just calling Felix. He's the surgeon looking after me. He said to call if I get any significant pain.'

Jude looked surprised. 'Felix Carucci?'

'You know him?'

Jude pulled a face. 'He's kind of my stepdad.'

Tabatha looked serious. 'No way! He saved my life. He's wonderful.'

Seb ended the call and looked at Jude. 'Did I hear that Felix is your stepdad?'

'Yeah. He lives with my mum, she's a surgeon at the hospital too. Claire Brodie. They're getting married soon.'

'Wow. We know Claire too, don't we? Small world,' Seb said. 'Do they live in town?'

'Across the road. It works out really well, we see a lot of them.'

Marcus was sitting next to Tabatha on the edge of the sofa, listening.

'When did you have your accident?' he asked her suddenly.

'Can't remember exactly. November,' Tabatha said.

'Sixteenth of November,' Seb said quietly.

'And you say you had a new heart? From a donor?'

Tabatha nodded. 'Uh huh. They tried to fix my heart, but it was too damaged, thank God for a donor heart. I was so lucky.'

'Why d'you ask?' Seb said, frowning.

Marcus had gone white as sheet. He was sat staring at the floor like he couldn't process what he was thinking.

'Marcus,' Jude said. 'What's up?'

Marcus stood suddenly and walked towards the back door. Jude followed him.

'Hey,' he said. 'What's up?'

Marcus looked back towards Tabatha on the sofa. 'I'm OK,' he said quietly. 'I just need to get my head around something.'

'What?' Jude looked really concerned.

'I think she might have Dad's heart,' Marcus said softly.

'Oh man.' Jude pulled a face.

'I need to go. To think about this.'

'OK. See you later?' Jude asked.

Marcus said goodbye and left through the back gate down onto the beach.

Tabatha glanced at Jude, worried.

'Is Marcus OK?' she asked, frowning.

'Something we did or said?' Seb said.

Jude walked over and sat next to Tabatha on the sofa, scratching Jack behind the ears.

'Marcus lost his dad about a month ago now. He was a soldier; he'd been missing for years, but he came back. He was messed up. He'd been really badly tortured and stuff for years. He ended up losing his legs and he couldn't deal with it. Any of it. He tried to end it, but in the end Marcus and his mum had to switch him off.' Jude looked at Seb. 'He was an organ donor, and he was at the big hospital where you were. Marcus thinks you might have his dad's heart.'

'The rule is that we're not allowed to know who the donor was,' Seb said. 'So we'll never know for sure.'

'Maybe so, but he was switched off around the same time as your accident. He's putting two and two together.' Jude looked towards the door where Marcus had left. 'Hope he's OK.'

Tabatha hugged Jack to her. 'I don't know how to feel about this apart from grateful,' she said. 'Do you think I should talk to him?' she asked Jude.

'Give him some time first. He has to sort out his head and then after that he'll be alright. He thought it was good that his dad was a donor and that he could help out loads of people when he died.' He squeezed Tabatha's hand. 'He'll come around.'

Foxy was in the climbing centre. There was a lull between bookings, and he was winding ropes absently and looking out to sea, enjoying the quiet. The door opened and Marcus walked in.

'Hey, buddy. You climbing?' Foxy asked then looked at Marcus with concern. 'What's up?'

Marcus looked confused. 'I don't know,' he said in a small voice.

Ten minutes later, Foxy had a rough idea what was bothering Marcus. He found him a cereal bar and quietly watched him as he munched through it.

'What's really the issue here?' Foxy pushed.

'Dunno. I just feel weird about it.'

'Do you think your dad would be cool knowing that it was someone you knew and that she's a nice girl?'

'S'pose.'

'Do you fancy her? Is that the issue?'

'Dunno.'

'Either you do, or you don't.'

'She likes Jude, I think,' Marcus said gloomily. 'Besides it would be too weird.'

'But you're OK if Jude gets to know her?'

Marcus shrugged.

Amused, Foxy said, 'He's probably just getting to know her. Christ, Marcus, chill out, it's not like they're shacking up and having kids.'

Marcus rolled his eyes. 'Suppose so. I don't know why it's weird. I wonder if there's part of Dad's soul in Tabatha?'

'Come with me.'

Foxy walked out to the Land Rover and popped the bonnet. He gestured for Marcus to look under the bonnet with him.

'See that?' Foxy pointed.

'Yes,' Marcus frowned at Foxy.

'That's the fuel pump. Takes the fuel and pumps it around the engine.'

'Why are you telling me this?'

'That's what a heart is. Just a pump to get the blood around the body. It doesn't have a soul or feelings. It's the brain that does that. So, in answer to your question, I don't think there's part of your dad's soul in Tabatha, she's just using his pump. Just like if I took this pump out and put it in another car.'

'Right. I see. So do you think I'm being stupid about this?'

Foxy thought for a moment. 'Not stupid. I think you're overthinking it slightly.'

'Maybe I am.'

'Marcus, you don't know for sure. It might be a coincidence.'

'Hmm.'

They walked back into the centre.

'Tell you what, stay, have a climb, clear your head.'

'Sure?'

'Go for it,' Foxy said, chuckling as Marcus had already toed off his boots.

Carla came out from behind the counter. 'You're good with him.'

'He's a good lad. Everything OK?'

'Yes. Penny, Steve's contact, just rang. I told her that I'd heard from him, and she agreed it was right to block his number. She says she's still digging.'

'But he's not called you again though?'

'Don't know. I blocked him.'

'So ideally I need to put off killing him until I can track him down then?'

'Exactly.'

* * *

For the first time in his life, Jimmy was having a dither about what to wear. What did the pilot of an ultra-fast speedboat wear who was up to no good? He was going out with Alexy, who always looked like the rich gangster. Jimmy surveyed his wardrobe of warm shirts, faded jeans and surf T-shirts. In the end, he settled for jeans, a black T-shirt and his black leather jacket. He thought he looked quite cool. He sauntered down the stairs to the kitchen where Marie, his partner, looked at him and guffawed loudly.

'What have you come as?' she said, trying to keep a straight face. 'Trying to look cool for the lobsters?'

'I think I look cool,' Jimmy said defensively.

'Jimmy Ryan, the days of you being cool are long behind you. So it's a good thing I love you anyway,' she added, seeing his crestfallen face.

'Well, I'm wearing this today. I'll be back late, so don't stay up.'

Marie eyed him suspiciously. 'And what are you doing today, Jimmy? You know it's Christmas Eve tomorrow?'

'I've been asked to deliver a package to Liverpool in a speedboat. My boat is too slow.'

Marie held up her hand. 'I don't even want to know. But if it's shady… you know the consequences and I won't sit by your hospital bed for a second time.'

'It's just a delivery,' Jimmy said, rolling his eyes. 'I'm being paid really well for it.'

'You aren't Deliveroo, Jimmy.'

'I'm not discussing it,' Jimmy said.

'Well, if you're all day on a speedboat you'll need a warm jumper and a coat. It's freezing outside.'

Jimmy stomped back up the stairs to source a thick jumper. He returned with a big warm roll neck jumper on and sullenly grabbed his all-weather coat. Marie handed him a bag.

'Lunch,' she said. 'Have a good day playing *Miami Vice*.'

Jimmy left and headed, grumpily, down towards the harbour. He heard a van toot and looked around to see Alexy behind the wheel of a large black van. Jimmy climbed into the front, and they headed off to the docks.

Jimmy looked at the speedboat in amazement. Now *this* was a fast boat.

'This is ours, right?' he asked Alexy.

'Yes. Problem?' Alexy asked.

'You know this is a Superhawk Predator, right?'

'It is fast boat.' Alexy pulled a face. 'I think.'

Jimmy looked at the sleek lines and the closed cockpit and regretted leaving his leather jacket behind.

Alexy snapped his fingers and one of his men jumped into the van and reversed it back towards the dockside. Alexy opened the door and dragged out two men, beaten and bloody, and threw them unceremoniously down on the floor.

'Jimmy, we go now.'

Jimmy started the boat. He closed his eyes and enjoyed the sound of the throaty powerful engine.

'Hold on to something. I'm not hanging about.'

* * *

Will was on the phone trying to organise repairs to the harbour wall where a boat had crashed into it. He knew he had to cordon the quayside area off to make sure it was safe, but had no idea what lurked in the mysterious store cupboard that might help him do that. Every time he ventured near the door something fell out.

As he ended his call, he heard a knock on the door and Danny stood in front of him.

'Hello, Will,' he said.

'Danny, how are you?'

'Very good, thank you. I've been busy cooking and I would like to ask you if you would like to come to mine for tea tonight. With me and Anna.'

He frowned when Will didn't respond immediately. 'I want to say thank you for saving me. I made you this too.' He thrust the paper bag at Will.

'What's this?' Will peered in the bag.

'Oat and raisin cookie.'

Will broke off a bit and ate it. 'This is really good, Danny,' he said in surprise.

'Will you come to tea?'

'What's on the menu?'

'Danny's homemade chicken and bacon pie,' he said proudly. 'It's my specialty.'

'Wow, I'm in. What time?'

'Dinner is at 6.30 p.m. I'm very pleased you said yes. Anna said you probably wouldn't want to.'

'She did, did she?' Will said. 'What can I bring?'

Danny looked confused. '*I'm* cooking. You don't need to bring anything.'

'Yes, but when someone asks you for tea at their house, you should bring something,' Will said gently.

'I'd not heard that rule,' he said doubtfully.

'It's not a rule. It's a thing to do.'

Danny frowned. 'I'm very confused now.'

'Don't be,' Will said. 'Leave it to me. Where do you live, Danny?'

Danny painstakingly explained to Will where they lived.

'OK then. See you later,' Will said, smiling.

'Maybe try and aim for 6 p.m. though?'

'OK. I'll do my best.'

'Bye, Will.'

Will plumped for a bottle of wine and some chocolates. He figured that was safer than a bunch of flowers since he thought Danny might get even more confused. It was 6.05 p.m. when he knocked on the door.

Will admired the house. The walls were light blue, with bright white trim and windows. The bright blue front door was three steps below street level. There was a warm glow from the windows and the front of the cottage had been decorated with tasteful fairly lights. Will reckoned you could see the bay from the first floor. The door swung open, and Danny stood there in an apron.

'Hello. Will. Come in. You don't have to take your shoes off here. Some people are quite funny about that.'

'Thanks. These are for you both,' he said, passing over the wine and the chocolates.

'Oh I'll take that, thanks,' Anna said, swooping in on the wine. 'I could do with a glass after the day I've had.' She turned to Danny. 'Danny, Will still has his coat on.'

'Oh yes.' Danny unceremoniously dragged Will's coat off him while Anna watched, rolling her eyes.

She whispered to Will. 'He's very excited. Sorry.'

'Don't be.' Will followed Danny through the house. 'So, Danny...?' he trailed off when he saw Danny standing expectantly by a chess game.

'Danny love, Will might not play.'

Danny's face fell and Will was sure he saw him become a little tearful.

'I'd love a game, as long as I can have a glass of that wine?'

'Consider it done. How are you settling in?' Anna asked.

'Good. I just have no idea where anything is.' He explained he had to cordon off a bit of the quayside, which was tomorrow's job, but said he had no idea whether he actually had anything to do it with. Danny looked excited.

'In the store cupboard there is hazard tape, fold out metal fencing and cones that you can use for that.'

'Do you know where all that stuff is then?' Will asked him.

Danny nodded.

'Would you like to come and help me tomorrow?' Will ventured.

Danny frowned. 'It's Christmas Eve tomorrow. I have got a lot to do.'

'Danny,' Anna chided. 'It'll take you half an hour to help Will. You can fit it in.'

Danny turned back to Will. 'Let's play.'

Will kissed Anna lightly on the cheek and patted Danny on the shoulder as he said goodbye. Dinner had been spectacular, and Danny was quite the cook, but got flustered and upset easily. He'd made a pavlova for pudding, which was one of Will's weaknesses. As well as being a fantastic cook, Danny was a demon chess player and they had played five games, with Will losing each one.

'Thanks, I've had a great time,' said Will. 'How about I cook next time for you both?'

'Oh, you don't have to do that,' said Anna.

'Why not? It's what friends do, isn't it?' Will asked, thinking that this woman had no idea how gorgeous she was. He was sure, however, that she would take a dim view of his previous evening's activities with the widow of his best friend.

'Are you going to Maggie's party tomorrow night?' Will asked.

'We are.'

'Good. Danny, I'll see you first thing to help me cordon that area off.' He turned to Anna and winked. 'And I'll see you at Maggie's tomorrow. Thanks again. Night.'

* * *

Night had fallen and the air was clear and cold. Jimmy had been pushing the boat to its limits and they had made good time. He eased off the throttle as they turned into the River Mersey. Jimmy had a fairly clear idea of where they were going and he dropped the lights down on the boat, leaving just low running lights.

As they got closer to the large red-brick, five-storey hospital Jimmy's stomach started churning. To him, the building looked empty, no lights were visible. Jimmy felt Alexy's presence next to his elbow and Alexy murmured to slow down further.

'Do you want me to get next to that loading dock?' Jimmy asked quietly, looking at the men on the floor of the boat.

'What is loading dock?' Alexy asked quietly, frowning and pointing. 'Sticky out thing?'

Jimmy smiled. 'Sticky out thing.'

'Close, but quiet,' Alexy said.

Jimmy expertly cut the engines and allowed the boat to drift next to the loading platform. He looped a rope around a cleat and with the current, this held the boat long enough for them to unceremoniously dump Ringo and Paul onto the dock. Jimmy quickly untied the boat. Alexy produced a semi-automatic weapon, which he trained on the doorway and then motioned to Jimmy to start the engines.

The noise of the engines was deafening in the quiet night air. A door next to the dock opened and a man stood in the lit doorway with a large gun in his hands.

Jimmy felt his knees wobble. He turned his back quickly so his face wouldn't be seen.

Alexy was relaxed. He called out, 'No shooting. Special delivery for The Surgeon. They will tell you the message.' He nodded to Jimmy and then held to the side of the boat tightly, the gun still trained on the man.

Jimmy floored the boat, the back of his neck prickling with the anticipation of a bullet landing in it. He breathed with relief as they powered up the river and out into the channel. Alexy put the gun down and turned to Jimmy smiling.

'Job is done,' he said and sat down in a comfortable chair. He rested his legs on the chair opposite and closed his eyes. 'Alexy is off for Christmas resting now.'

CHAPTER 23

Ensconced in his swanky hotel, Dr Jamie Hunter realised he'd eaten something that seriously disagreed with him; the likelihood being that he'd caught something disgusting from his mother's filthy hovel of a house. Since about an hour after his arrival in Castleby he had been unable to leave his room, suffering from vomiting and diarrhoea for hours. Luckily, he always carried Dioralyte and some other remedies, so he had taken those and was beginning to feel human again.

He breakfasted in his room and was relieved to feel his stomach had improved as he had no desire to be rushing to the bathroom, clutching his backside. He vowed to rest up a little more and snooze, perhaps have a light lunch in the restaurant overlooking the bay. He set an alarm on his phone and took himself back to bed in the hope that he would sleep the last of the bug off and awake feeling refreshed, so he could venture out and find Carla.

Danny had arrived at Will's office proudly wearing his 'Deputy Harbour Master' fleece. Anna had dropped him at the quayside as she had some medical supplies to be stored in Will's office for the next ferry.

As she stacked the boxes neatly, she said quietly to Will, 'He won't get in the way. He knows his way around more than you think, Gav used to say he was a real help.'

'It's fine,' Will assured her.

'I've got it!' Danny said, emerging from the store cupboard with hazard tape and an armful of fold-up metal fencing.

'Wow. What else is in there?'

'Lots,' Danny said seriously. 'It is very messy though. I'll tidy it up after Christmas.'

'Deal,' said Will. 'Let's get started.'

As they stepped out of Will's office, Anna's phone rang, and she answered it. She pulled a face and held the phone away from her ear slightly at the loud tirade. After a difficult conversation, she ended the call and tutted loudly.

'Problem?' Will asked.

'Woman in the holiday let in Compass Row is saying that food has been stolen. She wants the locks changed.'

'What? Anything else taken?'

'Nope. I think I've heard it all now,' she said. 'Stealing food? Never heard anything so bloody ridiculous in all my life.'

'What food has been nicked?'

'She says cheese, crackers and trifle – classic attack of the teenage munchies if you ask me. I must go. See you later, Danny,' she called and headed to the car.

'Bye, Anna,' said Danny, waving. He turned to Will. 'I've got to get on, I'm meeting Teddy in a little while.'

'Teddy?'

'He's my brother.'

Will frowned. 'He doesn't live with you?'

Danny looked upset. 'No. I wish he did, so he doesn't have to live with Dad. He hates it there. Dad treats him badly.'

'Is he older than you?'

'Yes. He likes to take photographs. He's very good. I need to get on, I don't want to be late for Teddy.'

* * *

Steve had watched the recording of Toby interviewing Levinson Lucas in London four times, and he was having a bad feeling. He trusted his gut and it was telling him something wasn't right, plus he was even more convinced that the bloke was a total dick. He whined constantly about Seb not having a funeral for Cassie, claiming everyone was desperate to say goodbye properly.

There was a light knock: PC Garland put his head around the door and handed Steve an envelope.

'Some guy's just dropped this off. It's a USB of the CCTV from the studio space that's on the outskirts of town. Apparently, it's all very self-explanatory.'

'Great. Thanks.'

He inserted the USB and waited impatiently for the software to scan it to make sure it was virus free.

'Tea,' Jonesey said, pushing open the door with his foot and plonking down a cup on Steve's desk. He produced a slightly squashed mince pie from one pocket and put it next to Steve's tea and then stuffed another in his mouth.

'Ta,' said Steve absently. He loaded the files up and searched for the date of Cassie's accident. He selected a few hours earlier and

249

played it on a slow fast forward. Settling back with his tea, he looked around for the mince pie.

'Where's that mince…' he said, looking at Jonesey's bulging cheeks. 'Did you eat my mince pie?'

'Course not,' said Jonesey guiltily. 'I'll get you one now though.' He disappeared.

Steve watched the screen and increased the speed of the fast forward until he saw what he was looking for. He watched in disbelief.

'Jesus,' he muttered, rewinding and playing it again.

Jonesey reappeared with another two mince pies and handed one to Steve, his eyes fixed on the screen as he slowly sat down.

'Wait… Is that?'

'Think so.'

Both men winced at the same time as they watched.

'Bet that fucking hurt,' murmured Jonesey. 'Play it again.'

The two watched as a green Ford Fiesta pulled up opposite the petrol station. A tall, thin figure got out and went next door to the small supermarket, emerging a few minutes later and climbing back into the Fiesta, and the car did an awkward four-point turn and passed the Porsche that Cassie and Tabatha were in. Abruptly, the Fiesta stopped, turned around awkwardly, and slowly returned, stopping across the street from the garage and switching off its lights.

Steve peered at the screen. He could see someone in the car taking pictures. He enlarged the image but couldn't get a clear view of the face, because the camera obscured it. After a minute, an old truck drove slowly past and stopped. Edwyn Lewis climbed out of the passenger side and the truck drove off.

They watched as Edwyn strode over to the green Fiesta and opened the door. He grabbed the person inside, dragging them out of the car onto the ground then repeatedly kicked them. It looked like he was shouting as he was kicking. The person on the ground had curled into a protective ball against the onslaught. Edwyn bent down and grabbed the figure by the back of the collar and rammed their head into the side of the car. Following that, the figure slumped to the ground.

'Ouch,' said Jonesey.

'Who is that?' Steve said, craning his neck to see the image. 'I can't see their face.'

'Go back a bit... there, check that out, said Jonesey, pointing with a mince pie in his hand.

'What?'

'That huge tattoo on the arm as he pushes against the car,' he said, stuffing the mince pie in his mouth. He closed his eyes in ecstasy. 'God, I love Christmas.'

'What tattoo?'

Jonesey rolled his eyes and licked his fingers. 'There,' he said, pointing.

Steve paused the film and zoomed in, peering at the screen.

'So, the delicious PC Warren is going to Maggie's later, I'm going to be all over her like a cheap suit tonight. Total charm offensive, she will—'

'Jonesey,' Steve said absently, staring at the screen. 'Get onto Michelle, the woman who was pushed off the cliff. Ask her if she remembers the guy having a tattoo.'

'OK.'

Steve glanced at him. 'Like now.'

'Oh. Right.' Jonesey got up, turning in the doorway. 'Er, what is that tattoo anyway?'

'I think it might be some sort of face, we'll need to see if it can be enlarged though. Go on, off you go.'

Steve focused on the screen before him. He watched as Edwyn dragged the person to the passenger side, opened the door and shoved them in, slamming the door angrily. He then strode around to the driver's side, got in and drove off.

Steve sat pondering. He rewound the film again and watched specifically for Cassie's Porsche and the timeline there. He watched her arrive at the pumps, fill the tank and then go inside. He didn't see any evidence of the man who Cassie had been arguing with arriving or departing, which puzzled him. He couldn't understand how the guy had appeared *inside* the petrol station. He watched Cassie leave the petrol station holding her phone and climb into the car next to Tabatha. She left a few moments before Edwyn, who then drove in the same direction.

Jonesey reappeared, breathless. 'She doesn't remember a tattoo, but she said he was wearing a coat so she wouldn't have seen his arms anyway.'

'Bugger. Can you get the evidence list from the accident for me, please? I want to see where Cassie's phone went. She had it when she left the garage.'

'Tech have it. It's totally smashed.'

'OK. Take PC Warren and—'

Jonesey inhaled sharply. 'Oh, you beauty! Where am I going with my future wife?'

'Wind your neck in. Take Warren, go to the garage and find out where that bloke would have got in and left again. And check for any CCTV that might show something else from a different angle.'

'I'm all over it, Guv.' He smoothed down his uniform and looked at Steve. 'How do I look?'

'Like a twat. Go.'

Steve's mobile rang and, noting the number, gently pushed his office door shut.

'Miller.'

'Hello, Steve, it's Pearl. How are you?'

'Very well. Yourself?'

'Good, thank you. I just wanted to share that we have returned two certain individuals to their original sender, with a very polite message.' She chuckled. 'Well, very polite for Mickey.'

'Good to know. Dare I ask whether they had a pulse?'

'Of course they did. How else would they have been able to relay the message?'

'Excellent.'

'We have asked politely that The Surgeon come and have a civilised discussion with us, so we wait to hear whether he will accept our offer. In the meantime, we remain vigilant.'

'As will I, Pearl.'

'Excellent. This relationship is working very well so far. For what it's worth, I understand how conflicting this must be for you. You have a good Christmas, Steve.'

'Same to you, Pearl.'

Steve had promised Kate he would knock off at a reasonable time to go to the party. He arrived at Kate's house, which was on the Castle Mount, perched above Maggie's cafe and the climbing centre. Kate beckoned him inside.

'Oh... hello to you too,' he murmured as she pulled him in the front door and kissed him. Steve's phone rang and he looked at the display. He glanced at Kate.

'Two minutes, then I'm all yours,' he said.

'Better be,' she said, walking backwards up the stairs in front of him unbuttoning her shirt.

'Wait... do that slowly...' he said before barking into his phone. 'What, Jonesey?'

'The door to the back is always ajar because they've got a nasty damp problem in there and it helps with the smell. So our mate came in and left by the back door, I reckon.'

'You have to ask yourself why,' Steve said as Kate's shirt flew down the stairs and landed on his head.

'There is CCTV on the back door. But it's downloaded to some bloke's house who's away for Christmas and not back until the day after Boxing Day. I've got his details and I've called to see if he can access remotely as a matter of urgency.'

'Good lad.'

'Also, the pet shop has CCTV in their car park, and I reckon it might cover their back area. I've left an urgent message for their manager, who's out delivering, to call me back before they go home. I reckon something will come up.'

'Anyone remember anything the night Cassie was killed?' Steve asked as Kate's bra flew down the stairs and hit Steve on the shoulder, dangling seductively.

'Nope. I did the usual and asked people to call if they remember anything.'

'OK. Great. Thanks for that. Get off home now. See you in a bit.'

'So, Guv… about PC Warren–'

'Gotta go, Jonesey, something's come up.'

Steve ended the call and took the stairs three at a time.

CHAPTER 24

Teeney knocked on Jenny's door at 7 p.m. Jenny opened the door to see one of the most beautiful women she had ever seen standing next to him.

'Ready to go?' Teeney asked, looking very handsome. 'Jenny, this is Flavia. She's Italian. She's a model, here for Christmas.' He turned to Flavia, speaking in a stream of fluent Italian.

Flavia giggled and bent to kiss his cheek. She turned to Jenny. 'Buonasera,' she said, nodding.

Jenny repeated the greeting in, what she considered to be, her best horrendous Italian and slammed the door shut behind her.

'You didn't have to come and get me,' she said to Teeney.

'I said I would. It adds to my mystical charm if I go to Maggie's with a beautiful woman on each arm.' He translated his comment for Flavia who laughed delightedly.

'Does she speak any English?'

'Not a bloody word. I'm not planning on spending too long chatting tonight, if you get my drift,' he said out of the corner of his mouth.

'You rogue. Where did you meet her?'

'Over by the docks. The Agency have hired a big warehouse and they needed it made secure for all their gear. The shoot is over a few days and nights, and I'm doing building security. We got chatting, and she seemed to quite like me.'

They rounded the corner and saw Maggie's. Outside lights had been strung up across the narrow lane and tables and chairs with heaters stood on the deck. On the beach in front, Foxy was prodding a large fire. Christmas music was being gently played and already there was a murmur of conversation and laughter.

Maggie fussed over Doug and Jesse when they arrived, and Jude escaped, making his way over to Tabatha. He squeezed in next to her.

'Hello,' he said. 'You look much better than yesterday.'

'Apart from my concussion.'

He rolled his eyes. 'Here's me being all manly and carrying you up some steps and you go on about the small matter of a concussion.'

'I feel sure Romeo didn't knock Juliet out in his escapades.'

'Picky, picky.'

Tabatha reached for his hand and kissed his cheek. 'Seriously though, thank you for yesterday.'

Jude looked down at their entwined hands. He liked the sensation. He liked her kissing him too.

'Anytime,' he said, blushing furiously.

'Oh, I see what you mean!' Jesse said, craning her neck to check out Jude and Tabatha. 'She's so pretty. Isn't she like her mother? Look how dopey Jude looks. He's got it bad. You know what this means, don't you?'

256

'Oh God, what?' said Doug, his mind going to a land of teenage pregnancies and unsafe sex.

Jesse adopted a serious face. 'It means that there is some serious piss taking to be done.'

'I don't think that's the wisest idea,' Doug said wryly. 'He was pretty sensitive about doing his hair the other day, Christ knows what else is off-limits.'

Will and Suzy arrived and Doug introduced them to Jesse. Doug motioned Will over to get a drink, while Suzy and Jesse started chatting about dogs.

'Few weeks in now. How are you finding it?' Doug asked lightly.

Will thought for a moment. 'I love it. I think a big part of that is, I feel part of the community already.' He eyed Doug. 'I'm sure you've had a hand in that, so thank you.'

'I haven't done anything. You did wonders for your rep by helping out on the rescue.'

'Hmm, what's gonna happen about the ferry?'

Doug lowered his voice. 'I've been meaning to float something with you. You must have some clout in the sailing community?'

'None whatsoever,' Will said. 'People think I died in the accident and I'm pretty happy to let that ride. Why?'

'Just wondered. One of the idiot boys we rescued happens to be the son of a pretty large provider of sailing equipment and clothing in the industry.'

'What? Not Sail-Loft? As in *the* Sail-Loft?'

'Uh huh.'

'Is that so?' asked Will. 'I know them well. Perhaps they'd like to help out, while the ferry gets replaced.'

'I imagine it's pretty good PR for them too.'

'I imagine so. Leave it with me,' Will said, grabbing a wine for Suzy.

Doug felt a hand slip into his and he turned in surprise expecting to see Jesse, instead it was Anna standing there smiling, with Danny.

'You said you'd hold my hand if I came to the party,' she said.

'I did, didn't I?' Doug kissed her cheek. 'Nice to see you here. Hello, Danny. How are you?'

'Hello, Doug,' Danny said. 'I played chess with Will last night and I beat him every time!'

'That's because you are a total hustler when it comes to chess,' Doug said wryly.

'I'm just very good at chess,' Danny said matter-of-factly.

'Yes, you are. What have you been up to today?'

'I've been very busy. I've helped Will out with the store cupboard and some fencing off. I delivered presents to people. I saw Teddy and gave him his present and I went to see Brother Joseph in hospital, and I went to do some errands for Miles as he still feels very funny.'

'How is Brother Joseph?'

'I think he won't make it home,' said Danny. 'Very sad. He wants to die on his island he said.'

'That's sad.'

'Brother Joseph says it's God's decision and not his.'

'Why does Miles still feel funny? Did he say?'

Danny screwed up his face trying to remember. 'He said he has post-concussion symptoms.'

'Do you mean post-concussion syndrome?'

'Yes, that one. Hard to remember. I had to practice saying it so I would remember it.'

'Poor Miles. So, Danny, what's on your Christmas list?'

Danny smiled delightedly. 'I have asked for a new PS game and a virtual headset, so I can play games with some of my friends online.'

'You're being careful there?'

'Yes. Anna makes sure I'm safe.' He looked sad. 'I miss playing games with Gavin though.'

Unexpectedly, Doug's eyes filled with tears: he blinked them away. He missed his best friend, especially at things like the party tonight where he would have been goofing about.

'I think you miss him just as much as me,' Danny said with surprising insight. 'Oh, look, there's Will. I've bought him a book on chess for Christmas, it was 50p in the charity shop. Don't tell him though. I have to go now, I see cake.'

Will strolled out onto the deck and saw Anna staring into the fire, holding a glass of white wine.

'Fancy seeing you here. As usual, you look drop-dead gorgeous.'

'Oh stop,' Anna said, rolling her eyes.

'I'm serious. You have no idea how utterly gorgeous you are, do you?'

Anna looked exasperated. 'Does this approach work for you?'

'Just saying what I see.'

'I've been googling you,' she said.

'Oh?'

'Why didn't you say you were *that* Will Scully?'

'Same reason you didn't say you were *that* Anna Lewis.'

'Hardly the same.'

'Er... pertains to relevance, Your Honour,' he said in a mock plummy voice.

'This is quite the change for you,' she said. 'The heady heights of the racing circuit and the lifestyle of the rich and famous, and now harbour master at Castleby. Down to earth with a bump, I suspect.'

'Have you been speaking to my interview panel by any chance?'

'It's quite the change. I would question your staying power.'

'I don't want that life. Since the accident, everything's changed. *I've* changed. And, for what it's worth,' he said dryly, 'my staying power is excellent.'

'I saw the accident. You were very lucky.'

'That depends how you look at it.'

'Your crewmate died.'

'My best friend died,' he corrected.

'You almost did from what I saw.'

Will felt a lump in his throat and looked at the fire blinking.

'Afterwards, you gave up racing completely?'

'Yup.'

'You miss it?'

'Nope.'

Will was quiet for a moment.

'You had quite the reputation,' Anna said lightly, sipping her wine.

'For what?'

'Being a heartbreaker.'

'Ah, the press can't be trusted, you know.'

'Ahh, so all the women were fake news?' Anna said, amused.

'Not all, I've just never met the right girl.'

'Not even once?'

'Maybe once. Years ago, there was a girl.'

'What happened?'

'Tragically, she had no idea and married my best friend.'

'Ah.'

'After that I figured it wasn't fair to be with someone and ask them to stand by while I was all over the world and rarely home.'

'Very noble of you,' Anna said dryly.

'I'm serious. That's not a proper relationship for anyone. Someone who's away nine months of the year.'

'Depends what sort of relationship it is, I suppose. People in the forces seem to manage it.'

'What about you, Anna?' Will moved closer, studying her. 'You're gorgeous. Gavin's been gone a while now. Do you think about moving on?'

'No.'

'Not ever?'

'No,' she said firmly.

'Don't you think Gav would want you to be happy?'

'I am happy. What makes you think I need a man in my life to make me happy?'

'I meant, start again. Marry again. Love someone again, be loved again.' He moved closer.

'I'm fairly confident that's not a veiled proposal,' she said dryly. 'Stop that by the way.'

'Stop what?'

'Leaning in… You know what you're doing.'

'I'm not leaning.'

'Yes, you are.'

Will sipped his beer. 'What's so bad about starting again with someone else?'

Anna stared into the fire. 'Because it doesn't happen twice,' she said softly.

'Maybe it does.'

'I can't do it again,' she said softly.

'Do what again?' Will touched her lightly on the arm.

'Love someone so totally and then lose them. I can't do it again. It'd kill me,' she said.

'You might not lose them.'

'I can't take that chance,' she said, tears glistening in her eyes. 'I need to find Maggie. See you later, Will.'

Steve and Kate arrived, slightly later than anticipated.

'Darlings!' Maggie shrieked. 'I thought you weren't going to make it.'

'So did I at one point,' Steve said, receiving a jab in the ribs from Kate.

Maggie fussed over them and dragged them into the noise, where Steve came face to face with Jenny.

'Inspector Miller!' Jenny said. 'Nice to see you.'

Steve spent an enjoyable ten minutes with Jenny hearing about the house, Archie, and a seagull that had frightened the life out of her, crashing in through a window upstairs.

'No sign of Sniffy?' he asked.

'No. I saw him the other day outside the bakery. He looked very unhappy, so I bought him a sausage roll and a hot drink.'

'Sucker.'

'What's his story?'

'Usual. Likes the drugs too much to get his shit together. He's tried and tried, but he comes back to it constantly. He's been in and out of recovery units, but he just can't stop himself.'

'That's so sad.'

'It is, and it will be the death of him. But he knows that and accepts it. I learnt fairly early on that you can't help people who don't want to help themselves. Did Teeney call for you earlier?'

'Oh, I can't thank you enough for introducing me to Teeney,' Jenny gushed. 'He's been fantastic, helping me out with the builders too.'

'He's a good lad.'

'Have you checked out his date? She is drop-dead gorgeous!'

'She is,' Steve agreed. 'He has quite the way with the ladies.'

Sebastian appeared. 'Hi, guys,' he said. 'Merry Christmas.'

'You too,' responded Steve. 'How's Tabatha?'

'She's very good. Enjoying Jack very much.' He looked awkward for a moment. 'I know it's not appropriate, but any news?'

262

'Nothing of any significance but give me a few days and I'll come and update you.'

'Fair enough. Sorry to ask when you're off duty.'

'He's never off duty,' said Kate, slipping her arms around him. 'Hi there, I'm Kate.'

Steve kissed her cheek. 'Kate's a local GP. She's never off duty either.'

Steve's phone rang. He looked at the display and saw it was Jim Murphy, the pathologist.

'See?' Kate said, rolling her eyes.

'Excuse me, I've got to take this,' he said, heading outside, waving at Carla as he passed her.

Stepping out he walked away from the party, answering the phone.

'Murph, it's late, mate. You still at work?'

'You're my very last call before I go home and enjoy being pampered by my long-suffering husband,' he said.

'Lucky me.'

'Cassie Warner's baby.'

Steve looked around to check where Seb was.

'DNA says hubby isn't the daddy.'

'Shit.'

'I imagine he'll say a lot worse.'

'It's a match from the sample from London.'

'Levinson Lucas?'

'The very same. Anyway, I'm outta here. Have a very merry one, my friend.'

'Cheers, Murph. You too, mate.'

Steve ended the call and leant against the wall, his mind processing the information and where he went from there.

'Excuse me.' A tall, well-dressed man approached Steve. He detected a very faint Liverpool accent. 'I don't suppose you happen to know Carla Fox?'

Steve pretended to think for a moment his brain quickly processing who this could be.

'I know Carla,' he said pleasantly, holding out his hand. 'Steve Miller and you are?'

'Jamie Hunter. A friend from work. I knew she was here; I just haven't been able to ring her. Problem with her phone, I think.'

'She was here,' Steve said thoughtfully. 'But her and her ex-husband have taken off to Scotland for Christmas.'

'Oh.' Jamie looked surprised. 'You sure? Her phone–' He stopped himself.

'Went earlier,' Steve supplemented.

'Oh well.' Jamie looked over Steve's shoulder. 'Is that a party?'

'Yes. Sorry, it's invitation only. The host is a right ball buster, no gatecrashers. Are you staying locally?'

'Yes. Up at The Bay Manor.'

'Very nice,' said Steve, smiling. 'You around for long?'

'Probably until after Christmas.'

'Oh well. Enjoy it here. Anyway, I'd better get back in. Sorry I couldn't help. Have a good Christmas. Nice to meet you.'

'You too.'

Steve watched as Jamie ambled up the road. It was all he could do not to go after him and arrest him. He ducked back into the party and cornered Foxy quietly.

'You're not going to believe this. Carla's unwanted friend is here.'

Foxy stared at Steve in disbelief.

'What?'

'I've literally just stopped him from coming in. He's staying at The Bay Manor.'

'What does he want?'

'To find Carla. I think he's got a tracker on her phone. I told him you'd gone to Scotland together, so she needs to switch off her phone or find it and disable it.'

'Shit, has he gone?'

'Looked that way. You've met him though; you know what he looks like?'

'Yup,' Foxy said grimly.

'I'll call Penny and let her know he's here. Let's find out if she has enough to charge him. Stick close to Carla.'

'OK.'

Steve went back outside and made a call. Disappointingly Penny had only found two nurses who felt that something might have happened to them, and she didn't feel there was enough evidence to stick. She promised she would keep at it and try to find more. Frustrated, Steve went back to the party and told Foxy.

'We'll just have to keep an eye out then,' said Foxy. 'He's not coming anywhere near her.'

'Don't go doing anything stupid.'

'You did say you'd help bury the body.'

'I know the manager up at the Manor. I'll get a heads up when he leaves.'

'Good plan. I'll make sure she switches that phone off.'

The party was heaving – Maggie's parties were legendary. The outside deck was crammed with people enjoying the heat from the fire.

Tabatha was looking for her dad, she wanted to head home, and needed to check it was OK if Jude came along to hang out. She found Sebastian chatting to Bree, Jenny and Suzy, and tugged his arm.

'Dad, I'm heading home. Is it OK if Jude comes and hangs out for a bit?'

'Sure. Do me a favour while I remember, ping me Jude's number so I have it?'

She tutted and Seb said, 'Those are the rules, kiddo.'

She sent him Jude's number. 'See you later, Dad.'

'Enjoy yourself,' said Bree, grinning.

'Aunty Bree,' scolded Tabatha. 'You've got a one-track mind.'

'What's the problem with that?' Bree said innocently. 'Have a nice time, darling, see you in a while. If you can't be good, be careful.'

Tabatha hugged Maggie goodbye while Jude went to tell Doug where he was going.

Doug raised an eyebrow. 'You got your phone?'

'Yup.'

'All charged?'

Jude rolled his eyes. 'Yup.'

'Call me if you need me.'

Jude and Tabatha strolled up the road together in the quiet night air, their fingers interlinked.

'How's Marcus?'

'He's OK,' Jude said.

They rounded the corner and heard Jack barking frantically.

'That's Jack.' Tabatha was worried. 'What's happened?'

Rushing to the front door, Tabatha scrabbled with the key. She pushed the door open, and Jack threw himself at her, licking her face.

'What's the matter?' she said, cuddling the shaking bundle. 'Is this because we went out?'

They walked into the kitchen and opened the door for Jack. He trotted about outside and then came back in again.

'Do you think he was frightened?' Tabatha asked.

Jude shrugged. 'Maybe he heard something.'

'Seems OK now though. I'm starving, do you want some toast?'

'Absolutely,' said Jude. 'Always hungry.'

Tabatha smiled. 'Right, toast. Do you want tea?'

'Go for it. I'll do tea. You do toast.'

Tabatha got busy. 'Tell me about the accident you had with Marcus.'

'You don't wanna hear that.'

'I do.'

Jude sighed. 'We were stupid.'

'Come on.'

Tabatha sat on a stool and watched Jude make tea as he talked. She wondered for a moment if he had any idea how much he was like his father. He had the same mannerisms, eyes, build, and he had Doug's way about him: thoughtful and kind.

'Marcus fell down the sinkhole, and you climbed down to get him, and then supported him when he climbed back up with a broken arm?' she said, amazed. 'How the hell did you do that?'

'I was climbing beneath him so he could rest on me, and I could push him up when he got into trouble.'

'So how did you hurt your hands?'

Jude explained it was heaving up the rucksacks from the bottom of the shaft that had taken all the skin off his hands. He'd needed the food and water for Marcus, and then the subsequent landslide where he had tried to hold Marcus upright on the ropes when he had passed out.

'My hero,' she said, impressed.

'He would have done the same for me.'

'Still pretty brave.'

'Nah.' He blushed.

'Who found you in the end?' she asked.

'Foxy and Rudi came out with Marcus's mum. Solo tracked our scent up the hill.'

'Clever dog.'

'Foxy found Solo in a war zone and rescued him. He was an army dog. Super bright.'

Jack started barking again and Tabatha went out into the hall.

'Jack?' she called, heading up the stairs. 'Jack?'

Tabatha followed the noise of Jack's barking into her dad's bedroom and saw Jack barking at something in the corner.

Flipping on the light, she said sternly, 'Jack, stop barking.'

Jack came over and sat next to Tabatha. She noticed a photo of her mother lying on the floor, the glass cracked.

'Oh no,' she said softly, picking it up gently. 'Come on, Jack.'

She went downstairs, with Jack trotting along behind her and went back into the kitchen. Jude was buttering toast.

'What was he barking at?' he asked.

'No idea, but I think he might have knocked this off Dad's bedside table.'

Jude took the frame. 'You are so like your mum.'

'I don't see it.'

'People say I'm like Dad, but I don't see it either,' he said ruefully.

She laughed. 'You are *so* like your dad it's uncanny.'

'See? I don't see it. Now, what do you want on your toast?'

The pair of them had eaten the toast and flaked out on the sofa in front of the TV. Before long, they were both asleep, with Jack sprawled across Tabatha's lap. Tabatha woke suddenly, remembered she needed to take her tablets and pushed Jack off her. In the kitchen, she slugged down her tablets with a glass of water and heard a noise above. She climbed the stairs, expecting it to be Jack in her dad's room again.

'Jack, what is it with you…' she said, pushing open the door. She screamed when she saw a shadowy figure sat on her dad's bed, with one of her mother's jumpers screwed up in his hand.

268

CHAPTER 25

Stanley, Pearl's right-hand man, worshipped Pearl with every bone in his body. He had done so for decades, ever since they had been at primary school together in East London. Stanley had been a small child, prone to illness and being bullied. Stanley's mother was always out working, and his father was a useless drunk who liked to beat up Stanley and his mother whenever the pubs were shut.

At the age of ten, Pearl had seen Stanley being beaten up by some larger kids and had waded in, dragged them off Stanley and given one of them a hefty punch in the face. Pearl had taken Stanley home, patched him up and made the starving boy a sandwich. Stanley had worshipped her ever since. Wherever Pearl went, Stanley went. He would rather die than let anything happen to her.

Tonight, Stanley was upset because Pearl was cross with him. She shouted at him and said she was sick and tired of having to constantly give him instructions, and by now he should be able to anticipate what she needed and when. She told him that if he didn't buck his ideas up she would replace him.

Stanley's heart was broken. He didn't want a life without being near Pearl. She sent him out of the house and told him to go and think about what she had said.

Stanley went for a walk and thought about Pearl's words. As he walked, his phone rang and he answered it gruffly.

'The Surgeon has received your message,' a voice said with a strong Liverpool accent. 'He'll have a discussion. He's on his way.' The line went dead.

Stanley swore loudly, Pearl would freak. He rang the number back with no luck. He realised he'd walked along the road and was at the entrance to the drive of the hotel that overlooked Mickey and Pearl's house. He liked it in there. He often drank in the bar, because he could keep an eye on things from up there. He walked up the drive; he would have a drink and think about how to tell Pearl and Mickey that The Surgeon was on his way.

Dr Jamie Hunter was frustrated. Carla's phone was telling him she was in Castleby, or that was the last location. Yet the guy he met at the party had said Carla had gone to Scotland. Surely she would take her phone with her? His expectations of seeing Carla again had been high. He had even brought his special liquid along to drop into her drink if she wasn't being overly receptive to his advances again. Heading back to his hotel, he decided to have a drink in the bar. He also wanted to find out what time the pretty receptionist knocked off work, and whether she might like a drink or two.

When he arrived, he noticed the receptionist was serving behind the bar. It was fairly quiet, apart from a few couples and a large bald man who was sitting at the bar nursing a pint.

'Well, hello there,' Jamie said, adopting his most winning smile. He sat a few seats away from the large man. 'Nice to see you again.'

The receptionist smiled. 'What can I get you?'

'A glass of your best Merlot, please,' Jamie said. 'Take a drink for yourself.'

'Thank you,' she said. 'This on a tab?'

Jamie nodded. She poured him a glass and placed a fresh bowl of nibbles next to it.

'How's your day been?' she asked pleasantly while she polished glasses.

'Not bad,' Jamie said. 'Yours?'

'Busy,' she said. 'Are you here on your own, or are you meeting friends?'

'I've been travelling and working away, so I'm taking a much-needed break before I go back to work. I've a friend locally, hopefully we'll catch up in the next few days.'

'Where've you been then?'

'I was in the Sudan and then Liverpool, then here.'

'Goodness. What were you doing in the Sudan and then Liverpool?'

'I'm a surgeon. I was training the army in the Sudan and then I had some business in Liverpool.'

'Very impressive,' she said. 'What sort of surgeon?'

'Trauma mainly. I do a lot of work with people who've been hurt in traumatic circumstances.'

'Interesting work.'

'It's very rewarding.'

A couple approached the bar and she excused herself to serve them.

Stanley was beside himself. The bloke next to him at the bar was only the bloody surgeon from Liverpool! Talking about people being hurt in traumatic circumstances! He was sure of it. He wasn't on his way;

271

he was already here! He thought quickly, quite the feat for Stanley who wasn't the quickest thinker in the world.

He tapped out a quick text to Maxim, telling him to meet him in the hotel car park ASAP. Maxim replied immediately, saying he was on his way. Stanley slid off the bar stool and noticed the surgeon had asked for a refill.

He met Maxim in the car park.

'What so urgent?' Maxim asked in his pidgin English.

'The fucking surgeon from Liverpool is here. In the fucking hotel. Bold as fucking brass.'

'I don't understand this bold brass,' muttered Maxim. 'What are we doing? What does Pearl say?'

'Nothing yet. Let's take care of him first and then tell them.' Stanley said, imagining how pleased Pearl would be with him.

'If you are sure,' Maxim said doubtfully.

'Yes. Let's get him out here and into the car. Take him somewhere safe,' Stanley said.

'Usual way?' Maxim asked, smiling.

'Yup.'

'Which one is it?'

'That one, I reckon. Dicks like him drive those,' Stanley said, pointing to the Range Rover. He peered at a car park ticket in the window. 'Liverpool, dated yesterday,' he said triumphantly. 'Definitely this one.'

Maxim went and fiddled with the car. Stanley watched in admiration. There wasn't a car that Maxim couldn't break into and do what he wanted to it. He left Maxim to it and went back to the bar, sitting himself down. Suddenly the blare of a car alarm went off loudly and Stanley looked out of the window.

'It's the Range Rover,' he said loudly to no one in particular.

'Oh damn.' Jamie reached into his pocket. Drawing out a key fob he pressed it and the alarm stopped suddenly. 'Don't know what that was about,' Jamie said, frowning.

Stanley resumed his drink and the alarm sounded again. Again, Jamie pressed the key fob and it stopped.

'Sorry, folks,' said Jamie, looking around.

The alarm went off a third time and Stanley said, 'I've had this with Range Rovers before, you have to get in and start it and that resets it.'

'Well, that's a bloody faff,' Jamie said, sliding off his stool. 'I'll try that. Thank you.'

'My pleasure,' Stanley said.

Jamie walked briskly out of the front door and pressed the key fob again. A few moments later, Stanley finished his pint. He stepped out the front door and wandered across the car park. He stopped at Jamie's Range Rover, where a smiling Maxim was sitting comfortably behind the wheel. Jamie slumped in the seat next to him.

'Where we go?' Maxim asked.

'Big shed,' Stanley replied, taking the keys to Maxim's car from him. He strolled to the car, taking a moment to text their contact who would come and take Jamie's car away and sell it. He wouldn't be needing it again.

* * *

The man on the bed jumped at Tabatha's scream and bolted from the room. He pushed her out of the way so roughly that she crashed into a chair and fell, hitting her head on Sebastian's bedside table.

Downstairs, Jude was woken by Tabatha's scream, falling off the sofa in surprise. He scrambled to his feet and tripped over Jack who thought this was all a big game. As Jude rounded the corner to go up the stairs, a man rushed into him. He pushed Jude out of the way and, winded, he slipped on the polished hallway floor before he could grab a hold of the man.

The man ran towards the back of the house and left through the back door. Slightly dazed, Jude picked himself up and called Doug as he ran up the stairs.

Doug answered on the second ring. 'What's up?'

'Dad,' Jude said breathlessly. 'There's a guy in Tabatha's house, I think he's hurt her.'

'Two minutes. I'll be there in two minutes.'

Jude continued up the stairs and found Tabatha lying on the floor. He skidded to his knees beside her.

'Tabatha?'

Her eyelids fluttered open, and she tried to sit up. Jude pushed her back down gently.

'Stay there,' he said. He rushed to the bathroom and ran a flannel under a cold tap, wringing it out. He ran back, and laid it over Tabatha's forehead, where a large bump was forming.

'Jude!' shouted Doug.

'Up here,' he called.

Jude heard feet thumping up the stairs and Doug, Seb and Steve arrived, out of breath, their faces full of concern, closely followed by Kate, Bree and Jesse.

'Oh Christ,' Seb said, striding towards Tabatha.

Bree's hand flew to her mouth when she saw Tabatha on the floor. 'Darling!' she squeaked, becoming tearful.

'I'm OK. He pushed me over and I fell against the bedside table. I just felt a bit dizzy for a moment.'

'Let me have a look.' Kate pushed Seb aside gently and knelt next to Tabatha. She checked her over gently and asked her to sit up. She ran through various checks with her, while Doug checked the house.

'What happened?' demanded Seb.

Jude recounted everything he could remember, from Jack barking, the cracked picture of Cassie, then him waking up when he heard Tabatha scream. He described the man as best he could, but in the darkness, he hadn't got a very good look at him.

Steve sat down beside Tabatha. 'Tell me what happened.'

Tabatha added to Jude's story. 'He was just sitting in here on the bed, holding Mum's grey jumper. Then he bolted.'

'Can you describe him?'

'I didn't really see his face. He was quite tall, bit taller than Jude. Thin.'

'Young? Old?' Steve prompted.

'Erm, I would guess young by how quick he was, but I didn't get a good look.'

'What was he wearing?' Steve asked.

'Dark hoodie. I can't remember.'

'Did he take anything else?'

Jude looked over. 'He was holding something soft, I felt it as he crashed into me. He went out the back door.'

Doug came back. 'I'm guessing he legged it over the wall.'

'How did he get in?' Steve wondered out loud.

'When we got home, Jack was barking his head off, we could hear it from outside,' Tabatha said.

'But how could he have got in?' Bree quizzed.

Sebastian looked around. 'No idea. I'm pretty religious about locking up because we've had a few experiences in London of paparazzi breaking in looking for a story.'

'Nothing's broken. No windows forced?' Steve pushed.

Doug shook his head. 'There's nothing, I've checked around.'

Bree said, 'I wonder if he got in while we were getting Jack from the beach earlier. We were all down there it was only a few minutes but...'

'Maybe,' Seb said doubtfully.

'Tabatha, do you feel OK to come downstairs? I just want to check your blood pressure; your dad says you've got a machine here.'

'I don't like it at all,' Seb said to Steve when she was out of earshot. 'Do you think Tabatha's safe here?'

'I've got no reason to think otherwise,' Steve said. 'He didn't hurt her, he wanted her out of the way so he could escape. If he wanted to hurt her, he would have.'

Seb said quietly, 'This is about Cass, isn't it?'

'I reckon so,' Steve replied.

'Anything to do with the pictures up the road?'

'Perhaps. I don't think anyone's at risk though.'

'How can you say that?' Seb asked, raking his hands through his hair in frustration.

'Because if that was the case, it would have happened already.'

'Hardly a reassurance,' Seb grumbled.

Seb closed the door on everyone and sent Tabatha to bed. He checked on her and then returned downstairs. He sat down next to Bree at the table and took a sip of her wine.

'She OK?' Bree asked quietly.

'Yeah. Sleeping.'

'Are you?' she persisted.

Seb closed his eyes and dropped his head onto his arms on the table and let out a loud sigh.

'I feel like I'm holding on by my fingernails,' he mumbled into his arms.

Bree stroked his hair. 'Hang in there. It'll get better.'

'Why does it feel like it won't?' he whispered.

'It will, darling. It will,' she said, continuing to stroke his hair. 'Now go to bed, darling, before I do something stupid. I've had way too much wine to be sensible and I'm finding your vulnerability to be like catnip. Off you go.'

Sebastian raised his head and looked at Bree. 'Don't say things like that.'

Bree got up and walked to the back door to get some air, she breathed deeply.

'Go to bed, Sebastian,' she said. 'Please.'

* * *

Dr Jamie Hunter woke up with a terrible headache to find himself tied so securely to a chair that he couldn't feel his hands anymore.

'Hello?' he yelled, struggling against his ties, his brain battling to process his current situation. He tried to remember what had happened. He had been having a drink, his car alarm had gone off and he had gone to start the car. He didn't recall anything else.

'Hello?' he yelled. 'Anybody here? HELLO? Somebody HELP ME!'

Stanley had gone through Jamie's pockets while he was unconscious and found four vials of liquid. He had been around long enough to know exactly what it was. His hands had shaken with rage at the very idea that this man might have planned to use it on his Pearl.

He heard Jamie shouting and grabbed a bottle of water. He tipped most of it out and then poured the contents of one vial in. He handed the bottle to Maxim who had been watching him, and gestured with his head.

'Time he had a drink.'

Maxim left, returning a few minutes later. Jamie's cries grew quiet.

Stanley grinned. 'He'll be out for hours. Let's go and see Pearl.'

As Stanley and Maxim pulled into Pearl and Mickey's drive, Stanley's phone rang.

'Hello?'

A man with a strong Liverpudlian accent said, 'The Surgeon will be there Friday at 6 p.m. Text me somewhere to meet. He'll have a civilised chat over dinner with your boss – no hardware. I'll wait to hear from you, oh and he's gluten free.'

The call ended and Stanley tried to process what he had just heard.

'What?' Maxim asked.

'Someone saying The Surgeon will be here Friday at 6 p.m.'

Maxim's eyes widened. 'Who's in big shed then?'

Pearl received the news surprisingly calmly.

'Let me get this clear, Stanley,' she said carefully, accepting a cup of tea in her preferred bone china cup and saucer. She lit her cigarette and took a sip of her tea. 'You were at the Manor having a drink and you overheard a man say he was a surgeon, and he has just come from Liverpool?'

'And that he dealt with traumatic injuries,' Stanley added.

'Right…'

Stanley nodded. 'Just before that I'd had a call saying the message had been received and The Surgeon was on his way.'

Pearl took a delicate drag of her cigarette. 'And you put two and two together, Stanley.'

'It was a posh hotel, and I thought, what if he was actually here? Checking us out already? I just wanted to keep you safe, Pearl.'

'Very admirable, Stanley. Do we actually know who the man that you have is? Do we have a name?'

'Jamie Hunter. Whoever he is, he's scum. Total scum,' Stanley said firmly.

Pearl frowned. 'Why do you say that?'

'I found cherry meth on him. Four nice, neat little bottles. He was obviously gonna use it on someone.'

Pearl raised an eyebrow. 'A serial date rapist?'

278

'Seems so,' Stanley said grimly.

Pearl pursed her lips. 'If he's that sort of man, then well done, Stanley. You know how I feel about men that do things like that to women. I don't care who it is, there's no reason for him to have that unless he is going to use it. Let me discuss whether we dispose of him with Mickey. I'd like it to be something painful to teach him a lesson. Perhaps I'll let Maxim have some fun.' She smiled at Stanley. 'Well done, Stanley darling.'

Stanley basked in Pearl's praise.

'I'll have the other vials, please, can't be letting that on the loose. Now, we think the real surgeon's name is Nathan White, don't we? But we can't be too careful, you may well in fact have the right surgeon. So, we'll hold off doing anything until someone turns up at 6 p.m. Friday. Let's set up a meet at Luigi's. Let's hire the whole restaurant, and make sure we fill it with friends. Yes?'

'Yes, Pearl. Oh, and he's gluten free.'

Pearl grinned mischievously. 'I'm sure we can create something special for him. I will speak to Luigi.' Pearl finished her cigarette. 'Text them the address. Agree no hardware, but between you and me, our friends in the restaurant will carry. I would like my usual table. OK?'

She stood, smoothing down her dress and kissed Stanley on the cheek.

'I'm sorry I shouted at you, Stanley. You've done very well. Now I must help Mickey get organised, and call Jimmy. Mickey's taking his trip to Liverpool just in time for the Surgeon's trip here.'

'OK, Pearl. Sorry if I messed up.'

Pearl looked at Stanley. 'I know you do it to keep me safe,' she said quietly, laying her small hand on his huge face. 'I'll always look after you, Stanley. You know that. You're my family.'

Stanley swallowed the huge lump in his throat and nodded. He left the room walking quickly, so Pearl wouldn't see the tears in his eyes.

* * *

The next morning Steve put a call into the manager at The Bay Manor, who was more than a little puzzled. Jamie had been drinking in the bar, gone out to his car and not returned, leaving a bar tab unsigned and a glass of Merlot untouched. The manager had checked his room and his bed had not been slept in.

'Maybe he got lucky,' Steve said.

'He's booked in and paid up until the day after tomorrow, so I'll hold the room until then.'

'Keep me posted if he turns up?' Steve had asked.

'Will do. Happy Christmas.'

'You too.'

Steve passed on the information to Foxy who had been equally puzzled.

'Something you're not telling me?' Steve persisted.

'Absolutely nothing.'

'Scouts honour? Seriously, mate, have you done a black ops on me?'

'Absolutely not.'

'Hmm. Carla's phone still off?'

'Yup.'

'OK. I'll keep you posted.'

CHAPTER 26

After Christmas, business resumed for the Camorra. While Pearl waited in Castleby for her meeting with The Surgeon, Mickey went to Liverpool for a meeting of his own. Once again, Jimmy had driven the speedboat and this time stayed in the marina with it.

Mickey had hired the entire restaurant and called on Alexy's contacts to make sure no one saw, heard, or said anything. On his arrival, Mickey selected a table and settled down with Alexy, ordering sparkling water for them all. Maxim was on the next table watching silently.

A few minutes after the prearranged time, the restaurant door opened and a very short, dark-haired man swaggered in with two larger men in tow. The small man stood in front of Mickey.

'You Mickey Camorra?' he said in a thick Liverpudlian accent.

Mickey stood, towering over the man. 'I am. You must be Freddy Castro.'

The small man puffed out his chest, and made a performance of pulling out a chair and sitting down. He clicked his fingers and shouted to the waiter.

'Scotch. Rocks. Now.'

The waiter raised an eyebrow. Freddy flashed his large gaudy diamond studded Rolex, looking at the time.

'I'm a very busy man. I think you'll find my reputation precedes me. My contacts tell me you want to have a chat with me. What's so important for a Friday lunchtime?'

Mickey regarded the man with cold eyes. This small man was everything that he hated. Wannabe gangsters who had no respect, and certainly no class or taste, who thought they were hard men. In Mickey's view, this guy had short man syndrome in spades. At the lack of chat from him, Freddy frowned at Mickey.

'So come on,' he said impatiently. 'Let's talk then.'

Mickey glowered at Freddy, his bright blue eyes cold, weighing him up.

Freddy leant forward. 'Cat got your tongue, eh?' He laughed nervously and looked around the restaurant, his eyes settling on Alexy. 'Does this bloke not talk then?' he asked, pointing at Mickey. Leaning forwards, he clicked his fingers in Mickey's face.

'Hello? Anyone at home?'

Alexy inhaled sharply and looked at Mickey. Mickey studied Freddy and then with an imperceptible nod, whipped out a handgun and shot Freddy through the forehead at the same time as Alexy and Maxim shot each of Freddy's associates.

'Jumped up little fucking prick,' Mickey said. 'I'm not working with that.'

He turned to Alexy. 'Set up what we agreed. One hour. Here. Maxim, there'll be a flash tasteless motor out there. Find the keys and put the boys in it would you? Then I think we'll have some lunch.' He beckoned the waiter over.

'Sorry about that.' He gestured to the three dead men and said in a conversational tone, 'You know, I can't stand it when people are rude to waiters. It's so unnecessary. My colleague won't be needing that Scotch now. We'll have some lunch menus though, please?'

'Certainly, sir,' the waiter said nervously.

Alexy caught his arm as he passed by and gave him a roll of bank notes.

'For your trouble,' he said quietly. 'We are friends now, yes?'

'Thank you, y-yes,' the waiter stammered. 'We… we have a loading bay around the corner, if that will help with…' He gestured to the dead men. 'And they were in that souped up white Mercedes jeep parked over the road.'

'Perfect,' Maxim said, looking in the pockets of each of the thugs. He retrieved a set of keys and headed out of the restaurant.

Alexy bent down and hefted the larger of the three men onto his shoulder before following the waiter out of the main restaurant.

Ten minutes later, all three bodies had been put in the Mercedes jeep. Maxim covered them with a blanket he'd found in the boot. He parked the car in a dark corner of a multistorey; wiped it down and left it to rot.

Returning to the restaurant, he quietly thanked the waiter who had been frantically clearing up the extensive blood splatter from the nearby tables and was hastily changing tablecloths. The three ordered lunch and waited for the next meeting.

* * *

Two days off for Christmas was enough for Steve. He had been catching up on paperwork and grumpily chased the numerous things he was sick of chasing. Jonesey appeared, complete with two coffees and a large box of shortbread.

'How can you even bear to eat?' Steve groaned, sick of the sight of food.

'Whaaat?' said Jonesey. 'Never.' He took a huge mouthful of shortbread. 'I love Christmas. Shortbread, stollen and mince pies for breakfast.'

'Ugh.' Steve's computer pinged, alerting him to the arrival of an email. He clicked on the link. 'Finally,' he said grumpily.

Together they watched the grainy black-and-white images on the CCTV from the pet shop car park.

'I can't see shit,' Jonesey moaned, peering at the screen. 'I think we're looking in that corner.'

'Scroll through to just before the time,' Steve said. 'Can you not get my mouse all sticky while you're doing it though?'

'There,' Jonesey said with a mouthful of shortbread. 'That's the corner of a car. What is that?'

'Is that the corner of a Peugeot?'

'Maybe.'

'Let's play the footage from the front and we'll see if it came past the garage.'

'We would have seen it surely?'

Steve leant forward to watch as the footage from the front of the garage was replayed. They watched Cassie pull in and then played it for another few minutes seeing a few more cars pass by the garage.

'There.' Jonesey pointed with a sugary finger. 'That's a Peugeot. Bet you that's a match for the one round the back. What colour is that?'

'White? Silver, maybe? Can we get a registration?' Steve said, peering at the screen. 'Can you enlarge that?'

Jonesey managed to enlarge the image and they made out a partial number plate.

'Open the CCTV from the gallery. See if that shows anything.'

They both watched the footage.

'Wrong angle.'

'Let's run it. Get Warren on it and say I need it ASAP.'

Jonesey was out of the office door before Steve had finished the sentence. He picked up the phone and rang the garage again, insisting that the footage from the rear of the garage was sent within the next ten minutes or he would be getting a warrant for it.

Encouragingly, after a few minutes his computer pinged and the file of the CCTV from the rear of the garage arrived.

As mentioned by Jonesey, the door to the back of the garage was ajar. Steve scrolled forwards to the timeframe for when Cassie's car arrived on the forecourt, sat back and waited.

'Bingo,' he said, watching a Peugeot creep into the car park and park next to a row of bins.

Steve played the footage five times and still couldn't see the whole number plate or the occupant clearly. Jonesey walked in grinning and waving a piece of paper.

'She's definitely playing hard to get,' he said, plonking himself down. 'At Maggie's party, she kept talking to that Sebastian bloke all night, I didn't get a bloody look in.'

'He's a good-looking bloke,' Steve said absently.

'What am I? Chopped liver?' Jonesey said grumpily. 'He's way too old for her anyway.'

'Perhaps she was attracted to someone who's more interested in her rather than the buffet table.'

'It was a good spread,' Jonesey said indignantly. 'I always appreciate a good buffet. Anyway, see anything?'

'Fuck all,' said Steve. 'I think this bloke knows the cameras are there, keeps his face covered the whole time. I can't decide whether that's a passenger or just a shadow. What do you see?'

Jonesey peered at the screen.

'Could be a shadow, could be a passenger.'

'Registration?'

'Warren narrowed it down to about twenty something using this partial plate.'

'OK. Names, addresses, previous and then we'll review if we can find any links.'

'OK.'

'Get moving then.'

'Now?'

Steve rolled his eyes. 'Of course now.'

'Well, it's tea break.'

'Jonesey, I will kick your arse…'

'I'm going!' Jonesey said, running out the door hastily.

Steve grumpily chased the analyst dealing with the phone data, who reluctantly sent over what they had, but stressed they were still waiting for more to come in.

Steve scrolled through it. Cassie's phone had been busy. Texts sent and received during the night before she died, right through to the early hours. A number of calls taken and made on the day she died. Plus a call was received around the time Cassie was at the petrol station. He noted no activity after the time of the accident.

He went back to the CCTV and noted the time Cassie was at the petrol station and then cross-checked it with the garage's own CCTV; the time period matched.

He checked Bree's phone. Very busy up until the day of Cassie's accident where it seemed to go quiet at 4.54 p.m. and then there was a flurry of texts at 5.05 a.m.

Steve looked at the location data for the phones. At the time of the accident, Cassie and Tabatha's phone showed them exactly where he would expect them to be, in the vicinity of the accident. Sebastian's phone showed his at his London home. Bree's phone showed her listed London address up until 4.54 p.m. and then nothing.

Steve saw the presence of two more phones in the vicinity of the accident when it occurred. One of which had called 999. He asked for mapping analysis of the phone use. He listened to the 999 calls repeatedly and still could not conclude anything.

That done, Steve decided he needed to try and find out more about the mysterious Rusty, plus he wanted to check in on Tabatha.

Steve bumped into Tabatha as he was strolling down the high street. She had Jack on the lead and was carrying a bag from the bakery.

'Hello, Tabatha,' he said pleasantly. 'How are you? I was just coming to see if you'd remembered anything else from the other night.'

Tabatha smiled. 'I'm OK. Aunty Bree has been fussing around me something rotten, so I had to escape. I did think of something though.'

Steve dragged his notepad out. 'Oh?'

'He smelt funny.'

'Smelt funny?'

'Yeah. Like woodsmoke, sweat and washing that's been left in the machine too long.' She rolled her eyes. 'Dad's worst habit.'

'OK.' Steve wrote it down. 'Anything else?'

'Nope. Have you asked Jude?'

He shook his head. 'I will though. Thanks. Call me if you remember anything else.'

'OK. Bye.'

Steve walked quickly down the road, he had seen Teddy disappearing around the corner towards Maggie's and he wanted to catch him. Steve walked around the back to find Teddy planting up some pots.

'Hey, Teddy. How was your Christmas?'

Teddy looked nervous. 'Fine, thank you, Mr Steve.'

'Did you go home?' Steve asked gently.

'I was at the council depot,' Teddy said, his eyes filled with tears. 'Please don't tell Dad or put me in prison.'

'I won't do either of those things, Teddy,' Steve said quietly. 'Did you not have a Christmas; did you not go home?'

Teddy shook his head fiercely. 'No. Me and Danny had a Christmas in the shelter overlooking the harbour on Christmas Eve. He bought me a donut and some films for my camera.'

'Wow. Cool present. Could you not have gone to Danny's?'

He shook his head. 'If Dad had found out he would have hurt Anna and Danny and I don't want that.'

'Right.'

'I gave Danny a picture of him, Anna and Gavin. I took it when they were on the beach one day. They didn't know I was there.'

'Did he like it?'

'Very much. He cried,' Teddy said.

'Sometimes tears are good.'

'That's what he said. Good tears, Teddy. These are good tears.' He sighed. 'I don't think I've ever cried good tears.'

'Maybe one day,' Steve said.

'Maybe one day,' echoed Teddy.

'Have you seen your father since the other day?'

'When he broke my mug?'

'Yes.'

'No. Barry said he'd come looking for me.'

'Have you seen Rusty?'

Teddy shook his head. 'No. I've not seen him for ages. Barry said Dad was looking for Rusty too.'

'No ideas where he would be?'

Teddy shook his head. 'No.'

'Does he have any tattoos?'

'I don't know, Mr Steve. I don't see him that much.'

'OK, I'll keep an eye out. Promise to tell me if you see Rusty?'

'Promise, Mr Steve.'

Steve crossed the road and poked his head into the climbing centre. Foxy was behind the counter finishing up with a customer.

'Has he turned up?' Foxy asked.

Steve shook his head. 'Haven't heard a dicky bird. The hotel rang to say he'd not been back and that they've packed up his stuff and let his room.'

'Weird. To come and then vanish.'

'Hmm. You're absolutely sure you didn't have anything to do with it?'

'Mate, come on,' Foxy said, exasperated.

'He'll turn up,' Steve said. 'Blokes like him always do.'

'Hopefully not too soon,' Foxy said grimly.

'Carla OK?'

'Fine. Enjoying the break.'

'I'll let you know if I hear anything.'

'Good man.'

Steve's phone rang as he walked back to the station.

'Hello, Pearl,' he said. 'How are you?'

'I'm very well, thank you, Steve, and you?'

'Very good. Very pleased to see no signs of any collateral damage yet.'

'Well, let's not relax just yet,' she said with an amused tone. 'I just wanted to make you aware that negotiations are happening today and this evening, so some of that collateral damage may well appear at some point.'

'Will you be OK?'

'I'm sure everything will be fine.'

'I don't want you in danger, Pearl.'

'Lovely of you to worry, darling,' she said, chuckling. 'I'm having discussions with Mr White this evening in Luigi's at 6 p.m. But I have a restaurant full of friends, so I won't be in any danger.'

'Are you sure, Pearl? I'm happy to be there in the background.'

'You are too sweet, but I'll be fine,' she insisted.

'Where's Mickey?'

'He's making new friends in Liverpool, there is a little collateral damage there but that's someone else's problem, isn't it? Besides, Mickey said he was genuinely doing everyone a service.'

'Will you call me later to tell me how it went?'

'Of course. You have a good evening now.'

'Stay safe, Pearl.'

* * *

Darkness had settled, and the night was cold but clear. Pearl climbed out of the car gracefully, helped by Stanley, and they both walked into Luigi's restaurant. Luigi kissed her warmly on both cheeks and ushered her reverently to her preferred table. Pearl settled herself and ordered a chilled Chardonnay and some sparkling water. Stanley sat on the table a few feet away. She looked at her watch. It was 6.05 p.m. and Pearl was a stickler for punctuality.

She looked out of the window when she heard the sound of a powerful car and watched as an attractive man got out. Pearl raised an eyebrow. An Aston Martin. Not the flash white drug dealers' Range Rover she had expected. The restaurant door opened and a handsome man about the same age as Pearl walked in. He was average height, nicely dressed in a suit, with salt and pepper curly hair, cut short at the sides. Pearl noted that the suit looked impeccably tailored, rather than off the shelf.

He approached Luigi and spoke quietly, and Luigi ushered him over to Pearl's table.

'You must be Pearl.' He stopped politely by the table. Pearl offered a hand.

'I'm charmed,' he said, shaking her hand gently, eyeing her with interest.

'Please.' Pearl gestured to the place opposite her. 'Do you have any colleagues with you? They're welcome to come in for dinner.'

He shook his head and settled himself. 'No colleagues.'

'Some people might call that brave.'

He shrugged. 'I would question why I need help when I'm here for a business discussion over dinner.'

Pearl inclined her head. 'Perhaps we move in different circles, Mr White. Do you prefer to be called Mr White or The Surgeon?' Pearl asked, watching as he unrolled his napkin and arranged it fastidiously on his lap.

'Nathan is fine,' he said, smiling. 'I assume it's acceptable to call you Pearl?'

'It is. I'm pleased to meet you, Nathan. Thank you for coming. The food is quite excellent here I think you'll find.'

Luigi approached and asked Nathan for a drink order.

'Just sparkling water, please.'

'Nothing else?' Pearl enquired. 'Luigi has quite the impressive wine cellar.'

'Nothing else,' said Nathan. 'Are we waiting for Mr Camorra?'

'Sadly not,' Pearl said. 'Mr Camorra is dealing with some business elsewhere; he's been delayed, I'm afraid. Are you happy to discuss business with me?'

Nathan smiled charmingly. 'Of course. I am delighted to hear that I have a beautiful lady all to myself for the evening.'

'You flatter me, Mr White.'

'Nathan, please.'

'Let's order. I have worked up quite the appetite today, Nathan.' She called over to Luigi. 'Perhaps you'd like to come and tell us about the specials tonight, Luigi?'

The two ordered their meals and Pearl picked up her wine. 'Let's make a toast to new friends,' she said, smiling.

In Liverpool, Mickey held up his glass. 'Ross, let's make a toast to new ventures together,' he said.

Ross Bishop picked up his glass and raised it. 'Looking forward to it,' he said.

Ross was a born and bred Liverpudlian. For years he had been treated like shit by Freddy Castro while he did all the work and Freddy took the credit. Ross was delighted to hear that Freddy no longer had a pulse.

Ross was a talented thief and excellent curator of low lifes who he could recruit to sell drugs or run errands. He combined the two over the years to make him indispensable, while also making Freddy look good. Mickey Camorra had offered him the opportunity to run the whole operation with his support and Ross knew a good deal when he was presented with one. He knew he needed help, and he needed a solid reputation of utter ruthlessness to stop others muscling in. Mickey Camorra certainly provided that: his reputation was legendary.

Mickey had agreed to stand back when the time came, providing there was no creep into Mickey's activities or areas, and he maintained receipt of his agreed cut.

Ross was relieved. He had been summoned to a meeting where he had assumed certain death would occur. Instead, he found he had been given the keys to the kingdom.

'So where is Freddy?' he ventured.

'Dead. In boot of car. In car park,' Alexy said nonchalantly.

'And what about The Surgeon?'

'He's lucky enough to be having dinner with my wife,' Mickey said.

Ross widened his eyes. 'Right... but...'

'Don't you worry about that. I think he'll get to know my wife and will want to stay.'

Ross pulled a face. 'I wouldn't trust him with my wife. He's a good-looking bloke with a lot of class.'

Mickey's eyes narrowed. 'You saying I'm none of those things?'

Ross swallowed. 'Nope… I didn't mean… I…'

'Relax. I'm fucking with you.'

Ross looked relieved. 'But he's definitely not coming back here?'

Alexy patted his arm. 'Relax, my friend. Enough business. It will all work out in wash. Now, who is for vodka?'

* * *

Pearl delicately finished her starter and took a sip of wine.

'You were a doctor once? Did I hear that correctly? A surgeon?'

'You are well informed. Yes, I was.'

'What happened? It's a noble profession.'

'I lost a patient who meant a lot to me. I had difficulty coping, so I turned to drugs.' He gave a half laugh. 'Can't have a surgeon tripping out while patients are dying on the table, can we? I was struck off and realised there was so much more money to be made in selling drugs, particularly to those in the medical profession.'

'So you had a conscience once, and then lost it for money?'

'If that's how you view it. From what I hear, your organisation has very little conscience at all.'

'Oh, I think that's a little harsh. We have a conscience. We only sell good quality products. We won't sell rubbish. We only punish people who deserve it. I like to call that being fair and just.'

'I think we'll have to agree to disagree,' Nathan murmured.

'From what I hear, Mr White, your product is poor. We have standards that we insist are maintained.'

'I don't agree. That eats into profits.'

Pearl sat back in her chair, picking up her wineglass.

'I very much see it as a civic duty to provide good quality product. Drugs are everywhere. People are deluding themselves if they think otherwise. I hear these ridiculous people who say there are no drugs in their town. They are quite stupid. Our organisation provides a service to meet that need, and we pride ourselves in supplying the best possible service. I will not be part of a service that is poor quality.'

'That mindset affects profits.'

'But has other more significant benefits.'

Nathan sipped his water and inclined his head to the waiter who had removed his plate.

'Will you share what those benefits are?'

'Not this early on in our discussions,' Pearl said. 'So, Nathan, are you married? A family?'

'I like to keep my private life private.'

'I'm just asking out of interest. I find it hard to picture what sort of woman,' she stopped herself and added as an afterthought, 'or man, would be your type. Whether you'd feel the need to fan the flames of your ego with a younger "model" or whether you would prefer a match nearer your own age,' she mused, watching him. 'These things interest me. Your car told me a lot about you.'

Nathan watched Pearl with amusement.

'Pearl, are you flirting with me?'

'Of course not, Nathan, I'm just nosey by nature.'

'What did my car tell you about me then?'

'That you like tradition, quality… classic things.'

'Perhaps I just like what they represent.' Nathan nodded thanks to the waiter who delivered his main course.

'Thank you,' Pearl said to the waiter who set down her plate and topped up their water glasses.

Pearl watched him, like a cat stalking its prey.

'I think you do like what things like that represent. I don't think you came from money. I think you had an average upbringing, middle-class I'd say. Not private school, but the boy was too bright for the local comprehensive, but not bright enough back then for the local grammar. You like women, but not enough to share yourself. *All* of yourself. So you choose your women based on how you feel at the time. It's always short lived. You don't want a girlfriend or a wife; you just require a willing body.' She sipped her wine. 'How am I doing so far?'

'Oh, please carry on,' he said, eating his dinner, a hint of a smile on his lips.

'I think you enjoyed being a surgeon. The adoration and god complex. The power. I think you enjoyed the money, but perhaps it wasn't quite enough. You drive an Aston Martin; your suits are hand tailored in Savile Row and you wear an extremely rare Patek Philippe watch. You like the good things in life. But you like them to be understated.' She took a delicate mouthful of food and studied him. 'But it's not enough, is it? You want more. Now, is it more money? More power? I don't think you're doing this for the celebrity.'

She ate some more and sipped her wine.

'So which is it, Nathan?'

'You have surprised me, Pearl,' Nathan said, smiling. 'I wasn't expecting that. It's very rare people surprise me.'

Pearl's eyes sparkled. 'How have I surprised you?'

Nathan finished his dinner and leant back in his chair.

'Your assessment of me is quite accurate. Yes, middle-class parents. Average education. I loved the power of medicine, but I wanted more. More money, more power. I won't apologise for any of that. But what I want to know is, how the girl born in the East End knows a rare Patek Philippe when she sees one? *That* surprised me.'

'I like to be unpredictable. May I see it?' she enquired, holding her hand out.

Nathan undid his wristwatch and handed it over. Pearl studied it closely, holding it reverently.

'Utterly beautiful. Incredibly rare... well, unique. The aviator prototype in chromed nickel, with splittable centre seconds with Guillaume balance and black hour angle dial calibrated for 360°,' she breathed. 'Absolutely beautiful. Pre-owned obviously, and manufactured in... approximately 1936, I'd say, I think it is only one of a few with the splittable centre seconds. I would guess this was bought at auction, probably Christie's, in the region of about £1.5 million pounds. Do you know why it's this large?' She stroked it lovingly.

Nathan shook his head.

'It's because the pilots wore them outside of their flight jackets and needed to see them, hence the face being this size. I would be afraid to wear it, it's so rare.'

Nathan raised an eyebrow. 'You're the unique one, Pearl. There were two made I think, but I could be wrong. I wear it because I like it and it's a watch. Doesn't matter about the cost. So, I repeat the question. How do you know so much about watches?'

Pearl passed it back carefully. 'Another life in the Burlington Arcade and Bond Street.' She smiled. 'Happy days, and I paid attention. It's more of a hobby now.'

The waiter came and removed their plates, asking quietly if they would like a dessert menu. Pearl declined, but ordered a double espresso and Nathan requested the same.

Pearl leant her elbows on the table.

'So, Nathan. To business. Out of interest, why here? What made you want to send your scouts to our area. You know who we are. Why not come and have a gentlemanly discussion first to test the water?'

Nathan twirled his water glass. 'I think the question should be, why not here? With the greatest respect, you don't factor into it at all. Your reputation doesn't matter to me. I am not at all bothered or intimidated by it. In fact, these are very small hurdles to be overcome for me, which can be done very quickly and easily.'

Pearl arched an eyebrow and Nathan chuckled.

'Pearl, I find you utterly gorgeous, charming and bright. I would have liked to meet you under different circumstances and get to know you. I wanted to come here tonight to meet you and to see for myself who is behind the Camorra reputation. I realise I have underestimated you, but that doesn't change anything. I will still be taking over all of your businesses with fairly immediate effect.' He broke off as the waiter delivered their espressos. 'So the question is, will you go quietly or will we have to force you to go, and where you're concerned I am very reluctant to make things unpleasant.'

'But you are prepared to make things unpleasant?'

'Absolutely.'

'Interesting. You're convinced it'll be that easy?'

Nathan shrugged. 'Of course. The thing is, it's not personal. It's business. I like you very much, but I can't let that affect my plans to control the coast from Liverpool down to the very tip of Cornwall.'

'You seem confident you'll succeed.'

'I've not failed so far. Nothing and nobody gets in my way. Yours is an insignificant organisation that can be easily crushed.'

'Perhaps you've not failed because you've just not met your match,' she said lightly.

Nathan's lips twitched. 'Perhaps I haven't. But the plans are in place, and I won't be swayed by petty distractions.'

'What do you consider to be a petty distraction?'

'Well, you are certainly a distraction, for starters,' Nathan said, looking Pearl in the eye. 'But petty distractions would be trying to negotiate a price for your business, when in all honesty, I'm just going to take it. All of it. Every single thing.'

Pearl mused for a moment. 'I see. You do have quite the ambition. Out of interest when do you expect to execute your plan?'

'Fairly soon. I know I'm stealing a line from a film, but resistance really is futile.'

Pearl laughed delightedly. 'A Patek Philippe wearer *and* a trekkie! I think you are the one who is quite unique, Mr White.'

'Ah. Now that's sad. Are we back to me being Mr White?'

'I think it's only fair now the battle lines have been drawn.'

Nathan drank his espresso in one gulp and placed his cup down carefully. He dabbed the corners of his mouth with his napkin.

'Pearl, I have thoroughly enjoyed my evening. Much more than I ever expected to. I mean that genuinely. So I've made a decision where you're concerned.'

'And what might that be?' Pearl sipped her coffee delicately.

'That you come on the journey with me. You intrigue me. I think I'd like to have you along for the ride.'

Pearl hid a smile. 'Now I think you are flirting with me. It's a flattering offer, but I don't think Mr Camorra will be willing to let me go. You know, in some small way, Mr White, I quite admire your arrogance to even consider that I might be interested. And now, I think it's time for you to go. Dinner is on me.'

Nathan considered her for a moment and then stood. He bent to kiss Pearl's cheek.

'Thank you. You are one of a kind, Pearl. It's been an absolute pleasure. If you change your mind, here's my private number.' He dropped an embossed card on the table.

'I'm sorry it had to end this way,' he said.

Pearl smiled at him. 'Oh, so am I, Mr White. So am I.'

CHAPTER 27

In Liverpool, Mickey had instructed Ross to get rid of Ringo and Paul. He had no need for them and wanted them gone. Ross promised faithfully he would oblige.

Mickey faced him with his cold stare. 'I'm trusting you, but if I believe that the trust has been broken, you will die. We can make each other a lot of money. Are we clear?'

'Crystal.'

'Right, let's start spreading word there's a new king in town.' Mickey clapped him on the back. 'I'll be back in a few days. See how you are. See whether we need to retire anyone else. OK?'

'OK, boss.'

Jimmy had been on the boat all day. He had taken himself off quickly to buy food, and he was enjoying the luxury of the boat while stuffing his face and watching TV. Not bad work for ten grand, he marvelled.

His phone rang, making him jump. It was Alexy.

'Put engine on. We are to leave soon,' Alexy instructed.

'OK,' said Jimmy, starting the engines. He cleared up his rubbish and watched a taxi come down into the marina and stop. Alexy, Maxim and Mickey got out and strode quickly towards the boat.

'Home, Jimmy,' Mickey said.

Pearl stayed in the restaurant and watched Nathan leave. As he stepped out of the restaurant, he staggered slightly en route to his car. She smiled to herself. Much as she loathed it, the cherry meth that Stanley had procured from the other surgeon was certainly effective. She almost laughed out loud, Pearl Camorra using a date rape drug.

She watched as Nathan managed to get into his car and then slumped forward onto the wheel. Luigi stood next to Pearl and looked out of the window.

'Job done, Mrs Camorra,' he said. 'I hope you enjoyed your dinner.'

'It was as wonderful as ever, Luigi,' she said. 'Quite the last supper for my friend.' She stood gracefully and raised her voice. 'Many thanks, everybody, you are good friends to us. Dinner is on me.'

There was a ripple of murmurs of thanks and Luigi brought Pearl's coat over.

'Thank you, darling,' she said, shrugging into it. 'You really are a good friend.' She pecked him on the cheek and left, followed by Stanley.

Pearl's car arrived driven by one of their oldest serving men, Tommy. Stanley lumbered over to the car where Nathan was out cold behind the wheel and opened the door. Pearl strolled over and looked at him.

'Shame really,' she said. 'Tommy, take him to the farm. Mickey will want to see him before we dispose of him. I want him stripped and the car gone ASAP, in case anyone's tracking him.'

Tommy nodded. He and Stanley moved Nathan to the passenger seat.

'One minute,' Pearl said, leaning in. Carefully she lifted his wrist and gently undid the watch. 'I'll see it goes to a good home,' she murmured, stepping backwards and nodding to Tommy. 'Be careful, Tommy. I'll get Stanley to meet you there when we've run an errand and he's dropped me off.'

Pearl climbed into her car and turned to Stanley, who was sitting behind the wheel.

'I want to pay a visit to the other guy.'

'Date rape guy?'

'The very one.'

* * *

Steve had worked late and then taken a trip up to The Bay Manor Hotel to see whether Jamie Hunter had reappeared. He was also worried about Pearl. He looked at his watch, it was nearly nine and he'd not had a call from her yet. He estimated that she couldn't still be having dinner.

As he drove up the drive, his car was almost hit by a large Maserati taking up the whole road. He wrenched the wheel to the left and stood on the brakes, with the other car seemingly oblivious, apart from an angry burst on the horn.

Wandering into the bar area he noticed with interest the excellent view of Pearl and Mickey's house.

'Steve, nice to see you.' A woman in a smart suit appeared at his elbow. 'Late to be working, isn't it?'

'You know me, never off the clock, Tina,' he said. 'Any news on our friend Jamie Hunter?'

She shook her head. 'Nothing. Can't understand it. Left an overnight bag and everything.'

'Can I have a look?' Steve asked.

'Sure, it's in my office.' As she led him through the foyer, the receptionist called her over. 'Go in, Steve, I'll catch you up.'

Steve lifted the overnight bag onto Tina's desk and unpacked it. All the usual things you would expect for a few days away. He noted that the man had expensive taste in clothes. He emptied the bag and out of habit felt around in the lining and found the outline of a small box.

He dug round a little more and found a hidden zip which exposed a small black leather case with a zip on three sides. Steve opened it and found a collection of small vials.

'You fucker,' Steve said to himself, pocketing the case. If Jamie came back, he could have the overnight bag, but not the stash.

'Anything?' Tina asked from the doorway.

'Nah. Nothing important apart from the fact that he likes his designer brands. You been busy?'

Tina rolled her eyes. 'I've had a couple staying from Liverpool. Well, a couple who want separate rooms but look like they're together? Absolute pain in the arse. Nothing was right, everything was wrong. In and out at all different times. She's just gone out, you must have passed her. All very odd.'

'When do they leave?'

'Tomorrow, I think. I'll be happily waving them off at the door.'

'Hoping they won't return?'

'Exactly. Got time for a quick drink? I was just gonna grab an espresso?'

'Don't mind if I do.'

Tina busied herself at the coffee machine in the bar and Steve wandered over to the window to look at the view.

'Stunning, isn't it?' Tina said, passing him the coffee.

'It is.'

'I love that house,' Tina said. 'I bet it's amazing inside.'

A guest interrupted them, asking Tina for something and she excused herself. Steve looked at the Camorra house, he had a good view from this angle. His eyes tracked the property from the cedarwood gates and parking area, down to where the huge manicured lawn stopped and the large hedge on the narrow lane was.

A flash of light in the darkness caught his eye and he leant forward to get a better look. He saw it again. A small light bobbing at the bottom of the garden. Steve frowned and watched as the light zigzagged its way up the garden and then went off. Steve strained to see. The outside lights to the house weren't on; that probably meant Pearl wasn't home yet. He knew Mickey was in Liverpool. Who the hell was this? It certainly wasn't a gardener at this hour.

Steve stepped out onto the outside balcony, his eyes adjusting even more, and he looked at where he had first seen the light. In the darkness he was sure he could make out a large car at the boundary fence.

Suddenly worried, Steve went back inside.

'Tina,' he said as he passed by her. 'If he turns up again, call me. Thanks for the coffee.'

Steve climbed into his car and sped down the drive.

* * *

Pearl and Stanley arrived at the barn where they were keeping Jamie Hunter. Stanley insisted that Pearl enter after him in case there was any danger. Stanley unlocked the door, pushed it open and stood back for a moment. Years of experience taught him to stand aside and wait

303

for crazed prisoners to rush the door, if they had managed to get themselves free.

Reassured that this wasn't going to be the case today, Stanley flicked on the lights and walked towards where he had left Jamie tied to a chair.

He stopped in his tracks and put a hand out to stop Pearl.

'Pearl, I don't want you to see this.'

'Oh, Stanley,' Pearl said, impatiently pushing him aside. 'Don't be ridiculous. I want to look into the face of a man who likes to drug women and then probably rape them.' She walked past Stanley's bulk and then stopped.

'Oh dear,' she said, stepping carefully over a pile of vomit on the floor in her high black stiletto Louboutin's. 'I wonder what happened here?' She moved closer to Jamie and peered at his face. She turned to Stanley. 'Is he dead?'

Stanley moved closer to Jamie and checked his neck for a pulse. He nodded.

'Oh dear,' Pearl sighed. 'Maxim will be so terribly disappointed. I had promised him some fun with him.' She tilted her head and looked at Jamie, dead in the chair with a face so swollen that both eyes had shut. 'What do you think it was?'

Stanley had seen this before with druggies. 'I reckon he was allergic to it, or it was a bad mix,' he said.

'Oh well,' Pearl said. 'One less job to do then!'

'Yes, Pearl. Shall I take him to the pig farm?'

Pearl chewed her lip thoughtfully.

'No. I want him found. I want the drugs found on him too. Make sure the leftover vials are in his pockets. I want the papers to know what this scum was. He might have been a surgeon, but I'd lay money that he was a sexual predator.' She walked around the dead body. 'I want him found somewhere public, please.'

He nodded. 'I'll do it when I've dropped you off.'

Pearl shook her head. 'No, get one of the others to do it. Somewhere he'll be found easily; perhaps dump him in the water. Although I'm loathed to waste the time of the lovely fellows on the lifeboat if he drifts out to sea.'

'We'll dump him in the harbour,' Stanley said. 'Then he'll be found early. Let me take you home, Pearl.'

'Lovely. Well, it's certainly been quite the evening. We should call Tommy, check he's OK and our guest hasn't suffered the same fate.'

'I'll do it on the way home.'

'Thank you, Stanley.'

Stanley waited for the large cedarwood gates to open and pulled into the drive, parking near the entrance for Pearl. He opened her car door.

'Thank you, Stanley,' Pearl said. 'Go and get Tommy.'

'Do you want me to come in and check around?'

'I'm sure it's all fine. Tommy has our guest safely incapacitated; he just needs taking home. Off you go.'

'Night, Pearl.'

'Goodnight, Stanley.'

Pearl closed the door gently and walked through the dark house towards the kitchen. She helped herself to a bottle of wine, took two glasses and her cigarettes, and pulled open the large bifold doors next to the pool. She lit the gas fire pit, settled herself into a chair and wrapped a blanket around her. Slipping off her stilettos she placed them carefully next to her.

'Please don't crouch in the shadows like a common thief,' she called. 'I expect better than that. If you're going to visit me in my home, then we will do it graciously. Would you like a glass of wine?'

There was a rustle and a woman walked out of the shadows. She was a little shorter than Pearl and slight. She had shoulder length blonde curly hair and Pearl estimated she was in her thirties. She was wearing black jeans, boots and a black leather jacket. She carried a large hunting knife.

'I adore your outfit,' Pearl said. 'Did you purchase it especially for trying to break into my home, or is this the usual getup for you?'

The woman came and stood in front of her.

'What have you done with him?' she said through gritted teeth, brandishing the knife.

Pearl eyed the knife with disdain and ignored it. 'With whom?'

'Don't play games with me,' the woman said menacingly. 'Where is Nathan?'

Pearl poured her some wine and handed it over.

'Sit,' she said. 'I refuse to have a conversation with you standing over me like an overzealous traffic warden. We can be convivial.'

The woman didn't take the glass and Pearl carried on offering it.

'It *is* quite the excellent white,' she said.

Finally, the woman accepted the wine.

'Good,' Pearl murmured, carefully lighting a cigarette. She inhaled deeply.

'I miss not being able to smoke in restaurants,' she mused out loud. She took another drag, sipped her wine and regarded the woman closely.

'Now,' she said. 'This is being polite and convivial. I'm Pearl. It's very nice to meet you. And you are?'

'Becca,' the woman said shortly, the wine in one hand and the knife still in the other.

'And what is Nathan to you?'

'I work for Nathan. I'm his personal assistant.'

Pearl raised an eyebrow as she took another drag of her cigarette.

'I deduce by your demeanour that your relationship is slightly more than that.'

Becca refused to meet Pearl's eyes. 'I've worked for him for a long time,' she said defensively.

'You love him.'

Becca remained silent.

'Yet he doesn't love you.' Pearl said. 'Really, Becca, us women must hold on to a modicum of self-respect with these men. Nathan will never love anyone, he's just not wired that way. He's too arrogant, too self-centred.'

'You don't know him,' Becca accused.

'Oh, I think I got to know him well enough this evening. He's smart, completely devoid of any emotion and utterly ruthless.' Pearl took another drag of her cigarette, letting the smoke curl softly from her nose. 'He actually had the audacity to ask me to join him on his quest to take over the coastline from Liverpool to Cornwall.' She laughed. 'Can you imagine?'

'Don't be ridiculous,' Becca hissed. 'He only met with you because he enjoys seeing the whites of people's eyes before he ruins them. He gets a kick out of it.'

'Yet here we are,' said Pearl. 'You and me drinking wine in a convivial way, and Nathan is nowhere to be seen.'

'Where is he?'

'Somewhere safe.'

'Is he alive?'

'Not for much longer.'

'You can't do that.'

'I think you'll find I can,' said Pearl. 'Nathan made the mistake of underestimating us. I knew he would be here with at least one other person. But we actually expected more. The arrogance of the pair of you astounds me. I've been watching your clumsy attempts to climb over the back fence and make your way up the garden. Do you not think we have a state-of-the-art security system? The slightest thing gets sent to my phone. I've been watching you with some amusement.'

'How do you know there aren't more of us?' Becca sneered.

Pearl rolled her eyes. 'For the love of God, your arrogance. I know everything that goes on here. You say to me that Nathan came here to see the whites of our eyes before he killed us and took all that we had, yet we also took a little trip up to Liverpool. We thought we'd take everything *you* had.'

Becca's eyes widened.

'I think you'll find there's a new king in town,' Pearl said. 'Put there by us. Controlled by us. I suggest you look for work, you're out of a job.'

'Freddy will take over.'

'Freddy and his thugs are dead. You, my dear, are finished, as is Nathan.'

'You fucking bitch!' screamed Becca and launched herself at Pearl. Pearl grabbed one of her shoes and hit her hard in the face with it. Becca's own momentum drove the spike of the long heel deep through one eye and into her brain. Becca dropped like a stone. She slumped to the floor; the left side of her face obscured by Pearl's shoe as it hung out of her eye socket.

Pearl stood and looked down at Becca.

'And Mickey says Louboutins are a waste of money.' She chuckled. 'I beg to differ.'

Pearl picked up her phone. She watched the screen and then stepped lightly over Becca's prone form, going inside and returning with a beer, which she placed on the table. She made herself comfortable again, lit another cigarette and sipped her wine.

Steve was running up the steep hill at the bottom of Pearl's garden. He had managed to heave himself over the wide hedge. He fell into something prickly, which badly scratched his face and hands, and ripped his suit. He kept slipping on the wet grass. In the gloom he had seen Pearl sitting with someone outside who had launched themselves at her, but from this angle, Steve couldn't see Pearl anymore.

'Pearl!' he shouted breathlessly as he reached the top of the hill. 'Pearl!'

He reached the edge of the raised area and saw Pearl sitting calmly by the fire, smoking a cigarette. He looked over and saw the dead woman wearing a shoe on her face.

'For fuck's sake, Pearl!' he exploded, gasping as he rested his hands on his knees, bending over to get his breath. 'I thought she'd fucking killed you!'

Pearl smiled. 'Sit down and get your breath back, darling,' she said. 'I love how you appear to be so concerned for my welfare. Terribly gallant! I feel quite giddy.'

'Are you kidding?' Steve said between breaths. 'If Mickey comes home to find you hurt or dead, I'm fish food.'

'I've brought you out a beer.' Pearl flipped the top off. 'Calm yourself down.'

Steve grabbed the beer and stepped over the prone body of Becca.

'Who's your guest?'

'Oh? The intruder who tried to attack me?'

'If you like. Nice shoe.'

'A favourite of mine. She is the partner, lover, whatever to our Mr Nathan White.'

'And how was dinner with Mr White?'

'Very productive.'

'Where is Mr White now?'

'Resting.'

'Permanently?'

'I couldn't possibly say.'

'Any other collateral damage?'

'A little.'

'I don't want to know.'

Pearl flicked her cigarette into the flames. Steve took a grateful slug of his beer.

'I need to deal with your guest,' Steve said.

Pearl shook her head. 'No need, I can deal with it.'

'Absolutely not, Pearl. Stuff like this will lose me my job. You won't have anything to worry about. I was here, she broke in with intent to kill you. You fought back. I won't be prosecuting, nor will the CPS. You have it all on CCTV?'

'I do. Including your rather graceful entrance into my hawthorn bushes. Your face is very badly scratched, darling, it's a shame to ruin something so handsome.'

'Oh stop,' Steve said. 'Don't let Mickey hear you say that, I'll be dead by morning. I need to call it in. OK?'

'If you say so.'

Steve finished his beer and made the call. Before long, the beautiful house was bathed in the reflection of blue lights.

CHAPTER 28

Will was at work early. He had called into Maggie's for a bacon roll and a coffee and headed back along the quayside to his office. A heavy fog rested gently on the shoulders of the town, giving the place a slightly eerie feel in the dim early morning light.

Out of habit, Will glanced down into the harbour, nearly dropping his breakfast when he saw the body of a man floating face down, knocking gently against the wide stone steps that led up from the water to the quayside.

'Shit,' he muttered, putting his breakfast down and opening his office door to grab a long pole with a hook on it.

He snagged the back of the man's jacket, his back protesting, and hoisted him up the stone steps until he was completely out of the water.

Will only had to look at him to know he was dead. Mindful of evidence, he didn't touch him, but ran back to his office, grabbing a foil survival blanket which he shook out and then placed lightly over the body. He cordoned off the route and called the police.

'What happened to your face?' Will asked Steve, watching him lift the corner of the foil blanket.

'Fell into some prickly bushes chasing a suspect,' Steve said, looking at the man. 'I know who this is.'

'Who is it?'

'He's a surgeon. Been missing from the hotel up on the cliff for a few nights now.'

'Now you know why.'

Jonesey was peering over Steve's shoulder and shuddered. He sat on the quayside next to Will.

'What time did you find him?'

'About twenty-five minutes ago. I'd got coffee and a bacon roll from Maggie and then came here.'

Jonesey looked at the foil wrapped sandwich on the quayside. 'You not eating that then?'

Will shook his head. 'Nope. One look at that man's face put me off my breakfast.'

'I'll eat it,' Jonesey offered. He scowled at Steve when he tutted. 'What? I'm performing a civic duty here. Too much food waste around.'

'Help yourself,' Will said, standing up. 'I'll be in the office if you need me.'

Steve made a call which was answered on the first ring.

'Murph...'

'Whatever it is, the answer's no.'

'Floater in the harbour.'

'Hmm. Go on.'

'I know this bloke, he's a surgeon, been missing for a few days. Blown up like a balloon. He's on his way to you.'

'Good, I need something to break the monotony, flu season is so boring.'

'I'll be sure to be on the lookout for some interesting bodies to brighten up your days.'

'I would appreciate that. I suppose you want initial thoughts like yesterday?'

'Please.'

'And the moon on a bloody stick too no doubt,' muttered Murph.

'Stop moaning. Get busy.'

'Up yours.' Murph ended the call.

Steve sent Jonesey up to the hotel to collect Jamie's overnight bag.

The climbing centre wasn't open yet, so Steve jogged up the outside stairs to Foxy's flat above. He knocked on the door, and Solo started barking.

Foxy opened the door. 'Everything alright? Blimey, what happened to you?'

'Prickly bush. Carla here?'

Foxy called over his shoulder. 'Carla.'

Carla appeared rubbing her wet hair with a towel.

'Hey, Steve. Everything OK? Fancy some coffee?'

'Great, thanks. Small one, please.'

'What happened to your face?' she asked.

'I fell into a prickly bush,' he said, grumpy with everyone asking him. 'Anyway, I have some news. Not to be shared in any way with anyone until we go public. Understood?'

Carla and Foxy looked confused. 'Understood.'

Foxy handed him a coffee. 'Sounds serious.'

Steve sat down. 'Jamie Hunter was found dead this morning,' he said quietly.

'*What?*' Carla said in disbelief.

'He's been missing from the hotel for a few days and was found in the harbour this morning. They've just taken him away.'

'Jesus,' Foxy said, walking over to the window. 'Who found him?'

'Will. Put him off his breakfast,' Steve said dryly.

'I can't believe it,' Carla said, staring at Foxy. 'I just can't believe it.'

Steve looked at Foxy. 'I hate to do it, mate, but I have to ask. I need you to promise me you had nothing to do with it. Not Rudi or Mack either.'

Foxy looked Steve steadily in the eye. 'I had nothing to do with it. I swear. Besides it's not my style. If I'd done it, he wouldn't have been found. Ever.'

'Remind me never to cross you,' Steve said. He looked over at Carla who was sat staring into nothing. 'Carla, are you OK?'

'Yes. Just shocked. This changes everything,' she whispered.

Steve finished his coffee. 'I need to go. This is between us, right? I'll call Penny, let her know.'

'Let me know if you can, you know... how he died.'

'If I can,' he said. 'See you later, guys, and not a word.'

Steve walked through the town, his mind buzzing. His phone rang, it was Tina from the hotel. He tutted expecting the reason she was calling was because Jonesey had messed up.

'Hey,' he said, answering. 'What's up?'

'There's something a bit odd.'

'What's that?'

'We had those two guests from Liverpool, remember me saying? Neither of them came back last night. Bit unusual, which is why I thought I'd ring.'

'OK. Names?'

'Becca Edwards and Nathan White.'

Steve closed his eyes, he had forgotten. The woman Pearl had killed. She had been staying at the hotel. She had nearly run him over.

'Becca Edwards won't be returning. She met with an accident last night. And I'm fairly confident that Mr White won't be either. If you could pack up both of their things and let Jonesey have them that would be great.'

'Right.'

'Have they paid for the room?'

'Yeah. Nothing owed.'

'Great. Thanks, Tina.'

'Steve, can you keep this quiet, please? Three people staying here have gone missing in the last week, this is the stuff of nightmares for our PR.'

'My lips are sealed.'

'I knew I liked you for a reason.'

'See you, Tina.'

* * *

Will had got over his early morning shock and was getting ready for a small surprise. He had asked Anna, Danny, Miles and Gemma to come down to the harbour at a very specific time. He'd also mentioned to Doug that he might want to be in the vicinity around then too. A few minutes before eleven, Will wandered out of his office to see Anna's car making its way along the quayside. She parked next to Will's truck, and the four of them got out.

'Good morning,' Will said. 'Miles, how are you doing?'

'Better, thanks,' Miles said. 'Every day I feel a little better.'

Gemma nudged him. 'He's so worried about the ferry though. The insurance company are dragging their feet, so he's worrying about hiring something big enough to take everything over,' Gemma said.

'Wyn has been taking some stuff over using the tourist ferry but it's getting too rough for it now.'

'We'll have to see what we can do about that,' Will said. 'Come on.' He beckoned them over to the higher part of the quayside so they could view the open sea beyond the harbour. In the distance, a bright yellow boat with a bright blue double keel motored towards them.

'She looks a bit like Ocean Ranger.' Danny pointed. 'She's a very pretty boat.'

The boat powered into the harbour and gracefully moored next to the stone steps. A very tall man with a tanned, weathered face killed the engine and strode up the steps towards Will.

'Will, my boy,' he said, pumping Will's hand enthusiastically. 'I miss you on the circuit. Can't persuade you to race again?'

'Good to see you, Don,' Will said, grinning. 'I'm going to ignore that request. Thanks for doing this.'

'Oh, it's my pleasure. Least I can do,' he said. He turned to face everyone. 'Now who have we here?'

Will nodded to Doug who had just arrived.

'Don, this is Miles and Gemma, they owned the ferry that sank. This is Danny and Anna. Danny has always helped out on the ferry doing the Kirby Island runs and Miles couldn't do the ferry runs without him; and this is Doug, he's the skipper of the lifeboat.'

Don was going around shaking hands with everyone.

Danny shook his hand politely. 'On ferry day, I'm always given a piece of cake by Gemma,' he said seriously. 'I never know what it's going to be, but I always hope for my favourite.'

'And what's your favourite?'

'Double chocolate fudge cake.'

'What's not to like?' Don smiled.

Danny frowned. 'Well, I don't like anything with marzipan or cherries.'

Anna laughed. 'Danny, he didn't mean it like that.' She turned to Will. 'What's this all about, Will?'

Will gestured to Don. 'Over to you, mate.'

Don grew serious. 'I'm here because I can't apologise enough to you all. It was my son and his friends who caused the accident. Their utter recklessness and stupidity. There aren't words to say how sorry I am and how disgusted I am with their behaviour. Let me reassure you that he will be paying for this for the foreseeable future. Will has told me how the supply ferry is such an integral part of the community and what a loss it is. So, this boat is a gift from Sail-Loft to you and the community. I will also replace everything that was lost at sea.'

Miles and Gemma looked at each other in astonishment.

'R-really?' Miles stammered, tears in his eyes.

Don nodded. 'When Will called me and told me what a lifeline it is for Kirby Island, as well as the local community, I had to do something.'

Miles stepped forward and grasped Don's hand.

'I can't thank you enough. This is amazing. Unexpected. Wonderful.' He had tears in his eyes as he looked at the boat.

Gemma kissed Don's cheek. 'This is wonderful. I don't know what to say! Thank you isn't enough!' she said. 'Danny! Isn't it wonderful?'

Danny was standing looking at the boat and at Don.

'I can't see a name. What's she called? She must have a name.'

'She doesn't have a name yet,' Don said. 'What would you like to call her?'

Danny's eyes widened. 'I can name her?'

'You can.'

Danny turned to Miles and Gemma. 'What shall we call her?'

'You choose, Danny,' Gemma urged.

Danny's eyes sparkled. 'The Tide Runner.'

'Oh I love that,' Anna agreed.

317

'Perfect,' Gemma said.

Don beamed. 'The Tide Runner she is. I'll get that sorted for you.'

Danny breathed happily. 'This is very exciting. I can't believe I've named a boat today.'

Don jangled the keys. 'Who wants to come out for a quick spin?'

'Me!' called Danny, jumping aboard. 'Come on, Anna.'

Miles, Anna and Gemma climbed aboard, and Don looked up at Will.

'You coming?'

Will shook his head. 'Sorry, mate. Too much on. You go and enjoy.'

Will and Doug stood on the quayside and watched the boat gently leave the harbour.

Doug nudged Will. 'You dark horse. How the hell did you manage to pull this off? Him giving us a whole boat?'

'He can afford it.'

'Super generous.'

'He wants to make amends.'

'I think he's achieved that. You'd better get the word out that the ferry is back in action.'

'Oh Jesus,' Will said. 'I'm not ready to go through that again just yet.'

'I don't think you'll have a choice, mate,' Doug said, laughing and clapping him on the shoulder as he walked off. 'Good job, Will.'

Will returned to his office and managed to catch up on some paperwork until he heard Danny's excited voice and the burble of the ferry engine. He stepped out of the office and watched the four climb off and wave goodbye to Don who was taking the ferry back to be named.

Danny was talking excitedly to Miles and Gemma, and Anna smiled at Will as he wandered over.

'Now that was an amazing thing to do,' she said.

'It needed to be done. Doug's idea. Not mine.'

'But you called in the favour. Must have been hard.'

'It was for a good cause.'

'I think you might be a good man.'

'Are you warming to me, Anna?'

She rolled her eyes. 'You're doing it again.'

'Doing what?'

'Leaning in.'

Will looked hurt. 'I thought you were warming to me.'

'Stop it. I need to go. That bloody woman up the road has been moaning again about food going missing. Thank God she's going home tomorrow. I need to go and fall on my sword.'

'Good luck with that,' Will said mildly.

Danny walked over and beamed at Will.

'Danny,' Will said. 'Are you and Anna free to come for dinner tomorrow night? It's my turn to cook.'

Danny nodded enthusiastically. 'Yes, we'll be free. Anna never goes out, so she'll be free.'

'Oi!' Anna nudged him. 'I might be busy.'

'Are you?'

'Well no, but I don't like people to assume,' she said huffily.

'So dinner tomorrow night. Let me guess, Danny, 6.30 p.m. with a game of chess beforehand if you arrive earlier?'

'Yes, please.' Danny beamed.

'Good.' He glanced at Anna. 'OK with you?'

She rolled her eyes. 'Alright then. What do I bring?'

'Nothing. Just you.'

She looked at her watch. 'I've really got to go.'

'See you tomorrow.'

She beckoned to Danny, who waved at Will as he climbed into the car.

'See you tomorrow, Will. I can't wait!'

* * *

Seb was standing in the garden enjoying the afternoon winter sunshine, watching Suzy's training session on the beach with Jack. Tabatha and Jude were helping. Steve had called and told him that the coroner would be releasing the body soon. They just needed final confirmation that all the evidence had been collected.

To his surprise, Sebastian felt positive about being able to bury Cassie. They had decided what they wanted.

He chuckled as he watched Jack grappling with being obedient and getting sidetracked by other dogs and exciting things found in the sand.

Bree stepped out of the door holding two mugs of coffee and passed one to Seb.

'Well thank you,' he said.

'Welcome,' she said, refusing to meet his eye. She sat on the table putting distance between them and rested her feet on a chair.

'Are you alright?' he enquired, mildly amused by her behaviour.

'Fine, thanks,' she said, watching Tabatha.

'Are we going to talk about the other night?'

'Nothing to talk about,' she said shortly.

'You sure?'

'Yes.'

'Bree, darling…'

'Don't call me that.'

'What?'

'Darling. Don't call me that.'

'Bree, I've called you darling for years. Why is it suddenly an issue now?'

'It just is.'

Seb moved closer to her and gave her a nudge.

'What gives, Gabriella?' he said softly. 'I am probably your oldest friend now. You can tell me anything.'

'How I wish that were true,' she said wistfully.

'I mean it. You can.'

'That's the thing, Seb,' she said, sighing. 'I really can't.'

Seb frowned. 'What's going on, Bree? You get all weird on me Christmas Eve and now you're being weird again. Something's up.'

'It's nothing.'

'Bullshit. I'm worried about you.'

'You don't need to worry about me.'

He took her hand and squeezed it. 'But I do.'

She snatched her hand away.

'I can't do this, Sebastian.'

'Do what exactly?'

'Play happy families.'

Sebastian looked confused. 'We're not playing at happy families. You'll always be part of our family. Cassie would have wanted that.'

'But what do you want, Sebastian?' she said, staring out to sea. 'Everything's different now.'

'Of course it's different. We all have to adjust...' His voice cracked and he looked away. 'She would have wanted us to be there for each other.'

'What else would she have wanted?' Bree asked.

'Family was everything to Cass,' Seb said firmly. 'You're part of our family.'

'When it suited her,' Bree said bitterly. 'Family was everything when it suited her.'

'What do you mean?' Seb asked. 'Bree? What are you saying?'

Bree opened her mouth to speak and then closed it again.

'I need to walk.' Bree pushed herself off the table and walked back into the house.

Sebastian watched her go, frowning. There had been a distinct shift in Bree since Christmas Eve when she had ordered him to bed. Since then, she had been weird.

Seb finished his coffee and watched Tabatha on the beach. She looked incredibly happy. He laughed when he saw Jude run after, pick her up and twirl her around with Jack jumping up and barking.

Suzy looked up and waved. He held up a coffee cup and pointed at it. She gave him a thumbs up and held up five fingers. He returned the thumbs up and went inside to put the coffee on.

Suzy arrived rosy and breathless.

'Jack's doing so well!' she said. 'Few more weeks and we'll have it nailed.'

Seb found himself a little disappointed to hear that this might mean the end of seeing her regularly and found himself slightly puzzled by it. He enjoyed Suzy's company. She was uncomplicated, funny, dry and sarcastic. In many ways, she was the polar opposite of Cassie. He chided himself for comparing.

She settled herself in a kitchen chair.

'What are you frowning at?'

'Didn't realise I was, sorry,' he said.

He put coffee on the table and added milk and the biscuit jar.

'Where's Bree?' Suzy said, looking around.

'Gone out.'

'She OK?' ventured Suzy.

'Being a bit weird,' Seb said, pulling a face.

'Weird how?' Suzy pinched a biscuit.

Seb looked a little embarrassed.

'She was a little drunk Christmas Eve, and she said something odd.'

'Ah.'

'And now she won't talk about it.'

'Ah.'

'Is that all you're going to say?'

'No.'

Seb looked at her enquiringly. She rolled her eyes.

'I think it's difficult,' she said. 'To be friends with a man who you find attractive and not expect at least one of you to have deeper feelings than friendship.'

'What? I've known Bree forever.'

Suzy pulled a face that implied he was being stupid. 'That doesn't stop her feeling a certain way about *you*.'

'You think she has feelings... for me?'

'Maybe that's why she's being weird.'

'But she was Cassie's best friend.'

'So what? She can't help how she feels.'

Seb stared gloomily into his coffee. 'I don't know how to feel about that. I've never looked at her that way.'

'Perhaps you should.'

'I haven't even buried Cassie yet,' he muttered.

Suzy clapped a hand over her heart. 'Love waits for no man,' she said theatrically.

'Oh stop it,' Seb said grumpily.

'You need to sort this.' She helped herself to another biscuit. 'Or it'll fester. I can't stand things that fester.' She pointed at him. 'Festering is no good for anyone.'

A faint scream rang out suddenly. Seb jumped and ran to look over the wall to the beach. Seeing Tabatha was fine, he was puzzled.

'Where the hell did that come from?'

Suzy came to the back door.

'Jenny's back door is open. Maybe it was her?'

They heard barking.

'That's Archie barking,' Suzy said, rushing through the gate to the beach and clambering over the rocks to Jenny's gate.

They followed the sound of Archie barking and ran into Jenny's place, searching until they found her sprawled unconscious on one of the upper staircases, blood on her forehead.

'Jenny!' cried Suzy. 'Jenny, are you OK?'

She was unresponsive.

'Call an ambulance,' instructed Jenny. 'She's breathing but unconscious.'

Seb pulled out his phone, dialled and went through the various questions.

'Do you think we should move her?' Seb said.

'We don't know how far she fell,' Suzy said. 'I wouldn't want to move her in case we do some damage. Go and look upstairs. See if there's an idea of what happened.'

Seb passed the phone over to Suzy and made his way upstairs. He spent time methodically checking the rooms on every level. On the top floor he saw that Jenny had been decorating. He pushed open the last door and splattered across the new white walls were the words 'Gow Awaye,' in red paint.

'Shit,' muttered Seb, suddenly remembering what Steve had told him about a room filled with pictures of Cassie. He heard sirens outside and ran downstairs to Jenny.

'I need my phone,' he said.

'What did you find?' she asked, passing it over.

'Go away written on the wall.'

'What?'

A loud knock had Suzy running downstairs to let the ambulance team in. Seb ran back up the stairs and called Steve immediately, frustrated when the phone went straight to answerphone. He left a message saying it was urgent and could he call him immediately.

* * *

Steve was in the car, oblivious to the fact that his phone was on silent. As he passed the outskirts of town, he swung along one of the main roads. He spotted new Heras fencing around the old hotel the local pond life favoured as a doss house and drug den. He spotted a bundle on the pavement. It looked like clothes, until he realised it was a person.

'Christ,' he muttered. Steve pulled over and activated the emergency lights on his unmarked car. Pulling on some nitrile gloves, he approached the heap on the pavement.

'Hey,' he said loudly. 'Police.'

He gently touched a shoulder and realised the person was Sniffy.

'Sniffy?' Steve said. 'What the hell? It's freezing.'

Sniffy slowly blinked and focused on Steve. 'Huh...' he said, sounding spaced out.

'Sniffy,' Steve said. 'You hurt?'

'Got beat up,' he said. His eyes closed again, he was drifting off. 'Then I found some money, so I bought me a little pick me up.' He mumbled happily. 'Nothing hurts now.'

'Are you not in the hotel anymore?' Steve asked.

Sniffy tried to nuzzle Steve's shoulder. Steve pulled a face and moved away slightly.

'Can't get in anymore,' he murmured. 'Locked out.'

He waved a wonky finger at Steve.

'Why did I have to get out of the big house and the other guy gets to stay? Not fair to old Sniffy.'

A big piece of jigsaw suddenly fell into place in Steve's mind.

'Which guy, Sniffy?' he said, knowing the answer.

'The weird boy.'

'Why's he weird?'

'Not right in the head.'

'What's his name?'

'Dunno.'

'Describe him?'

'Tall, thin, red hair.'

Steve swore under his breath and heaved Sniffy upright.

'Come with me.'

'Where we going? I don't want to go… I've not done anything wrong. You can't arrest me.' He closed his eyes and carried on muttering softly. 'I just rung the filth that's all… I didn't see nuthin'… those poor girls… poor girls… Sniffy tried to help.'

'Sniffy.' Steve tried to wrestle the dead weight towards the car. 'What are you on about? It's not safe here. Come on, I'm taking you in. I don't want you on the streets in this state.'

'You going to nick me?' he slurred.

'Nope. You're a danger to yourself.'

He put Sniffy in the rear seat of his car where he immediately started snoring loudly, stopping occasionally to sniff.

Steve drove to the station and went to butter up the custody sergeant.

'One night and one night only,' the sergeant called to Steve's back as he went to get Sniffy out of the car.

Steve left Sniffy in the cells and dug out his phone. He saw a message and missed call from Seb. He listened as he went back to his car and then quickly pulled around the front of the station. He grabbed Jonesey and they drove, at speed, down to Jenny's house.

CHAPTER 29

Steve, Jonesey and Seb stood in Jenny's house and surveyed the writing on the wall.

'Someone's not gone to school,' announced Jonesey, unwrapping a toffee and chewing on it loudly. 'Dreadful spelling. Is this connected to the thing at your place Christmas Eve?' he asked Seb.

'You tell me,' said Seb grimly.

'How are they getting in?' mused Steve. 'Do you think Jenny fell or was she pushed?'

'Back door was open,' Seb said.

'This paint was done a while ago though,' Steve said. 'Otherwise, the really thick bits on some of the letters would still be a little wet.'

'Shall we get forensics in?' Jonesey asked.

'To look for what?' Steve said. 'Have you had a thorough look round, Seb?'

'Not that thorough.'

'OK, let's start at the very top and work down. Jonesey, get a stepladder.'

Jonesey headed off, while Steve studied the writing. Something was niggling at the back of his mind, just out of reach.

'Where do you want it?' Jonesey called as he carried the ladder up the stairs.

'Here,' said Steve. 'Into the loft.'

'They'll be spiders in there,' Jonesey said doubtfully.

'Offer them a toffee then,' Steve said dryly. 'Get up there. I'll hold the ladder.'

Jonesey gave Steve a dirty look and climbed the ladder, pushing up into the loft hatch. He shoved it up and it clattered loudly on the boarded area of the loft.

'Can't see anything up here. Looks empty,' he called down. 'Ugh there's spiders' webs up here.'

'Mind out, I'm coming up,' Steve said. 'Let's do this properly.'

Steve climbed up and stepped into the loft brushing off his hands. He flicked his phone light on and peered into the dark corners. Jonesey was wandering about unwrapping another toffee.

'Told you there was nothing here.' He leaned backwards on a wall and folded his arms, giving Steve a knowing look. 'But you never listen— Whoooah!'

A large part of the wall where Jonesey had been leaning fell backwards and a cavernous space was exposed. Steve stepped forwards to see if Jonesey was OK and suddenly everything made sense.

'This is a false wall,' he said. 'Look, this space spans all the houses.'

To one side, Steve saw a mattress, empty packets of food lying beside it, a few framed photographs of Cassie Warner and a grey cashmere jumper.

'Seb!' Steve called. 'Come up!'

Seb's head appeared and he boosted himself into the loft space and stood silently looking around.

'Has someone been living up here?' Seb asked with a shocked expression. Looking around, he picked up Cassie's jumper.

'Looks that way. Things are making sense now.'

'You know who it is,' Seb said accusingly.

'I think I do. I'm not completely sure though. I just need to find them. They can't come back here.' He dialled a number.

'Teeney, I need something urgent.' He listened for a moment. 'I don't know how you do it, mate.' He chuckled. 'Right yeah. Jenny's place. We think she's either fallen or been attacked and has fallen down the stairs... Hey, calm down... I don't know yet, but listen, someone's been living in the loft space above the houses.' He listened. 'Yeah... Like a false wall. I need locks and padlocks on all the loft hatches. They're getting in somehow. Do you mind?' Steve was silent for a moment. 'Soon as, please. We had an incident with whoever it was turning up in the house and knocking over a poorly girl, so I don't want it happening again, even if I have to pay for it myself.'

'I'll pay,' Seb said. 'Don't worry about that.'

'OK. That'll be great, thanks. Yes. I will, soon as I get an update.' Steve ended the call.

'Teeney is on his way back, he'll be an hour or so.'

'Good,' Seb said. 'I can't stand the thought that someone's been prowling about up here.'

Seb's phone rang. 'It's Suzy,' he said. 'Hello, Suzy? I've got Steve here, can I put you on speaker?'

Suzy's voice came over the phone. 'Hey. Jenny's being kept in. Nasty bump on the head, they'll probably send her home tomorrow.'

'Any broken bones or anything?'

'Dislocated shoulder and two fingers. All fixed now. Guess she landed on them.'

329

'She was lucky if she fell a long way,' Seb said. 'Do you need a lift home?'

'I've just bumped into Kate, she was at the hospital this afternoon, she's giving me a lift home in about half an hour. Seb, can you take Archie home? He knows Jack. So he'll be OK with him.'

'Did she say what happened?' Steve asked.

'She said she felt someone push her. She didn't see who.'

* * *

Night was falling and Mickey Camorra strolled over the expanse of the large barn towards Nathan White. He regarded him with cold blue eyes. Tommy, who had been looking after Nathan, had been very wary of him and reluctantly admitted to Mickey, that he thought he had overmedicated him. As a result, Nathan was still out cold.

'So this is Mr White,' Mickey said, strolling around him. 'How long has he been out?'

'Since last night, boss,' Tommy said.

'Dope him up again. Let's take him night fishing.'

Tommy frowned. 'I can do that, boss, you don't need to get your hands dirty.'

Mickey prowled around Nathan. 'On this occasion, Tommy, I need to. This man wanted to take everything I had. Including my wife. He won't be drawing breath again.' Mickey rubbed his hands. 'Give him a shot of something bad. Something we've confiscated off one of his own scrotes, that should tip him over the edge. He's a known ex junkie. This is a fall from grace. He'll be OK in his skivvies. People will think he went swimming when he was tripping. Get him ready and chuck him in the back of one of the vans. We'll ask a friend for a favour.'

Jimmy was at home snoring in front of the TV. He had driven the speedboat all night while the others slept, and he was knackered. True to Alexy's word, when they arrived back at the dock and Jimmy moored the boat, they had given him a lift home and ten grand.

Jimmy had been relieved that Marie, his partner, was out working. She had recently qualified as a nurse and worked long shifts so she wouldn't be back until following morning.

Jimmy had treated himself to a Chinese takeaway and fallen asleep shortly afterwards. A sharp rap on his front door frightened the life out of him. He staggered over to answer it and almost wet himself when he found Mickey Camorra on his doorstep.

'Jimmy,' Mickey said. 'I need you for a little night fishing trip and then we're all done.'

'Now?' Jimmy said stupidly.

'It *is* night,' Mickey said, raising an eyebrow.

'Course, yes. Right.' He tried to step out the door and Mickey put an arm out to stop him.

'Shoes, Jimmy? Perhaps some warm clothes? Night fishing can get chilly.'

'Right, yes.' Jimmy went bright red, realising what an idiot he looked in front of Mickey.

'We'll wait in the van,' Mickey said. 'Give you time to get yourself together.'

'Oh OK. Great, thanks.'

'That means hurry the fuck up,' Mickey growled.

Jimmy stepped back inside, grabbed his fishing shoes and warm clothes and hurried outside. Just as he got to the van, he remembered he'd forgotten the key to the boat, so he scuttled back to his cottage.

When he finally climbed in, Mickey raised an eyebrow. 'Have we got everything we need?'

'Yes.'

'Sure?'

'Yes, Mickey.'

'Off we go, Tommy.'

They parked the van on the quayside, and Tommy unceremoniously threw Nathan onto the deck of Jimmy's boat.

'Is he dead?' Jimmy whispered to Tommy.

Tommy shook his head. 'He will be shortly.'

Mickey stepped onto the boat and took a seat, he smiled at Jimmy.

'Bit of a change from what we've been used to eh, Jimmy?'

Jimmy smiled ruefully. 'Yeah. Sorry. Not very grand.'

'Let's go,' Mickey said.

Jimmy started the boat and motored gently out of the harbour. Mercifully, the tide was on his side, and it was actually a good night for fishing.

'Where do you want to go?' asked Jimmy.

'Far out. I don't want this scum anywhere near here when he washes up. *If* he washes up.'

Jimmy set a course avoiding the night work on the wind farm, out to sea. They motored for a while out into the open channel and eventually Jimmy said, 'We're on the edge of the fishing lanes here. The currents are fairly strong so anytime from here is a good place to drop your friend.'

Mickey walked over to Nathan White and removed the cover. He was still unconscious. Mickey picked him up effortlessly and tipped him over the side. He watched impassively as Nathan sank gently away and then said to Jimmy, 'Home.'

* * *

The police station received a call from the owner of a local caravan park, complaining of an abandoned vehicle. Eventually the message that it was the green Ford Fiesta had found its way to Steve. It was

332

the car he had been looking for. He sent forensics to retrieve it and give it a good going over, urgently. He also chased the analyst again: he was still waiting on some location data for the phones that were of interest.

Frustrated, Steve called Murphy, the pathologist, in the hope that he could at least wrap up one outstanding thing.

'Well, if it isn't the ever-demanding Inspector Miller,' Murph said dryly.

'You love it. So, floater in the harbour, cause of death, please.'

'Your floater died from a massive allergic reaction to our old friend gamma-hydroxybutyrate, also known as GHB, cherry meth, liquid ecstasy, you get the drift. His system didn't like it. He had a series of seizures and then a massive heart attack.'

'Right, so massive overdose. Self-inflicted?'

'No way of knowing but he had previously been bound by the wrists. Let me caveat that by saying, I had a gentleman in here about a month ago who met a very similar fate. He died at the hands of Miss Whiplash in her S&M cave, so the fact that he had ligature marks around the wrist doesn't mean he was held against his will. He had a pocket full of the stuff too, so he was no stranger to it.'

'Great. Thanks for that.'

'Can I go now?'

'Dismissed. Thanks.'

Steve ended the call and had an idea. He made another call and waited for an answer.

'Hello, Inspector Miller.'

'Hello, Pearl. How are you today?'

'I am very well, thank you. How's that handsome face of yours after it's encounter with my hawthorn bushes?'

'I live to fight another day.'

Pearl laughed. 'As we all do, darling. Now, what can I do for you?'

'Just a quick question about collateral damage.'

'Oh?'

'Any steers on a Dr Jamie Hunter found in the harbour?'

Silence came from Pearl's end of the call.

'Pearl, help me out here,' Steve cautioned.

Pearl exhaled heavily. '*Off the record*, Stanley got a little confused. He was at the hotel and thought that Mr Hunter was our friend from Liverpool, so he took him to a place to ask him some questions and when Stanley went back to visit him, he had died.'

'I see.'

'I won't apologise though, Steve. The man had cherry meth on him and to me that means he liked to date rape; that he was a predator. I simply will not tolerate men who do that sort of thing to women. I am hoping that there will be an element of public disgrace too if we can rely on the newspapers to do their jobs properly on this occasion.'

Steve was silent for a while. 'Pearl, all I'll say is that this is the second time you've performed, what I like to call, a public service. He was exactly what you say he was, prosecuting him would have been incredibly difficult.'

Pearl inhaled sharply. 'Well, his demise was no more than he deserved.'

'Exactly. There are a number of women who would agree. Perhaps death by misfortune is the answer.'

'I'm very pleased about that, and Stanley will be delighted.'

'Glad we've cleared that up. I'm not going to pursue it. How is Mr White?'

'He's left us permanently, I'm afraid.'

'Will I be seeing him at all?'

'I doubt that very much.'

'Good to know. Thanks, Pearl. You take care now.'

'Goodbye, Inspector. Do pop in for a drink next time you're passing.'

'I don't think Mickey would appreciate that.'

She laughed. 'You're probably right. Bye now.'

Steve smiled fondly as he ended the call and threw his mobile on the desk. He liked Pearl very much. She was classy and bright and had superb morals when it came to certain pond life. He was slightly relieved that he had worked together with the Camorra and had lived to tell the tale.

He tapped out a text to Jerry in Organised Crime to say the matter of the Camorra and The Surgeon had been resolved. Jerry replied instantly with 'Full debrief this week, please! Well done for staying alive! Let's focus on getting Mickey!' Followed by a thumbs-up emoji.

* * *

Will was looking forward to dinner with Anna and Danny. He had nipped out for a few minutes at lunchtime to get some ingredients for his trademark fish pie and called into Maggie's for a sandwich on his way back. Outside he noticed Teddy, lovingly planting up some of Maggie's outside troughs.

'Hi there. It's Teddy, isn't it?' Will asked.

Teddy jumped and looked fearfully at Will.

'Y-yes,' he stammered.

'My name's Will. I'm the harbour master here. Danny helps me out sometimes.'

Teddy's whole face changed. 'Oh yes. You look like a captain in your uniform,' he said, smiling. 'Danny likes you very much. You rescued him. He told me about the untidy store cupboard, and he told me about the new ferry, but it's a *big* secret until she has her name painted on her. I'm going to come and take pictures,' he said, his eyes bright with enthusiasm.

'Sounds cool,' said Will. 'Look, I'm cooking dinner for Danny and Anna later and I wondered if you wanted to come too.'

'But you don't know me,' Teddy said doubtfully. 'Why would you want me there?'

'Why not?' said Will. 'I always cook way too much. Anyway, it'll be a nice surprise for Danny.'

'I don't know where your house is,' Teddy said.

'I live in the loft above the Sea Cadet's hall. In the harbour.'

'That's got a blue door,' said Teddy. 'A round window in it like a boat. I like that window. Gavin used to live there before he married Anna.'

'I like that window too,' said Will. 'See? We have something in common already. Plus, Maggie knows me pretty well now.'

'Yes. OK if you know Mrs Maggie too then.' He nodded. 'I'd like to see Danny then.'

'Good,' said Will. 'Six o'clock?'

Teddy looked at his Mickey Mouse watch and pointed to it. 'At six o'clock I shall be there.'

'Great. Just knock and come up.'

'I just open the door and come upstairs?'

'Yes. Surprise for Danny though?'

Teddy giggled. 'I like surprises.'

Anna arrived at Will's with Danny who was in a high state of excitement. He had brought his chess set with him and he insisted on setting it up as soon as he arrived. Will was juggling things in the kitchen and Anna strolled over to his drawing board.

'This is amazing!' she called over. 'Did you design this?'

'Yup.'

'It's brilliant. Danny, come and look.'

Danny walked over and looked at the drawing. 'What is it?'

'It's a racing boat,' Will said.

'Like the one you crashed?' Danny asked.

Will winced.

Anna looked horrified. 'Danny!'

'Did I say something wrong?' he asked.

'It's OK, Danny,' Will said. 'I am designing a boat that's safer if it hits a freak wave like we did.'

'What's a freak wave?' Danny asked.

There was a knock at the door and Will winked at Anna who looked at Will questioningly.

'Someone else coming?' she asked.

'Surprise for Danny,' Will said quietly, walking over to the top of the stairs.

'Come on up,' he said, smiling.

'Who else is here?' Danny said, frowning.

Teddy hesitantly stepped into room, and Danny jumped to his feet and rushed over.

'Teddy!' he said, delighted. 'Have you come for tea too?'

'Will asked me, he said it would be a good surprise.' He looked worried for a moment. 'Is it a good surprise, Danny?'

'It's a great surprise!' Danny dragged Teddy over towards the chess game. 'We can play before tea,' he said, steering Teddy to sit down opposite him.

'OK,' Teddy said, sighing happily and shrugging off his coat.

Anna watched the exchange before going to sit at the kitchen counter where she watched Will.

'That was a nice thing to do,' she said, pouring herself a glass of wine.

Will shrugged as he pottered about finishing the preparations for dinner.

'I was talking to Steve about him a while ago. Steve said he'd had a hard life. The dad was—'

'Don't even go there,' Anna said grimly, looking over at the boys. 'The man is a monster and should have been locked up years ago. Gav did everything he could to try and get the man prosecuted. I do worry about Teddy; he was too old for social services to place with Gavin.'

'You're worried he's being hurt?'

'Yes, plus it's the mental cruelty that bothers me. But I've tried and tried, and Teddy and Rusty are adults, so the rules are different. For some reason social services don't consider them to be vulnerable adults. I've tried to get Teddy away from the old man, but he won't have it. Last time I got Teddy at our house, the old man came and literally dragged him away, gave me a black eye. It was awful.'

'I heard he had a go at him outside Maggie's the other day. So who's Rusty?'

'Teddy's twin. He's very different.'

'In what way?'

'Not in a good way. He's cruel. The old man loves him. He's always favoured him, and I don't know why.'

'Does Rusty live with him?' Will asked.

'Rusty does his own thing. No one knows where he is half the time.'

A loud burst of delighted laughter came from Danny and Teddy, and Will and Anna looked over.

'He's beaten me!' Danny said. 'Nobody beats me!'

Teddy smiled and looked over at Anna and Will.

'Happiest I've seen him for ages,' Anna said quietly.

'Who's ready for dinner?' Will asked.

Anna insisted on washing up after dinner and made Teddy and Danny dry up. Will sat on the sofa and watched them, enjoying his wine. When they had finished, Danny insisted on playing one more game of chess with Teddy.

'I have to beat him!' he said determinedly.

'One more game,' said Anna. 'Then home. Teddy, do you have work tomorrow?'

'Yes. Me and Barry are planting up the roundabouts,' said Teddy. 'Then I have to go and see Mrs Maggie.'

'Busy day then,' observed Anna as she watched the boys transfixed on their game.

'How is the looking forwards and not backwards going?' Will asked her as she sat on the sofa next to him.

She smiled and sipped her wine. 'When I remember to do it, it goes well. But I read this thing about loss, I can't remember where, and it seemed to make sense.'

'What was it?'

'That grief is just love with nowhere to go.'

Will was quiet for a moment. 'Makes perfect sense,' he said.

'I wonder to myself, does it stop? Do I ever get over this? Will I always feel this way?' she mused.

'I always thought that it's not about *not* loving who you've lost anymore, it's the fact that you *accept* that they have gone. So it's just acceptance of the loss. You still love them.'

Anna thought for a moment. 'Makes sense.'

He nudged her. 'Good.'

'You're doing it again.'

'What?'

'Leaning in.'

'Sorry.'

Danny was clapping his hands which meant he had beaten Teddy. Anna finished her wine.

'Come on, guys, time to go.'

Danny packed up his chess game carefully.

'Teddy, where are you sleeping tonight?' Anna said quietly.

Teddy looked worried. 'I don't want to go home. I haven't been there.'

'Why don't you come and stay with us?' Anna said. 'Danny's got a spare bed in his room.'

'But what if…'

'No one will know, Teddy,' Anna said. 'Our secret. Come home. Have a nice bath and a warm bed. No one will tell your dad.'

'Promise you won't tell,' he said nervously.

'It's our secret!' whispered Anna.

'Come on, Teddy,' said Danny. 'We can tell stories like we used to.'

'OK,' Teddy said shyly.

'Yes!' Danny fist-bumped the air.

'Thanks for a lovely dinner, Will,' she said. Both boys nodded.

'I don't normally like fish pie,' Danny said. 'But yours was very nice. I'll eat it again.'

'I liked it. It's as nice as Mrs Maggie's,' Teddy added.

'I'm glad you both liked it,' Will said. 'Thank you for coming.'

Will kissed Anna's cheek.

'You're leaning in again,' she said, smiling.

'Can't blame a man for trying,' Will grinned. 'Bye, guys.'

Will watched the three of them walk across the harbour, saw Teddy trail along behind them nervously looking around. He watched as Anna threw her arm around Danny and beckoned Teddy to come into the other one. Will caught of flash of Teddy's huge smile at Anna's casual affectionate embrace. He sighed. She was quite the woman.

CHAPTER 30

Sophie arrived to pick up Marcus from climbing and found the centre empty apart from a few climbers outside and Foxy on his own.

'Hey you,' she said, feeling ridiculously pleased to see him.

'Hi!' he exclaimed. 'How's it going? I've been meaning to swing by.'

'You're busy. It's fine,' she said.

'How's your dad? He's been home for a bit now, hasn't he?'

Sophie's dad had dementia and had been getting progressively worse. Sophie had managed to get him into respite care for a few weeks, but he had come home again recently.

Sophie exhaled heavily. 'Thank God Carol's with him. I think if he asks me once more if he's got to pay to use the toilet, I'm going to go mad. He's got over whether he has to wear his school uniform and pay in cheques, but now the latest obsession is that we can't afford the electricity, so he keeps switching everything off, including the fridge freezer. He keeps asking me if Mum has enough nighties and I just don't know what to say to that.' She rubbed her face, tired. 'Carol's got him back into respite care for a week at the end of next week. I just don't know whether this is sustainable if this disease is progressing as quickly as it seems to be.'

Foxy pulled a sympathetic face. 'Can I do anything?'

'Not really. How's Carla?'

Foxy gave her a wry smile. 'Hanging in there.'

'No decisions yet?'

'No, but everything's different now she says.'

'How so?'

'Between you and me. That body in the harbour was the bloke who raped her. He'd come looking for her.'

Sophie stared at him. 'You didn't...'

Foxy put his hands on his hips and said grumpily, 'What *is* it with people thinking it was me?'

'You did used to kill people for living.'

'Well I don't anymore,' he snapped.

'Just asking,' she said. 'So, this must change how she feels about it.'

'It does.'

'What do you think she'll do?'

'No idea. The workings of the female mind are a mystery to me.'

'Is she in?'

'Nope. Don't know where she is. She went out a few hours ago.'

'OK. Tell her I'll catch up with her soon.'

'You going?'

'Yes, I'm Sophie Cabs. Marcus is off to see a girl this afternoon and needs a lift.'

'Young love.'

'Don't even go there,' she said.

'He's at Maggie's.'

Sophie turned to leave. 'Well, if he's not here, he'd be there. See you later.'

'See ya.'

Carla had been up early that morning. She had taken Sophie's advice and seen a counsellor in a town further away. She'd spent an hour discussing how she felt with a very sympathetic woman and at the end of it still wasn't sure how she felt about the baby. She had developed a banging headache and was feeling slightly sick too, so she took herself off to have a coffee and a snack in the hope that she would feel better.

She felt a little less sick after she had eaten, but her headache persisted, so she took two paracetamol. As she sat with her coffee watching the world go by, she mulled over her situation. Things felt different now she knew Jamie was dead. She felt freer to decide without fear of him finding out.

The press had got hold of his death and reported him to be quite the sexual predator, with undisclosed sources saying that he was a serial date rapist. Whatever he was, she still had a decision to make, and it was becoming harder by the day. An hour later, her headache was worse, and she was beginning to feel terrible, so she drove back to Castleby, scribbled Foxy a note and went to bed to try and sleep it off.

* * *

Steve was catching up with paperwork when he received the report on the green Ford Fiesta from forensics. Scanning it, he tried to make sense of it. The were multiple DNA profiles in the car, but two of them were related. Steve carried on scanning. There was the presence of blood, from the related profiles, on the dashboard and steering wheel, suggesting they were in an accident and had hit their heads.

343

As he carried on reading, he sat a little straighter. Traces of Cassie Warner's blood had been found on the passenger car door handle and two specks in the passenger footwell. There was also a miniscule spot on the left-hand side of the steering wheel.

Steve stared at the report. That meant someone from the car *was* at the scene and had *then* got back in the car, surely? He tried to figure out how it would have got on the car door on the left and then the left-hand side of the steering wheel. Was it the passenger? he mused. Maybe they had grabbed the wheel? He focused back onto the report. Would Cassie have been in the Fiesta?

The gist of the paintwork analysis showed that, essentially, the Fiesta had been in contact with a silver vehicle. The silver paintwork was a match for a Peugeot. He dug out the analysis of the Porsche and saw traces of the same silver paint on that too.

Steve tried to get his brain around the findings. He called the accident investigator and had a lengthy discussion.

He eventually made sense of most of it and took a moment to try and process it, but still had a question about whether there had been a car coming in the opposite direction when the crash happened.

He picked up the phone. 'Jonesey, get in here.'

'With tea?'

'Go on then.'

Jonesey arrived after a few minutes balancing two cups of tea and a bag of Maltesers.

'Here'ya,' said Jonesey, putting the tea down, almost slopping it over the side. He sat down, opened the bag of Maltesers and shoved one in his mouth.

'What's poppin' then?' he said, slurping his tea noisily.

Steve held out a hand for a Malteser and Jonesey shook some out for him.

'You tell me. Progress on Rusty, please.'

'Oh right.' He chucked another Malteser in and sucked it noisily. 'So, our friend Rusty. He's a ghost. I can't find anything else on him apart from a note of a verbal caution because he was caught stealing food years back.'

'Education?'

'None that I can see past about year 3 in primary school. Nothing from secondary school, no childhood inoculations. No NHS records, GP, anything. Note about Edwyn being visited by the education beaks for the kid's truancy, but no names.'

'But the other two had records? Teddy and Danny?'

'Yes. Patchy though.'

Steve opened his mouth, clicked his fingers and pointed. Jonesey chucked a Malteser in his mouth. Steve grinned and motioned to repeat it. They both laughed.

'My thinking is that Rusty was definitely the one who wrote on Jenny's wall,' Jonesey said, chucking another Malteser to Steve. 'Think about the spelling, totally phonetic.'

'I agree,' Steve mused. 'So we have a twenty-six-year-old man; we don't know where he lives, he has no education. No driving licence – although he does drive – who we think is a bit of a loose cannon. We think he might have been the one living at Jenny's and he possibly has a thing for Cassie Warner, but now Teeney has been in, he can't get in. So where do you go, if you don't want to go home?'

'Sleep rough?'

'Maybe. Teddy said he'd heard Rusty and Edwyn having a row a few weeks back. Edwyn took a stick to Rusty, and then Rusty threatened him with a shotgun.'

'When was it?'

'He couldn't remember. The woman, Michelle who was pushed off the cliff, she said it was a bloke with reddish hair who looked like Teddy. He had a cut on his head.'

'Do you think Edwyn and Rusty had something to do with it?'

'Forensics on the Fiesta say there was blood on the front driver's and passenger side dashboard. We know the DNA profiles are related, but we don't know if it's a match to them though.'

'Why was there blood on the dashboard, air bags should have gone off?'

'Air bags didn't deploy apparently.'

'Another one, please.' Steve opened his mouth and ducked to catch the wayward Malteser.

'Think back though, Edwyn had a mark on his forehead when we saw him, the woman said Rusty had a mark on his head *and* we saw the car at the garage.'

'That certainly explains it,' Jonesey said.

Steve's phone rang and as he answered it, he caught another Malteser and tried not to laugh. A voice told him that the mobile phone data had been emailed over. Steve waited impatiently for it to arrive. He waited a further few minutes and then picked up the phone to the analyst who was actually crunching the data.

'Hi, Hannah. So I'm not chasing, but–'

She sounded exasperated. 'So you know the data has literally landed in my inbox, like this second? And this is you not chasing then, Inspector Miller?'

'I wondered if you had anything preliminary for me.'

'I'm not sure where to start, I'm still sorting the other stuff out.'

'What do you mean?'

'It's complex. Cassie Warner's phone was very busy right up until the accident and all the night before. She repeatedly called and received calls from, what we think is, a burner phone, because it's not registered, but is of interest to us – let's call it burner A. She also made and received calls to and from Gabriella Logan's phone.'

'Nothing at all on who the burners are linked to?'

'Nope. Burner B isn't *ever* on. So, Cassie and Gabriella's phone both show contact with burner phone A. In fact, sometimes, when one call ended from one, the other rang, almost like a three-way conversation.'

'Right.'

'I'm still mapping that phone's activity. There were no calls from or to any of their phones from burner phone B, but it was switched on in the vicinity of the accident – remember it's not *that* accurate location wise – on the night of the accident. It made the 999 call.'

'OK.'

'But looks like burner phone A was in the vicinity of the accident scene and the garage where she stopped for petrol on the night of the accident, but it's not that accurate.'

'Right. So, it's safe to conclude that Cassie, Bree and the owner of burner phone A all knew each other.'

'Yes.'

'And you think the owner of burner phone B didn't know them but was near the accident.'

'Near enough to call 999. Now, the location data for the burners. On the day of the accident burner A was around Chelsea, and central London during the day, then… oh wait, it was near here at the time of the accident, and then appeared to go straight back to Chelsea.'

'Wow. Some drive. And burner phone B?'

'Just switched on once on the night of the accident. Inactive before and since then.'

'Anything else?'

'Nope. Not for now.'

'OK. Thanks.'

'No problem, can I get back to it?'

'Yup. Thanks.' Steve ended the call.

Steve was thoughtful, then he picked up the phone again and dialled Toby who had interviewed Levinson Lucas in London.

'Toby,' he said cheerfully.

'Please tell me I haven't got to go and see that dick again,' Toby said by way of a greeting.

'Quick question about him.'

'Go on.'

'Did you happen to see a car on the property?'

'Can't remember. But you're in luck. I've gotta go over that way tonight, I'll have a snoop about and see what I can see.'

'Thanks, mate.'

'You know it'll be a prick's car, don't you? Whatever he drives.'

Steve chuckled. 'More than likely. Keep me posted though. There's a pint in it.'

'How you spoil me,' he said dryly. 'I'll let you know.'

Steve hung up and turned to Jonesey, who had produced an iced bun and was tucking in.

'Fuck's sake, Jonesey, do you ever stop eating?' Steve snapped. 'I want to bring Edwyn Lewis in.'

'Good luck with that then,' Jonesey said, pulling a face and stuffing the last of his bun into his mouth.

'I want you to go with another officer and get him.'

'Whaaat?' Jonesey mumbled with hamster cheeks.

'Soon as you can.'

'Can I take PC Warren?'

'Nope. Take Garland, he's the size of a house, then Edwyn might be less likely to kick your head in.'

'You're not selling it to me,' grumbled Jonesey.

'Get cracking. Also, give Gabriella Logan a heads up that we'd like to see her first thing tomorrow morning. You can call her and ask her to come in at nine and see me.'

'Just her?'

'She's welcome to bring a solicitor if she feels like she needs one.'

'I'll let her know.'

Jonesey was silently thanking God that Steve had made him take PC Garland to bring in Edwyn Lewis for questioning. He was nursing a split lip and bruised balls. Christ knows how it would have gone if he'd turned up with petite PC Warren.

Garland pulled into the yard at the station and drove around to the door of the custody suite.

'I'll take our friend in,' he murmured. 'Don't want any more damage happening to your crown jewels.'

He walked around to the rear door of the car and yanked Edwyn Lewis out painfully by the handcuffs. He marched him towards the custody suite.

Steve had been informed that Edwyn Lewis was residing unhappily in interview room two. He headed for it and then beckoned Garland out of the room, into the corridor.

'Did he come quietly?' he asked.

'Nope.' Garland grinned. 'Jonesey got a fat lip and a kick in the balls.'

Steve stifled a bark of laughter. 'He OK?'

'He'll live. That's one vicious old git though,' he said, gesturing in the room.

'You don't know the half of it,' Steve said grimly. 'Thanks for getting him.'

'No probs, Guv.'

Steve entered the interview room and sat down opposite Edwyn. Steve started the tape recorder and introduced himself and Edwyn for the tape.

'I hear you gave one of my officers a fat lip and a kick in the balls,' Steve said.

'He was asking for it.'

'I see. I'm told you've waived the right to a solicitor. Are you sure?'

Edwyn's eyes narrowed. 'Useless fuckers anyway.'

'I'd like a chat about a car of yours, Edwyn, and your movements on the night of Saturday 16th November.'

Edwyn shrugged and folded his arms. 'Ain't got nothing to say to you fuckers.'

'You have a green Ford Fiesta?' Steve shuffled his papers and read off a registration number. 'Correct?'

Edwyn looked away.

'Can you respond for the tape, please?' Steve asked.

'No comment.'

'As I understand it, you own the car, which incidentally has no current MOT, tax or insurance, but you let others drive it. Noticeably, your son Rusty and on occasion, Teddy. Yet neither of them have passed their driving test.'

'No comment.'

'This car has been found abandoned and we have it in for forensic testing.'

'Good for you.'

'Are you denying that you have this car?'

'No comment.'

'Here's what we have. I have video footage of a man, who I believe to be your son Rusty, driving the car. Then you arrive, physically assault him, climb in the car and drive off in it. Here are some stills from that tape.'

Edwyn ignored them.

'I would like to know what occurred in the time period between you assaulting Rusty and driving off, and when you arrived home where you had a very vocal argument, resulting in Rusty pointing a shotgun at you?'

'No comment.'

'Were you involved in any sort of accident?'

'No comment.'

'Did you encounter any other person or persons on the journey?'

'No comment.'

'Would you like to comment on your car potentially being at the scene of a murder?'

'No comment.'

'Do you have any comments regarding your car having traces of paintwork from another car, which is part of the murder enquiry, as well as having blood from the murder victim present?'

'No comment.'

'OK.' Steve stood up. 'I'll need a DNA sample, Mr Lewis, and then we'll reconvene. Interview terminated for now.'

Steve looked at Garland. 'Fingerprints and DNA sample. High priority. Mr Lewis, I will be releasing you after this but talking to you again in the very near future.'

Edwyn sneered.

PC Garland dragged a resistant Edwyn off to the custody suite.

Steve went down to his office and left a message that the DNA sample was on its way and that it was a high priority.

* * *

Foxy was worried, he hadn't seen Carla all day. He closed the climbing centre after the last evening class and climbed the stairs wearily to the flat, Solo trailing at his heels. The flat was in darkness, but Carla's car was next to his. He walked into the lounge and dumped his phone and keys on the table, and saw Carla's note.

'Bad head, going to bed.'

Foxy frowned and headed into the bedroom. Carla was asleep, in the dim light she looked pale and sweaty, but he could see she was shivering. Foxy felt her head, she was hot. She mumbled in her sleep and turned over.

Foxy went back to the lounge and made some dinner for himself, he debated waking up Carla, but knew from years together that when Carla felt ill, all she wanted to do was sleep, so he left her to it.

Foxy had grumpily relocated himself to bed with Carla in the small hours of the morning when he had awoken in his chair with a stiff neck. A few hours later, the crying seagulls woke him, and he lay for a moment enjoying the sounds. He looked over at Carla, who was on her side with her back to him, and he gently threw back the covers trying not to wake her.

He sat on the edge of the bed for a moment and blinked himself awake. He frowned when he looked down at his hand and realised that his side was covered in blood.

Panicked, he stood up and threw the covers back. There was a pool of blood around Carla.

'Carla!' He ran around to her side and knelt by her. 'Carla,' he said loudly, desperately trying to rouse her. Her face was flushed, her hair sticking to her head with sweat. Her forehead was red hot.

'Carla!' he shouted. 'Wake up.'

He ran into the lounge, grabbed his phone and called an ambulance. He ran a towel under the cold tap and ran back to wet Carla's face and neck with it.'

'Carla. Come on, baby,' he said, desperately laying the cool towel on her forehead and looking for signs that she coming around, but she remained unconscious.

The wait for the ambulance was interminable. He was at the limits of his frustration when he heard a distant siren. It occurred to him that he needed to dress in order to go to the hospital with her. He rang Mike and asked him to open up telling him Carla had been taken ill. He threw on trousers and a shirt and ran out to the top of the outside stairs as he heard the sirens get closer. He ran down the steps.

'It's my wife,' he said. 'She's in the early stages of pregnancy, she had a bad headache yesterday, she was sweaty and feverish last night. There's blood all over the bed and I can't bring her round.'

The two paramedics headed up the stairs into Foxy's flat, Maggie had come running out of the cafe as Foxy was following them.

'Carla?' she asked.

Foxy nodded.

'Let me know what I can do,' Maggie called out to him as he ran up the last few steps.

Foxy watched as they loaded her into the back of the ambulance, still unconscious. He hated the sense of helplessness. He jumped in the back of the ambulance and held her unresponsive hand tightly as the sirens blared through the streets.

CHAPTER 31

Foxy sat on the uncomfortable chair in the hospital corridor and waited. His phone rang and he answered it quietly when he saw Sophie's name.

'What's happened? Maggie said Carla's been taken in.'

'Yup.'

'Is she OK?'

'She's in surgery.' He swallowed the lump in his throat.

'Now?

'Yup.'

'Has she lost the baby?'

'Guess so. There was blood everywhere.'

'Are you doing OK?' Sophie's voice was soft.

'I'm not worried about me.'

'I am. Do you want company? Someone to keep you supplied with food?'

'I wish.'

'I'll come.'

'I'll be OK. Don't come.'

'I'll call you later, see if there's news?'

'Yup.'

'Mr Fox?' A woman in scrubs was standing in front of him.

'Gotta go.'

'Shout if you need me. Lots of love.'

Foxy ended the call.

'Hi there,' she said. 'I'm Dr Michaels. I've just operated on your wife.' She pointed to the chair next to him. 'May I?'

Foxy nodded and the doctor sat down with a large sigh.

Foxy glanced at her. 'It's ex-wife actually. But we're close. She's been staying with me.'

'Nice that you're close,' she said. 'My ex-husband can't even be civil to me. Everything is via snippy texts. I'm sorry but Carla's lost the baby, I'm afraid.'

'I suspected as much.'

'Had you been trying long?'

Foxy shook his head. 'It wasn't mine. Strictly between you and me, she was raped. The pregnancy had caused quite the dilemma for her.'

'I see.'

'Blessing in disguise I would call it. I think she would too. How is she?'

'She's running a high fever. She's got some sort of virus we can't identify. Very high temperature, she's weak, and struggling to maintain consciousness. We've got her on a broad spectrum of medication in the hopes it will help her through it. She lost a lot of blood, she haemorrhaged quite badly. It's unlikely she'll have any more children though. I'll be keeping her in for a good few days yet.'

'Can I see her?'

'Of course, but just for a minute. She's in intensive care until we can get this fever under control. She's drifting in and out of consciousness. If you could mask, gown and glove up that would be great. More to protect you from this awful thing she has.'

'No problem.'

Foxy left ICU, stripping off his protective gear. It had frightened him seeing Carla that way and not much frightened him. She looked terrible. Her skin was clammy, the colour on her cheeks was high, but the rest of her face was pale. She hadn't realised it was him. She hadn't come around long enough to know, and he had been ushered out by a quiet male nurse after a few minutes.

'Foxy?' He turned to see Lottie, Rudi's girlfriend, standing behind him with a coffee and a sandwich.

'Hey, Lottie,' he said, kissing her cheek absentmindedly. 'What are you doing here?'

'Delivering sustenance to you from Sophie. She's worried about you.'

Unexpectedly Foxy's eyes filled with tears.

'Hey!' Lottie pulled him over to sit on some chairs. 'Come on.'

'Sorry,' he said, wiping his eyes with the back of his hand. 'Stupid. Crept up on me. She's in a bad way, isn't she?'

Lottie patted his arm. 'She's in the best place.' She passed him the coffee.

Foxy sipped at it gratefully. He realised he was starving. Life in the forces had taught him to eat and drink when he could. Hunger and dehydration led to weakness and bad decisions. He eyed the sandwich.

'That for me?'

Lottie handed it over and he devoured it in about three bites.

'Better?' she said.

'Thanks.'

'You look shattered. I'm ordering you home. Nothing you can do here, plus, Rudi's coming to get you. Any change and they'll call you. I'll pop back to see her later and text you an update. OK?'

Foxy was grateful. 'Thanks, Lottie. You're a diamond.'

Her phone pinged. 'Rudi's out front,' she said, texting a reply. She kissed him gently on the cheek. 'Go.'

Foxy gave her a quick hug goodbye and left to meet Rudi.

'Cheers, mate,' Foxy said as he climbed out of Rudi's truck wearily.

He slammed the door and went to go in the climbing centre when Maggie rushed out of her cafe opposite.

'Foxy my love. How's that lovely girl?'

Foxy walked past Teddy who was busy outside Maggie's painting a wooden flower trough.

'She's in intensive care. She's got a virus they can't get a handle on. She looks awful, Mags.' His voice cracked.

Maggie enveloped him in an enormous hug. Then she stepped back and held his giant arms and looked at him.

'She's in the best place. You can't do anything else for her at the moment. We just have to hope.'

Foxy nodded, a huge lump in his throat. Maggie patted him on the arm.

'Now, don't be cross with me. I hope you don't mind, my love. I got Gary the Beds to deliver you a new mattress and get rid of the old one. I've made it all up for you and sorted out those bloody sheets and duvet, and I've tidied up from the paramedics. That's one less thing you have to worry about, and there's a plate of dinner in the microwave.'

Foxy couldn't help himself. A tear rolled down his cheek. 'You are too good, Maggie,' he said softly. 'Too good to me.'

Maggie gently wiped his tear away and gave him a brisk squeeze. 'I do it because I love you and you're family. Now go and see Mike. That poor boy's been rushed off his feet today.'

She bustled back inside, and Teddy came to stand next to him.

'She loves you Mrs Maggie does,' he said, slowly wiping his hands. 'It's nice when Mrs Maggie loves you, isn't it?'

'Yes, it is, Teddy.' He sighed. 'Yes, it is.'

* * *

Bree arrived at the police station just before 9 a.m. holding a large takeaway coffee and looking very relaxed. PC Warren ushered her into an interview room and informed Steve. He gathered up his file and notebook and was just about to leave his office when his phone rang.

'Miller,' he barked into it.

'It's Toby.'

'Hey, mate. Just about to interview a suspect.'

'I'll be quick, last night I swung by your friend and mine, dickhead of the century. He's got a posh Jag. F-TYPE.'

'What colour?'

'Blackboard... you know, dull black.'

'OK.'

'Told you. Dick's car.'

Steve laughed.

'But it gets better,' Toby continued. 'He has a housekeeper who lives in. Want to know what her car is?'

'Yes.'

'A silver Peugeot.'

'Does he use it?'

'Well, I saw him stepping out of it last night. Snapped a little cheeky pic too.'

'Hang on one sec.' Steve grabbed a spreadsheet from his desk. 'Give me the registration.'

Toby rattled it off.

'I need your forensics to go and get that car as a matter of urgency.'

'Really?'

'A silver Peugeot was at the scene of Cassie Warner's accident. We've also got the partial plate on CCTV.'

'I'm on it.'

'Appreciate it. Can you do me a favour, get your forensics guys to talk to ours? I need results ASAP. I expect toes will be trod on.'

'Will do.'

'Oh, and tell dickhead not to leave town. Take his passport.'

'With pleasure.'

'Ring you later. Thanks again, mate,' Steve said.

Steve pushed his way into the interview room.

'Good morning, Bree,' he said pleasantly. 'Thanks for coming in.'

'No problem.'

'How's Tabatha doing?'

'She's good. She's quite smitten with young Jude.'

'He's a sound lad that one.'

'Everyone says he's just like his father.'

'They're not wrong.' He shuffled his files, activated the recorder and went through the preliminaries.

'Bree, we're just going over some questions today, you're not under caution, but you are welcome to a solicitor if you would feel more comfortable?'

She inclined her head. 'I think I'll be fine.'

'OK. Let's get started.'

He consulted his notes. 'Before we start, is there anything that's come to mind since we last spoke that you might want to share?'

'Such as?'

'You tell me.'

She looked blank. 'Nothing I can think of.'

'OK, let's make a start. Bree, do you recognise this phone number here, please?'

Steve pushed a piece of paper across the table and read out the number for the tape.

Bree looked at the number and shrugged again. 'I have no idea. I can barely even remember *my* number; this means nothing to me.'

'If I tell you this number is unregistered, would that shed any light?'

'What do you mean, unregistered?'

'Like a burner phone. Come on, Bree, you've been around the block long enough to know what a burner phone is.'

'I have no idea,' she repeated.

'A lot of celebrities use burner phones so their accounts and phones can't be hacked,' Steve said.

'Really?' She shifted in her chair.

'Bree, please don't insult my intelligence. I have your phone records.' He took out a sheet of paper and consulted it.

'I don't recall giving you permission to access those.'

'This is a murder investigation; I don't need your permission.'

Bree folded her arms defensively.

Steve continued. 'You had quite a series of conversations the day before and the day of Cassie's death, didn't you?'

'I've told you I saw her that day.'

'Yes, and you also had a number of conversations too.'

'We spoke a lot.'

'This amount is verging on ridiculous.'

'Not really.'

'You also had a number of conversations with this other phone number, yet you say you don't know who it is.'

Bree took a long drink of her coffee.

'Do you have your phone on you, Bree?'

'No.'

'Is that not unusual? In your job particularly, not to have your phone on you?'

'Not really. I need a break from it.'

Steve sat back in his chair and produced his phone from his pocket and tapped out a number. A phone rang from the depths of Bree's jacket.

'Would you look at that. You do have it after all,' Steve said flatly.

Bree's face was like stone.

'Who does the burner phone belong to, Bree?' Steve asked softly.

Bree stared at the ceiling and exhaled deeply. 'Levinson Lucas.'

'Interview suspended; I'll be back in 2 minutes.' Steve stood and paused the recorder. He stepped out of the door and pulled his phone out of his pocket. Toby answered on the second ring.

'Toby, I need you to bring in Levinson Lucas for questioning under caution.'

'Really? Excellent. Couldn't happen to a nicer twat.'

'I've got preliminary evidence he was at the murder scene.'

'Excellent. Do you want him brought down to you? I fancy a trip away. I can probably swing it since it's a murder.'

'Can you? I'll put you up.'

'It'll be fine. Boss is half expecting it since you spoke to him. See you in a few hours.'

Steve ended the call and went back to resume the interview.

'Right.' He looked at his notes. 'You had quite the three-way chats with each other the day before and the day of Cassie's death.'

Bree shrugged. 'It might look that way, but I'm sure it was just coincidental.'

'I see. And out of interest, what might that be?'

Bree looked defensive. 'Oh I don't know, maybe Levinson saying something in the press that affected Cassie.'

'Did that happen a lot?'

'Sometimes. Usually I could head it off.'

'So what was it?'

'I don't recall.'

'I'll give you a minute to think about it.' Steve leant back in his chair and watched her.

'It wasn't like that…'

'Wasn't like what, Bree?'

Bree sighed deeply. 'We were arguing. All three of us.'

'About?'

Bree tutted. 'How is this relevant? What we argued about before she died?'

'It's relevant.'

'It's nothing.'

'I'm interested in her state of mind. Things have come to light.' Steve pushed.

'Such as?'

'I'm not at liberty to say at this point. I'll ask again. What did you talk about?'

'Her behaviour,' Bree said quietly.

'What about her behaviour?'

'It was getting out of hand.'

'In what way?'

Bree cleared her throat and shifted in her chair. 'This goes no further. I cannot have Sebastian and Tabatha finding out about this. I love them both too much.'

'I can't guarantee that.'

Bree bit her lip. 'Cassie liked to have flings with her leading men.'

Steve was genuinely surprised. 'Really?'

'Oh yeah. If anyone took the time to analyse it, they would see that I represented most of the leading men Cassie acted with. I mopped up all the damage.'

She looked at the ceiling, tears brimming and said bitterly, 'The wonderful and great Cassie Warner, the new Hollywood darling, with the wonderful husband and daughter, but it just wasn't enough. We needed *more* adoration, *more* attention. So we slept with our co-stars. It made for a better picture apparently.'

'Does Sebastian know?'

'I don't know. I don't think so. It would break him… and Tabs.'

'Tell me about Levinson?'

Bree snorted. 'Stupid idiot fell for her. And I mean big time. He was being ridiculous about it. He wanted to announce their love. Wanted her to tell Sebastian. Live together, be a golden couple. He got these blind rages, no one could control him when he was like it. He was a bomb waiting to go off that one. I was seeing him that day to tell him to find a new PR person. I'd just had enough of it.'

'Did you and Cassie argue about you leaving Levinson?'

'Yes. She wanted to be protected and she didn't trust anyone else to do it.'

'Anything else going on I should be aware of?'

Bree shifted uncomfortably in her chair. 'Such as?'

'You tell me.'

'You know about the baby, don't you?'

'I do.'

'She didn't know whose it was.'

Steve looked at her. 'But?'

'She thought it was Levinson's.'

'Tell me more about Levinson.'

'In what way?'

'Tell me how he was with Cassie.'

'Possessive. Desperate. Obsessed.'

'How did Cassie feel about it?'

Bree pulled a face. 'Part of her bloody loved it. Loved the idea of someone being obsessed with her. Their love for her being so intense,' she said viciously, looking angry. 'But then she began to find it difficult to control him. He became a loose cannon.'

'How so?'

'He wanted her to tell Seb. He wanted her to have Christmas with him. He didn't want her disappearing for weeks on end to Wales and not seeing him. He tried to forbid it. He threatened all sorts.'

Steve raised an eyebrow. 'Such as?'

'Going to the press. Releasing photos, interviews. Proper career ending stuff.'

'What happened?'

Bree finished her coffee and tapped the empty cup idly on the table. 'They argued. At the costume fitting, that day. She read him the riot act. Told him to leave her family alone. Told him it was over.'

'How did he take that?'

'Not well. He flew into a rage.'

'Had she been planning to end it?'

'Of course! As soon as the film was a wrap. That was her style,' she said bitterly. 'Finish the film, finish the affair!' She looked away from Steve shaking her head.

'You seem very bitter,' Steve observed.

'Am I?'

'Seems that way.'

'I need the loo.'

'No problem. Interview suspended.'

Steve poked his head out of the door and beckoned to PC Warren.

'Accompany our guest for a comfort break, please?'

'Guv,' she said, stepping into the room and motioning Bree down the corridor.

Steve mulled over their discussion so far. He had a very nasty feeling about the whole thing, and he knew to trust these feelings. He also felt heartbreakingly sorry for Sebastian, knowing he would have to tell him the majority of the story before the press got hold of it. Steve knew exactly how it felt to be betrayed when someone you loved cheated on you.

His thoughts were interrupted by PC Warren ushering Bree back into the room, who sat down in front of Steve. Steve resumed the interview.

'To continue, Cassie and Levinson argued on the day that she died.'

'Yes.'

'And she broke it off, or threatened to break it off?'

'Yes.'

'Why that day in particular?'

'Well, he didn't want her to be away from him for Christmas and he suspected she might be pregnant.'

'*He* suspected?'

'Yeah. They rowed about it, and she stormed out, saying it was over.'

'What happened then?'

'I've got no idea.'

'Well, the phone calls continued.'

She waved a hand dismissively. 'Oh it was the usual "he said, she said" calls. Me trying to reason with them both and then I got bored and switched my phone off.'

'So you have no idea what Levinson did after their row?'

'No.' She shifted in her chair.

Steve sensed she was lying.

'When did you speak to him again?'

'The day after the accident, I think.'

'How was he?'

'Distraught. Broken. Inconsolable. Wailing like a wounded animal.'

Steve consulted his notes for a moment.

'Do you happen to know what car Levinson drives?'

'Matte black F-TYPE Jag,' she rattled off.

'Nothing else?'

'Not that I'm aware of.'

'Nothing to be inconspicuous? Hide from his adoring fans?'

'I don't know.'

Steve watched her silently. She shifted uncomfortably.

'I really don't know!' she exclaimed.

Steve closed the file. 'OK. That's it for today. I'm not done yet though. I'll need you again at some point, probably tomorrow.'

'Well, I was going to go home. There is such a thing as outstaying your welcome.'

'Find a hotel then. Don't leave town. I hear The Bay Manor on the hill has a few unexpected vacancies,' Steve said shortly. 'I'll call you when I need you. Thanks for coming in.'

He opened the door and motioned to PC Warren, who escorted Bree to the front desk. He watched her go, shaking his head. He was feeling sorrier for Seb by the minute. Nothing was as it seemed.

Bree returned to Sebastian's and stayed in her room, citing a headache. She just couldn't face him.

Later, she heard him knocking gently at the door and asking if she wanted anything to eat. She couldn't even bring herself to answer him. She heard him talking to Jenny who was back from hospital, and it sounded like Seb was cooking her dinner.

Bree lay in the darkness and cursed herself over and over for being so stupid. If she had been honest, none of this would have happened. She couldn't see a way out that wouldn't involve Sebastian looking at her with his gorgeous big eyes full of hurt and pain. It would be the end. No more holidays together, no more time together. She rolled over burying her face in the pillow and sobbed.

* * *

Carla was in a bad way. Dr Michaels had phoned Foxy and asked him to come in. He arrived at the hospital and ran to intensive care, frustrated by the endless wait to be let in after he'd rung the buzzer.

Dr Michaels guided him to a small room off the main area.

'How are you?' she asked him.

'We're not here to talk about me,' he said. 'Tell me about Carla.'

'OK. So we think she is in something called septic shock.'

'Isn't that blood poisoning?'

'Basically, septic shock is the severe result of uncontrolled and untreated sepsis.'

'That's bad, isn't it?'

'It couldn't really get any more serious,' she said. 'We think Carla's miscarriage was caused by something called a septic abortion and this just means the baby was aborted naturally by an infection in her uterus. We're trying to treat that, but the fever is pretty bad. You should know we have some serious concerns about whether she'll make it.'

Foxy stared at the doctor. 'But she was fine yesterday and the day before,' he said stupidly, trying to process what Dr Michaels was saying.

'Infections like this happen fast and take hold quickly. She's not regained consciousness and she's finding it difficult to breathe. There is a mammoth battle going on with the infection and the antibiotics

367

at the moment. Now, do you mind me asking whether you're her next of kin? I need to make sure.'

'Yes. I still am.'

'OK. Would you like to see her?'

Foxy nodded, not trusting himself to speak. The thought of losing Carla was a reality and he felt helpless and ridiculously tearful. Anger at his inability to help, or do anything, crept over him.

He donned protective gear and Dr Michaels said quietly, 'Only a few minutes. OK?'

Foxy pulled up a chair and held Carla's hand. She looked terrible and Foxy was truly terrified she wouldn't make it through.

'Carls,' he said, fighting back the tears. 'Come on now. Doc says you've got to fight this. I'll be here. I'm not leaving you. I'll help you fight this. We'll do it together, Carls. Come on. You're stronger than you think. Fight this, Carla.'

Carla was delirious. In her mind, her daughter Charlie was at the other end of the ward. Carla couldn't understand why she was there. She knew she had died, so what was she doing at the hospital? Charlie was frowning and shaking her head. Carla was so pleased to see her she tried to run towards her, but Charlie held up her hand firmly and shook her head. Then Charlie pointed and Carla turned around to look. She saw Foxy sitting by her bedside, resting his head on her hand.

Charlie started walking away. Carla called out, but Charlie kept looking back and shaking her head and pointing at Foxy. Carla watched Charlie's figure recede until she couldn't see it anymore.

'Fight for me, Carla,' she heard Foxy say and felt his warm hand squeezing hers.

Hours later, Foxy left the hospital. He was a useless presence and also wasn't allowed to stay in ICU any longer. So he sat outside for a while just to be close.

He was sure Carla had no idea he was there, but he hoped she had heard him. He drove back to Castleby, grateful both Tom and Mike were at the climbing centre all day.

The centre was closed by the time Foxy got home. He climbed out of his Defender and trudged up the stairs towards his flat. He frowned, the lights were on and he opened the door to the smell of cooking.

Foxy walked in the door. He was shattered and emotional.

Without saying a word, Sophie walked over and gave him a huge hug. He exhaled deeply as he returned it.

'I needed that,' he said, stepping away and making a fuss of Solo. 'What are you doing here, Soph? Not that it's not nice to see you. Who's with your dad?'

'Dad's fine. I've come to make sure you have a good meal. You look wrung out.' She handed him a beer. 'What's the latest?'

Foxy took his time repeating what the doctor had said and struggled to finish his sentence as he was hit by a tide of emotion.

'I don't know what to say,' she said. 'We just have to hope she can fight this.'

Foxy exhaled loudly and rubbed his hands over his face. 'I feel so helpless,' he said. 'Why didn't I see it? Why didn't I try and wake her the night before or get her to hospital?'

'Because you didn't know,' Sophie said. 'There's no way you could have known. 'Look, dinner's going to be about half an hour. Take the beer and the dog. Walk on the beach and clear your head. Come back and eat in a bit.'

Foxy gave her a half smile. 'Thanks, Soph,' he said softly. 'Thanks for being here.'

He whistled for Solo and headed down the steps towards the beach, Solo following faithfully at his heels.

CHAPTER 32

New year had come and gone without ceremony. Dr Kate Cooper rubbed a tired hand over her eyes and was about to call for her next patient when her door opened.

'Hello, Doctor, I've got an extremely large swelling that I need you to inspect,' Steve said, walking into the room and pulling her up into a long kiss.

'I think I remember you,' she said, smiling, and kissed him again. 'Problem patient. How on earth did you get past the rottweiler?'

The rottweiler was the name they both had for Margaret, the doctor's receptionist who ruled the reception desk with a rod of steel.

'Urgent police business,' he said, nuzzling her neck.

'To what do I owe the honour?' She was enjoying the feel of him.

'I just wanted to pop in and tell you I love you,' he said, grinning. 'Oh, and I'll be flat out for the next few days. Case is about to break, so I'll be at the station all hours. Plus, Toby from London has brought a suspect down and he's staying at mine.'

'I hate having two houses,' she said, pulling him close.

'We should do something about that then.' He kissed her again. 'You should move in with me.'

'Oh should I?' she said, eyebrow raised.

He nodded enthusiastically. 'Uh huh. It'll give you a chance to see for yourself these large swellings I keep getting.'

'Would we say large?' she said, grinning.

'Cheeky cow.'

She laughed. 'Obviously, I meant enormous.'

'Obviously.'

He studied her face and rubbed a thumb over her cheek. 'Are you OK? You look tired.'

'I'm fine. I just miss you. Go on. Suspects to torment and all that. Do you think you'll be done by Saturday? I've got the day off and I'm not on call.'

'I'll do my best, even if I have to resort to beating a confession out of my suspects.'

'Little harsh.'

'But effective.' He kissed her again. 'See you, Doc. Unless there's an outside chance of a quick bunk up.'

'GO!' she said as he left the room winking at her. She sighed at his retreating back. 'Gorgeous man.' She smiled as she waited for the next patient.

Levinson Lucas arrived in the back of a police car, complaining loudly about mistreatment. Toby left him in an interview room to stew.

Ever the Lothario, Toby took it upon himself to ask PC Warren if she could show him where he could get a coffee and a sandwich. Jonesey spotted the pair and marched off to find Steve.

'Your mate is hitting on PC Warren,' he announced crossly at Steve's office door.

'Is he now?' Steve said, amused. 'Where is he?'

'Kitchen,' grumped Jonesey. 'Put me off my afternoon bun that has.'

Steve headed into the kitchen and saw Toby making PC Warren giggle. She spotted Steve and stood, pulling her uniform straight.

'Guv.' She blushed.

'PC Warren,' Steve said amused. 'Perhaps you'll take our new guest a sandwich and a coffee, please.'

'Guv.' She scuttled out.

'Stop hitting on my staff.' Steve clapped Toby on the back. 'Good to see you, mate. Thanks for bringing him down.'

Toby's eyes were full of mischief.

'What a fucking dick he is. Crapped on all the way down like some petulant child. Tell me we're gonna have some fun with him?'

'Oh yeah. Come find me when you've eaten, and we'll interview him.'

'Music to my ears.' Toby grinned.

Steve returned to his office and called the head of forensics who answered the phone in his usual brisk, but snippy style.

'Ah, Detective. I imagine you're calling regarding the silver Peugeot?'

'I am.'

'My colleagues in the Met are running tests for me under my direction. I have it on the highest priority. I would imagine your absolute priority is matching the paintwork to the silver paintwork found on the other cars at the accident and also placing the suspect in the car?'

'Bang on.'

'Well it doesn't take a genius. Now, do I have prints and DNA from your suspect?'

'Yes, but I'm going to add one more person to it, they'll come to you tomorrow.'

'I suggest you keep your fingers crossed then, Inspector.'

'I'm just about to start with the suspect, so any early heads up will be great.'

'I'll do my best, but we all need to sleep. Goodbye.'

Frustrated, Steve ended the call and looked up to see Toby lounging in the doorway. A grumpy Jonesey behind him in the corridor.

'Jonesey, can you call Gabriella Logan and ask her come in for prints and DNA. If she asks why, tell her it's to eliminate her.'

'Tonight?'

'Yeah, or first thing.'

'On it.'

Steve turned to Toby. 'Let the games begin.'

Steve held the door open for Toby and went and sat down, putting a file carefully on the table. Toby placed his large notebook in front of him and made himself comfortable.

Levinson was sitting opposite with his arms folded and an indignant expression on his face. Steve reached over and pressed record on the tape machine: listed off the date, time and names of those present.

Levinson looked at Steve, eyebrows raised. 'Do you know who I am?' he asked haughtily.

'Mr Lucas,' Steve said, ignoring the look and flicking through his file. 'We wish to discuss the day before and the day of Cassie Warner's death. You appear to have waived the right to a solicitor. Are you sure you don't want one?'

'I have nothing to hide,' he said, his chin raised defiantly.

'Previously, you've spoken to my colleague here, but I just want to recap things for the record.'

'Can I get some sparkling water, please?'

'This isn't a restaurant, Mr Lucas. We can get you some tap water in a moment.'

Levinson Lucas folded his arms and looked mutinously at Steve.

Steve continued. 'So, Mr Lucas, tell me about your movements with Ms Warner on the day before her death.'

'I've told you all this,' he said peevishly, looking at Toby.

'I'd like you to tell me,' Steve said pleasantly.

'We were working on set. We filmed the last of the scenes for that particular set and then we broke for filming for six weeks, until we resume abroad.'

'So you saw each other.'

'Obviously if we were filming together.'

'I assume you're not in every single scene together though.'

'Well, no. But we saw each other *on set* that day.'

'How was she in herself?'

Levinson sighed. 'Fine. She was looking forward to getting away and having a break.'

'Did you see anyone else that day who wasn't film crew?'

He thought for a moment. 'Yes, her friend turned up.'

'Would that be Gabriella Logan?'

'Yes.'

'Who is also your PR person as I understand it?'

'She is.'

'Did you spend time together as a three that day?'

Levinson shrugged. 'We might have chatted together; I don't remember what about.'

'I see. And did you see Ms Warner the day she died?'

'I had a costume fitting, she was there and then I went home.'

'And stayed at home?'

'Yes.'

'All night?'

'Yes.'

'Did you speak to anyone?'

'I doubt it.'

'Do you have a mobile phone, Mr Lucas?'

'Of course I do.'

'May I have the number?'

Levison pulled a phone from his pocket and reeled off the number.

'Can't remember it?' Steve asked.

'I have a terrible memory.'

'Must be difficult in your job then, learning lines and so on?'

'I'm better with words than numbers.'

'Do you have a car that you use, Mr Lucas?'

'Of course. I have a Jaguar F-TYPE.'

'Right. Any other cars you use and drive?'

'No.'

'Are you absolutely sure about that?'

'Yes.'

'Do you drive yourself to set?'

'I have a driver if it's an early start or a late finish.'

'Always the same driver?'

'I don't know. I don't look at them or speak to them.'

'Right. I just want you to confirm to me that this is the only mobile phone number you have.'

'Have I not just said that?' he said testily.

'I just want to be sure that the number you gave me is the only number you have,' Steve persisted.

Levinson rolled his eyes.

'And that you don't have a burner phone for example,' Steve said.

'I don't know what a burner phone is,' Levinson said.

'I find that hard to believe.'

'Why?' Levinson asked snippily.

'Because a few films ago you played a detective who found a stash of burner phones in a house search if I recall.'

Toby folded his arms. 'I saw that film. Yes, it was a drugs raid. You found drugs in the wall and burner phones under the floor.'

'Mr Lucas, are you sure you don't want a solicitor?'

Levinson was quiet for a moment. 'You can't hold me for long anyway, can you? You'll have to let me go soon.'

'I can hold you for ninety-six hours if I choose to, Mr Lucas, which I may just do, so I suggest you make yourself comfortable.'

Out of his peripheral vision, Steve saw Toby fake a cough to cover a large smile.

Levinson looked at Steve. 'I'd like my solicitor now, please.'

'We'll suspend the interview until he arrives. Will he be coming from London?'

'Yes,' Levinson said sullenly.

'I suggest we reconvene in the morning then. Interview suspended.'

Steve gathered his files up. 'Obviously for your safety, Mr Lucas, as you are here under caution, you will remain in the cells for the evening until your solicitor arrives.'

'Absolutely not.'

Steve opened the door and called, 'PC Garland, if you could take Mr Lucas to our custody sergeant?'

'No problem, Guv.' Garland stepped forward and gestured for Levinson to leave the room.

'We'll resume tomorrow,' Steve called as Levinson was escorted by the elbow down the corridor.

Steve looked at his watch. It was nearly 11 p.m. There was very little he could do so he and Toby headed back to Steve's for a few hours' sleep.

* * *

Foxy had been awoken in the very early hours by his phone ringing. Dr Michaels informed him that Carla had taken a turn for the worst and was now on a ventilator; she was very weak and not responding as well as they had hoped. She intimated to Foxy that he might want to come in and see her. His preference being for straight talking, he asked her what was at the forefront of his mind.

'Is she going to make it? What are the odds?'

'Next few hours are critical,' she said. 'I would look at it as though she has around a thirty per cent chance of pulling through. You ought to say goodbye in case she deteriorates suddenly.'

Foxy was silent for a moment while he processed the information.

'I'm so sorry it's not better news.'

'If I had got her into you the night before, would it have made a difference?'

'In all honesty, probably not. We'll shortly be at a point where we can't try anything else, it's going to be up to Carla soon. I think she can hear though.'

'What makes you say that?'

'She was delirious before we ventilated her. Kept saying repeatedly that she couldn't come now because Dad had asked her to fight for him.'

Foxy felt a weird sensation pass over him. 'What?'

'That's what she said. Over and over. She said I can't come now, Dad's asked me to fight for him. Maybe she thought she was talking to one of your children? Do you have children together?'

'We had a daughter. She died.'

'I see. What was her name?'

'Charlie.'

'She was saying that name. But, as I said, she was delirious. The mind plays funny tricks.'

'Thanks, Doctor, I'll be in shortly.'

Foxy ended the call and thought hard. He remembered talking to Carla yesterday and saying that he needed her to fight for him. In a way, he found it a comfort if she was seeing Charlie. He hoped to God she'd pull through.

Years ago he had realised that his love for Carla was strong, but time had evolved it into something else. A comfortable and safe loving relationship. Like long-term companions or best friends would have. When she wasn't there, he missed her. When he had issues, often he'd wonder what she would say. He didn't want to lose Carla from his life. He prayed she would make it.

* * *

Steve and Toby arrived at the station the next morning. Steve went to see the Superintendent to keep him abreast of proceedings. He also requested, in principle, obtaining an extension of time for Levinson from a magistrate if he felt he needed it. The Superintendent agreed but droned on about the public face of the police and having a celebrity at the station and Steve took a dim view. He informed the Superintendent that he didn't care if this man was a celebrity or not, if he had murdered Cassie Warner in cold blood then he would go down for it. As usual, Steve left the Superintendent's office frustrated and swearing under his breath.

He found Toby chatting up PC Warren in the kitchen again. Jonesey was sitting in the corner looking on murderously and taking refuge in a sausage roll.

'Jonesey,' Steve said. 'Where are the results of the bloody fingerprint Murph sent over that he found on Cassie Warner?'

Jonesey looked blank. 'What bloody fingerprint?'

Steve felt frustration bubbling up inside. 'Fuck's sake, Jonesey,' he exploded. 'If you stopped eating for long enough to get your fucking brain in gear, we might have half a case.'

'But I don't know anything about it!' he said, standing up, crumbs scattering down the front of his uniform.

Steve tried to calm himself down. 'There's a bloody fingerprint that Murph found on Cassie Warner's jawline. He sent it over to fingerprints to compare from our files. Chase it up or get it sent again. Compare it to known people we have on this enquiry.'

'Sorry, Guv, I really didn't know anything about it.'

'You were in the room with me!'

Jonesey looked sheepish. 'I probably wasn't paying attention.'

'Jonesey, I need this like YESTERDAY. Understand me?'

'I'm on it, Guv.'

'Then I need you to get on to Jenny Miller and get a statement about her accident, see if she remembers anything else.'

'Guv.'

* * *

Bree arrived at reception and PC Warren took her for fingerprints and DNA collection. Steve had requested that she either wait or come back after lunch to speak to him again. Bree had chosen to wait, not wanting to have to face Sebastian.

Levinson Lucas's solicitor arrived and regarded the police station reception area with a haughty air of distaste. This irritated the PC on reception so much that he had taken great pleasure in making the solicitor wait. Then he sat a very smelly homeless lady on the seat directly next to him at the earliest opportunity. The PC rang Steve.

'Solicitor is here for Mr Lucas.'

'OK, I'll get someone to bring him in.'

'No rush, Guv. No rush at all.'

'Why do you say that?'

'Annoyed me. Turned up in a poncy pinstripe suit, looked down his nose at everything with a right old dog shit moustache. So I've sat him next to smelly Mary for ten minutes before we run her down to the doctor's. Give him the full effect.'

Steve laughed loudly. 'I'll take my sweet time then.'

'Knew you'd understand.'

Steve's phone rang again. This time it was the snippy tones of the head of forensics.

'You're in luck. The silver Peugeot from London is an exact match to the paint found on the car at the scene and the green Ford Fiesta.'

'Could it be argued that any silver Peugeot would throw up the same result?'

'Not in this case. Large panels of this car have been resprayed with a slightly different mix of silver paint, so the combination of the two are fairly unique I would say.'

'What about inside the car?'

'Oh it gets better. Fingerprints from Mr Lucas are present, as well as DNA, plus the miniscule presence of Cassie Warner's blood in the footwell and traces on the steering wheel.'

'Superb news.'

'Your new fingerprints have just been sent over and I'll wait for the DNA file, but I'll get onto that as a priority. You have the suspect in custody as you say, so let's see if we can throw the kitchen sink at them, shall we?'

'I like your style.'

'I'll be in touch.'

Steve went to the canteen to find Toby.

'PC Warren, you are here to work and not entertain southerners,' he said loudly. 'Mr Lucas's solicitor is here. Please put him in an interview room and go and get Mr Lucas.'

'Guv.'

'I'll help.' Jonesey scrambled up.

'I need the results of that fingerprint,' Steve warned.

'Never arrived, so I've had Murph send it again and the fingerprint technician is on it now. Super high priority. Costing me a bloody custard tart that is.'

Steve looked at Toby. 'You ready to rock and roll?'

'Oh yeah.' Toby gave a cruel smile.

CHAPTER 33

Steve allowed Levinson some time with his solicitor before him and Toby entered the room.

As they walked in Steve overheard the solicitor say, 'Don't worry Levinson you'll be out of here by lunchtime, these local hicks have no idea what they're doing.'

Steve took an instant dislike to the solicitor, which wasn't particularly unusual for Steve, he often disliked the slick suits who tried to undermine cases to get their clients off. He resumed the tape recording and went through the introductions.

'Mr Lucas,' Steve began. 'Picking up from yesterday, I asked you if you had more than one mobile phone number.' He reeled off a phone number. 'This was the number you said was the one phone you used, but I asked you if you had any more mobile phones, such as a burner phone.' He consulted his notes. 'You purported not to know what a burner phone was and then requested your solicitor. So, Mr Lucas. I will ask you again. Do you possess a burner phone?'

Levinson Lucas shifted in his seat and looked at his solicitor.

'I've got no comment to make about that,' he said haughtily.

Steve looked at Toby and then the solicitor. 'Is this how it's going to be?'

The solicitor raised an eyebrow.

'Mr Lucas, I asked you yesterday whether you had access to another car, and you said no. Is that correct?'

'Yes.'

'To clarify, you do not drive any other car?'

'Correct.'

'Just to be absolutely clear. You have no comment on whether you own a burner phone, and you claim to *not* have use of, or drive, another car.'

'Correct.'

'Can I ask who Lorensa Morales is, please?'

'She's my housekeeper.'

'Can you confirm that she owns a silver Peugeot?' He read out the number plate and showed Levinson a picture.

'I don't recall.'

'Does Ms Morales live at your house?'

'Yes. She has her own quarters.'

'So the car will be at your house.'

'I suppose so, I've not noticed it.'

'I see. Do you consider yourself not to be very observant?

'I beg your pardon?'

'Surely your property is not so big that you wouldn't notice a silver car parked in your driveway most days.' Steve turned to Toby. 'Perhaps you'd like to refresh Mr Lucas's memory with your photos taken a few days ago?'

Toby showed pictures of Levinson's house, which clearly showed Levinson's Jaguar and the silver Peugeot on the drive together.

Levinson looked at the pictures impassively.

'So, despite it being there, you don't notice it?' Steve said.

Levinson crossed his arms.

Steve pushed. 'To clarify, you haven't noticed a silver car belonging to your housekeeper parked in your driveway?'

Levinson just stared at him.

'An answer for the tape, please, Mr Lucas.'

'I am unaware of it.'

'And you don't have a burner phone?'

'I have no comment about that.'

'Excellent. Well, I am compelled to inform you, Mr Lucas, that I have witness testimony stating you do have a burner phone. I also have the phone records from that phone, placing a number of calls between yourself, Gabriella Logan and Cassie Warner. I also have the location data for that phone in the vicinity of your London address. So I ask you again. Do you have a burner phone?'

'No comment.'

Steve carried on. 'We seized the silver Peugeot belonging to your housekeeper. We have forensically investigated this car and have discovered your fingerprints, your DNA, and blood from Cassie Warner on the driver's side floor and steering wheel. So, just to fully clarify, that would be the silver Peugeot that you don't drive, or don't notice parked in the driveway of your home.'

Levinson had gone deathly pale and looked at his solicitor.

'No comment,' he said tightly.

Two sharp raps on the door heralded code for an urgent message. Steve stood and said, 'Excuse me for one moment. DI Miller leaving the room.'

Steve found Jonesey hopping about in the corridor grinning.

'What?'

'That bloody fingerprint from Murphy on Cassie Warner's face is a partial match to Levinson Lucas's prints.'

'Good job, Jonesey.'

'Thanks. By the way, Jenny Miller just remembers a shove from behind.'

'OK. Thanks.'

Steve returned to the interview room and sat down.

'DI Miller returning.' He glanced at Levinson. 'We were talking about the car that you aren't aware of and don't have the use of, that had your DNA and fingerprints in. We also have the location of the burner phone that you have no comment on in the vicinity of the accident on the night of Cassie Warner's death and in the vicinity of your home.'

'That proves nothing,' Levinson said.

Steve continued. 'During the Cassie Warner's postmortem we recovered a bloody fingerprint on her face. The PM concluded that she had been suffocated by someone holding her nose and covering her mouth and I propose that someone was you.'

'That's preposterous!' Levinson gasped. 'You have no evidence of that.'

'Mr Lucas, it has just been confirmed that the fingerprint was a partial match to one of your fingerprints.'

Steve sat back and watched Levinson's face get paler as the enormity of the situation sank in. He turned to Levinson's solicitor and said in a conversational tone, 'I hope you've brought your PJs with you. This is going to take some time; us local hicks take ages to get organised. I'll leave you alone for a little while now so you can have a think about what you recall and what you don't recall. Then we'll resume and take a full statement. Interview terminated.'

Steve and Toby left the interview room and Toby clapped Steve on the back.

'You are a fucking legend, mate. His face. Part of me wished I'd taken a picture to sell to the tabloids. I could retire on what I'd get for it.'

'I'll certainly get a kick out of his fall from grace, arrogant twat,' Steve muttered. 'Are you staying around for his statement or are you heading off?'

'Gaffer wants me back. So, I'll head back. Thanks for the bed for the night. Shame we didn't get to go out on the lash.'

'If it comes to court you'll have to give evidence, you interviewed him first. We'll do it then.'

'Hold you to that.'

'Thanks, Toby. Appreciate everything you've done.'

'Give PC Warren my warmest regards, won't you.'

'Bugger off.'

Steve returned to his office and thought about the car accident. Mentally he tried to piece together what had happened on the road, but it wasn't clear to him, especially whether there had been a car coming in the opposite direction. His phone rang.

'Miller.'

'Inspector, more good news,' the Head of Forensics said. 'The prints you sent this morning match those found on the passenger side of the Silver Peugeot. The DNA will take longer.'

'What?' Steve said distractedly.

'I repeat. The prints that you sent this morning were a match to that found—'

'Yes, I heard that part,' Steve interrupted, frustrated. 'The name you have on the prints?'

'Gabriella Logan. Let me see... yes, a PC Warren sent them over. I confirm they are a match.'

'Oh.'

'Not expecting that, Inspector?'

'Not at all.'

'We're finishing running the other sample now… an Edwyn Lewis, against the green Ford Fiesta too. Results should be available in a few hours. We need to double check DNA. You know, dot the Is and cross the Ts and so on.'

'Thanks.'

'I'll be in touch.'

Steve put the phone down. He tried to understand what Bree could have been doing in the silver Peugeot. Then it occurred to him that she could have been in that car at any time. He frowned and then suddenly remembered that she was at the station, she had opted to wait after giving her samples. He called through to reception and asked her to be brought into an interview room.

Bree sat waiting nervously. She had tried to call Levinson the previous evening and neither of his phones were on. She was dreading Steve's questioning. She was also at the point where she just wanted to go home, away from all of this. Away from Sebastian's concerned questions.

Steve entered the room and sat down. He activated the tape recorder and went through the preliminaries.

'We'll continue from our previous interview. Are you sure you don't want a solicitor?'

'I'm fine, thank you.'

'I just want to recap your movements on the day Cassie died.'

'I've told you all this.'

'Yes, you had a lunch with someone, yes, that's checked out. But what about after that?'

'Well, I went home.'

'What did you do?'

'Watched TV, looked at my phone. Usual stuff.'

'You looked at your phone? Like what? Twitter? Instagram?'

'Yes.'

'I thought you said your phone was switched off because you got tired of all the calls?'

'Maybe I was on my iPad then.'

'I see.'

'Did you order any food to be delivered or anything?'

'No. I'd had a big lunch, I wasn't hungry.'

'OK. I just need some background on Levinson Lucas's cars. Does he just drive the Jag?'

'Not very often. He prefers to be driven. He thinks it's better for his image.' She rolled her eyes.

'So there are no other cars that you are aware of?'

'No.'

'Any other cars you've travelled in with him?'

'No.'

Steve leant back in his chair and watched her. She shifted uncomfortably.

'Are you absolutely sure about that, Bree?'

'Yes,' she said firmly.

'It's just that we've found your fingerprints along with Levinson's in the car that belongs to his housekeeper.'

Bree stayed silent.

'Just to be clear, I'm referring to the silver Peugeot and not the Jag,' Steve finished.

Bree stared at Steve, her face draining of colour.

'Why don't you tell me when you were last in this car, Bree?' Steve said softly.

'I really don't even remember...' she faltered.

'It's important you try to remember.'

'What are you accusing me of?' Her voice shook.

'I just want to know your best recollection of when you were last in the silver Peugeot, please.'

Bree ran her hands through her hair and Steve noticed they were shaking. There was a loud tap on the door.

'Interview suspended.'

Steve left the room. Jonesey was waiting outside with a handful of paper and a half-eaten Mars bar.

'Have you interrupted me for a half-time snack?'

'What? No.' Jonesey looked affronted. 'I've just had the analyst calling about the cell phone data. She missed something. So I've checked and checked again. This number here?' He pointed to a number and next to it was scribbled Bree's name. 'Well this number here was switched off on the day Cassie died. Last location London. But this is what she missed. It was switched back on for a few minutes in the vicinity of Cassie Warner's accident and a 999 call was made, but then it was shut off again just as the call was answered. Next time it was switched on it was back in London.'

A chill ran down Steve's back. 'This says her phone was in the vicinity of the accident. She must have known Levinson killed her.'

'Exactly! What a fucking bitch!' Jonesey exclaimed in a loud stage whisper, looking indignant. 'There she is, lording it about with the husband without a care in the world, and all along she knew. Fuck! With friends like that who needs enemies?'

Steve leant against the wall for a moment. He couldn't quite believe the duplicity of the woman. To appear nice and caring, a little bitter about Cassie, a little in love with Sebastian, while all the time keeping a dreadful secret.

'Well done, Jonesey,' he said.

Steve took a deep breath and walked back into the room. He watched Bree as he sat down and tried to ensure his face remained impassive. He pressed record and informed Bree that the interview was continuing under caution.

'I'm waiting for an answer, Bree. For you to clarify when you were last in the silver Peugeot.'

'I don't recall,' she said, twisting a ring on her finger nervously.

'I think you do.'

'Well, you tell me then,' she said obstinately, folding her arms.

Steve sat back in his chair and studied Bree. She shifted uncomfortably under his gaze.

'Why are you staring at me?'

'Here's what I think happened,' he said. 'I think you had your lunch out then and went home. I think Levinson turned up. Angry, desperate, obsessed. Wanted to know where Cassie's house was in Wales. Threatened all sorts. I think *you* decided to go with him because you thought maybe you could talk him around on the way?' He leant forward. 'How am I doing so far?'

* * *

Sebastian was on the beach with Tabatha. They were throwing balls for Jack and Alfie. Laughing at Jack when he got sidetracked and chased seagulls.

'Dad, why do the police keep talking to Aunty Bree?' Tabatha asked.

'No idea,' Sebastian said, frowning.

'Do you think she's OK?'

'I don't know, darling; she won't talk to me.'

'Have you tried?'

Sebastian looked affronted. 'Of course I've tried.'

'Perhaps you need to try harder,' Tabatha observed dryly. 'Jude has a theory.'

'Would this be the Jude who is now your boyfriend?'

'Shut up, Dad,' she said, blushing furiously.

'So, what's your boyfriend's theory?'

'That she's in love with you. Completely.'

Sebastian thought back to her comment on Christmas Eve and the half-finished conversation they'd had a few days previously.

'Rubbish,' he said dismissively, feeling uncomfortable at the prospect. 'I've never looked at her that way.'

'Question is, Dad, do you *want* to look at her that way?'

'She's a friend, nothing more. I've told you, I've never looked at her that way.'

'Hmm. Suzy's your friend and I see you totally checking her out.'

'What?' Seb looked flustered.

'Just saying, Dad.' She grinned widely. 'Suzy's gorgeous. You're not a monk either. Mum would want you to be happy. To love again.'

'What? But your mum… she… look, I can't think like that. It's too soon. I'm not…'

'But is it? Too soon? I don't think so. Life is short, Dad. We both know it. Grab it when you can if it means happiness.' She looked at him with eyes that were older than her teenage years. Suddenly she was all business again. 'Are you OK to drop Alfie back to Jenny's? She said she'd be up and about tomorrow and able to walk him.'

'No problem.' Seb stared at this creature who, not long ago, was waddling around the beach in a sunhat with a bucket and spade, and was now giving him advice on his love life.

* * *

Bree looked at Steve in horror. *He knew.* He knew she had been in the car with Levinson. She had wild thoughts of trying to kill herself so the truth wouldn't come out and she wouldn't have to face the consequences. She couldn't deal with it. She certainly couldn't deal with Sebastian and Tabatha knowing. She would be ruined. Her reputation, her business. A tear rolled down her cheek and she made no effort to brush it away.

'I tried to stop it,' she said desperately. 'I tried.'

392

'I wonder whether part of you perhaps wanted Sebastian to find out because of how you feel about him?'

'What makes you think I feel any particular way about Sebastian?' She raised her chin defiantly.

'I think we're way past that, aren't we?' Steve said quietly. 'It would have been great, wouldn't it? In some way? Seb finding out about Cassie and her infidelities on set. It would have destroyed him surely. Then you could have stepped in and been supportive.'

'Is that what you think of me?' Bree whispered. Her eyes filled with tears. 'You think I would be so manipulative?'

'You tell me,' Steve said. 'What happened in the car?'

'I think I might need a solicitor,' she said.

'Do you have a solicitor?'

'I do.'

'Let me guess. They're in London.'

Bree nodded.

'OK. You can make the call and then we'll wait. You'll need to remain in custody until they arrive.'

Bree's eyes filled with tears again.

'It's not up for discussion, Bree.'

Steve returned to his office and found an email confirming what he already knew; that Edwyn Lewis's prints and DNA were present in the green Ford Fiesta. This further reinforced the theory Edwyn had been in some sort of contact with the murder scene. Steve suspected that Rusty was the passenger, but he needed his DNA to confirm it.

Frustrated about the whole situation with Bree and Levinson, Steve wanted to take action immediately, so he marched out of his office to find Jonesey and Garland.

'Jonesey,' he barked as he caught him plying PC Warren with a packet of crisps. 'Get Garland, a taser and some vests. Tell Sarge we're leaving in five minutes to arrest Edwyn Lewis. Meet me out back.'

'Guv,' said Jonesey, pushing himself off the desk.

Steve drove aggressively towards Edwyn Lewis's house. The police radio burbled and Jonesey checked in with control.

'Disturbance just reported at Edwyn Lewis's place.'

'Tell them we're on it and request backup. The bloke's a psycho.'

Jonesey called it in.

Steve arrived at the Lewis house and pulled to a halt in the road next to a large hedge.

'Everyone in a vest?' he checked. 'Right, let's go in slowly. Body cams on.'

Steve edged slowly through the entrance in the overgrown hedge. Hesitantly, the three of them walked into the yard in front of the dirty white bungalow. Angry, raised voices could be heard towards the back of the building. Steve motioned to Jonesey and Garland to follow him. As they rounded the corner, they saw father and son facing each other.

Edwyn Lewis was holding a shortened scaffold pole. In front of him was a tall, thin man in his twenties with reddish hair, who was pointing a sawn-off shotgun at Edwyn. He wore a ragged black Metallica vest top, a large tattoo on his arm could be clearly seen. In the freezing air his lips looked almost blue, despite the high flush on his cheeks. Tears were pouring down his face and he was shaking his head at Edwyn.

Neither noticed Steve.

'I think we've found Rusty,' Jonesey said out of the corner of his mouth. 'See that tattoo, that's Cassie Warner's face.'

Rusty was weeping and looked trance-like.

'All these years,' he said bitterly, the gun shaking. 'All these years of you beating me. *Hurting* me.' His voice shook. 'Really hurting me… doing those *things* to me. Calling me *special*. Doing those things again and again and again. Telling me it was our secret because I was so special. Well, I'm not special anymore. Not for you. Not for your *special* friends. You killed the only thing I ever cared about. The only thing I ever loved. So now I am going to kill you.'

'She was a stupid actress! You didn't love her. You're sick in the fucking head!' Edwyn roared. 'She was a tart, a floozy, a whore! She wasn't going to be interested in a fucking half-wit like you. You're dreaming. Just like your mother. A fucking waste of space. Only ever good for one thing and even then it wasn't that great. You saw her in a film and then thought she'd want you? YOU? You're sick in the head. She was out of your league. Everyone is out of your fucking league. You were born a fucking dimwit. Stupid. Thick. Damaged. A fucking idiot!'

'Yeah, well I was good enough for you and your mates, wasn't I?'

'All something like you is ever good for. Fucking useless at everything else.'

'You killed her. You were driving. You ran her off the road.'

'You were the sad fucker stalking her. Waiting for her to come down. You knew she was coming down. You waited for her. You sick fuck. You disgust me. You're sick in the fucking head. I should have let them take you and lock you up.'

'YOU KILLED HER!' yelled Rusty, hoisting the gun higher.

'I DIDN'T KILL HER!' Edwyn bellowed, taking a step forwards. 'It was that car behind us, trying to get past, ramming us, it pushed us into her car.'

'YOU killed her,' wailed Rusty, dropping to his knees, sobbing, still holding the gun. 'You killed her, and I loved her. She was nice to me.'

'She said one thing to you and then probably laughed about you behind your back. The stupid thick boy hanging about like a lovesick fucking idiot.'

'It wasn't like that. She was nice to me. She *knew* me. She gave me food once and a jumper. She was nice to me. She could have *loved* me.'

Edwyn shook his head. 'What the fuck did I ever do to get such fucking idiot sons?' he shouted. 'She felt sorry for the sick fuck that hung about like a bad fucking smell.'

'NO!'

'Yes. She was a fucking whore like all the other women in the world.'

'Take that back,' Rusty shouted.

'NO! I've had enough of this. You don't hold a gun to me, you little shit. How dare you. Who the fuck do you think you are?'

Steve heard the faint wail of a siren in the distance. He moved out of position, nodding to Jonesey and Garland who had their tasers ready.

'POLICE! Put down the weapon now, Rusty. Edwyn drop the pole.'

Both men looked at Steve in surprise when he stepped out. Steve saw everything happen as if time had slowed down.

Edwyn looked at Rusty and raised the scaffold pole like it was a baseball bat, ready to hit him with it. Rusty's head turned at the movement and he bought up the barrel of the gun, shooting Edwyn in the chest at close range.

'DROP THE GUN, RUSTY!' shouted Steve.

Terrified, Rusty threw the gun away and stared at Steve who was running towards him. He dropped to the ground and curled himself up into a small ball and started crying.

Backup pulled into the drive, bathing the white bungalow in flashing blue lights in the twilight.

Steve kicked the shotgun away and approached Edwyn Lewis. The damage to his chest was irreversible. Edwyn was gasping for breath, blood bubbling from his mouth, fingers clawing at the ground.

He reached a hand out to Steve and tried desperately to talk. Steve ignored it and stood watching impassively as the final few moments of Edwyn Lewis's life ebbed away.

CHAPTER 34

It was late evening when Steve finally left the station. He walked down through the town, called into the supermarket and bought a few bottles of beer. He wanted to sit and mentally sift through the horrors he'd heard before taking it inside to Kate's. He needed to process it, so it didn't taint the sweet time he had with her.

He sat on one of the picnic benches outside Maggie's, which was in darkness, and watched the sea roll in. It calmed him and allowed him to focus. Cracking open a beer he drank deeply and then exhaled heavily. He was beyond exhausted. Rusty had been incredibly difficult to interview. He veered from being angry to incredibly upset, with the two moods being at the absolute extreme.

Steve had discovered Rusty had been living in the lofts of Compass Row for years, preferring to spend time away from his father, which was understandable now Steve had heard the systematic abuse he had suffered.

Rusty had first moved into Compass Row when he met Cassie on the beach one day. She was nice to him, chatted to him and gave him a sandwich. She had been on her own then and he claimed they had been friends, often chatting. She had given him an old jumper of Seb's and looked out for him a little.

Rusty became besotted with her. He followed her home and watched the place. He broke in to the end house (now Jenny's), and realised that he could get across all the loft spaces and into Cassie's house too. He liked to do that. To be around her things. He felt close to her. He cried for days when she went away.

Rusty said he always knew when she was coming down because the housekeeper came in and gave the house a good clean, changed the beds and filled up the fridge. If there was food in the fridge, Rusty knew she was coming. He knew which road she drove in on and sometimes liked to wait for her and follow her into town if he could find a car to use.

He liked to take pictures of her and saved up his money to buy disposable cameras. But when he didn't have any money, he would borrow Teddy's camera if he could find it. Sometimes Teddy took his camera back though, so he never got to see the pictures.

Rusty talked very matter-of-factly about the level of abuse he had suffered from an early age. His father preferred him for sex; Teddy and Danny for physical violence. Rusty talked about his father and his father's friends, who routinely sexually abused him in the caravan at the rear of the property. Rusty said he thought sometimes the men gave his dad money to be with him. Rusty broke down and cried, saying how much they hurt him.

Rusty wasn't starved of food like Teddy had been. Rusty said he was given Teddy's food, bought nice clothes and sometimes had a nice treat like ice cream or chocolate, but there was always some sort of payment to be made. His father would often force himself on him after giving him a treat. Rusty hated treats.

He talked about the violence growing up. He talked about how Edwyn had beaten Teddy with a metal pole. Rusty said he wanted to take Teddy to hospital afterwards, but Edwyn had refused and locked Rusty in the caravan. He said Teddy slept for four days after the beating and wouldn't wake up. When he did, he wasn't the same. He couldn't think very fast afterwards and was slow at doing normal things. Rusty said neither him nor Teddy ever really went to school, and he was sad about that.

He said when Danny came along nothing changed, only that Teddy and Danny were beaten more. Rusty said his father threw Danny across the room once when he was a baby and he didn't wake up for a whole day. After that he was a much quieter baby. Rusty said he wasn't close to Danny and Teddy. He said he didn't want to see them because they knew what he was. That he was dirty and it was his fault his father did those things to him.

Steve closed his eyes and exhaled deeply. He finished his beer and took another. Once they had talked about Rusty's home life, they had moved onto the accident. After all of the reconstructing the police had done, the accident had been surprisingly simple.

Rusty said he had come around from the beating, and a silver car had been following them too closely on the narrow winding road into Castleby.

Edwyn was angry about it and was shouting and braking hard to try and force them back. The silver car had seemed desperate to get past and bumped the back of the Fiesta, which shunted it into the Porsche. The Porsche had shot forwards, fishtailing. The silver car had then overtaken, forcing the Fiesta aside, scraping its side. It had then pulled in front of the Fiesta, braking hard, making the Fiesta slam into the back of it. Both Rusty and his father hit their heads when the air bags hadn't deployed.

The silver car had surged forward into the rear of the Porsche and sent it swerving. Rusty said he'd seen a bright light coming the other way which had blinded him. Then the Porsche braked hard and swerved, flying off the road.

Rusty had cried as if his heart was broken as he recounted seeing Cassie's car disappear from sight. He wailed as he told them how he had wanted Edwyn to stop the car so he could get out to go to Cassie, but Edwyn carried on driving. Rusty looked over his shoulder as they drove off and said he had seen a man get out of the silver car, slide down the bank and disappear from sight. He said he saw a woman get out too and follow him.

Tearfully, Rusty recounted that he had finally got out of the car while it was still moving and had run back up the road. He saw the man who had been driving the silver car leaning into the Porsche. He was shouting and crying; the woman was standing just behind him. Rusty said the woman had been screaming and crying at the man and that he had pulled her away by the hair. She screamed that she didn't want to get back in the car and that they needed to call the police. Rusty said the man dragged her away.

Rusty had crept down the hill and saw Cassie was dead. He sobbed as he told Steve how she looked and that he thought the girl next to her was dead too. He said he was sorry and that he had taken some pictures of her with Teddy's camera, because he wanted to remember her. He said tearfully that he had loved her and that no one had loved her like he had.

Steve asked Rusty if he had called 999, but Rusty said he didn't own a phone. He didn't know who called the police.

Steve remembered producing the photographs that he had found in Jenny's house and asking Rusty if these were the pictures he had taken. Rusty said yes and then Steve showed him the blurry picture of a man through the car window that had come from Teddy's most recent camera film.

Rusty said he wasn't a nice man and that he had hurt him in the caravan, but didn't know who he was or who had taken it. He assumed Teddy must have taken it. Rusty kept weeping and saying he was sorry he took pictures of Cassie when she was dead. He said that he thought he'd seen Cassie on the cliffs one day and thought for a moment that she hadn't died after all, but then he realised it wasn't her. He admitted to getting angry with the woman and pushing her. He also admitted to pushing Jenny down the stairs. He wanted her to leave so he could be left alone to live there, to be near Cassie's things.

With Rusty tearful and exhausted, Steve figured he had enough of an idea what happened, so he stopped the interview and Rusty was taken to a cell for the night.

It had always bothered Steve who it was that could have called the police that night and he vowed to listen to the recording again in the morning. He felt a presence next to him and turned to see Kate watching him.

'I saw you down here. Drinking and thinking,' she said lightly. 'Tough day?'

'And then some,' he said wryly.

'Is that why you're out here?'

'Didn't want to bring it in.'

'Want to talk about it?'

'No.'

'Sure?'

'Yup.'

'Wanna do something else?'

'Like?'

'Got any of those swellings to show me?'

'Oh yeah.'

* * *

Steve woke ridiculously early the next morning and silently climbed out of bed and got ready for work. He kissed Kate goodbye softly and left her a note before heading to the station. It was even too early for Maggie's to be open. At the station Steve sat at his desk and thought about Rusty's account of the night of the accident.

Levinson so far had refused to admit he had killed Cassie. He maintained he was trying to give her CPR, which was why his fingerprint was on her face, but Steve didn't believe a word of it. The truth, and pivotal evidence, partly rested on Bree's account of the night in question, so Steve would have a chat with her once her solicitor had turned up.

He made a quick decision and went back into town, heading for the council depot.

Teddy was where Steve expected him to be: fast asleep in the van they used. Steve knocked softly on the window. Teddy opened an eye and shot upright in his seat.

'It's OK, Teddy,' Steve said. 'I know it's early, want to come and have breakfast with me?'

Teddy eagerly climbed out of the truck and trailed after Steve down the road to Maggie's, rubbing his eyes and hair. They chose what to eat and Steve pointed Teddy over to a table and waited for Maggie to make drinks.

'Hear it all kicked off at the Lewis place,' Maggie said softly. 'Does he know yet?'

'He will in a minute,' said Steve, picking up the drinks and going over to Teddy.

'Here you go,' Steve said, passing him his special mug that Maggie had replaced for him.

'Thank you, Mr Steve. Why are we having breakfast together?'

'I've got something to tell you. It's pretty important. And I have a question.'

Teddy sipped his tea and looked at him with wide eyes. 'OK.'

Steve struggled for a moment. 'Do you remember when we got your pictures developed in an hour, Teddy?'

Teddy nodded. 'I still can't believe that. An hour!'

'Do you remember the photograph of the man in the car… it was quite blurry, and you said Rusty must have taken it?'

'Yes…' Teddy said cagily.

'Rusty says he didn't take it.'

Teddy looked guilty and avoided Steve's eye.

'You found Rusty then.'

'I won't be cross, Teddy. You should know that by now. We're mates, aren't we?'

'Yes.'

'Can you tell me where you took the photograph?'

'I don't like to think about it.'

'It's OK.'

'You'll be cross that I didn't tell you.'

'It's OK. Tell me now.'

Teddy's eyes filled with tears. He whispered. 'It was a man that hurt Rusty.'

'In the caravan?'

Teddy's eyes were like saucers. 'You know about the caravan?'

'Rusty told me.'

Teddy shook his head and screwed his eyes shut. 'Rusty was in the caravan. I was asleep in the barn, and I woke up and heard Rusty screaming. The man was hurting him. He managed to get away, Rusty said he'd hit him, and the man ran out of the caravan and got in his car. I saw him and took a picture because I thought I ought to tell someone what the man had done to Rusty. 'Cause he hurt him. I knew he wanted it to stop. He didn't say much to me, but he said that.'

404

'Did you know who the man was?'

Teddy shook his head. 'No. Never seen him around and I see most people around. Are you cross with me? About the photograph?'

'No. Course not. But, Teddy, I've got something else to tell you. It changes everything. It's about your dad.'

Teddy inhaled sharply and looked around fearfully, poised to run. Steve patted his arm.

'It's OK. It's OK. Your dad isn't ever going to hurt you again.'

'Never?' Teddy asked doubtfully. '*Never ever?*'

'No.'

'Why's that? Is he going away?'

'Teddy, your dad was killed last night. He's dead.'

Teddy stared at him. 'Dead? Who killed him?'

'Rusty did. He shot him.'

'Was he being nice to Rusty again in the caravan? Was that why he did it?'

'They argued and your dad was going to hurt him, and Rusty shot him.' Steve glanced at Teddy. 'Are you alright? It's big news.'

Teddy picked up his tea and sipped it. 'So if he's dead. That means he can't hurt me, Rusty or Danny anymore?'

'Yes.'

Teddy's eyes filled with tears. One escaped and rolled down his cheek leaving a clear trail in the grime.

'I'm sorry, Teddy. I didn't want to upset you,' Steve said softly.

Teddy sniffed and wiped his nose with the back of his hand. 'It's OK, Mr Steve. These are good tears. Danny calls them happy tears.'

Steve walked Teddy back to work and left him with Barry after having a quick word. It was still early, so Steve went via Anna's house and told her the news quietly.

'Is Teddy OK?' she asked.

'I've just dropped him off at work. He cried, but says it was good tears.'

'Oh bless him. I'll go and find him after work and see if I can persuade him to come here for a bit if he wants to.'

'Any support you need with social services or anything, Anna, just say. The systematic abuse he's suffered makes him a vulnerable adult. I'll do everything I can to keep him safe.'

'Thanks, Steve. Where's Rusty?'

'In custody. He has his own problems. Not sure what the CPS will do.'

'I'll let Danny know.'

'Thanks, Anna. I mean it. Anything I can do.'

Steve returned to the station and entered reception at the same time as Bree's solicitor arrived. Steve signed her in and escorted her to an interview room. He sent a PC off to collect Bree so they could have some time together.

Steve tapped out a text to Sebastian asking if he could come to the station that day. Sebastian replied saying he'd be in early afternoon as he had some work calls. Steve was dreading telling Sebastian, but he had promised; he felt a strong duty to tell him before the tabloids got to it, which he knew was inevitable. Steve made some calls, replied to some emails and then collected his files before heading to the interview room.

'Morning,' he said as he sat down and activated the tape recorder before running through the introductions.

Steve addressed Bree. 'We suspended the interview yesterday because we got to the point where I was asking you what happened in the car, and you requested your solicitor. Is that correct?'

Bree nodded.

'For the tape, please.'

'Correct.'

'So, what happened in the car, please?'

Bree looked at her solicitor and exhaled heavily.

'Levinson was crazy. He'd lost it. He was obsessed. He was driving like a mad thing all the way. Ranting and raving about Cassie. About telling Sebastian so that he and Cassie could be together. It was like I wasn't there... all these crazy plans about their future, what they would do, films they would make. Like he had a life plan all mapped out.'

'Why did you get in the car with him?'

'Because I thought I could talk him out of going down there on the way.'

'What did you say to try and talk to him out of it?'

'I couldn't get a word in. When I did talk, he looked at me like he was surprised to find me in the car.'

'He drove all the way to Castleby without knowing where to go?'

'He did know it was Castleby, he just didn't know where they lived.' Bree rested her elbows on the table and held her head in her hands. 'I genuinely thought he listened to me. That I could tell him not to do this. He just wasn't hearing anything I said.' She lifted her head, tears glistening in her eyes. 'I wish I'd never got in the fucking car with him.'

'What happened in the car?'

She sighed deeply. 'We somehow managed to catch up with them, I don't know how. She drove everywhere like she was rallying. But he spotted the car as it pulled into a garage. He was saying that he didn't want Tabatha to see him, he'd seen her in the front seat, so he drove around the back of the garage and managed to get in that way. I don't know what happened in there, but when he came out, he was white lipped with anger.' She gave a half laugh. 'And that is never a good sign with him.'

'Does he get violent?'

Bree folded her arms. 'He has got rough with people, yes.'

'How rough?'

'Enough to require a gag order and a payoff.'

Steve raised an eyebrow.

'That man doesn't know how to control himself, let alone listen when someone is saying no.'

'No as in… forced himself on someone?'

'Yes, that's hardly relevant now.'

'I think it goes towards character,' he said, glancing at the solicitor.

'Well, yes then. On two occasions.'

'Right. We'll need those names. After the garage, you don't know what was said?'

'Nope. But he got in the car and was livid, muttering that she couldn't order him about, who did she think she was and that no one was going to tell him what to do. He said he was going to really make her pay.'

'What did you think that meant?'

'I don't know. I hated the sound of it. I knew what he was like. As soon as he stopped in Castleby I was going to get out and try and get away. Warn them.'

'What happened?'

'As we left the garage he got a call from his agent, saying Cassie was threatening to pull out of the film. He needed that film. He was running out of money and was desperate to be cast in a different sort of role; this film would have done it for him.'

'What was his reaction?'

Bree closed her eyes. 'Every day, I think if he hadn't got that call at that time, then Cassie would definitely still be alive.'

'Really?'

Bree looked serious and leant forward to emphasise her point.

'Absolutely. It was like a red mist settled on him afterwards. He had no idea I was with him. He was driving crazily; no regard for anyone's safety, like he was possessed. Overtaking on bends, tailgating, flashing people to get out of the way. I've never seen anything like it. It was like he couldn't hear what I was saying, I was shouting and screaming at him to stop. I grabbed the wheel but he hit me hard and carried on like nothing had happened. We came up behind a green car and it was going quite slow. Levinson was screaming at them, honking his horn, flashing his lights, yelling out of the window... He looked... he looked...'

'What?'

'Pure evil,' she said quietly.

'Then what happened?'

'He couldn't get past the green car, and then he just went for it, just before a bend. He clipped the green car, and we hit them on the side and then he cut in front of it behind the Porsche... God, he was going so fast...' She shook her head. 'So fast. He was angry and shouting at the green car and he braked hard. They slammed into the back of us.' Tears poured down Bree's cheeks. 'I was so frightened. I thought he was going to kill us.'

'Go on,' Steve said, passing her some tissues.

She swiped at her eyes. 'When they slammed into us... which was his fault! We shot forwards, right into the back of Cassie. I remember looking at Levinson and the look... the look on his face was awful. Evil, he was enjoying it. He floored the car again, like he was going to ram her again.'

'Did Cassie have control of the car?'

'It was fishtailing, the weather... It was so bad. We were nearly on a bend and then he rammed her again. He caught the side of the car and she sort of fishtailed a bit more and then we saw a headlight come around the bend.'

Steve's head snapped up. Rusty had talked about a light coming the other way but hadn't remembered anything else.

'Headlights or a headlight? From the other direction on the other side of the road?'

Bree nodded.

'Was it a car or a motorbike?'

Bree frowned. 'Yes, I remember now… I remember thinking it was a motorbike because it was one light. Then I realised it was a car with only one headlight. I screamed and tried to wrench the wheel, but he hit me again and then everything happened like it was slow motion.' Tears poured down her face unchecked. 'I remember it so vividly,' she whispered, staring into the distance. 'It was like I was watching a film. The Porsche swerved around the oncoming car, and went off the side of the road down into the trees. I saw the headlight of the other car. I heard screaming and wondered who it was, and then realised it was me.' She wiped her face with the back of her hand and sobbed. 'God. Poor Cassie, poor Tabatha. I can't bear it.'

'What happened next?'

'Levinson stopped the car. He just stopped. The green car went around us. Levinson was shouting and swearing, and he ran across the road and down the bank.'

'What about the other cars, can you recall what they were doing?'

Bree sniffed. 'I just don't remember. I managed to get out, and I ran down after Levinson to see if I could help the girls.'

'What did you see then, Bree?'

'He was shouting and crying at her… through the wreckage… I was behind him… I could see…'

'What did you see? What happened? What did Levinson do?'

'He was screaming at her. Yelling about her not leaving the movie, ruining him and she was wailing… calling for Tabatha, and then… and… then…' She gulped in air.

'Then what?'

'He had his hands over her face, and then everything went quiet.'

'Cassie went quiet?'

'Yes. Then I heard him crying and saying sorry, saying he didn't mean it.'

'In your opinion, what was he saying sorry for?'

'I don't want to think… I can't bear it.'

'Bree, what did you think Levinson was doing?'

Bree shuddered and covered her face with her hands again, silently crying, her shoulders heaving. Finally, she dropped her hands and raised her tear-stained face.

'I think… I think he killed her,' she said softly. 'She was alive one minute and then he had his hands on her face and then she was quiet. His rage, I've never seen anything… anyone like it. But I knew what he was capable of.'

'What did you do?'

She sniffed. 'I tried to dial 999, so I switched on my phone and then he was behind me. I was so scared. I thought he was going to kill me. He grabbed me, took my phone and switched it off. He dragged me back to the car.'

'Do you remember any other cars being there?'

She shook her head. 'I don't remember anything. He was dragging me by my hair, yelling at me.'

'What happened then?'

'We drove for hours and then suddenly we were home.'

'His home?'

'No mine. He drove me home. We got there and he dragged me out again. He threatened to tell everyone I was driving if this ever came out; if I ever said anything.' She sniffed and wiped her eyes. 'The man is a fucking psychopath.'

'At the accident you don't remember any other cars around? The one coming towards you. Where that car went?'

'I don't remember it at all.'

Steve pushed her. 'You can't recall anything else about the other cars?'

'Nope.' She wiped her eyes and blew her nose. 'What happens now?'

'You'll be charged, Bree.'

She inhaled sharply and her eyes filled with fresh tears. 'Will I go to prison?'

'Most likely. It's up to higher powers than me. The CPS will review it.'

'I'd like to know what my client will be charged with and when,' Bree's solicitor chipped in.

'We'll get to that,' Steve said grimly. 'It will be more than one charge though.'

Bree looked around the room in panic. 'Oh God. I can't go to prison.'

'I don't think it's an option. I will be charging you.'

CHAPTER 35

The next few hours were gruelling. Bree gave a formal statement and a charge sheet was prepared. In light of Bree's testimony and the other supporting evidence, Levinson was also charged but was still complaining and denying everything. Both were being put in front of a magistrate that afternoon; Levinson had been taken already and Bree was waiting in the custody suite to go.

Steve was shattered. He was grabbing a quick sandwich when Warren appeared, her eyes sparkling.

'Sebastian's in reception,' she said breathlessly, laying a dramatic hand over her eyes. 'Be still my beating heart.'

'Can you bring him into my office?' Steve said, mildly amused.

A few minutes later, there was a knock and Seb came in.

'Hey, Seb,' Steve said, managing a smile. 'Come in, sit down. How's Tabatha doing?'

'She's good. Flourishing. You'd never know. Unless you saw her run. That'll take some time, but she is good.' He recounted a few tales of the puppy.

'It must be a huge relief that she's better.'

Seb exhaled deeply. 'I'd never known fear like it. Hopefully, she'll get stronger and stronger.' He paused for a moment. 'Do you know where Bree is? I'm not sure if she came home last night.'

Steve took a breath and wondered where the hell he was going to start.

'What I'm going to tell you is going to be really upsetting, but I'm compelled to tell you because I don't want you reading about it in the press further down the line.'

'Upsetting?' Seb said cagily.

'I'm not sure where to start. Cassie's postmortem showed us a few surprises.'

'What sort of surprises?' Seb asked.

'She was a few months pregnant.'

Seb's eyes widened. 'Pregnant?'

'Unfortunately, the child wasn't yours.'

Sebastian's face drained of colour.

'Not mine?' He paused for a moment. 'But you know whose it was, right?'

'Yes. It was Levinson Lucas's child.'

Sebastian inhaled deeply and Steve saw a muscle pound in his jaw.

Steve shifted uncomfortably. 'Sebastian, this is really difficult, because if the press get hold of it...'

Sebastian looked stunned. 'There's more?'

'Apparently, it wasn't unusual that Cassie slept with her leading men. She said it made for a better picture.'

'Bree told you that, didn't she? Did she know?'

'Yes.'

'Did she know about Cassie and Lucas?'

'Yes.'

414

'Where is she?'

'In custody.'

Sebastian's face got paler. 'Custody?' he said faintly.

'I have three people in custody linked to your wife's death. One was a passenger, so he isn't culpable, and the other driver has since died. However, I have Levinson Lucas and Gabriella Logan in custody. I have arrested Levinson Lucas for Cassie's murder.'

Sebastian looked pale. 'And Bree?'

'I've charged her with a number of crimes, Seb.'

'What?' Sebastian looked incredulous. 'That can't be right.'

'I'm afraid it is.'

'I can't believe it,' he said, shaking his head in disbelief. Suddenly his head snapped up. 'What aren't you telling me?'

Steve sighed deeply. 'She was there. At the accident.'

Sebastian gaped. 'Bree was there?' he said faintly. 'All this time, she was there and saw it?' He stood up and paced around Steve's office raking his fingers through his hair. 'The things… the things she's been saying, how she was… and all the time she fucking *knew*?' He slumped back down in the chair and rested his elbows on his knees, his head in his hands. 'I can't believe she fucking *knew.*' He looked up at Steve. 'I don't understand what happened.'

'It's complicated and I'm still collating final statements. But the evidence shows Levinson was driving with Bree in the car. He was coming down to confront Cassie because she'd ended the affair. He wanted you told. Bree went along to try and talk him out of it. He rowed with Cassie at a petrol station and then was behind her trying to stop the car. His driving effectively forced her off the road. We think he then suffocated her by holding her nose and covering her mouth.'

'What?' Sebastian whispered.

'I don't know why. He was crazy by all accounts. He didn't want it to end.'

'So he killed her?'

'He was reportedly a very violent man.'

'But Bree… what did she do?'

'Her main crime is keeping quiet about it if the truth be known, not reporting the accident and so on.'

Sebastian looked up at Steve with red-rimmed eyes. 'I can't believe she, that she knew… She was my *friend*. How could she do that to us?'

'I don't know. I'm so sorry.'

'Can I see her? Speak to her?'

'Afraid not. She's due in court shortly to be formally charged along with Levinson. I want to throw the book at them both.'

Sebastian stood shakily. 'I can't believe this. I need to go. To think. I just can't process…' He turned back to Steve. 'Thank you. For telling me the truth. I just need to get my head around this, I think.'

'Seb, I'm so sorry it had to come from me. Come on, I'll see you out.'

Bree tried to make herself look presentable. She was facing court shortly and this would be the end of her life as she knew it. She was in total shock about the reality of her situation. Never once had she considered that she would be charged with anything related to Cassie's murder. In her mind, she hadn't done anything wrong apart from not speak up. Her heart ached for the betrayal that Sebastian would feel once he knew she had known all along. She had sobbed through the night at the loss of his friendship and the loss of the one man she had ever truly loved.

She was collected and led out of the custody suite by Garland. When they rounded the corridor, she came face to face with four PCs trying to hold down a prisoner who was yelling, writhing and kicking.

'Out the front way, idiot,' snapped the custody sergeant. 'Use the squad car out front. Jonesey's taking you.'

Garland had led Bree back through the corridors quietly, holding her arm gently, but firmly enough to propel her in the direction he wanted her to go in. They passed through reception, met Jonesey and stepped out into the wintry sunshine.

Bree saw the police car parked by the entrance in the front car park and realisation dawned on her. She wouldn't ever be able to just walk out of anywhere, ever again. She wouldn't be free, *ever again*. Her life as she knew it was over. Completely. She couldn't go back to her flat, couldn't have lunch with her friends, couldn't walk on the beach. She gasped and stumbled slightly at the enormity of the change, Garland steadied her. Tears poured down her cheeks as the fear took hold.

In front of her, on the edge of the car park she saw an old lady, with dirty clothes and a shopping trolley full of litter and carrier bags. She was trying to get the trolley up the kerb, into the car park. Garland looked at Jonesey and tutted.

'Blimey, Mary's back and she's got herself a trolley.' He called over to her. 'Mary, are you OK? What are you doing back here?'

Bree watched as Mary tripped on the kerb and fell face down on the pavement, pulling the trolley over with her, the contents scattering over the entrance to the car park.

'Oh Christ, she's down,' muttered Garland. He led Bree quickly over to the car. Jonesey was already going to help Mary who was lying on the pavement, wailing.

'Get in,' he said, opening the car door before running over to Mary.

Bree looked at the road, it was busy with traffic coming around the bend road faster than it should be. As if in a trance Bree walked towards the road, past the two officers who had their back to her lifting up Mary. She heard her name being called and she turned.

Sebastian was stood in the doorway of the police station next to Steve, his face was pale, his eyes red rimmed and a hurt expression on his face.

She looked into his eyes and saw everything she never wanted to see. Her truest fear was realised in that moment. He stared at her with anger and betrayal. He shook his head in disbelief and she saw tears on his face. Bree gulped and looked away. She closed her eyes and stepped out into the road.

Gabriella Logan died at the scene. The paramedics were unable to revive her after she was hit head on by an articulated lorry, forced under the front of the cab and dragged for a few metres.

Sebastian and Steve saw it play out second by second. Sebastian dropped to his knees in horror as he watched the woman who had been his friend for over a decade, get hit by the lorry and pushed beneath it. Steve had dragged him back inside the station and without knowing who else to call, phoned Suzy. He explained what had happened and asked her to come and get Sebastian. Suzy arrived quickly and ushered Sebastian gently into her van to drive him home.

That afternoon, Levison Lucas was remanded in custody to await trial after being charged with all the offences Steve hoped for. Bree's testimony had been the piece to bring it all together. The CPS had called to inform him, and had also reminded him to step up the search for whoever had called 999 as they would likely need them for the trial.

Steve had reluctantly briefed the Superintendent who was apoplectic about the loss of a suspect on their watch. As usual Steve left his office swearing under his breath. He returned to his own office and sat grumpily at his desk. Something was niggling him. He knew that there was something he was missing. He just needed to remember what. As was his habit, he instructed his subconscious to tell him what it was, switched off his computer and left for the day.

Suzy had taken Sebastian home. He sat silently in her van, his head resting on the window as she drove the short distance to his house. She was worried about him. Steve had briefly outlined the basics for her. Cassie's death was murder and Bree had been involved. On her way to being formally charged, Bree stepped out in front of a lorry and was killed almost instantly. Sebastian had seen it happen.

She pulled into Sebastian's drive and sat for a moment in silence. She realised he had no idea they were home. She climbed out of the van, walked around to the passenger side and gently opened the door.

'Come on, Seb,' she said, taking his arm gently. 'Come inside.'

She walked him up the steps towards the front door and he mechanically got keys out and opened the door. He said trance-like, 'Bree's stuff is here. I don't know what to do with it. What do I do with it?'

Suzy guided him down towards the kitchen. There was a note on the side from Tabatha saying she was at Jude's and would be home later.

'Don't worry, I'll take care of Bree's things.' She sat him down on the sofa and opened the cupboards until she found a bottle of brandy. She poured him a generous measure.

'Drink it, you're in shock,' she said.

Sebastian drained the glass and pulled a face. He leant forwards putting his arms on his knees and buried his head in his hands. Suzy stood back quietly watching his shoulders heave as he cried silently. She felt utterly helpless. In the end she sat close to him and rubbed his back as he cried.

Her phone buzzed quietly, and she slipped outside to answer it, so she didn't disturb him. By the time she came back in, Sebastian had stopped crying and had fallen asleep on the sofa. Suzy covered him with a blanket and watched him for a moment. Sighing, she texted Steve asking whether it was OK to pack up Bree's clothes and Steve agreed. She went upstairs to Bree's room, packed her stuff into an empty bag she found, and tidied up as best she could.

Quietly, she walked back downstairs and found Seb awake and in the kitchen. He looked sheepishly around the open door of the fridge.

'Sorry about the meltdown,' he said ruefully. 'Bit of a shock.'

'It's fine,' Suzy said. She reached up and picked something out of his hair. 'You've got a feather in your hair.'

Seb caught her hand and looked at her.

'Look,' he said quietly. His thumb gently stroking her wrist. 'Sorry… and thanks for bringing me home and sorting things out. You're a good friend.'

'It's OK,' she said, blushing. 'It's fine.'

'Well, I appreciate it,' he said. 'And sorry for blubbing like an idiot.'

'Anytime.'

He rested his head on the edge of the fridge door. 'I'm a bit all over the place today.' He stepped closer to her. 'I think I'm in danger of making some rash decisions.'

'I should er… go,' she said awkwardly.

'I was going to offer to cook, but I see that Tabatha has eaten the contents of the fridge.'

'I really should go,' Suzy said, grabbing her bag.

'Suzy.'

'What?'

'Thanks for earlier.' He bent and kissed her cheek gently, lingering slightly as if unsure of something.

'No problem,' she said lightly. 'I'm due to see you guys the day after tomorrow for some training with Jack. Do you want to reschedule?'

'No. I'll see you then. I need to round up Tabatha and tell her everything.'

'The truth? About Bree?'

'Lying about it makes me no different from Bree.'

'True. If you need to reschedule, just say.'

'Thanks, Suzy. See you.'

Seb watched as Suzy let herself out of the door. He sighed deeply, he felt the anger of betrayal mounting and tried to control it before he saw Tabatha.

Seb sat Tabatha down and told her about Bree and Cassie. He didn't tell her about Cassie's affairs or about her being pregnant with another man's child.

Tabatha was in shock. She sat at the kitchen table, stunned. Unusually quiet.

'What, so she just walked out into the road?' she said suddenly after an eternity of being silent.

'Uh huh.'

'And you saw it?'

'I did.'

'How horrible for you, Dad.'

'Um... I think so.'

'So, she knew Levinson killed Mum? She knew that?'

'Yes. We don't need to keep re-hashing it,' Seb said.

She held up a hand to stop him talking. 'I'm processing, Dad. So, she knew about it all, but kept quiet. She let that man go about his daily shit and she said nothing.'

'Tabby cat...'

'No!' Tabatha stood up and paced angrily. 'She knew, Dad! She fucking knew! She came here, stayed with us. Heard us talk about Mum, helped us plan the funeral and all the time SHE FUCKING KNEW!'

'Tabatha! I won't have you using language like that.' Seb raised his voice.

'Well, I think the situation requires it,' she shot back angrily. 'Dad, how are you not mad about this? I'm really fucking mad about this.'

Seb sighed deeply. 'I'm sad more than anything else. Stop swearing.'

Tabatha frowned. 'Sorry you feel that way, Dad. If I was you, I'd be fucking livid though.'

'Tabatha,' Seb warned.

'What?' she said innocently. 'Just saying it like it is. I can't help but be angry. I won't have people betraying us, Dad. I just won't. That's what she did and in my view, she did it in the worst way too.'

'I know, love. Try not to be angry.'

'Can't help it. It's how I'll get through it. Harness the beast.'

'What?'

'The beast. The anger. Harness the anger. Use it.'

'I'm not an angry person.'

'Perhaps you should try it.'

'Perhaps I should.'

'I think we should burn her stuff.'

'I think that's a step too far.'

'I don't.'

'Suzy's packed it up for me.'

'Suzy's been here?'

'She brought me back from the police station.'

'And?'

'And nothing.' He looked sheepish. 'I had a bit of a meltdown on her.'

'Oh God. Did you cry? You did, didn't you? God, Dad, no one likes a crier. No one will sleep with you if you blub everywhere.'

'Oh, well I'm sorry,' Seb said indignantly. 'I did apologise.'

'We're going to have to embark on some serious damage control,' muttered Tabatha. 'We can't have her thinking that you're a total loser.'

'What?'

'Nothing. Is there anything to eat?'

* * *

Foxy was sitting next to Carla in intensive care. He held her hand and watched her pale face. He was at the point where he didn't know what to do; what to say. Dr Michaels checked Carla's stats and adjusted something on a drip.

'Hi there,' she said softly to Foxy.

'How's she doing?'

Dr Michaels lifted each of Carla's eyelids and flashed a light in.

'Hmm,' she murmured and checked more readings.

'Is that a good hmm or a bad hmm?'

Dr Michaels leant on the end of the bed. 'Her fever has reduced, but she's still not out of the woods yet. Her responses are sluggish and I'm not happy about that, so we're going to run another battery of tests. She's still a real worry. It's a waiting game, I'm afraid. She's pretty out of it. I'm concerned that she's slipping further away from us.'

'Is it OK if I stay longer?'

'Of course, but get some rest at home. I'll call you if there's any change.'

'Thanks, Doc.'

Foxy was asleep in the armchair. He'd spent hours with Carla and had then come home, sat in the dark watching the lights of the wind farm being constructed far out to sea. He'd watched a storm track across the horizon, seeing the occasional forks of lightning dart from the heavy undercarriage of dark clouds.

'Dad.' The words were spoken softly.

'DAD!' Louder. More urgent.

Foxy woke suddenly and looked around.

'Dad.'

He looked over and in the opposite armchair sat Charlie, his fifteen-year-old daughter. Foxy looked at her.

'You're not real,' he said softly, sleepily. 'I wish you were.'

'Whatever,' she said impatiently, and for a second Foxy wondered if she was actually there in the room with him.

'Are you real?'

'Dad. Focus,' she said. 'I'm taking Mum. She can't fight anymore. She can be with me. I just wanted you to know so you wouldn't worry. We'll be together.'

'Don't take her, love. It's not her time.'

'It is her time. She's too weak, Dad. I'll keep her safe. She says she can't fight anymore. She's too tired.'

She unfolded her long legs from the chair, came over and leant down, stroking his face.

'I love you, Dad. I miss you like crazy.'

'Love you too. Oh, I miss you so much,' he whispered, tears streaming down his face. His arms reached up to hold her small, beautiful face in his huge hands.

'Bye, Dad. I'll keep Mum safe.'

'Bye, darling. I love you. I love you both so much,' he whispered.

Foxy woke suddenly. Tears wet on his face. He remembered the dream. His mobile rang loud and insistent in the darkness. He answered it knowing instantly.

'She's gone, hasn't she?' he asked before anyone could speak.

'Mr Fox, it's Dr Michaels and yes, I'm afraid so. Just a few moments ago. I'm so very sorry for your loss.'

'What happened?'

Dr Michaels sighed. 'I don't know, it's like she suddenly gave up. She died looking very peaceful though, if that's any consolation.'

'It is. Thank you, Doctor. For everything you've done,' he managed to croak out.

'Goodbye, Mr Fox.'

Foxy sat back in his chair and closed his eyes.

'It's OK, Dad, she's with me now,' a faint voice said softly. 'We love you, Dad.'

CHAPTER 36

Steve's subconscious had not performed as requested. He woke up to find no answers had presented themselves during the night, and he had stomped off grumpily to work.

He sat at his desk ignoring the repeated email requests from the Superintendent's snotty secretary for his written report on yesterday's death in custody. Instead, he stewed about the 999 call. He was missing something. He knew it.

He had replayed the message time and time again and still couldn't come up with anything. Then he thought about listening to it through headphones to see whether the sound was any different; perhaps he was missing some faint sound that was a giveaway. He scrabbled about in his drawer and spent a frustrating five minutes trying to untangle a tight knot in the wire of his headphones.

Finally, he plugged them in and pressed play. He fiddled about with the volume and then listened carefully. He listened again, frowning deeply and then fiddled with the volume some more.

There it was. He listened again and shook his head.

'No fucking way,' he shouted, pushing himself angrily off his chair, almost garroting himself with the headphones. He flung them off and strode out of the station and down the road. Shaking his head for not making the connection sooner.

He headed through the town towards the Loafing About Bakery and marched down the alleyway that ran along the back of it.

'Anything tasty?' he asked the pair of feet that were dangling from the large bin. The feet suddenly disappeared and there was a rustling from its depths. Steve waited, watching with amusement. Slowly the lid lifted, and a pair of eyes looked out.

'Just the man I want to talk to,' said Steve dryly.

'Fuck's sake,' Sniffy muttered. 'I'm not doing anything wrong; all this is being thrown away anyway.'

'That's not what I want to talk to you about.'

Sniffy pushed the lid fully open and rested his arms on the edge.

'Well, as I'm keeping office hours here today, what can I do for you?'

Steve couldn't help smiling. 'You need to come to the station, Sniffy.'

'Can't do that,' he said, rooting around behind him and producing a squashed croissant, which he offered to Steve.

'No thanks,' Steve said. Sniffy shrugged and took a large bite. 'Tell me why you can't come to the station?'

'Because I have stuff to do today.'

'Such as?'

'Meetings and stuff,' he said, refusing to meet Steve's eyes.

Steve raised an eyebrow and suppressed a smile. 'Meetings?'

'Meetings.'

'These meetings wouldn't involve you handing over money and then spending the rest of the afternoon off your face?'

'Might be.'

'That's not happening today.'

'You filth are a bunch of fucking killjoys. Innocent people, going about their business, and you come and ruin their day.'

'What a hard life you lead with us persecuting you so much.' Steve dialled a number, which was answered promptly.

'Jonesey, bring a squad car down to the Loafing About Bakery, will you?' He listened for a moment. 'No, I won't. Hurry up.'

Sniffy had disappeared back into the bin and emerged with a variety of pastries which he hurriedly stuffed into his pockets.

'Out,' ordered Steve.

Sniffy tutted and climbed out, dropping down on the ground next to Steve, accompanied strongly by the odour of bins. Steve propelled Sniffy towards the road where the squad car had just arrived. Steve opened the back door and pushed Sniffy inside.

'Put him in an interview room. I'll see you back there in a minute.'

Jonesey looked at Steve. 'What? Why aren't you coming? What *is* that smell?'

'I'll see you in a minute. Oh, Sniffy's got pastries on him.'

'Oohh what pastries?'

'Ones from the dustbin.'

Steve walked back to the station and arrived within a few minutes of Jonesey, who was in the corridor moaning about the smell in the car.

'Which interview room is he in?'

'This one.' Jonesey inclined his head.

'Two teas, Jonesey, if you'd be so kind,' Steve said, pushing open the door.

'Guv.'

Steve sat himself down and looked at Sniffy who had emptied his pockets. There was a variety of squashed pastries arranged on the table.

'Help yourself,' Sniffy said, pointing.

'I'm good, thanks. Right, let's get started. You're not under caution, we are just having a chat. But I'm going to record it. You know yourself you can be a bit flaky.'

'Rude,' muttered Sniffy.

Steve pressed record and went through the preliminaries.

'Sniffy, I want you to tell me about the car that used to be parked outside the place at Compass Row when you were dossing there.'

'What about it?'

'When did you get it?'

'Ages ago. Don't remember.'

'It's unlike you to leave town, Sniffy. So why did you have the car?'

Sniffy shrugged and sniffed.

'Come on.'

'You'll nick me. I don't want to incimm… inclimmmi…'

'Incriminate.'

'That one.'

'You won't.'

'But you'll nick me,' he whined.

'I won't. It's a done deal, isn't it? I can't prove anything. I just want to know what happened on a certain night, with that car.'

'You trying to fit me up?'

'No, Sniffy. I just want to know what happened.'

'It was weeks ago.'

'I know. Still relevant.'

Sniffy picked at a squashed cinnamon roll. 'So, I had to get some gear for a bloke.'

'Right.'

'I owed him some cash. He said this job would pay it off.'

'Right. How much gear?'

Sniffy shifted uncomfortably. 'Enough.'

'How did you get there?'

'Hitched a ride.'

'So you hitched a ride to the docks. And then how did you get back?'

'He had a car that was hookey. Gave me a phone. Told me to just give the car to the guy and chuck the phone once I got there safe.'

'The gear was stashed in the car, and he gave you a burner phone.'

'Yeah.'

'Still got the phone?'

'Course not. Dumped it.'

'What happened on the way back, Sniffy?'

Sniffy shifted uncomfortably in his chair and inspected his pastries closely. Jonesey chose that moment to deliver two teas. For a second he eyed up the pastries and then thought better of it.

Sniffy slurped his tea. 'There's fucking sugar in this.'

'You'll live.'

'Sugar's bad for your teeth.'

'So's heroin, Sniffy. So, what happened on the way back?'

'How do you know something happened on the way back?'

'Sniffy,' Steve warned. 'I want to know what happened. Tell me, and I won't nick you.'

Sniffy leant back in his seat and slurped his tea. 'Sure?'

Steve rolled his eyes. 'Come on... thought you had meetings to get to.'

Sniffy folded his arms. 'So I goes to the docks to get the car. He didn't tell me the car was fucking knackered, crying out to be stopped it was. Anyway, I come back on the back lanes. Fucking horrible night it was, pissing down, branches and shit all over the road.'

'And then?'

'And then I come around a corner and there's a car my side of the road swerving about, then it goes off the road.'

'Did you stop?'

Sniffy shifted uncomfortably in his chair. 'I couldn't, could I?' he hissed. 'I had a car full of fucking dope.' He folded his arms. 'Oh hello, officer, yes there was an accident, car went over the side. Oh what's this in my car? Ten years in fucking prison that's what's in my car. So no, I didn't stop.'

'Did you do anything?'

Sniffy was silent for a moment. 'You know, don't you?'

'You rang 999.'

'I stopped further on and ran back through the woods. I saw the bloke fucking arguing with some woman about not calling the police and he grabbed her phone. So I ran back to the car and used the burner phone.'

'See anything else?'

'No.'

'Where did you dump the phone?'

'Threw it off the cliffs,' he said, sniffing. 'How did you know it was me?'

Steve pointed at him. 'That's how. Your sniffing. Always worse when you're nervous. I heard it on the recording. Plus, the car that was where you were dossing was stolen and had a broken headlight and brake light, and both of those were mentioned by people involved in the accident. I just hadn't linked the two until I heard the call.'

'You can't prove it was me.'

'I probably can't and to be honest I'm not sure whether we'll have to. I don't think the CPS will consider you a reliable witness.'

'Well they can fuck right off,' he said indignantly. 'I'm reliable.'

'I'll be sure to pass that on.' Steve looked at Sniffy critically. 'You thought about getting clean, Sniffy? Get a life and stop chasing the dragon?'

Sniffy shook his head. 'Tried that. I'll always come back to the dragon. Don't wanna give it up.'

Steve knew he was fighting a losing battle.

'Let's write up a statement and then you can go.'

'Really?' He looked surprised.

'I've got what I need from you, and I'll find you if I need any more.'

'OK.'

'You dossing at the hotel?'

'Nah. They've closed it all up and the water's off now.'

'Where are you dossing?'

'Here and there.'

'I heard a rumour that the old cafe in the top car park has gone out of business. Might be somewhere to doss.'

Sniffy's eyes lit up. 'Maybe I'll take a stroll up there.'

'You do that, Sniffy.'

Steve returned to his office after letting Sniffy out of reception. He looked at the email from the CPS. They were weighing up the case of whether to charge Rusty with his father's murder, but taking into account the significant sexual and domestic abuse he had suffered throughout his childhood. Adult social care were also involved. Steve supposed the extenuating circumstances of his upbringing might affect the likelihood of him getting a prison sentence, but it was up to someone else now. He felt extreme sadness for the three boys and the ways their lives had turned out.

Anna had said that Teddy had stayed with them since Steve told them of his father's death. She said he was doing well and seemed happy. He just needed to realise that it could be home if he wanted it. Whenever he left, Teddy always asked her quietly if it was OK if he came back. Steve told her again that he would do everything he could to help her keep the boys together.

* * *

After the call, Foxy had fallen asleep again in his chair and was woken by a soft tapping on his front door. He heaved himself up and went to answer it, finding Sophie outside clutching a large paper bag. Wordlessly he opened the door. Sophie came in and put her arms around him, giving him a hug.

'I'm so sorry,' she said. 'So, so sorry. Lottie called me, she was on duty last night and thought you might need a friend.' She put her hand on his face and looked up at him, concerned.

'You doing OK?' she said.

Foxy didn't trust himself to speak.

'Come on,' Sophie murmured. 'I've brought you breakfast. Hit the shower. You'll feel better.'

Foxy went to shower and Sophie busied herself. She let Solo out, opened a window and plumped up a few cushions. When she heard the shower stop, she busied herself unpacking the paper bag. Foxy returned in jeans with wet hair and pulling on a T-shirt.

'I'm starving,' he announced and sat down at the table eyeing the food appreciatively.

'Can't have you wasting away,' Sophie said dryly.

Foxy sat for a moment and then started his food, making appreciative noises.

'You not having any?' he asked, his fork in midair.

'Already eaten,' Sophie said. 'Look, I don't know how I can help, but I want to.'

Foxy stopped eating for a moment. 'I had a weird dream-like thing last night,' he said, sipping his coffee.

'Why was it weird?'

'You'll think I've lost it.'

'Try me.'

'Charlie spoke to me last night.'

Sophie raised an eyebrow. 'You dreamt that?'

'Suppose so. She was calling my name… and I woke up and she was sitting in that chair. She told me she was taking Carla, that Carla would be OK with her and that she would keep her safe. She said Carla was tired and couldn't fight anymore.'

'Wow,' said Sophie softly.

'Then she said she missed me like crazy,' he whispered. 'Soph, it was so real. I touched her face.'

'Oh, Rob.' Sophie's eyes were full of tears.

'Then she said again that she was taking Carla, and then two seconds later the phone rang, and it was the doctor saying Carla had just passed away.' He sighed. 'The doctor said the other day that Carla had been talking to someone called Charlie.'

'Do you think they're together now?' Sophie asked quietly.

'I want to think like that. I don't know how Carla could have been OK one minute and then dead the next.'

'Lottie said it was bad, they couldn't get a handle on it.'

'I can't help thinking that it was the baby that killed her.'

'I don't think it was… that was just one of the things that started a chain of events in her body. You know what it's like, Rob. If the body's vulnerable, it's prone to attack. Like a fort or something with a weak defence point, all sorts can happen in that area and then it's game over.'

'Are you using military examples on me?'

'Are they working? I thought they were inspired.'

He pushed his plate away.

'It doesn't feel real, that she's gone.'

'It won't for a while.'

'I need to sort stuff out, I suppose. Tell people. Her friends.'

'Can I help?'

'Appreciate that,' he said, squeezing her hand.

'Here if you need me,' she said. 'When Sam died, you came over and told me you were here for me. Well, bestie, I'm here for you, OK?'

'OK.'

'Want me to open up for you? I've cleared my day.'

'That would be great. Thanks. Mike and Tom aren't due in till later.'

'No problem. You get your head together a bit. There's a whole raft of people out there for you. You know that, right? You're part of this family now.'

Foxy had a flashback to a night when he first met the lifeboat crew and Jesse had said to him, *'This is good for new roots. Give it time, let it happen and you end up with family here.'* He smiled as he remembered. It was so true. He did have family here now.

'Thanks, Soph,' he said, not trusting himself to speak anymore. He swallowed the lump in his throat.

There was another knock at the door and Rudi barrelled in, closely followed by Mack.

'Mate,' Rudi said. Stepping forward he enveloped Foxy into a hug. Mack followed and the three of them stood together.

'Here for you, mate,' Mack said quietly.

* * *

Sebastian and Tabatha attended Cassie's short cremation. It was just the two of them and the service was mercifully quick. Sebastian remained quiet and stoic. Standing next to Tabatha he held tightly on to her hand as she cried quietly.

Cassie's favourite song played and the celebrant talked about how loving and tight-knit the family was. How Cassie adored her family, and it was all Sebastian could do not to stand up and call the woman a fucking liar. He managed to get through the thirty-minute service without making Tabatha aware of how utterly betrayed he felt by his wife cheating on him with different men, on a fairly consistent basis.

As he listened to the celebrant drone on, he tried to unpick how he felt about Cassie. He felt hurt, and deeply deceived. He couldn't believe that she would do something like that to him when she professed to love him so deeply.

He mused that she was an even better actress than he had given her credit for, believing her lies for so many years. It felt easier to be angry about the lies and the cheating, so he decided that was how he would be. As Tabatha had said, he was harnessing the beast to help him through it.

The service finally ended, and Sebastian arranged a quick turnaround of the ashes. He didn't want to be waiting for days, prolonging the agony.

He wanted it over and done with, but he couldn't tell Tabatha that. The ashes were due the next day and part of Seb didn't want them anywhere near him. The way he felt he would gladly dump them in the bin. But that wasn't fair on Tabatha.

They arrived home in a sombre mood, and Tabatha disappeared to the beach with Jack. Still in his black suit, Sebastian mechanically started packing Cassie's clothes and shoes into some large bin liners. He figured he'd drop them at the clothes bank. The doorbell rang and when he answered it, he found Suzy on the doorstep. She eyed him up and down in his suit.

'What is it with men looking totally gorgeous in a good suit?' she said. 'Even my ugly brother looks drop-dead gorgeous in a suit.' She tilted her head, inspecting him. 'You really didn't have to dress up for me, you know.'

'Alas, this is not for you,' Seb said, standing aside so she could come in. 'As for your brother being ugly, that man is too good-looking for his own good. If I batted for that side, I'd definitely be tempted.'

'Hmm, so it's for work?'

'Funeral.'

'Shit. Sorry.' Suzy clapped a hand over her mouth. 'Cassie? God. Seb, I'm so sorry. I'll come another day.'

'Don't,' he said over his shoulder, walking towards the kitchen. 'Coffee?'

'Thanks.' She followed him.

He leant against the kitchen counter while the coffee machine burbled, and faced her.

'Apparently, I completely embarrassed myself by having a meltdown on you, and I've been told in no uncertain terms that no one likes a crier.' He pulled a face. 'Tabatha's words. Not mine. So I feel I must apologise profusely.'

Suzy chuckled. 'Don't be silly.'

'I mean it,' he said softly. 'Sorry.'

She waved his words away dismissively. 'It's fine. Blimey, if you think that was a meltdown you should've seen me after my husband left me for his eighteen-year-old secretary.'

Sebastian pulled a face. 'Ouch.'

'Exactly.'

'He must have been a fucking idiot,' he said, looking at her steadily.

'In so many ways,' she joked. She sat down and watched him while he made coffee. 'So, tell me to mind my own business, but I get the impression that the meltdown wasn't just about Bree. I sense there's a raft of other stuff going on.'

'What makes you think that?'

'You've just had a service for your wife, and yet here you are acting like you've been to a funeral for someone you hardly knew.'

Sebastian kept his back to Suzy and paused for a moment.

'You can talk to me, you know,' she said softly.

Seb put the coffee on the table, added mugs and some milk and sat down next to Suzy. He shrugged off his jacket, loosened his black tie and rolled up the sleeves of his crisp white shirt.

'Few things have come to light,' he said, sighing. 'Turns out I really didn't know her at all.'

'Oh?' Suzy said, helping herself to coffee and pouring some for Seb.

He rubbed his face. 'Give him his credit, Steve is pretty fucking good at his job.'

'What is it? Come on.'

'Cassie was pregnant with another man's child it turns out.'

'Shit.'

'She was also a prolific cheater with most of her leading men too. Apparently, it made for a better picture.'

'And you had no idea?'

He shook his head. 'And the Oscar for best performance of a lying, cheating wife goes to the great Cassie Warner.'

'My God. You must be devastated.'

Sebastian exhaled heavily. 'I'm not devastated, Suzy. I'm just really fucking angry. So angry. But I can't tell Tabatha. She mustn't know, it'll kill her. I just feel such a fool. Such a fucking idiot for trusting Cassie, for never questioning her, for thinking she loved me.'

Suzy leant forwards and laid a hand on his arm. 'I know *exactly* how you feel,' she said. 'I've been there. Exactly where you are. You wonder if everyone knew. Were they laughing about it? How much of it was a lie. Even the really special memories. Were they a lie?' She leant back in her chair. 'What was actually real and what wasn't?'

'I'm there,' Seb mused. 'Exactly there.'

'It'll get better,' she said, sipping her coffee and helping herself to the biscuit tin. 'You just need to find something cathartic. Help you deal with it.'

'What did you do? Besides eat everyone's biscuits?'

'I got him to buy me out of the business, and I bought a house I loved that I knew he would hate. I set up the business I'd always wanted to and that he was always dead against. I got a lot of satisfaction from that.' She sat forwards in her chair. 'You should write a drama about this. It's what you do. Not the same exactly, obviously, but with the same parallels.'

'Not a bad idea.'

'Then don't kill off the cheater until you've said everything to them you would have wanted to say if Cassie was still alive.' She helped herself to another biscuit. 'Now that would be cathartic.'

'I like your thinking.'

CHAPTER 37

Mickey and Pearl Camorra were on their way back from Liverpool. Mickey had felt it was important to show their faces and for Pearl to assess who he had put in charge.

'I don't trust him,' Pearl said as soon as they got in the car. 'He's planning something.'

'What makes you think he would be so stupid?' Mickey asked.

'Because he's there, and you're elsewhere, darling,' Pearl replied. 'And when the cat's away, the mice can play. And this one looks like he might. What do we know about him?'

'Not a lot. I got rid of his competition and promoted him. He saw me get rid of those two henchmen. I would have thought that was enough of a warning to know that he can't be crossing me.'

'I think he's got too confident too quickly. We might need to remind him that he needs us. I think we need an inside man,' mused

Pearl. 'If there isn't one already. Perhaps I should ask Steve what he knows.'

'You have a soft spot for that copper.'

'Perhaps I do. He rushed quite gallantly to my rescue when that psycho bitch tried to kill me.'

'Hmm.'

'Plus, I like his moral compass very much. He looks the other way when we dispose of people who really deserve to die. I quite like that in him, unusual in a policeman.'

'Do I need to be worried?'

'Stop it, darling. I'm old enough to be his mother. Well almost. But he is deliciously handsome.' She tittered.

'Pearl,' Mickey growled.

'I'm just teasing, darling,' she said, laughing. 'You're too easy to get worked up.'

'You don't normally complain about me getting worked up,' he said, tugging her towards him for a kiss.

'Who said I was complaining?' Pearl said. 'I'll speak to Steve and see what his colleagues know about this man and then I think we take a view. Then we can decide if we need an inside man. Alexy has mentioned it before. He has various extended family up there he can reach out to again if the price is right.'

'Hmm. I don't want a repeat of all the trouble we've just sorted out,' Mickey said.

'Oh I don't know,' Pearl murmured. 'It certainly had its moments.'

* * *

Will had news. He took a quick break and headed over to Anna's. He knocked on the bright blue door and waited. Feet thundered down the stairs and Danny flung the door open,

'Hello, Will,' he said. 'Have you come to play chess with me?'

441

'No, but I'm happy to have a very quick game.'

'Come in, come in,' said Danny enthusiastically. 'TEDDY! Will's here to play chess with us!'

'Am I going to be hustled by the both of you?' Will asked, pretending to grumpy.

'He's only joking,' Anna said, seeing the look of dismay on Danny's face. 'What can we do for you, Will?'

'Well, I've come to ask Danny and Teddy if they're busy tomorrow.'

'Oh what do you have planned?'

'Ferry day,' Will said. 'The new boat's being delivered this afternoon, so we need to let people know it's ferry day tomorrow. I wondered if you boys wanted to help?'

Danny nodded excitedly. 'TEDDY!' he yelled.

Teddy appeared and Will blinked in surprise. He looked healthy; he'd had a haircut and was clean and tidy. He smiled at Will shyly.

'Hello, Mr Will,' he said.

'Teddy! The ferry is coming later this afternoon. You can take pictures!' Danny said. 'And it's ferry day tomorrow!'

'I'm not working tomorrow,' Teddy said. 'I can come and take pictures.'

'I wondered if you wanted to help out too, Teddy,' Will said.

'I don't know if I'm allowed,' Teddy said doubtfully.

'Well, I was hoping you would. Miles and Gemma have said they'd appreciate the help since Miles isn't one hundred per cent yet,' Will said, producing a carrier bag. 'Plus, I got you both these and it would be shame to waste them.' He produced two T-shirts and passed one to each of the boys.

Danny held his up and did a dance of delight. 'Teddy! We've got one each!'

Teddy was looking at the T-shirt. They were a bright blue, the same blue as the new ferry and on the front in yellow block capitals it read 'FERRY CREW'. On the reverse, it had each of their names in capitals and then underneath it read in cursive writing, 'The Tide Runner'.

'I've never had a T-shirt with my name on it before,' Teddy said quietly.

'These are so COOL,' said Danny, rushing off. 'I'm trying mine on. Come ON, Teddy!'

Teddy followed him up the stairs.

Anna leant against the door to the kitchen. 'That was a nice thing to do,' she said. 'Thank you.'

Will shrugged. 'Teddy looks good.'

'It's amazing what food, a bath and a haircut can do, as a start anyway.'

'Is he staying here for good?'

'I've told him this is home for as long as he wants it, and he seems a little more settled. His nightmares have calmed down.'

'You are a good woman,' Will said.

The boys came thundering back down the stairs wearing their T-shirts and looking very happy.

Danny laughed. 'We tried each other's on too, but then Teddy said that would be silly, as mine would say Teddy and his would say Danny!'

'They look good,' Will said. 'So! Report for duty at 11 a.m. tomorrow morning for ferry day?'

Both boys nodded.

'Good.' Will rubbed his hands. 'Right, quick game of chess and then I'm off.'

'Me first!' cried Danny.

The new ferry had arrived by the time Will got back to the harbour. One of Don's staff had piloted the boat over, and he was talking through the new equipment with Miles and Gemma. Will watched them carefully taking notes and trying out the equipment. He was pleased that Don had come up trumps with a good ferry that had good equipment. He turned to see Doug, Jesse and Brock approaching.

'Hey, guys.'

'Lovely boat,' Jesse said. 'She sounds wonderful. I wanted to come and have a nose.'

'Ever the mechanic.' Doug rolled his eyes. He gestured to the boat. 'The town has a lot to thank you for, Will. This wouldn't have happened without you.'

'Er, it was you who gave me the idea and told me it was Don's son. So this is down to you as much as me.'

'Stop with the mutual ego stroking,' laughed Jesse. 'Will, we're off to the pub in a bit for a few beers. Do you fancy joining us?'

'Why not?' Will said. 'Thanks for asking. Means a lot,' he added.

'Those big shoes you had to fill are fitting pretty well, I think.' Doug said, winking at him and throwing an arm across Jesse's shoulders. 'See you in a bit, mate. We'll save you a seat.'

Will watched them go. Life was good. He was happier than he had been in a long time. All he had to do was to persuade Anna to come out to dinner with him, and he'd be even happier. He couldn't stop thinking about her.

* * *

The next day Cassie's ashes arrived; Seb and Tabatha took them down to the beach.

'How do you want to do this, Dad?'

Sebastian resisted the urge to tell her to upend it and dump the lot in the shallows or find the nearest bin.

'Up to you, darling,' he murmured.

444

Tabatha kicked off her shoes and rolled up her jeans. 'I'm going to wade in and sprinkle it in. Do you want to?'

'You do it, love. You say your goodbyes.'

'Don't you want to do this?'

'You do it, darling. Go on.'

Tabatha picked up a bag of rose petals in Cassie's favourite colour that she had been drying and walked into the shallows. Sebastian watched with folded arms as she sprinkled a handful of rose petals and then a handful of Cassie. He watched her scatter the final remains of dust and then she swished her hand in the sea. Sebastian felt awful for her. Tears were on her cheeks, and she came back and stood next to Seb.

'You OK, Tabby Cat?'

'Just us now, Dad,' Tabatha said quietly.

'Just us,' echoed Seb.

He turned and walked back to the house.

'Bye, Mum,' said Tabatha softly, following Seb into the house.

Tabatha sat at the kitchen table.

'Dry your feet, it's freezing out there, and have a hot drink.'

Tabatha dried her feet and found a pair of warm socks. She sat in the chair and pulled them on.

'So as it's just us now, Dad,' she said in her matter-of-fact way.

'Yup,' Seb said, stirring a hot chocolate for her. 'It is.'

'This means we're honest about everything and share everything.'

'Everything?'

'Well, not the yucky stuff, obvs,' she said, rolling her eyes. 'But we have to agree to be honest, right?'

'Right,' he said, delivering the hot chocolate.

'So that means you're honest with me when I ask you stuff. Right?'

'Right. Where are we going with this?'

Tabatha took his hand and pulled him to sit down next to her.

'So this means you tell me the full story about Mum.'

'What full story?'

'Don't do that, Dad,' she said quietly. 'I'm not stupid. She was sleeping with Levinson, wasn't she?'

Sebastian inhaled sharply.

'I knew it,' Tabatha said. 'I want the whole truth, please. There's things I remember from being little that aren't adding up either. I don't think Levinson was the only one.'

'Tabby Cat,' Sebastian said desperately.

'You didn't know, did you?' said Tabatha sadly. 'About any of them?'

'No. I didn't. I thought… She…' He gulped. 'I feel such a fool.'

Tabatha stood suddenly and flung her arms around him.

'It's OK, Dad. We'll be OK. Always.'

Sebastian hugged her back and closed his eyes. 'Always.'

'Wuv you, Dad.'

Seb squeezed her tightly. 'Wuv you too.'

* * *

Pearl was sitting outside on the terrace enjoying the wintry sunshine with a glass of chilled wine and a cigarette. She picked up her phone and looked at her watch. Right on time it rang, she checked the caller ID and answered.

'It's just starting, Mrs Camorra. I'll keep you on the line so you can hear.'

'Thank you.'

Pearl listened carefully.

'Good afternoon, ladies and gentlemen. Welcome to Christie's. Now, I would like to draw everyone's attention to our first lot, an incredibly rare piece, one of only two in the world. Sold by an anonymous seller. We have the Patek Philippe Aviator Prototype wristwatch in chromed nickel, with splittable centre seconds, Guillaume balance and black hour angle dial calibrated for 360°. This watch was manufactured in 1936. I would like to start the bidding at one and three quarter million pounds. Who will give me one point seven five million?'

Pearl sipped her wine and listened. She smiled broadly as the bids trickled in.

'Do I hear anything further on two point six million pounds? Two point six million, going once, going twice. Sold to the gentleman with paddle number 46, thank you.'

'The funds should be transferred shortly, Mrs Camorra,' said the clipped tones of the Christie's assistant.

'Thank you very much indeed.' Pearl ended the call and placed her phone carefully down on the table next to her.

'Who was that?' Mickey asked.

'Christie's.'

'Auction house? What have you bought now?' he said with a long-suffering air.

'I was selling.'

Mickey frowned. 'What were you selling?'

'Our friend, Mr White's watch.'

Mickey looked confused. 'His watch?'

'Mmhm.'

Mickey snorted. 'Don't know why you bothered; I expect it was a copy whatever it was. Bet you didn't get much for it.'

Pearl raised an eyebrow.

'How much did you get for it?' he asked.

'Two point six million pounds,' she said. 'Not bad for an evening's work, darling, don't you agree? It's at least enough to buy me a new pair of Louboutin's, such terribly useful shoes, you know.'

447

* * *

Steve was summoned to see the Chief Superintendent with a request to update him on the Cassie Warner murder and Edwyn Lewis's death. They were finishing up when the door opened, and the assistant reverently ushered in the Chief Constable.

The Chief Superintendent stood up and shook the Chief Constable's hand, introducing him to Steve.

'Sir,' said the Chief Superintendent. 'I wasn't expecting you today.'

'I was just passing. The higher powers are very pleased we've cleared up all that nasty business with Ms Warner. Not good for us to have celebrities murdered on our streets, is it?'

The Chief Constable placed a proprietary hand on Steve's shoulder, squeezing it. 'Now, I heard about the Lewis boy killing his father. I wanted to come and make sure that there's nothing that's going to cause us any problems on that one. I've heard you were there when it happened. I want this all put to bed quietly.'

'I was. All due to years of systematic abuse that was ignored,' Steve said. 'Very sorry state of affairs.'

'Quite. We have to manage this carefully. We can't have this looking like a failing on our part,' the Chief Constable murmured.

'With respect, sir, for those three boys, it was a failing on everyone's part. Sexual and physical abuse for much of their childhood has affected them for life. They'll never recover. We've all failed them.'

Steve glanced at the Chief Constable's hand still holding on to his shoulder and squeezing with a constant pressure. He noticed the large gold signet ring on his pinky and gently tried to step away, to regain his personal space.

'We just need to tread carefully, particularly with those boys,' the Chief Constable said, still squeezing. 'I want to make sure I leave with

448

all the loose ends tied up. Nothing looming in the shadows, so to speak. Everything squared away.'

The Superintendent glanced at Steve. 'The Chief Constable retires at the end of the month.' He turned to the Chief Constable. 'I'm sure Inspector Miller has it all covered.' He smiled dismissively at Steve. 'Keep me posted, Inspector Miller.'

Steve returned to his office. He needed to get the file together for Rusty Lewis, so he organised the paperwork scattered on his desk and filed it.

He idly flicked through the file and then he saw it. The blurry photograph that Teddy had taken. The one Steve initially thought had been taken at Cassie Warner's murder scene. But actually, Teddy had taken a picture of the man who had been hurting Rusty in the caravan. While the picture didn't show a clear face, it showed the clear definition of a gold pinky ring with a fleur-de-lis insignia.

Steve felt a light sweat break out and his bowels loosen. The ring was the exact replica of the one he had just seen on the Chief Constable's pinky finger.

He slowly struggled to process what he was seeing. He saw the blurry face in the picture and the enormity of what it meant sank in.

'Oh fuck,' he said, quietly dropping his head into his hands.

The End

ACKNOWLEDGEMENTS

Getting a book out into the bottomless pit of published matter is a huge team effort and as always there are loads of people that I owe genuine heartfelt thanks to.

As always, my first readers posse deserve their special mention. Sal, Jane, Mette, Tracy, Linda and Julie. Your views and comments on the raw drafts are always spot on and much appreciated.

As always, enormous love, respect and gratitude have to go to my wonderful 'dream team'. My editor, Heather Fitt, for her insight, guidance, knowledge sharing and for being so incredibly long-suffering with me. Abbie Rutherford for her wonderful forensic eye, (assisted gamely by the lovely Thorin). I have learnt so much from Heather and Abbie, I will be forever grateful. Thanks to Peter at Bespoke Book Covers for interpreting my mad ramblings and pictures and nailing the cover every time, and the gorgeous gals at

Literally PR who are so wonderfully efficient, hugely supportive, and an absolute joy to work with.

Thanks also to Stuart Gibbon (GIB consultancy) for enabling me to 'fact check', and also Dave Schudel for his advice on all things cell tower related.

A special shout has to go to my friend Julie for her wonderful support and 'critical eye' on the finished MS and for also putting me onto her lovely friend, who will remain anonymous. This friend went above and beyond to answer many of my questions on certain practices and procedures (in a certain organisation), despite the endless red tape and staggering levels of bureaucracy that he had to fight his way through. For him it must have been exceptionally onerous just to help out a struggling author he'd never met. For all his time and efforts, I will always be eternally grateful.

As always, love, thanks and endless gratitude go to my friends. For buying my books and *still* being interested and supportive (or at least pretending to be). Your lovely comments, texts and feedback mean the world.

Endless love is always reserved for Jane Bateup for her unbridled enthusiasm for any hint of an idea that might turn into a book. I love our story dissections over copious amounts of wine. She has complete faith in me and my writing, and I feel blessed to have her in my world.

A shout out to my wonderful sister, who has always been incredibly supportive of this journey in every single way. Her interest, support, enthusiasm, commitment, and love for the stories make me love her even more. She is one of my biggest advocates and I don't even have to bribe her (apart from the usual provision of red wine and chocolate).

I couldn't do *any* of this without 'my crew'. You guys let me escape into my fictional world for hours (and sometimes days), and you don't moan (too much) about it. I feel truly blessed to have you in my corner (well, most of the time anyway). Special love and thanks go to Andy, whose standard response to my increasingly regular statements of 'I think I need to go on a research trip to…' is now met with, 'Sure, when do we go?' I genuinely couldn't ask for more from my muse and silent research partner (I only wish you were tax deductible).

As always, I really want to thank my readers. Wholeheartedly. Your response and commitment to this series, and the characters make the hard struggle of self-publishing completely worthwhile. Whenever I am filled with doubt, weighed heavy under the numerous knockbacks and am struggling to carry on with it, your comments and reviews give me the strength to continue, even on the darkest of days. I love it when you tell me Foxy or Doug is your ideal man, or you desperately want to live in Castleby, it makes sharing the world I've created in my head totally worthwhile.

I know I've said it before, but I'll say it again. Huge love, respect and enormous gratitude go to the lovely reviewers on the online book tours. I love your commitment to the books and your excitement at the next book in the series. You are all completely inspirational and to me, you will always be part of the Castleby family (whether you like it or not). Thank you so much for your support and your commitment. I only wish one day I can get to the heady heights of really exciting 'book post' bundles for you all. Hopefully you guys will stick around for more from me, other journeys, characters and places are all in the pipeline, so it would be great if you'd come along with me on the journey.

Stick around, fingers crossed, there's lots more to come.

Thanks for reading this book and I hope you enjoyed it. As an independent author I really value all the reviews I get, so if you could take a couple of minutes to review this on amazon, I would be eternally grateful!

Printed in Great Britain
by Amazon